ÆGYPT ▲

ÆGYPT ▲
▲JOHN CROWLEY

BANTAM BOOKS

TORONTO · NEW YORK · LONDON · SYDNEY · AUCKLAND

ÆGYPT
Bantam hardcover edition / April 1987
Bantam paperback edition / January 1988
Bantam trade edition / March 1989

Grateful acknowledgment is made for permission to reprint excerpts from the
following: THE SOLITUDES OF LUIS DE GONGORA translated by Gilbert F.
Cunningham, copyright © 1968 by Johns Hopkins University Press. THE STORY
OF CHAMPIONS OF THE ROUND TABLE by Howard Pyle, published by
Dover Publications, Inc.

Library of Congress Cataloging-in-Publication Data

Crowley, John.
  Aegypt.

  I. Title.   II. Title: Egypt.
PS3553.R597A68   1987   813'.54   86-26482
ISBN 0-553-34592-3

Published simultaneously in the United States and Canada

Bantam Books are published by Bantam Books, a division of Bantam Doubleday
Dell Publishing Group, Inc. Its trademark, consisting of the words "Bantam
Books" and the portrayal of a rooster, is Registered in U.S. Patent and
Trademark Office and in other countries. Marca Registrada. Bantam Books,
666 Fifth Avenue, New York, New York 10103.

PRINTED IN THE UNITED STATES OF AMERICA

FG   0 9 8 7 6 5 4 3 2 1

AUTHOR'S NOTE

▲

More even than most books are, this is a book made out of other books. The author wishes to acknowledge his profound debt to those authors whose books he has chiefly plundered, and to offer his apologies for the uses to which he has put their work: to Joseph Campbell, to Elizabeth L. Eisenstein, to Mircea Eliade, to Peter French, to Hans Jonas, to Frank E. and Fritzie P. Manuel, to Giorgio di Santillana, to Stephen Schoenbaum, to Wayne Shumaker, to Keith Thomas, to Lynn Thorndike, to D. P. Walker, and, most of all, to the late Dame Frances Yates, out of whose rich scholarship this fantasia on her themes has been largely quarried.

I have also put to use the speculations of John Michell and Katherine Maltwood, Robert Graves, Lois Rose, and Richard Deacon. I have used the translations and notes to the *Hermetica* of Walter Scott, and Gilbert P. Cunningham's translation of the *Soledades* of Luis de Góngora.

But what follows is, still, a fiction, and the books that are mentioned, sought for, read, and quoted from within it must not be thought of as being any more real than the people and places, the cities, towns, and roads, the figures of history, the stars, stones, and roses which it also purports to contain.

ÆGYPT ▲

THE
PROLOGUE
IN HEAVEN

There were angels in the glass, two four six many of them, each one shuffling into his place in line like an alderman at the Lord Mayor's show. None was dressed in white; some wore fillets or wreaths of flowers and green leaves in their loose hair; all their eyes were strangely gay. They kept pressing in by one and two, always room for more, they linked arms or clasped their hands behind them, they looked out smiling at the two mortals who looked in at them. All their names began with A.

—See! said one of the two men. Listen!

—I see nothing, said the other, the elder of them, who had often spent fruitless hours alone before this very showstone, fruitless though he prepared himself with long prayer and intense concentration: I see nothing. I hear nothing.

—Annael. And Annachor. And Anilos. And Agobel, said the younger man. God keep us and protect us from every harm.

The stone they looked into was a globe of moleskin-colored quartz the size of a fist, and the skryer who looked into it came so close to it that his nose nearly touched it, and his eyes crossed; he lifted his hands up to it, enclosing it as a man might enclose a fluttering candle-flame, to keep it steady.

They had been at work not a quarter of an hour before the stone when the first creature appeared: their soft prayers and invocations had ceased, and for a time the only sound was the rattle of the mullions in a hard March wind that filled up the night. When the younger of them, Mr. Talbot, who knelt before the stone, began to tremble as though with cold, the other hugged his shoulder to still him; and when the shivering had not ceased, he had risen to stir the fire; and it was just then that the skryer said: *Look. Here is one. Here is another.*

Doctor Dee—the older man, whose stone it was—turned back from the fire. He felt a quick shiver, the hair rose on his neck, and a warmth started in his breastbone. He stood still, looking to where the candle flame glittered doubly, on the surface of the glass and in its depths. He felt the breaths in the room of the wind that blew outside, and heard its soft hoot in the chimney. But he saw nothing, no one, in his gray glass.

—Do you tell me, he said softly, and I will write what you say.

He put down the poker, and snatched up an old pen and dipped it. At the top of a paper he scribbled the date: *March 8th, 1582.* And waited, his wide round eyes gazing through round black-bound spectacles, for what he would be told. His own heartbeat was loud in his ears. Never before had a spirit come to a glass of his so quickly. He could not, himself, ever see the beings who were summoned, but he was accustomed to sitting or kneeling in prayer beside his mediums or skryers for an hour, two hours before some ambiguous glimpse was caught. Or none at all.

Not on this night: not on this night. Through the house, as though the March wind outside had now got in and was roaming the rooms, there was heard a patter of raps, thumps, and knockings; in the library the pages of books left open turned one by one. In her bedchamber Doctor Dee's wife awoke, and pulled aside the bed curtains to see the candle she had left burning for her husband gutter and go out.

Then the noises and the wind ceased, and there was a pause over the house and the town (over London and all England too, a still windless silence as of a held breath, a pause so sudden and complete that the Queen at Richmond awoke, and looked out her window to see the moon's face looking in at her). The young man held his hands up to the stone, and in a soft and indistinct voice, only a little louder than the skritching of the doctor's pen, he began to speak.

—Here is Annael, he said. Annael who says he is answerable to this stone. God his mercy on us.

—Annael, said Doctor Dee, and wrote. Yes.

—Annael who is the father of Michael and of Uriel. Annael who is the Explainer of God's works. He must answer what questions are put to him.

—Yes. The Explainer.

—Look now. Look how he opens his clothes and points to his bosom. God help us and keep us from every harm. In his bosom a glass; in the glass a window, a window that is like this window.

—I make speed to write.

—In the window, a little armed child, as it were a soldier infant, and she bearing a glass again, no a showstone like this one but not this one. And in that stone . . .

—In that stone, Doctor Dee said. He looked up from the shuddery scribble with which he had covered half a sheet. In that stone . . .

—God our father in heaven hallowed be thy name. Christ Jesus only begotten son our Lord have mercy on us. There is a greater thing now coming.

The skryer no longer saw or heard but was: in the center of the little stone that the little smiling child held out was a space so immense that the legions of Michael could not fill it. Into that space with awful speed his seeing soul was drawn, his throat tightened and his ears sang, he shot helplessly that way as though slipping over a precipice. There was not anything then but nothing.

And out of that immense emptiness, ringing infinite void at once larger than the universe and at its heart—out of that nothing a something was being extruded, with exquisite agony produced, like a drop. It was not possible for anything to be smaller or farther away than this drop of nothing, this seed of light; when it had traveled outward for æon upon æon it had grown only a little larger. At last, though, the inklings of a universe began to be assembled around it, the wake of its own strenuous passage, and the drop grew heavy; the drop became a shout, the shout a letter, the letter a child.

Through the meshing firmaments this one came, and through successive dark heavens pulled aside like drapes. The startled stars looked back at his shouted password, and drew apart to let him through; young, potent, his loose hair streaming backward and his eyes of fire, he strode to the border of the eighth sphere, and stood there as on a crowded quay.

Set out, set out. So far had he come already that the void from which he had started, the void larger than being, was growing small within him, was a seed only, a drop. He had forgotten each password as soon as he spoke it; had come to be clothed in his passage as in clothing, heavy and warm. After æons more, after inconceivable adventures, grown forgetful, unwise, old, by boat and train and plane he would come at last to Where? Whom was he to speak to? For whom was the letter, whom was the shout to awaken?

When he took ship he still knew. He took ship: those crowding the quay parted for him, murmuring: he put his foot upon a deck, he took the lines in his hands. He sailed under the sign of Cancer, painted on his bellied mainsail; at length there came to be two lights burning on his yardarms, were they Castor and Pollux? *Spes proxima:* far off, far far off, a planet like blue agate turned in space.

THE
PROLOGUE
ON EARTH

▲ ▲ ▲

A prayer said at bedtime to her guardian angel was enough, always, to wake his cousin Hildy at whatever hour she needed to get up: so she said. She said she would ask to be awakened at six or seven or seven-thirty, and go to sleep with a picture in her mind of the clock's face with its hands in that position, and when next she opened her eyes, that's what she would see.

He could not do this himself, and wasn't sure he believed Hildy could either, though he had no way to dispute it. Maybe— like Peter walking on water—he could use the Hildy method if he could only have enough faith, but he just didn't, and if he woke late he would miss Mass, with incalculable results; the priest would perhaps have to turn to the people, with his sad frog face, and ask if anyone there was capable of serving; and some man in work clothes would come up, and pull at the knees of his trousers, and kneel on the lower step there where *he* should be but was not.

So he woke by a brass alarm clock that stood on four feet and had a bell atop it that two clappers struck alternately, as though it were beating its brains out. It was so loud that the first moments of its ringing didn't even seem like sound, but like something else, a calamity, he was awake and sitting up before he understood what it was: the clock, hollering and walking on its feet across the bureau top. His cousin Bird in the other bed only stirred beneath her covers, and was still again as soon as he stilled the clock.

He was awake, but unable to get up. He turned on the lamp beside his bed; it had a shade that showed a dim landscape, and an outer shade, transparent, on which a train was pictured. There was a book beneath the lamp, overturned open the night before, and he picked it up. He almost always filled the time between having to wake up and having to get up with the book he had put down the night before. He was ten years old.

Often in later life Giordano Bruno would recall his Nolan childhood with affection. It appears frequently in his works: the Neapolitan sun on its golden fields and the vineyards that clad Mt. Cicala; the cuckoos, the melons, the taste of *mangiaguerra,* the thick black wine of the region. Nola was an ancient town, between Vesuvius and Mt. Cicala; in the sixteenth century its Roman ruins were still visible, the temple, the theater, small shrines of mysterious provenance. Ambrosius Leo had come to Nola early in the century, to plot the town, its circular walls, its twelve towers, and discover the geometries on which—like all ancient towns—Leo believed it must be based.

Bruno grew up in the suburb of Cicala, four or five houses clustered outside the old Nolan walls. His father, Gioan, was an old soldier, poor but proud, who had a pension and kept a garden plot. He used to take his son on expeditions up the mountainsides. Bruno recalled how, from the green slopes of Mt. Cicala, old Vesuvius looked bare and grim; but when they climbed Vesuvius, it turned out to be just as green, just as tilled, the grapes just as sweet; and when, at evening, he and his father looked back toward Mt. Cicala, from where they had come, Cicala was the one that seemed stony and deserted.

Bruno said at his trial that it was then he discovered that sight could deceive. Actually, he had discovered something far more central to his later thought: he had discovered Relativity.

Now the train on his lampshade, heated by the bulb, had begun with great slowness to advance through the dim landscape. The clock pointed at late numbers. Mass was at six-forty-five on weekday mornings, and he was serving every day for a week; after he served the earliest Sunday Mass, someone else would take over the daily duty, and he would do just Sundays, climbing the ladder of Mass hours up to the sung Mass at eleven. Then he'd begin again with a week of dark mornings.

This system was peculiar to the tiny clapboard church in the holler, invented by its priest to make the most of the only five or six altar boys he had; to the boys, though, it had the force of natural law: like the progress of the Mass itself, ineffectual, the priest said, unless every word was spoken.

> He was a boy who saw spirits in the beech and laurel woods; but he also could sit patiently at the feet of Father Teofilo of Nola, who taught him Latin and the laws of logic, and told him that the world was round. In his Dialogues Bruno sometimes gives the spokesman for his own philosophy that priest's name: Teofilo. He writes in the *De monade,* his last long Latin poem: *Far back in my boyhood the struggle began.*

By the time he had pulled on his sneakers and jeans and the two flannel shirts he wore one over the other, and gone the dim long journey through the house to the kitchen, his mother had appeared there, and had poured him milk. They spoke only the few words required, both too sleepy still to do more than ask and answer. He was aware that his mother resented the priest's insistence that a boy of ten was old enough to get up and walk to Mass at such an hour. Boys of ten, the priest had said, are up and working in these parts at that hour, working hard, too. His mother thought, though she didn't say it, that the priest had condemned himself out of his own mouth. Working!

In the light of the kitchen lamp, the day was night, but when he went out the door, the sky had a soft bloom, and the road down the hill was patent between dark hedges. The day was the eighth of March in 1952. From the broad porch he could see over the valley to the next hilltop, gray, leafless, and lifeless-seeming; yet he knew that people were living over there, had daffodils in their yards, were now plowing and planting, had fires lit. The church couldn't be seen, but it was there, under the wing of that hill. From the church, the porch he stood on couldn't be seen.

Relativity.

He wondered if, as well as Latin, the priest knew the laws of logic. The laws of logic! they tasted strangely rich to his thought, within the chewy consonants of the phrase. The priest had taught him only the Latin of the Mass, to be memorized phonetically. *Introibo ad altare Dei.*

He knew the earth was round, though; nobody had to tell him that.

Down in the valley beyond the town, a coal train that had lain unmoving all night, a caravan of dark beasts all alike, started with a long shudder. It might be a hundred cars long: he had often counted trains longer than that. The cars were being filled at the breaker near the pithead of the mine, and the train would take hours to be loaded and pass out of the town and the valley to wherever it went. The locomotive pulling it puffed slow and hard as an old man taking steps uphill: One. One. One. One.

His road led downward to the main road by the crick, which went to town and past the church and beyond. Thinking of early-morning dogs, he set out, thrusting his hands into the grimy familiar pockets of his jacket, familiar but not somehow his own. *I'm not from here,* he thought: and because that was true, it seemed to account for the shrinking he felt of the tender aliveness within him from the touch of this: this raw twilight, this road, that black train and its smoke. *I'm not from here; I'm from someplace different from this.* The road seemed longer than it ever did by day; at the bottom of the hill, the world was still dark, and dawn was far away.

I

VITA

O N E

▲

If ever some power with three wishes to grant were to appear before Pierce Moffett, he or she or it (djinn, fairy godmother, ring curiously inscribed) would find him not entirely unprepared, but not entirely ready either.

Once upon a time there had seemed to him no difficulty: you simply used the third of your three wishes to gain three more, and so on ad infinitum. And once upon a time too he had had no compunctions about making wishes that would result in horrendous distortions of his own and others' universes: that he could change heads with someone else for a day; that the British could have won the War of Independence (he had been profoundly Anglophile as a child); that the ocean could dry up, so that he could see from its shore the fabulous mountains and valleys, higher and deeper than any on land, which he had read lay in its depths.

With an endless chain of wishes, of course, he could theoretically repair the damage he inflicted; but as he grew older he became less sure of his wisdom and power to make all things come out right. And as the lessons of the dozens of cautionary tales he read sank in, tales of wishes horribly misused, wishes trickily turned against their wishers, misspoken or carelessly framed wishes tumbling the greedy, the thoughtless, the stupid into self-made abysses, he began to consider the question at more length. The monkey's paw: bring back my dead son: and the dreadful thing come knocking at the door. All right, make me a martini. And Midas, first and most terrible exemplar of all. It was not, Pierce decided, that those powers which grant wishes intend our destruction, or even our moral instruction: they are only compelled, by whatever circumstances, to do what we ask of them, no more, no less. Midas was not being taught a lesson about false and true values; the dæmon who granted his wish knew nothing of such values, did not know why Midas would wish his own destruction, and didn't care. The wish was granted, Midas embraced his wife—perhaps the dæmon was puzzled for a moment by Midas's despair, but, not being human himself, being power only, gave it little thought, and went away to other wishers, wise or foolish.

Literal-minded, deeply stupid from man's point of view, strong children able thoughtlessly to break the ordinary courses of things like toys, and break human hearts too that were unwise enough not to know how much they loved and needed the ordinary courses of things, such powers had to be dealt with carefully. Pierce Moffett, discovering in himself as he grew older a streak of caution, even fearfulness, coloring a mostly impulsive and greedy nature, saw that he would have to lay plans if he were to escape harmless with what he desired.

There turned out to be so many angles to consider—his changing desires even aside—that, a grown man now, professor, historian, he still hadn't completed his formulations. In the useless, vacant spaces of time that litter every life, in waiting rooms or holding patterns or—as on this particular August morning—when he sat staring out the tinted windows of long-distance buses, he often found himself mulling over possibilities, negotiating tricky turns of phrase, sharpening his clauses.

There were few things Pierce liked less than long rides on buses. He disliked being in motion at all, and when forced to travel tried to choose the briefest though most grinding means (the plane) or the most leisurely, with the greatest number of respites and amenities (the train). The bus was a poor third, tedious, protracted, and without any amenities at all. (The car, most people's choice, he couldn't take: Pierce had never learned to drive a car.) And his disdain and loathing for the bus was usually repaid in how it treated him: if he was not forced to wait for hours in squalid terminals for connections, he would be thrust in among colicky infants or seated next to liars with pungent breath who bent his ear and then slept on his shoulder; it was inevitable. This time, though, he had tried to meet the awful necessity halfway: having an appointment today in the city of Conurbana, a job offer at Peter Ramus College there, he had decided to take the slow uncrowded local, to travel in a leisurely way through the Faraway Hills, have a glimpse of places long known to him by name but still more or less imaginary; at least to get out into the country for a day, for sure he needed a break. And it did seem to him, as the bus left the expressways and carried him into summer lands, that he had chosen rightly; he felt suddenly able to shed by sheer motion a state of himself that had become binding and flavorless, and enter into another, or many others, like these scenes now being shown to him one by one, each seeming to be a threshold of happy possibilities.

He rose from his seat, taking from his canvas bag the book he had brought to beguile the time (it was the *Soledades* of Luis de Góngora in a new translation; he was to review it for a small quarterly) and made his way to the back of the bus, where smoking was permitted. He opened the book, but didn't look at it; he looked out at opulent August, shaded lawns where householders watered their grass, children dabbled in bright plastic pools, dogs panted on cool porches. At the outskirts of town the bus paused at a juncture, considering the possibilities offered by a tall green sign: New York City, but that's where they had come from; Conurbana, which Pierce did not yet want to contemplate; the Faraways. With a thoughtful shifting of gears, they chose the Faraway Hills, and when the bus after a series of smooth ascensions gained a height, Pierce supposed that those hills, green then blue, then so faint as to meld into the pale horizon and disappear, were they.

He rolled a cigarette and lit it.

The first two of his three wishes (and of course there would be three, Pierce had studied the triads that cluster everywhere in Northern mythology—whence it seemed most likely his fortune would come—and had his own ideas as to why it had to be three and not more or fewer) had for some time been in their present form. They seemed airtight, clinker-built, foolproof to him, he had even recommended them to others, like standard legal forms.

He wished, first of all, for the lifelong and long-lived mental and physical health and safety of himself and those whom he loved, nothing asked for in a subsequent wish to abrogate this. Something of a portmanteau wish, but an absolutely necessary piece of caution, considering.

Next he wished for an income, not burdensomely immense but sufficient, safe from the fluctuations of economic life, requiring next to no attention on his part and not distorting his natural career: a winning lottery ticket, along with some careful investment advice, being more the idea than, say, having some book he might write thrust magically onto the best-seller list with all the attendant talk-show and interview business, awful, whatever pleasure he might have in such fame and fortune spoiled by his knowledge that it was fake—that would be selling his soul to the devil, which by definition works out badly; no, he wanted something much more neutral.

Which left one more, the third wish, the odd one, the rogue wish. Pierce shuddered to think what would have become of him if one or another of his adolescent versions of this wish had been granted; at later times in his life he would have wasted it getting himself out of jams and troubles which he had got out of anyway without a wish's help. And even if, now, he could decide what he wanted, which he had never finally done, wisdom would be needed, and courage, and wits; here was danger, and the chance for strange bliss. The third wish was the world-changing one of the triad, and it was hedged around in his mind with strictures, taboos, imperatives moral and categorical: because, for Pierce Moffett anyway, the game was no fun unless all the consequences of any tentative third wish could be taken into account; unless he could imagine, with great and true vividness, what it would really be like to have it come true.

World peace and suchlike enormous altruisms he had long dismissed as unworkable or worse, at bottom solipsistic delusions of the Midas kind, only unselfish instead of selfish: obverse of the same counterfeit coin. No one could be wise enough to gauge the results of imposing such abstractions on the world, there was no way of knowing what alterations in human nature and life might be required to bring about such an end, and as the CVD Brothers had taught him at St. Guinefort's, if you will the end you must axiomatically will the means. Any power strong enough to remold the whole great world nearer to the heart's desire Pierce had in any case no desire to match wits with. No: whatever destiny a man's three wishes compelled him to, hilarious or tragic or sweet, it was his destiny, as they were his wishes: he should leave the world alone to wish its own.

Power: there was a sense in which, of course, all wishing was wishing for power, power over the ordinary circumstances of life one is subject to; but that was a different matter from actually wishing for power in the narrower sense, strength, subjection of others to your will, your enemies your footstool. This whole huge field of human desire was in some way alien to Pierce, power had never figured in his daydreams, he could somehow never manage to imagine power very vividly in his own hands, but only as it might be used against him; freedom *from* power was his only true wish in this line, and negative wishes had always seemed to him mean.

It had occurred to him (as it occurred to the Fisherman's Wife in the story) that it might be nice to be Pope. He happened to have a number of ideas about natural law, liturgy, and hermeneutics, and he thought a lot of good, in small ways, might be able to be done by a man of large historical sensibilities in such a job, able to enunciate God's will and impose it by fiat, no long-drawn-out contest of wills interposed between Sanctissimus and the carrying out of His pronouncements. But those gratifications could never make up for the awful tedium of official position; and in any case the hierarchy was probably not so responsive now to bulls and encyclicals as they ought to be, or had once been. Who the hell knew.

Love. Pierce Moffett had been both lucky and unlucky in love, his luck good and bad was among the causes of his being on this bus now through the Faraway Hills, love took up the greater part of his daydreaming one way or another; and no more than any man was he able not to toy with thoughts of hypnotic powers, unrefusable charms, the world his harem—or, conversely, of a single perfect being shaped exactly to his wants, of the kind that lonely academics described at such self-revealing length in the Personals columns of certain journals Pierce subscribed to. But no: it was no good using his third wish to compel the heart. It was wrong. Worse, it wouldn't work. There was no joy Pierce knew like the joy of finding himself freely chosen by the object of his desire, no joy even remotely like it. The astonished gratification of it, the sudden certainty, as though a hawk had chosen to fall out of the sky and settle on his wrist, still wild, still free, but his. Who would, who could compel that? The closed hearts of call-girls, the glum faces of last-chance pickups: Pierce drunk or coked enough could pretend for an hour or a night, as they could. But.

And if hawks flew then, choosing to fly as they had chosen to alight, and if he failed to understand why—well, he hadn't understood why they alighted in the first place, had he? And that was, that must be, all right, if one were going to love hawks in the first place. Gentle hawks, kind-unkind.

Chalkokrotos.

I wish, he thought, I wish, I wish . . .

Chalkokrotos, "bronze-rustling," where had he come up with that epithet, some goddess's: *chalkokrotos* for her bronze-colored hair and the rustle of her bangles on a certain night; *chalkokrotos* for her weapons and her wings.

Good lord, he thought, and fumbled with his book, crossing his legs. He tossed his cigarette to the floor amid the sordid litter there of other butts, and counseled himself that perhaps daydreaming was not a thing he should indulge himself in just now, this week, this summer. He looked out the window, but the day had ceased to flow in toward him, or rather he outward toward it. For the first time since he had decided on this jaunt, he felt that he was fleeing and not journeying, and what he fled took up all his attention.

When he was a boy, traveling from the fastness of his Kentucky home east and northward to New York City where his father lived, he had seen signs directing people to these very Faraway Hills he now rode through, though the immense Nash crowded with his kinfolk never followed the arrows that pointed that way.

It was Uncle Sam at the wheel (Uncle Sam looked a lot like the Uncle Sam who wears red white and blue, except for the goat's beard, and his suit, which was brown or gray, or wrinkled seersucker on these summer trips) and Pierce's mother beside him with the map, to navigate; and next to her, in strict rotation, one or another of the kids: Pierce, or one of Sam's four. The rest contested for space along the wide sofa of the back seat.

The Nash held them all, though just barely, the swollen sides and fat rear end of its prehistoric-monster shape bellied out (it seemed) with their numbers and their luggage. Sam called his car the Pregnant Sow. It was the first car Pierce knew well; the remembered smell of its gray upholstery and the plump feel of its passenger clutch-straps still meant Car to him. There was something penitential about those long trips in it that he would not forget, and though he held nothing against the Nash, "pleasure driving" would remain an oxymoron for Pierce the rest of his life.

Leaving the eroded and somehow unfinished-looking woods and hills of Kentucky, they would descend through country not much different though with now and then a further prospect of folded hills in sunlight that meant Pennsylvania; and then, by ritual passage through wide gates and the acquisition of a long ticket, they would enter onto the brand-new Pennsylvania Turnpike, and on its broad back be carried into country both new and old, country that was at once History and the gleaming clean Present as well. History and the blue-green distances of a free land, a new-found-land uncircumscribed and fruited, which Kentucky did not seem to him to be but which America was described as being in his school texts, was contained for him not only in the rolling hills they rolled through but in the roll of Pennsylvania names on his tongue and around his inward ear—Allegheny and Susquehanna, Schuylkill and Valley Forge, Brandywine and Tuscarora. They were never to see anything of Brandywine and such places, nothing except the turnpike restaurants located near them, clean, identical, sunlit places with identical menus and identical lollipops and waitresses—that were, however, not really identical at all, because each bore on its fieldstone front one of these lovely names. Pierce would ponder the difference between Downingtown and Crystal Spring as they sat around a long table breakfasting on exotic foods not found at home, tomato juice (orange only and always at home) or sausages in little burger-shapes, or Danish, and even oatmeal for Sam, who alone of them relished it.

And then on, through land forested and farmed and seeming underpopulated and yet to be explored (this illusion of turnpike travel, that the land is empty, even primeval, was more strong in those days when cars first left the old billboarded and well-trodden ways for the new-made cuts) and—best of all—into the series of tunnels whose beautifully masoned entrances would loom up suddenly and thrillingly: all the children would call out the name, for each tunnel had one, the name of the intransigent geographical feature it breached and left behind so neatly, so curtly—there was Blue Mountain and Laurel Hill, there was (once Pierce could say them all, like a poem, he no longer could) Allegheny and Tuscarora . . . One other?

"Tuscarora," Pierce said aloud, on his bus. O Pennsylvania of the names. Scranton and Harrisburg and Allentown were hard and dark with toil; but Tuscarora. Shenandoah. Kittatinny. (*That* was the last tunnel: Kittatinny Mountain! They plunged into darkness, but Pierce's heart had been lifted as though by music into a height of summer air.) Never once had the Nash left the turnpike, never followed signs inviting it to Lancaster or Lebanon, though the Amish lived there, or to Philadelphia, built long ago by the man on the Quaker Oats box; they went right on, up the Jersey Turnpike, a pale shadow of Pennsylvania's it seemed to Pierce, though just why he didn't know: perhaps it was only that they drew closer to New York and his old reality, passing out of History and the splendid Present into his own personal past, pressing on toward the Brooklyn streets that he would take up and put on like an old suit of clothes, too well known and growing smaller each time he came back to them.

There had always been other choices, up to the last minute, up to the Pulaski Skyway anyway and the hellish flats it crossed, after which the Holland Tunnel like an endless dark bathroom was inevitable. They could turn away (Pierce found the places on the map his mother held) to these strange Dutch-named places north, or south toward the Jersey Shore—the very word *shore* was for him full of the splash of salt surf, gull's cries, bleached boardwalks. On the way there they could visit unimaginable Cheesequake. Or they could turn toward the Faraway Hills, which did not seem so far, they could leave the turnpike just here, and in not too long a time they would find themselves passing the Jenny Jump Mountains and entering the Land of Make-Believe. It said so on the map.

He couldn't urge Sam to turn aside, really, the journey had too strong a logic, the Nash a juggernaut compelled by the turnpike habit. And he didn't really want not to see his father in Brooklyn. Yet he would wish silently: *I wish we could go now to this place,* his finger touching it, covering it: even—closing his eyes and throwing all caution to the winds—*I wish I were here right now*: not actually expecting the car's roar and his cousins' hubbub to be replaced by silence and birdsong, or the smell of the sun-hot upholstery by meadow odors: and a moment later opening his eyes again to the turnpike still shimmering ahead with false pools of silver water, and the billboards advertising the attractions to be found in the city fast approaching.

And a good thing too, on the whole, Pierce thought now, looking out at the meadows, ponds, and townlets of the place. It was all nice enough, surely, more than nice, desirable, and yet not really that otherwise, that place where the grass is always greener. He couldn't have known it as a boy—he didn't always know it as a man—but wishing is different from yearning. Yearning, a motion of the soul toward peace, resolution, restitution, or rest; a yen for happiness, which momentarily is figured in that duck pond overhung with maples, that fine stone house whose lace curtains beckon to cool rooms where the coverlet is turned down on the tall bed—a hard-won wisdom distinguished between such motions, which had fleeting objects, and true wishing, which carpentered an object of desire with such care that it could not disappoint.

Goshen. West Goshen. East Bethel. Bethel. A choice between Stonykill, three miles, and Fair Prospect, four, they chose Fair Prospect, good. *I wish I were here right now, in Fair Prospect in the Faraway Hills:* and there, or nearly there, he was, only a quarter-century later.

But something meanwhile seemed to have gone badly wrong with the bus he rode. It was laboring to complete a long curving climb less steep than many it had already swept over; somewhere deep within it there was a hard basso rhythm, as though its heart were pounding at its ribs. The noise subsided as the driver sought a gear it could be more comfortable in, then began again as the way steepened. They had slowed to a creep; it seemed evident they would not make the grade, but they did, just barely, the bus snorted and blew like a spent horse, and there was the fair prospect, framed by a dark side-wing of heavy-headed trees like a landscape by Claude: a sunlit foreground, a zigzag silver river greenly banked, a humid distance blending into pale sky and piled cloud. Leaf shadow swept over them, and a terrible jolting twang shook the bus—a torn ligament, a stroke, they had not made it after all. The bus shuddered all along its length, and the engine ceased. In silence—Pierce could hear the hiss of the tires on the road's surface—it coasted down the far side of the hill and into the village at the bottom, some stone and frame houses, a brick church, a single-span bridge over the river; and there, before the interested gaze of a few folks gathered on the porch of the gas station–general store, it came to rest.

Well, hell.

The driver let himself out, leaving his passengers in their seats, all still facing front as though traveling, only not traveling. There were sounds without of the engine compartment being opened, looked at, tinkered with; then the driver ducked into the store, and was gone some time. When he returned, he slid again into his seat and picked up his mike—though if he had faced them the fifteen or so people on the bus could have heard him well enough, maybe he was embarrassed—and said metallically, "Well, folks, I'm afraid we won't be going any further on this bus." Groans, murmurs. "I've

called down to Cascadia and they'll be sending on another bus just
as fast as they can. Be an hour or so. You're free to make yourselves
comfortable here on the bus, or get off, just as you like."

It had always astonished Pierce how, no matter what inconve-
niences they thrust on you, buses and their minions never let drop
the pretense that they were offering you comfort, luxury, even
delight. He thrust his book of Solitudes into the side pocket of his
bag, shouldered the bag, and got off, following the driver, who
intended it seemed to hide out in the store.

"Excuse me!"

What a day this was though, really, what a day! The real air
filling his lungs as he drew breath to call again was odorous and
sweet after the false air of the bus. "Excuse me!"

The driver turned, raising his eyebrows, could he be of any
service.

"I have a ticket to Conurbana," Pierce said. "I was supposed
to catch a connecting bus at Cascadia. Will I miss it?"

"What time?"

"Two."

"Looks like it. Sorry to say."

"Well, would they hold it?"

"Oh, I doubt that. Lots of folks on that Conurbana bus, you
know. They got to make their connections too." A small smile, facts
of life. "There's another though, I believe, from Cascadia, about
six."

"Fine," said Pierce, trying not to get testy, not this guy's fault
as far as he knew; "I have an appointment there at four-thirty."

"Hoo," said the driver. "Hoo boy."

He seemed genuinely grieved. Pierce shrugged, looked around
himself. A breath of breeze lifted the layered foliage of the trees that
overarched the village, passed, and restored the noontide stillness.
Pierce thought wildly of hiring a taxi, no, there would be no taxi
here, hitchhiking—he hadn't hitchhiked since college. Reason returned. He walked toward the store, rooting in his pockets for a
dime.

Up until this summer, Pierce Moffett had taught history and
literature at a small New York City college, one of the little institu-
tions which following the upheavals of the sixties had come to cater
chiefly to the searching young, the scholar-gypsies who had seemed

then to be forming into a colorful nomadic culture of their own, Bedouins camping within the bustle of the larger society, striking their tents and moving on when threatened with the encroachments of civilization, living hand-to-mouth on who knew what, drug sales and money from home. Barnabas College had come to be a caravanserai of theirs, and Pierce had for a time been a popular teacher there. His chief course, History 101—nicknamed Mystery 101 by his students—had been heavily subscribed at the beginnings of past semesters; he had the knack of seeming to have a great, a terrific secret to impart to them on his subject, a story to tell that had cost Pierce himself not a little in the learning, if they would only sit still to hear it. Lately, it was true, fewer and fewer had been sticking to the end; but that was not, or not chiefly, the reason Pierce would not be returning to Barnabas College in the fall.

Peter Ramus College, where he had been headed, was a rather different affair, as far as he could judge; an aged Huguenot foundation that still enforced a dress code (so he had been told, it couldn't be so), inhabiting smoked stone buildings in the suburbs of a declining city. Its picture was on the dean's letter, which Pierce pulled, somewhat crumpled and sweat-stained, from his pocket, the letter inviting him for an interview there: a little steel engraving of a domed building like a courthouse or a Christian Science church. Pierce could imagine the new poured-concrete dorms and labs it was now immured in. Below the picture was the college's phone number.

A tin sign advertising bread, the blond girl and her buttered slice much faded, was attached to the screen door of the little store; Pierce hadn't gone through such a door with such a sign on it in years. And inside the store was that cool and nameless odor, something like naphtha and raisins and cookie crumbs, which is the eternal smell of stores like this one; stores in the city which sold much the same goods never seemed to have it. Pierce felt swept into the past as he dialed the number.

There was no one alive at Peter Ramus at this August noon hour except other people's assistants; no one would reschedule his appointment, but he didn't dare cancel it outright; he left a number of vague messages that were only half-heartedly accepted, said he would call again from Cascadia, and hung up, in limbo.

By the front counter of the store he found a soda cooler, one of the sarcophagus kind that had used to stand in Delmont's store in his old hometown: the same dark red, with a heavy lid lined with zinc, and inside a dark pool of ice and water and cold bottles that clanked cavernously together when he chose one. He took a pair of dark glasses from a card of them by the roundel that held postcards; he considered buying a copy of the local paper, also piled there, but did not. It was called the *Faraway Crier*. He paid for the Coke and the glasses, smiling at the placid child who took his money as she smiled for him, and went back into the day, feeling weirdly at liberty, as though he had been set ashore, or had struggled ashore. He donned his new dark glasses, which turned the day even more into a landscape by Claude, amber-toned and richly dark: serene.

He had broken his journey, and with a lot maybe at stake, and a lot no doubt to pay for it in tedium or worse; it didn't matter, he couldn't for the moment care, since he neither much desired to go where he had been headed, nor much desired to return where he had started out from. If he wanted anything, it was simply to sit here at this wooden picnic table in the shade, to be not in motion, to sip this Coke and the deep peace of what seemed a still and universal holiday.

Serenity. Now you could wish for that, naming no conditions: a permanent inner vacation, escape made good. To somehow have this motionlessness which he drew in with the sweet air he inhaled for his inward weather always.

But there were problems too with wishing for moral qualities, serenity, large-mindedness. The interdiction (which Pierce thought obvious) against wishing for such things as artistic abilities—sit down at the piano, the Appassionata flows suddenly from your fingertips—applied in a way to wisdom too, to enlightenment, to heart-knowledge, useless unless earned, the earning of it being no doubt all that it consisted of.

The best thing. Pierce breathed deeply, he had come to these conclusions before. The best thing would simply be to refuse the offer altogether. Thanks but no thanks. Surely he was already wise enough—or at least well-read enough—to know that there was very likely something corrosive to common happiness in the very nature of granted wishes. He did know it. And yet. He could only hope that when the wishes came he *would* be wise, and not yearning; in good case; not transfixed by some object of desire; not in some dreadful circumstance from which he desperately needed relief: not, in other words, just now. Then, even if he could not refuse altogether, he might at least be able to take the next-wisest course, an option he had long since worked out that was sensible, usually all too sensible for him: and that was, his first two practical wishes for health and wealth having been asked and granted, to use his third wish simply to wish that he might forget the whole thing had ever happened; his safety and ease magically assured, to forget he had ever known wishes could be granted, to be returned to his (present) state of ignorance that such irruptions of power into the world, power placed at his unwise disposal, were really truly possible at all.

Really truly actually possible at all. Pierce drank Coke. From a side road beyond the church, a sheep wandered out onto the highway.

And of course it could be that just such a thing had already happened. That wisest set of wishes might right now be in the works, already granted, the genie having retreated into his lamp and the lamp into the past and the whole process into oblivion, Pierce ignorant now of his great good fortune and still toying with possibilities. On the face of it it seemed unlikely, considering his joblessness, and his mental health, which did not seem to him ruddy—but there would be no way to tell. He could have been visited this very morning. This day, this blue day, might be the first day of his fortune, this moment might be the first moment.

Several more sheep had come out from the side road and were wandering along the highway, huddling and bleating. One of the locals from the porch, who had seemed immovable, got up, hitched his pants, and walked out onto the highway to stop traffic, waving a warning hand at a pickup truck that was just then approaching, stay there, be patient. A dog circled the flock, barking now and then in a peremptory way, guiding the sheep (there were dozens now, more and more coming out from the side road as though conjured) toward the bridge over the river, which they seemed reluctant to enter upon. Then there strode out, amid the rear guard of the flock, a tall shepherd, crook in his hand, broad broken straw hat on his head. He looked toward the impatient pickup, grinning, as though not displeased to have caused this fuss; he crooked back into his fold a lamb that had thought to flee, and marshaled his charges with a call, bustling them over the bridge.

Pierce watched, aware of a chain of associations taking place within him without his choosing, inner files being gone through to a purpose he didn't know. Then the conclusion was abruptly handed to him. He rose slowly, not sure whether to believe himself. Then:

"Spofford," he said, and called: "Spofford!"

The shepherd turned, tilting his hat up to see Pierce hurrying after him, and one black-faced sheep turned too to look. The driver of the bus, coming out of the little store to gather and count his belated flock, saw one of his passengers wander off, meet the shepherd in the middle of the bridge, and fall suddenly into his arms.

"Pierce Moffett," the shepherd said, holding him at arm's length and grinning at him. "I'll be damned."

"It *is* you," Pierce said. "I thought it was."

"You come to visit? Hard to believe."

"Not exactly," Pierce said. "I didn't even plan to stop." He explained his predicament, Conurbana, thrown rod, canceled appointment.

"How do you like that," Spofford said. "Buswrecked."

"I seem to have blown it," Pierce said cheerfully. They both looked toward the beached bus, whose other passengers milled aimlessly around it.

"Hell with it," Spofford said suddenly. "Leave it. Come visit. I'm not far. Stay awhile. There's room. Stay as long as you like."

Pierce looked from the bus to the meadow across the river, where now the sheep were spreading out, chewing contentedly. "Stay?" he said.

"We've got to catch up," said the shepherd. "The old alma mater. The old neighborhood."

"I've left them both."

"No shit." He gestured with his crook toward the lands beyond the rise of the meadow. "My place is up," he said. "Around the mountain."

What the hell anyway, Pierce thought. A runaway mood had been in him all day, all week; all summer for that matter. He had got this far toward Duty and the Future and been thrown off course, no fault of his own. Okay. So be it. "What the hell," he said, a strange and sudden exhilaration rising from his breast to his throat. "What the hell, why not."

"Sure," Spofford said. He whistled a note that set the sheep in motion and took Pierce's arm; Pierce laughed, the dog barked, the whole straggling line of them left town.

This Spofford had once, some years before, been Pierce's student; he had been, in fact, among Pierce's first students at Barnabas College, trying out education on the GI Bill or its Vietnam equivalent. Pierce remembered him sitting in History One earnest and attentive in his fatigue jacket (SPOFFORD on the white tape over his breast pocket), seeming displaced and unlikely there. He was only three or four years younger than Pierce, whose first real gig that was ("gig" they called it in those days; Pierce had been doing a long gig in graduate school while Spofford did his gig in Vietnam). With the same GI money, Spofford had opened a small joinery shop in Pierce's low-rent neighborhood, doing fine spare pieces with a skill that Pierce envied and enjoyed watching. They'd become friends, had even briefly shared a girlfriend—quite literally one night, a night to remember—and though radically different in many ways, had, while drifting away from each other, never quite drifted apart. Spofford soon quit school, and then the city, taking his skills back to his native country, and Pierce would now and then get a letter in Spofford's miniscule and perfectly legible hand, noting his progress and inviting Pierce to visit.

And here at last he was. Spofford, nut-brown and hale, ragged straw hat and crook, looked well, suited; Pierce felt a surge of something like gratitude. The streets of the city were littered with Spoffords who had not escaped. When he grinned sidelong at Pierce—no doubt assessing Pierce in return—his teeth shone white in his big face, save for one central upper, dead and gray. "So here you are," he said, offering his world with a sweep of his arm.

Pierce looked over where he was. They had ascended the meadows of a tall hill's folded basis; its wooded heights rose beside them. The valley and its twinkling river lay below. There is almost a music in such summer views, an airy exhalation of soprano voices; Pierce didn't know whether the music which always used to accompany the opening scenes of pastoral cartoons, Disney's especially (music that the animated hills and trees sang, dancing slightly), was a transcription of this music he seemed now to hear, or whether this music was only his own memory of that. He laughed to hear it. "Nice," he said. "What river is that?"

"The Blackberry," Spofford said.

"Nice," said Pierce. "The Blackberry."

"The mountain is Mount Randa," Spofford said. "From the
top you can see over into three different states, up into New York,
down into Pennsylvania, over into New Jersey. A long view. There's
a monument up there, where a guy had a vision."

"Of three states?"

"I dunno. Something religious. He started a religion."

"Hm." Pierce could see no monument.

"We could climb it. There's a path."

"Hey, may be," said Pierce, his breath already short from this
gentle incline. The dog, Rover the drover, barked impatiently from
on ahead: his four-legged charges were getting on all right, his tall
ones were malingering.

"Are these guys yours, by the way?" Pierce asked, amid the
sheep, looking down into their silly upturned faces.

"Mine," said Spofford. "As of today." He tapped the hind legs
of a laggard with a practiced motion of his crook's end, it bleated
and hurried on. "Did some work for a guy this summer. Raising a
barn, carpentry. We made a trade."

"You needed sheep?"

"I like sheep," Spofford said mildly, surveying his own.

"Well, who doesn't," Pierce said laughing. "All we like sheep."
He sang it out, from Handel's *Messiah*: "All we like sheep. All we—
like—sheep. . . ."

Spofford took up the tune (he and Pierce had sung it together
in a come-all-ye version one winter in the Village) and so they went
singing up the meadow:

> All we like sheep
> All we like sheep
> Have gone astray; have gone astray
> Every one to his own way.

T W O

▲

The Blackbury River (not Blackberry, as Pierce heard it) arises as an unpromising stream in the Catskills in New York; fed by kills and brooks, it surpasses or incorporates its fellows and becomes a river as it nears the border, where it debouches into a mountain reservoir round and silver as a nickel, and called Nickel Lake for that reason or a different one. In Nickel Lake it cleanses itself of the silt gathered on its New York journey, and when it exits from the lake refreshed, it falls broadly over a series of stony rapids and low waterfalls amid the aspen woods that foot the northern Faraway Hills. In the long central valley of the Faraways it finds itself; when people speak of the Blackbury, they mean this river, widening and stretching and slowing to a stroll as it meanders across its pleasant floodplain. It has made a few shortcuts through this valley floor over the centuries as it matured; in 1857 folks found, after a week of violent spring rains, that it had broken right across one great curve of itself, leaving an oxbow lake behind and cutting two miles off the boating trip from Ashford Haven to Fair Prospect.

The Blackbury for most of its length has always been a useless sort of river; bordered as it is on both sides by the stony Faraways (Mount Randa rises in a series of ever-steeper removes from its western banks), it has no real ingress; clots of tree-topped islands every mile or so inhibit navigation. A stretch of fertile fields does well in corn and vegetables between the river and the mountains, though often disastrously flooded, and as it seeks an egress from the valley, its banks grow steeper and its course narrower, the land is more sharply folded and less farmed, the woods older, the banks less populous.

The river breaks from its valley through a gap called David's Gate, between stony palisades which are the eroded clubfoot of Mount Randa, and there is a sudden confluence there with the much smaller Shadow River, which has been curling and cutting its way along the steeper western side of Mount Randa before adding itself to the larger body; and there, built up on the palisades and reached by two bridges, one over the Shadow, one over the Blackbury, is the town of Blackbury Jambs: named for the enjambment of two rivers, or because it occupies the jambs of David's Gate—both opinions, and others, are held locally.

Sometimes, in the right weather or the right light, it is possible to see, from Blackbury Jambs, the two rivers rushing together and turning southward, but not mixing; the Blackbury's water, now silted again from its slow valley journey, less reflective, less brilliant, than the faster, colder Shadow; two kinds of water side by side for a moment, shouldering each other. Fish might swim, it seems, from one kind of river into another, as though passing through a curtain. Then the moment is gone; it is all one river. (There is local argument about this too, though; some claim that the sight of two rivers is an optical illusion, or even a legend, something never really seen at all. Those who have seen it—or know others well who have seen it—merely state the fact again. The argument goes on.)

You can get to Blackbury Jambs from the north by taking the river road along the eastern bank of the Blackbury, and crossing the bridge at South Blackbury; or you can cross farther up, at Fair Prospect, and take a smaller road over a hump or two of mountain, and come into town at the top—Blackbury Jambs being one of those towns that has a top and a bottom. Locals invariably do that; and as she once had been a local, and was on her way to becoming one again, that's how Rosie Mucho always did it when she came into the Jambs from her house in Stonykill, even though her old station wagon, huge as a boat, pitched and rolled like one too as she came over the mountain road.

Rosie Mucho (*née* Rosalind Rasmussen, and soon to be so again) had a longish list of errands, some pleasant, one not, one not even exactly an errand at all though Rosie had decided to think of it as one, had put it on the mental list along with the daycare center, the stop at Bluto's Automotive, and the library. In the car with her were her three-year-old daughter Sam, her two Australian sheep-dogs, her natal chart in a brown manila envelope, a historical novel

by Fellowes Kraft to be returned, and her husband's lunch, wrapped
in plastic wrap; and then too all the other oddments, baggage and
tackle that invariably accumulate in a car of this one's kind and age.
Beside her on the seat was the rear-view mirror, which only that
morning had come off, when Rosie tried to adjust it, from where it
was attached to the front window. It reflected nothing useful there,
only cast up into Rosie's face and her daughter's the brilliant August
morning and the leafy way.

The streets of Blackbury Jambs are a series of traverses leading
down to the waterfront main street that connects the two bridges.
Up above, the houses are often gaunt frame places with outside
staircases to the second floor, and wash hung on lines from windows, and steep front stairs; for the Jambs could not until recently
have been considered a pretty town, or a wealthy one; it was a
workingman's town. Now there are health-food stores and shops
with clever names on the ground floors of some houses, galleries in
the old warehouses; but still, especially in hard weather, an older,
less hopeful place still persists, a black and white photograph:
dirty-faced children, a sour church bell, coal smoke, smells of
five-o'clock supper. Rosie, who remembered, was cheered by the
new cleanliness and color of the town; amused, too, by its air of
dressing up. She wheeled the big car downward and then turned
onto a shady street, Maple Street, and pulled up—the steepness of
the street required some pulling—before a large house, one of that
kind whose hipped roof seems to bulge pregnantly and whose deep
porch is supported by fat pillars made of rubble. Up its side went
the usual stairway to an apartment on the second floor.

"Going to see Beau for a while?" asked her daughter Sam. It
was their usual euphemism for being left at daycare.

"Yup."

"C'n I come up?"

"You can come up," Rosie answered, pushing open the door of
the wagon, "or you can stay down in the yard." The brief, brownish
yard had its attractions: there was a changeable number of children
who lived in the house, and their toys—trucks and wagons and a
garish plastic motorcycle—lay here and there. Sam chose the yard,
and solemnly, as though it were duty not pleasure, mounted the
motorcycle. Crumb-crushing equipment, Rosie's husband Mike called
such things. Kids were crumb-crushers. Apartments with outside
stairways, like Beau's, were creeper apartments. Mike Mucho had

supported himself through school selling encyclopedias door to door and had picked up the lingo. Creeper apartments with crumb-crushing equipment in the front yard indicated good marks: young marrieds with kids.

Like so many other certainties, that one had passed. Nowadays daycare might be indicated, three or four or five single women, a couple of them with kids, a butch, a baker, and a candlemaker, and six or eight other kids taken in to help pay the rent—as here. And Beau upstairs could not be sold an encyclopedia, not one anyway of the kind Mike had once sold.

He should have stuck with that, Rosie thought, climbing up-ward. I bet he was good at it. I just bet. Helpful. Advisory. We're conducting a survey in your community, Mr. and Mrs. Mark. We want to place these books in your home, at no cost to you now or ever.

" 'Lo, Beau!" she called through the screen door. "You up?" She cupped her hands against the screen to look within.

"Hello, Rosie. Come on in."

He sat lotus-fashion on his white-clothed mattress, dressed in a white caftan. The little apartment was white too, walls ceiling and floors; a long strip of oriental carpeting connected an enameled metal kitchen table, the white bed, and a small balcony beyond, overlooking the town and the river. Beau's path.

"I can't stay," Rosie said, loitering just inside the door. "I didn't want to disturb you. Hey, don't unfold just for me."

Beau laughed, rising. "What is it?"

"Can I leave Sam for a while? I've got a bunch of stuff to do."

"Sure."

"Just for a couple of hours." She was aware she hadn't paid this month's bill, and didn't have a check; this wasn't supposed to be a day on which she left Sam here. Emergencies. Emergencies and money made her a little shy before Beau, who didn't seem to acknowledge either in an ordinary way.

"Sure," Beau said. "You want a cup of tea? Who's downstairs?"

"I didn't look in. I can't stay."

Beau began making tea anyway. Rosie watched him set water to boil on a hotplate, find tea and cups, set them out. He was still smiling slightly. He always was. Rosie thought maybe it was only the shape of his mouth that made it seem so, a turn-up of the delicate corners like an archaic Greek statue: a beautiful mouth, she thought.

A beautiful man. His sweep of curly black hair had a brilliant sheen, his velvet eyes were soft; his long narrow nose, that mouth, and the shapely beard, made him look like the best kind of Renaissance Jesus, strong young courtier become translucent with holiness.

"So what's up?" Beau said. "How's Mike?"

Rosie walked Beau's path toward the balcony, enfolding herself in her arms. "All right," she said. "He's having fun. A lot of fun. He's in his Down Passage Year."

"What's that?"

"Climacterics. His thing. Every seven years. Things go up and down. A sort of curve."

"Oh yes. I remember now. He explained it to me once. He referred to it."

Mike didn't like Beau, and didn't like Sam being given into his care. Beau had tried to draw him out once or twice when he'd dropped Sam off; Beau (Rosie had seen it) could draw almost anybody out, but not Mike. "Yeah," Rosie said. "Down Passage Year. Heading for the bottom of a cycle. He's feeling very tender. So he says. His needs, you know?" She laughed. "His needs are sticking out."

Beau opened a china cookie jar in the shape of a fat pig and took out a lumpy circle of something brown, Beau's own recipe probably, Rosie thought, he did the cooking as well as much of the baby-sitting for the women downstairs. He saw to them; that was his only job; somewhere, Rosie guessed, between guru and servant and pet for them. What other relations he had with them she didn't know; it wasn't that he or anyone hid them, only that they were too amorphous, or too superstandard, to ask questions about in a nosy way. For all Rosie knew, he was chaste as well as holy. Chaste: watching him chew with slow self-possession, she felt impelled to stroke him like a cat.

"I think," Beau said, "he's a young soul."

"Oh yeah?"

"I think," Beau said, "that might be why it's a hard trip for you." She'd never told him that life with Mike was a hard trip. "You're an old soul," Beau said. "And he's just not in the same place you are."

"An old soul, huh," Rosie said, laughing. "An old soul. A jolly old soul."

There was a shriek outside, and Beau without haste put down

his cup and went out. Sam and Donna, a fierce-faced child Rosie mistrusted, each held an arm of the plastic motorcycle, glaring at each other.

"Hi, Sam," Beau said, shielding his eyes like a scout.

"Hi, Beau." Still not releasing the vehicle. Donna shrieked threateningly again.

"Hey," Beau said. "Hey, what's all this energy, where's all that coming from? Hey, let's talk."

"I've got to run, Beau," Rosie said, fishing out her bunch of keys from her overalls. " 'Bye, Sam. You be nice. I'll be back soon." Sam had already begun negotiations with Beau, who knelt to hear both children, and barely noticed her mother pass. Rosie, starting her car, glanced back at them and had a sudden vision, an idea for a painting, that made her laugh. A big painting. It would be a version of that old religious picture that used to be everywhere, Jesus sitting on a rock and around him all these sweet-faced kids of all nations with shining eyes. Only, in her painting, around the same Jesus (Beau in his caftan) would be real kids, kids today: sticky-fingered kids armed with TV weapons, kids in plastic diapers, kids in filthy T-shirts lettered with smart remarks, belly buttons showing, orange-popsicle drool on their chins, bandaids on their knees; kids lugging superhero dolls and frayed blankies and five-and-dimery of every kind, riding red and yellow plastic motorcycles, making rum-rum noises. She laughed aloud, seeing it clearly. The Easy Jesus Daycare Center. Suffer the little crumb-crushers. At the end of Maple Street she had to stop, unable to make the turn, laughing hard, too hard, tears standing in her eyes.

She returned the novel, a week overdue, to the library that stands on Bridges Street, one of those thick, gray Romanesque concoctions that Andrew Carnegie used to give away across America, pillared, arched, rusticated and domed, at once fantastic and dispiriting. The stone steps are worn like old salt licks, partly by Rosie's young feet in years gone by; and in the entranceway there hangs a slab of prehistoric mud, turned to stone fifty million years ago with the track of a dinosaur clearly pressed into it. When Rosie was a child, she would stand before that paw, thinking: fifty million years ago; and in after years she had often described it to others, the old library where there hung an immense footprint of a prehistoric monster. Immense: the print, when Rosie returned to the Faraways fully grown, had shrunk to the size of a monkey's paw, or a human hand signaling *three:* trivially, laughably small. Well, so had she been herself, back then, fifty million years ago. She passed into the dim inside.

"And how was this one?" Phoebe asked her while she hunted up nickels for the fine. This was the same Phoebe to whom Rosie had once paid fines for *The Secret Garden* and *The Borrowers Abroad,* herself, too, grown a lot smaller.

"Good," said Rosie. "A good one."

"I've never read him," Phoebe said. "I suppose I should. Our local famous author."

"Oh, it's good," Rosie said. "You'd like it."

"They were very popular once." She turned *Darkling Plain* in her hands, regarding through the bottoms of her bifocals the edgeworn cover, a dim painting of armored men struggling together. "There's lots more."

"More where that came from, huh," Rosie said. She paid her fine and wandered into the stacks. Maybe she would try another. She was intending to save them for winter, when, if things turned out as she thought they would, she would be in need of long and easeful distractions, a place to go. But *Darkling Plain* had not satisfied, somehow; involving and colorful as it had been, it had seemed not a complete story; she wanted more. She ran her hand across the backs of them, unable to think how she might make a choice among them; she knew only the rudiments, if that, of the true histories they were based on (in fact she was hoping to learn a lot from them in the history line), and they all seemed more or less the same thing, each with its old-fashioned watercolor painting for a cover, overlaid with black script title, and each bearing at the bottom of the spine a little leaping wolfhound imprint. She drew one out: *Under Saturn,* a Novel of Wallenstein. More battles. Who was Wallenstein again? Another: this one's cover had a crowded Elizabethan scene, an inn-yard theater, orange-sellers, swells with swords, an apprentice or somebody who turned away from the scene and called out to the viewer, hand by his mouth, pointing to the players: *Lots of fun here, let's go.* Well, all right, this looked cheerful. It was called *Bitten Apples.*

She checked it out, and with its solid, deckle-edged weight under her arm felt oddly safe. Only one or two things left on the list before Mike's lunch. Mike's lunch was the last. She wrestled the great wagon out of its parking place, craning her neck to see whom she might run over; the power steering cried out, oil smoke farted from the tailpipe, the dogs barked. Rosie went west across the bridge and out of town, thinking: *the last.*

From Blackbury Jambs to Cascadia, the river takes on briefly a broad, quick lordliness; there are paper mills and furniture mills and a few tall brick chimneys along this stretch, and the river is walled and channeled here and there. Most of this work from the Iron Age is derelict now, the mills mostly stand windowless and the riparian works are crumbling; visitors to the Faraways in the last century complained bitterly about dark satanic mills and the intrusion of the Great God Dollar into sylvan loveliness, but the rosy brick and calm desuetude of the old factories seem harmless enough today, even romantic in certain weathers. One small ivy-clad block, once a chair factory, is a kind of monastery now; there are open services on weekends, and ecstatic dancing. The crowd there even makes and sells herbal remedies and cordials, but there are old cars in the yard, and crumb-crushing equipment, they aren't celibate who live there. Others of the old places are still marginally alive, doing a little warehousing or renting space to small businesses.

Rosie turned in at one of these, a corner of which housed Bluto's Automotive. Its sign showed a grinning, black-bearded cartoon brute in full stride, crushing a muffler in one paw and holding a wrench in the other; the resident mechanic, though, was a chinless, weedy guy with a thin fair beard and a prominent Adam's apple, scholarly-looking in rimless glasses. He looked at the rearview mirror Rosie handed him as though he'd never seen anything resembling it before, but if given time for study would figure out its purpose.

"It glues on," Rosie said.

He put its chrome foot to the spot on the window where it had come from. It didn't cling there.

"I can't see behind me," Rosie said. "Can't see where I've been."

"Epoxy," he said thoughtfully. "Give me a minute."

He went off with the mirror into his shop. Rosie let the patient dogs out of the car—they flowed smoothly out as soon as they understood it was permitted, and went racing after each other around the littered yard; they might, Rosie thought, melt like Sambo's tigers in this heat, churn themselves into buttermilk. She wandered to the brick embankment, iced with broken concrete, which ended the yard at the river's edge, and leaned her elbows there. Bending forward and stretching she could see, far downstream, the towers of Butterman's lifting themselves out of the river and the midday haze like a fairy castle.

Even along this deep and almost lakelike part of the Blackbury there are islands large and small that put out their heads; and on one of them someone named Butterman once built a castle. A real castle, with turrets and outworks and machicolations; across one red stone face he had his name carved in tall Gothic letters, BUTTERMAN'S, and inside there was a beer garden and a variety theater. The commonalty on excursion to the Faraways a hundred years ago needed to go no farther than here. A steamer then plied the river all summer long, starting from a special steel pier at Cascadia (Gateway to the Faraways) and calling at Butterman's on its way to Blackbury Jambs, and then again on its return to Cascadia. Butterman's is a ruin now, and the dock at Blackbury Jambs is gone, though the water-stairs remain; Rosie's uncle Boney could remember the steamer, and she often used to imagine it, holiday-makers in white clothes, the tooting steam whistle and the striped awnings. And though she had never been inside the ruin of Butterman's, she always meant to organize an expedition there, when she was grown up and needed no permission, because Butterman's, at least partly, was hers.

The Rasmussen holdings in the Faraways are not now as extensive as they once were; the big place in Cascadia was sold for a boys' school twenty years ago, and while Rosie was growing up in the Midwest with her father and mother, the whole tissue of properties somewhat unraveled. "Arcady," the summer place above Fair Prospect, with its fields and woods, is still theirs, though strictly speaking it belongs not to Boney Rasmussen, who lives there, but to the Rasmussen Foundation. As a child, Rosie hadn't perceived the decline, if it was one, of the Rasmussens; she had a Grandfather and a Grandmother Rasmussen in addition to Boney, a father too, and cousins, and her Sunday visits were always to one Rasmussen satrapy or another; but even in those days a kind of abstraction was setting in, was in fact well advanced, her own father's flight first to the West and then increasingly into his own fast-darkening soul (he died of an overdose of morphine when Rosie was fourteen) was only the extremest example of it. When Mike got the job here at The

Woods (partly through Boney's influence, the Rasmussen Foundation still contributed to the place's existence) and Rosie returned to the Faraways, she felt a little like a princess who had awakened after being asleep for a hundred years: grandparents were dead, known houses sold to strangers, cousins departed, new blacktop highways and plastic shopping centers laid over Rasmussen pastures and horse barns. Only Boney, her grandfather's older brother, oldest of them all, old even when Rosie was a child, still survived, outliving them all. And Butterman's, her castle, to the best anyway of Boney's remembrance, was still hers or his: her castle, that she had told stories of, to herself and others, during her long life elsewhere. Between her and Mike especially the castle had been a funny bond, Rosie's castle in the Faraways, her dowry, they would take possession when they moved back there together.

A trickle of sweat ran down her side beneath her T-shirt.

Spofford's party is tomorrow night, she thought; Full Moon party on the river. Her heart rose, or sank. Below her, in the glassy curls of the backwater, several ducks floated, turning idly in the current, dabbling, climbing onto rocks and shaking themselves head to tail always with the same small motion.

A swim. A long dive into dark water. Always that moment, as you leaped, when the desired water made you afraid, a moment in the middle of the air when you half-changed your mind, decided not to dive after all, a thrill of oh-no that was swept off by the cloven water's cold solidity and the bliss of being in it.

"Okay, hey," Gene the mechanic called to her.

She turned back to her car. Gene was stretched out in the front seat, looking at his work from different angles while the dogs sniffed his pants leg. In the western sky a huge pile of dense cloud had arisen: thunderheads. Rosie shuddered in the heat. A storm coming soon.

She drove back toward Blackbury Jambs, but instead of crossing the bridge into town she took the leftward way and went north along the Shadow River road. Now at high noon the river wasn't shadowy but spangled and glittering with sundrops, with shafts of sun reaching through silvery aspens and dark firs down into its deep bed. It ran gurgling happily over its waterfalls and around the tall boots of a fisherman who stood in it casting for trout.

The Shadow is a recreational river, or at least so billed, and has been for a long time. Down near the Jambs the vacation houses built amid the firs are stark geometries of glass and naked wood, with jutting decks and roofs sloping at surprising angles; they are "year-round" houses and several are lived in year-round by psychiatrists and administrators who work at The Woods, professionals on permanent vacation. Farther along the style changes to the passé chalet and A-frame types built ten and twenty years ago, interspersed with log cabins and even some trailers lugged laboriously into place and then fitted out with woodsheds, porches, carports, becoming immobile homes over time; but farther on than that, on the steps of Mount Merrow and Mount Whirligig, are the oldest settlements, clusters of bungalows and cabins, summer camps and boardinghouses dating from the Depression and before, beloved places cheerfully cheek-by-jowl around the shores of aging lakelets or strung along the river's banks wherever it widens momentarily; places that have names on boards over their doors, and whitewashed rocks bordering their brief front walks, flamingos and windmills and jungle gyms and seesaws arrayed around them.

Rosie called the general style of these encampments Tacky Tuckaway; their smallness had intrigued her as a child, their smallness and the neighborliness of their tiny lots, the noise their children and dogs and picnicking made. Her own child-life was lived on a larger scale, more widely spaced, less loud: these places had seemed child-sized to her. And her affection remained. She drove slowly through them on her way to The Woods or to Val's Faraway Lodge, never failing to notice something new and astonishing. Someone had bordered his pat of pine-needle-strewn ground with a cement wall, a turret at each corner, all stuck full of bits of colored glass, bottle bottoms, shiny scraps of this and that. The working-class people who came to vacation here, heavy-bellied men from Conurbana, couldn't rest, it seemed, they had to work; they built cement walls and stuck glass in them, they made carports and barbecue pits and trimmed their minute porches with fretwork. Or they had once anyway. More and more Rosie noticed empty cabins, camps for sale. Where did they go now instead, she wondered. Daze-Aweigh, what could that mean. Daze-Aweigh was 4 Sale. Oh: "days away." She drove past the Here You Are grocery store and the bait store, spelled Bate—Don't you know how to spell "bait," mister, sure I do but I always get a lot of folks come in to the store just to tell me how; these two stores and a squat cement-block church were all there was to Shadowland, a failed township that had once been laid out around these glens, centering on this crossroads.

Rosie paused at the crossroads. On ahead and down to the river was Val's; Rosie had wanted to go see Val, she had brought her chart with her for Val to look at and give advice, and she might have liked a quick drink too. She glanced at her watch. No. She turned left, and in a short time passed through a gateway, huge wooden posts roughly hewn, and onto a private road that led up the side of Mount Whirligig. The road was bordered with heavy wooden fencing; now and again trails and small roads led away, marked with finger boards directing walkers to the Grotto, the Falls, the Serpentine. At the end of the road, amid tended plantings, was a large wooden sign, rough handiwork but varnished and authoritative, that said THE WOODS CENTER FOR PSYCHOTHERAPY. A circular drive swept around this sign leading to the Center itself.

The Woods is a long, many-angled, four-story frame place, painted white, with fieldstone chimneys and deep verandas. It was built after World War I as a resort, the sort of place middle-class families would come to for a summer holiday in the mountains, to breathe healthful piny air and eat huge communal meals at long tables, chicken every Sunday, and sit on wicker chairs along the verandas or play bridge in the wide lounges; fireworks on the Fourth, and a hayride at season's end. It was never fancy; there were lace curtains in the rooms, but iron bedsteads and no rugs, and the toilet was down the hall. In the twenties a three-hole golf course was made, and some tennis courts put in. Evening entertainment was an upright piano with rolls. Despite a loyal though aging clientele, The Woods started to seem not much fun by the next war, and declined; Rosie remembered the dining room in the fifties, shabby and prison-like, the waitresses ancient. She thought it must have been among the last resorts anywhere to serve canned peas. It closed in 1958, and didn't reopen as a private psychiatric institution until 1965, when Rosie was living in the Midwest.

Wisely, the directors decided to leave the place as much as possible as they found it, beyond sprucing it up, replacing kitchens and bathrooms, and fitting in staff quarters and offices and infirmary. The Maxfield Parrish prints disappeared into the directors' offices or houses, and a moose head was removed from over the fieldstone fireplace, being thought perhaps unsettling; but the wicker furniture and the pine dining tables, the cool smell of the long

wood-clad halls, the lace curtains, all remain. The Woods as a
psychiatric center was to have the same tranquilizing properties it
had as a resort, and the principles it is run on are communal in
some of the same ways, not excepting group sings around the fire
and even hayrides. As stronger tranquilizers were developed over
the last decade, The Woods began to decline again; even the profoundly troubled who cannot live in the world can stay at home now
and still float on quiet seas far away. The people who come to The
Woods these days are for the most part not in desperate trouble,
though their unhappiness may lead them to think so; they are
people who, as the staff say to local people, "need a rest"; and The
Woods is as restful as it always was, though quite a lot more
expensive to stay in.

Rosie parked her panting wagon, which shuddered and heaved
for some time after the ignition was switched off—it didn't like
these mountain climbs—and apologized profoundly to the dogs.
"Just a little while, guys," she promised, and got out, only to return
for Mike's Saran-wrapped lunch, which lay on the front seat. It was
soggy with the heat, and, Rosie thought, probably more inedible even
than before. Who cares, who cares. Mike had recently decided to
change his diet, adopting a new and fairly severe one consisting
mostly of whole grains in certain combinations; Rosie cooked the
required cakes and compotes but refused to eat them. Beige food.

The Woods is divided into two wings by a broad portal running through its center, through which the porches and lawns on
the back side can be seen; from certain angles this portal makes the
whole place seem two-dimensional or fake, a cutout front merely, or
a standing screen, as though you could fold up its angled length and
put it away. Rosie's clogs echoed on the flags of this passage; she
avoided the eyes of one or two aimless people who loitered there
before the notice board—you could be hours here if you caught the
wrong person's attention—and went into the east wing through big
old screen doors that clacked behind her satisfyingly. She liked this
place, basically. Too bad. She asked for Dr. Mucho at the desk,
noticing by its clock that she was only minutes late.

"There it is," she said when he came. She gave him the food.
"I've got something to tell you."

The woman at the desk looked up slyly, interested. Mike,
cake in hand, glanced at her and at Rosie. He nodded thoughtfully,
entertaining the idea. Then he said, "Okay. Let's go to Woodpecker."

The various suites, rooms, crafts shops, and lounges at The
Woods have the names of local birds. On the doors are polished
wooden plaques in the shape of Kingfisher, Woodpecker, Robin.
Woodpecker is the staff lounge, almost deserted at lunchtime except for one or two other dieters. Mike sat at a table and picked at
the wrapping of his lunch, stuck to the bolus within. Rosie, feeling
the underarms of her shirt growing stained as a workman's, crossed
her arms before her, watching.

"So," she said. "The last lunch."

"Rosie," Mike said, not looking up, "don't be cryptic."

He should never have grown that mustache, Rosie thought.
Its drooping ends only emphasized the pout of his mouth and the
chub of his cheeks. She began to pace in a small circle, two steps,
turn, two steps. "I'm going to Boney's this afternoon. I'm packing
my stuff. I'm not coming back."

Still not looking at her, a mask of professional calm on his face,
Mike stood and got himself a plastic fork from a jar of them on the
next table. He sat again, poised the fork for use, but didn't use it.
"We agreed," he said, "that just now, just *now* and for a while,
there wasn't going to be any of this."

"No," she said. "*You* agreed."

A quick dart of Mike's eyes to the others in the room. "If you
want," he said carefully, "we can go somewhere, outside. . . ."

"I'm taking the calculator," she said. "If that's okay. I know
you use it all the time but I did pay for it and I can't do anything
without it."

"Rosie. You're acting out." He looked up at her at last, levelly,
candor and control projected from his narrow eyes. "You know, I
really feel like you're breaking a bond. Like a little kid. As though
you can't see me, see me as a person. We agreed that with my work
and my research and my, that we would put off any discussions."
His voice had sunk to a low murmur. "Until a turnaround time."

"Your Up Passage Year." Rosie stopped pacing. "We agreed
about Rose, too."

His head sank at that, as though it were unfair. His fork
counted four in the air. "We can't talk about this here, we can talk
if you want to talk about it. . . ."

"It's not to talk about," Rosie said. "It's an announcement."

"And Sam?" he said, looking up again.

"Sam's coming with me."

Mike began to nod slowly, saddened but not surprised. "Just like that," he said.

She flushed. This was the hard part. She had arguments for this part too, but they hadn't ever completely convinced her, and she didn't dare embark on them. "For a while," she said tersely.

"And be brought up," he said, "by Beau Brachman."

Quick as a cat attacked, Rosie shot back: "And who would you leave her with? Rose?"

Again Mike's head sank. Then he smiled, shook his head, chuckled, taking another tack. "Rosie," he said. "Rosie, Rosie, Rosie. Are you really jealous of her?" A grin began to spread across his face. "Really? Or is it something else? Something else about Rose, I mean."

She only stared, arms uncrossing.

"No, really, you and she being good buddies there for a while. That could be tense-making. Gee, we were *all* good buddies, you know, weren't we, one time there, one night." His voice had sunk again to a murmur, which the broad grin made horrible. "I *thought* maybe you had a little thing for her."

She couldn't throw the pie of grains, it wouldn't hold together, but she swept it up with both hands and pressed it into his grin so suddenly that he couldn't prevent it.

"There," she said, "there," more to herself than to anyone else, and turned away as Mike leaped up knocking over his chair and wiping bran from his face furiously. The others there had stood too and were hurrying over, but Rosie was gone, walking the wooden corridor steadily, quickly, in time with her steady hard heartbeats, and dusting bits of sticky meal from her fingers.

There, she said to herself again when she was seated in the suffocating car. *There. There there there.* The dogs sniffed and panted at her impatiently as she sat waiting for her heartbeat to slow.

Stupid. Stupid thing to do.

But what an awful, what an awful impossible man. She put the key in, turned it, nothing happened, she had a swift dreadful vision of a whole chain of events including return to The Woods, telephone calls, a wrecker, apologies, a ride home with Mike, and then saw that she had the car in the wrong gear. She fixed that, and the car started with a roar.

Almost as though he chose to be awful. Didn't have to be and chose to be. That couldn't be so, but it was just as though. It made it hard to forgive him. It always had, always. She reached up, tears beginning to burn and sparkle in the orbits of her eyes, to adjust the rear-view mirror. It came away in her hand.

THREE

▲

"What I'd like to do," Spofford said to Pierce, "is to get married."

They sat together on the porch of the little cabin that was Spofford's present home, catching up on each other's news. Out in the rocky meadow the sheep fed, raising their heads now and then as though to admire the view.

"Well," said Pierce. "You got somebody in mind?"

"Yup."

"And when?"

"Well, I don't know. Maybe not soon. She's sort of taken just at the moment."

"Married."

Spofford nodded. "To a Mucho person. Mike Mucho." As they talked Spofford shaped, with only a hatchet, a piece of stove wood into a maul, turning it this way and that to work it, chipping delicately. "So she's lying low now, being good. You can understand. But that's what the sheep are about, in a way. She likes sheep too. She'd like to keep some. So. We'd have that in common. Sheep used to be big around here, I mean it used to be a big enterprise. These hill pastures are perfect for sheep. I don't know why it went out. It could be big again."

The present spread Spofford had inherited from his parents when they moved recently to Florida: acres that the family had held for years, good for nothing but held anyway. Florida: Spofford spat. Talk about good for nothing. Pierce nodded; his own mother had recently drifted with the aged to that land.

"So anyway," Spofford said. "I've got this place, good for sheep, and I'm building a house. Or I'm going to start building it.

I've got ideas about what kind of house I want. I'm going to build it up on that crest, above the old orchard. It'll look both ways—see? There's an old foundation there, and a hearthstone. I like that. I could build on that. I've cut a lot of wood up there, it's curing now. I'll use that to build with. That's what this is for." He weighed the unfinished maul in his big brown hand. There was a tattoo on the back of the hand, a flying fish, faint, blue, like the veins there. "For splitting off shakes, pine shakes, for the roof."

"Don't they sell shingles?" Pierce asked. "I mean I would have thought shingles, roofing materials you know, would be for sale these days."

"Sure," Spofford said placidly. "I'd rather do it myself. It's sort of a gift, I guess—this house I mean. My own place. My own trees. Cut the trees, trees to make boards, boards to build the house; cut the maul, maul to cut shingles, shingles for the roof, roof to keep the rain out, if you see what I mean. . . ."

Pierce, hypnotized by Spofford's careful hands working and careful voice making plans, only nodded. The maul, no crude bludgeon but a true tool, beveled and shaped with an offhand grace, entranced him.

"A gift," Spofford said again, trying the maul's balance. "You'll meet her. There's a party tomorrow. A Full Moon party. Lots of people. She'll be there."

"Oh?" said Pierce. "What do people do at a Full Moon party?"

"The usual," Spofford said. "Swim. Eat. Drink. Take drugs."

"And what's this lady's name?"

"Rosalind."

Pierce laughed aloud. Spofford eyed him sidewise and said, "You never tumbled, right?"

"If you mean by that," Pierce said, "have I ever spoken vows, the answer is no."

"Aha," Spofford said.

"Tumbled, though," he said, "yes. Not once. More than once."

He laced his hands behind his head. Spofford went on working, and did not inquire further. The afternoon was strangely loud, cicadas in competition and a thousand other lesser insects filling up the air with a changeful hum. The sun crept toward concealment in the mountains behind them. "I quit my job," Pierce said at last, "because of a tumble."

"I thought you were fired."

"Quit, fired," Pierce said. "Let's not put too fine a point on it."

"And love was the reason."

"Love and money." *Chalkokrotos.* "It's a long story."

"And that's why the trip to Whatsits College, in Conurbana. Job hunting."

"Peter Ramus."

"I don't know if you'd like Conurbana so much," Spofford said. "Who the hell is Peter Amos?"

"I tell you what," Pierce said. "Just for the time being, as long as I've run off, let's not talk about Conurbana. Or Peter Ramus either. He invented, among other things, the outline."

Spofford laughed, and turned the smoothness of his maul against his palm. Pierce took off his brown spectacles: a darkness had come down suddenly as the sun reached the mountain's edge, and long shadows sprang out across the yellow grass.

She had led Pierce a pretty wild ride, and in fast company too. The danger she had always been a little bit in had excited him—it had excited her as well—and the excitement was magnified by the champagne she wanted and got, by the long nights on the town and the intense dawns alone together: all that was fueled by the coke, which in turn paid for it all or most of it—the remainder being the difficulty Pierce had at last come to. She thought of him as shelter; he had always, big-boned and ham-handed as he was, given the impression of great strength, not entirely an illusion; she thought of him as level-headed also, which was an error.

He had bought into her deals in a small way right from the start. He couldn't be sniffing up her capital for free, and it seemed sordid to buy from her in nickels and dimes; certainly he couldn't refrain, not if he was going to be with her through those long icy nights, and he didn't want to refrain even if he could have: the stuff she got was good, it was very good, Pierce red-eyed and jittery in class next day trying to explain the Enlightenment had no complaints.

"What was that," she asked him, "that she said, old lady Moldy Hairy Whatshername . . ."

"Lady Mary Wortley Montagu," Pierce said, classes done and his tongue untied again by coke and champagne. " 'Never complain, never explain.' "

"That's it," she said. "That's my motto. Never complain, never explain."

She kept to it. Business got better, and more dangerous. She got Pierce out of his old slum apartment, to which he had held on through thick and thin, and into a wide glassy concrete-floored place with a view over the fairy towers of the black bridge to Brooklyn. More central. He went deeply into debt to the Barnabas credit union over this deal, his never-large salary was going out those wide windows, she was snowballing her share of the rent into some big bucks.

"Snowballing," she said, and laughed.

He knew he was teetering, but teetering didn't mean falling. He knew himself to be afraid, though, and a man afraid and teetering could not help showing he might fall. He tried not to show it: he wanted above all that she not think he was not up to her. The sudden decisions she needed ratified—the apartment, money in huge wads and what to do with it, indulgences proposed that he had never even heard of—coke helped him with those, coke was decisive, but coke was funny: it made your reach seem swift and sure, but often it made you lurch and grab; the floor of the apartment was littered here and there with unswept crumbs of glass from wineglasses he had reached for too boldly, too coke-boldly. The bed was the only safe place. They clothed it in eiderdown and sunburst sheets and mirrored it and pillowed it. By the time it was full-rigged she had begun to spend nights elsewhere.

The telephone was a dreadful noise in that stone place at four in the morning. Pierce was alone, curled fetally on one edge of the big bed, it took what seemed hours to claw his way through the foamy bedclothes to the phone's cry.

It was the biggest deal, of course, the one that was to make him all his money back and double, that had gone wrong. In the ladies' john of the clubhouse of a baseball stadium, opening night of the season, and some really dreadful characters.

"Baseball stadium? What baseball stadium?"

"How do I know? I don't know anything about baseball."

It was all gone, money gone, stash gone, Pierce would never get the whole story.

"Just so you're safe, just so you're safe," he said.

"Oh, I'm safe. It isn't that. I owe you a lot of money."

"Forget it. Come home."

"I can't. I won't be coming over there for . . . a while. Change the phone. Change the locks. Really. But listen, listen. I'll pay it all back, like I said. And more. Just wait."

"It doesn't matter. Where are you? Where are you going?"

"I'll be all right."

"You can't just hide out alone. . . ."

"I won't be alone." There was a pause, a pause long enough to be filled with a story, or an apology, or an excuse. Then: "Goodbye, Pierce," she said.

On the day he first met her, she had been masked and naked, and he was being paid by her mother to caress her.

She was part Jew, part Gypsy on her mother's side, and mostly Romanian, or perhaps a full half something entirely different, on her father's side; she doubted her parentage. She thought her mother's marriage was white; her father, an old-fashioned Broadway boule-vardier, gentle and gay, had a secret hurt or weakness, never talked of much, which sent him early to bed and made him often vague, though always spiffy in a silk ascot and a neat white beard. He was "semiretired," a successful writer of sentimental songs and TV jingles once, and a violin virtuoso too. He was a good host, offering Christmas champagne and black Balkan cigarettes to Pierce even before he was introduced, questioning him closely and then striking an attentive pose (he was an exquisite striker of antique poses) though seeming not to hear the answers Pierce made.

It was her mother's cicisbeo, Sid, who was also Pierce's friend and landlord, who first brought her and Pierce together; and Sid who also later brought Pierce to her parents' apartment on a sleety Christmas night. Pierce's father, Axel, with whom Pierce usually spent Christmas, was in the hospital, and Sid, deeply sentimental about Christmas for reasons Pierce couldn't fathom, had insisted that after the grim visiting hours were over, Pierce accompany him to this little party rather than (as he had intended) go back to his empty apartment and read.

He recognized right off the ring on her left ring finger. She wore several rings, delicate silver ones, but the one on her left ring finger was an imitation Florentine one with a great glassy stone. When, at their first meeting, he had spent hours naked with her, he had had time to study it, among other marks now hidden from him. She took his hand with a smile of recognition, for she had seen *his* face. He had arrived late that day a month before, at that huge and overheated loft somewhere in the West Forties (he would never come upon the place again); the others had already doffed their winter things and were masked; Pierce remembered the oddity of coming in among them clothed but naked-faced when they were the opposite.

"We've met," she said, when her father tried to make an introduction, forgetful of Pierce's name. "Hi. 'Scuse me, Daddy, Effie wants to see you, everybody, she woke up."

Her mother—she called her putative father Daddy but her undeniable mother Effie, perhaps out of some desire to restrike a balance—was bedridden with 'flu, but wanted not to miss anything. Pierce brought in the box of chocolates which was all the cheer he had been able to acquire on a Christmas afternoon in Brooklyn, and these were opened and offered by Effie to the gathering around her bed.

"Is Olga here?" she asked. "Oh I hope she can come. You never know with Olga, but she promised." Effie wore pearls with her ecru satin bedjacket, an attractive woman much younger and seeming also to belong to a later decade than her husband, fifties to his twenties, or maybe twenties to his nineties.

Her daughter sat on the bed. "You know Pierce," she told Effie. "He's an actor. You've seen him." Effie ate a chocolate, smiling just the sly smile her daughter smiled.

"Oh," her father said (standing a little apart in the doorway, one hand except for the thumb inserted in his blazer pocket, the other holding champagne), "that's how you know Sid? The movies?"

"Sort of," Pierce said, no actor at all in fact, though when Sid had recruited him for a day's work, he'd assured Pierce that didn't matter a bit. Sid himself, though he could convincingly, even with a certain air, describe himself as being "in films," was in actuality a landlord, a born landlord in every sense, which is how Pierce had come to know him, Pierce's building required minute and constant attention from Sid, who would far rather have been at work on his other enterprises, in films.

"A dream sequence," Sid had explained to him as he tried to conjure heat from Pierce's stricken furnace that November. "A day's work is all. Less. And twenty dollars in it for you too, not that you need the money." Sid had just acquired the rights to a Japanese film, a piece of mild erotica that he thought might appeal to a certain audience, only it included no male nudity; a high court had recently allowed as how male nudity was not in itself grounds for prosecution, and Sid was sure his film could make money if it went to the absolute limit and could be so advertised. Noticing a scene where his much-tried heroine collapses into a deep sleep, Sid had thought of inserting a dream sequence just at that point, as full of naked men (and women) as he could make it, an Orgy Scene in fact, though "all simulated, all simulated," as Sid said, gesturing *No* with the wrench in his hand. And masked: the masks disguising the fact that the dream-revelers Sid had hired were neither Oriental nor appeared anywhere else in the film—as well as giving the proper surrealistic touch.

She was masked, then, when he was paired with her, and abstracted further by harsh lights that paled her tawny skin almost to transparency, unreal as a doll. Her mother, an amateur of several arts, had made the masks, and they were clever: just scarves of thin, silky stuff, almost transparent, on which Effie had painted Kabuki faces, beetling brows and outthrust chins. When the scarf was tied over the face, the features beneath gave some life and movement to the painted features—spooky and dreamlike indeed. Her mother had also, out of some fund at her disposal, paid for the shooting. Her husband knew nothing of it.

Pierce understood nothing of this at the time, they were all strangers to him then but Sid, it was only explained to him by Sid in a hurried whisper as they mounted the stairs together to her apartment at Christmas. Sid didn't whisper, though—Pierce couldn't remember him ever mentioning it—that Effie's own daughter had been among the dream-revelers. Or perhaps he *had* mentioned it, at some point, only it had not struck Pierce as it did now, among the family, at Christmas, drinking her father's champagne.

"Oh," she said, "there's the bell." She got up from her mother's bed with a bounce and went to answer it.

"Are you going to play later?" Effie asked her husband, who struck a new pose, shy, coy.

"Oh sure," Sid said. "You must, *must*. It wouldn't be Christmas."

"Olga's here," his daughter said, looking in.

"Oh, tell her to come in," Effie said. "I *have* to talk to her. Alone. Just for a while." She passed the box of chocolates to Sid, and tidied herself.

Olga was old, a sharp-eyed scarved head necklessly atop a

tiny and plump figure, a beachball in flowing garments and heavy gold. Pierce was briefly presented, and was offered a ringed child's hand and an absurdly deep, grandly accented "How do you do" that might have come from Bela Lugosi.

"My mother's cousin," she told Pierce when Olga had swept on into Effie's room. "From the Gypsy side." She took Pierce to the sideboard, where food was displayed, catered, she said, nobody in this house could cook. She talked rapidly, her long earrings that might have been Olga's trembling as she laughed or bent to the table, explaining family history, Christmas customs (Olga's visit, her father's recital on the violin). She lifted a cracker and caviar to her lips with her ringed hand; her breasts were free beneath a cashmere sweater, breasts he knew. She caught him looking. "Kind of funny, isn't it?" she said, smiling her frank sly smile.

He had writhed with her in exaggerated lust all morning, on hard platforms draped in dusty black theatrical velvets (the scene was laid in Nowhere, which was cheap). The action Sid had devised seemed to have been derived from the antique avant garde crossed with de Mille depravities, cavorting in abandon, and struck Pierce as operose and quite unerotic, but between takes he could simply look at her, absent behind her mask (once tied on, the masks were in place for the morning), and a strange jaybird freedom rising in him nearly made him giggle. She said she could use a smoke; she wondered what they were to do next; Pierce said he wasn't sure, he thought now all the men together were to menace the heroine, sort of set upon her—a dark-skinned girl whose mask wore sad raised eyebrows and a red anguished mouth. He wondered aloud if part of the terribleness of this poor Japanese girl's nightmare was that all the men she dreamed of were both hairy and circumcised. From behind her own painted cat's eyes—she was a Kabuki sphinx, only lacking wings—his partner looked them over, and laughed, seeing that it was so; she brushed, absently, with her Florentine-ringed hand, the glittering sweat from her breasts (this was hot work), and though with a delicacy of its own it had remained unmoved through all its appearance on film, Pierce's penis flexed and started.

"I remember the ring," he said, taking a cracker from her. Still Sphinx-like, more like her mask than he would have thought. "It's an interesting one."

"Ugly, isn't it?" she said. "But it's got a secret."

"Oh?"

She looked at him in an assessing sort of way for a moment, and then around the apartment. Sid and her father were greeting new guests (grandparents? one walked with a triple-footed cane). "C'mere," she said.

She led him down a corridor, past Effie's door, which was partly open; Olga and Effie, hands clasped, were talking in low voices.

"She'll tell your fortune later," she said to Pierce. "Really." She pushed Pierce through another door, into the bathroom, and closed the door behind them. "She's got cards, too, if you want cards." She extracted one dangling earring and laid it on the top of the toilet tank. Then she raised the hand that bore the ring, looking intently at its stone as though it were a fortune-telling crystal, and with the thumbnail of her other hand she opened a catch and lifted back the stone.

"A poison ring," Pierce said.

"Carefully, carefully," she said. Within the ring was a dab of white matter. Moving with skilled care she took up the earring, and with its shovellike silver pendant she dipped into the ring, brought out a load, and lifted it to her nostril; watching herself in the mirror above the sink, she inhaled it in a quick sniff, her nostril collapsing as though grasping it. "Why is it," she said, "I wonder why it is, that people think Gypsies can tell fortunes. Why is that?"

He could explain that. He watched, eyes wide, this bathroom a stranger place by far than that loft with its ersatz sex had been. She dipped the earring again and lifted it to him, feeding him, her mouth slightly open, kind nurse administering a powder, patient to sniff it all up, what a good boy. And again. "I could explain that," he said.

"What?"

"Why Gypsies can tell fortunes."

"Olga's good," she said. "You might learn something."

He could explain, he could explain, it was not that he knew nothing else but for sure he knew the reason for that, even as he watched her treat herself again he felt doors within him, behind him, blowing open one by one, doors into the country of that explanation, and it made him grin. She closed the ring, and looking in the mirror she put back on her earring, not before touching its powdered tip with the tip of her tongue.

She was turning back from the mirror when he caught her up,

easily and not swiftly but neatly, as in a dance or an embrace of stars on film, and she melded with him as she had not ever quite done in Sid's dream though willing enough it now seemed. Pierce marveled: it was as though he had been granted a wish, one of his adolescent wishes: that he could by some means know for sure beforehand that if he embraced a woman he would be welcomed; that he could somehow have already embraced her when the time for the first embrace was at hand.

There was a knock on the door. "Just a sec," she said over Pierce's shoulder. They held each other, listening to the footsteps recede; they kissed again, turning now irrevocably to fire and ice.

"Better go back," she said.

The living room was a new place, the books and pictures and the holly wound with tinsel and twinkling lights gayer now though somehow far off, amusing, richly festive.

"This lady is amazing," Sid said, passing them on his way to the buffet, and indicating the old Gypsy aunt with his thumb. "Don't miss her."

Olga had set up in a lamplit corner, a little table by her where she spread and gathered and spread a deck of cards.

"I'm next," she who had just been kissing him whispered to Pierce. "I'm going on a trip."

"Oh yes?" Pierce said. "Isn't that what *she's* supposed to tell *you?*"

"I need advice. I'm going to be gone a long time."

A sense of loss absurd and total fled over Pierce's heart, somehow only supercharging his present glee. "Where?"

"Europe. With a theater and mime troupe."

"Mime troupe?"

"Did you forget I'm into acting?" she said with a grin. "Sort of mimes. Spontaneous theater. We've got dates and everything." She took his arm. "I have a stage name," she whispered.

"What is it?"

A superstar expression, dreamy and self-mocking, came over her intelligent fox mask. "Diamond Solitaire," she said.

Olga beckoned from her corner with a hand, her other hand spreading and gathering her cards. "Listen," Pierce said. "Can we go someplace?"

"Sure," she said. "Later. Where?"

"My place."

"Sure."

Sure. He let her go, and went to look for more champagne; he was thirsty and gloating. There had come to be a steady tremble to him, a tremor, a standing wave of glee and triumph like the wave that stands in a silk banner in the wind.

What had Olga told him of himself that night? He couldn't afterward remember clearly; sitting by her he had felt himself for the first time to be truly an actor, and in a play witty and brilliant, which he also watched, a box-holder, first-nighter, wondering what turn the plot would take next and having loads of fun.

A hiatus in his work: he remembered something about that: an uncompleted thing, she wasn't sure what, a titanic sculpture (his thought, at her suggestion) which was to take far longer to complete than he had at first supposed, he should be patient. And—since he was thinking of moving far away (he didn't know that he was)—she gave him a piece of advice, that he should write away to the chambers of commerce in the towns he was considering, and ask about job opportunities and housing and so on there; which struck him as sensible, as eminently sensible and a surprise coming from an old Gypsy woman in what appeared to be a semitrance. He remembered snow falling outside the window in which the lamp stood reflected.

Snow was falling too outside the window of his own little bedroom hours later, a silk banner of snow standing in the ghostly streetlight, filling the night with its waving.

Sid's movie never opened. It was in that month or the next that there appeared in commercial theaters, uptown theaters, movies that broke open the whole box Sid was promising a quick peek into, broke it all open at last, and nothing done masked, nothing.

Oh antique innocence, Pierce thought, watching dawn come from the high tower to which she had at last led him; oh lost innocent days that we thought were so utterly, so brutally unrestrained.

Diamond Solitaire.

She had left for Europe in the spring, but she had come back; she had danced toward and away from him for a year before they became partners, and often enough had do-si-do'd away again thereafter, only to end up at the end of every figure facing him again, clap hands and promenade.

Not this time though. Why he was sure of it he didn't know, but he was sure.

He went back to the Barnabas credit union to "renegotiate" his loans, to sell, if they would take it, his soul to the company store. There was an anxious wait of a week or more while they studied his whole financial and academic picture (Pierce groaned aloud sleepless on the bed, thinking of the classes he had missed, the office hours he had canceled, it had all got to be a little too much in the past months, too many ashen dawns, too wide and safe a bed) and in the end the news, in two parts, was given to him by the dean of arts and sciences, Earl Sacrobosco.

The first part of the news was that they would be willing to renegotiate his loans, though on harsher terms than he had hoped for.

"What's with the money problems, Pierce?" Earl asked. "It really doesn't look good. You taking flutters on the market?"

Pierce was mum. Never complain, never explain.

The second part of the news was that a special course that Pierce had long brooded on, a syllabus for which he had recently devised and which he wanted to try out on young minds the following semester, had been turned down by the curriculum committee. Which in turn, Earl had to be frank with him, was not going to help him with the tenure committee, not combined with this loan business and, let's face it, Pierce's continued difficulty in playing with the team, so to speak. A word to the wise; it didn't appear at this juncture that Pierce had a good chance of being offered tenure at Barnabas.

"I get the general impression," Pierce said, "that I'm being fired."

"You have an assured contract for the next academic year," Earl said gravely. "I'm sure the whole picture will look different by then. Your coming in to see me is a step in that direction. The way I see it."

"On probation." A cold rage was blossoming in Pierce; fled, discarded, and now to be caned and humiliated—he had stood sufficient. "It's inadequate, Earl."

"Once these present difficulties have been . . ."

"It's just inadequate. I have taught here for some years, Earl. I don't really feel I need to prove myself as some kind of slavey."

He was trembling, and Earl saw it. Abashed, he said, "Well, let's get it all on paper. And think further . . ."

"No," said Pierce. He rose, almost knocking over his chair, anger always exaggerated his natural clumsiness. "Nope," he said, towering over Dr. Sacrobosco, who looked gratifyingly alarmed. "Forget it, Earl," he said, "that's it," and without another word—he could hear, through the roar in his ears, himself say not another word—he went out.

That's it, he said to himself as he went down the terrazzo halls of Barnabas unseeing; that's it, that's it, that is *it*. With this last iteration, though silent, went a sharp downward chop of his hand, as though he were cutting an invisible partner from his side.

In his tower again, he took out the slab of black obsidian and with a single-edged razor blade crushed on it the glittering crumbs of the last of his store, more precious than gold, by weight far more precious. He took a crisp new twenty from his wallet, not many more where that came from, rolled it into a tube, and with it up his nose he inhaled the matter on the stone in long ardent sniffs, exhaling carefully away from the stuff, and then wiping up the powdery remainder with a fingertip to wipe on the inside of his lower lip, where there were fine capillaries to absorb it.

God damn Earl Sacrobosco, he thought. Tenure committee. That was Earl and who else. No, he only wanted Pierce for his proletariat, that's all, piecework, day wages. And then the ax in June no doubt. And he thought Pierce would sit still for that, because of the loans.

Well, he's wrong, quite wrong; quite, quite wrong.

He took from the freezer a bottle of vodka—the champagne was gone, all gone—and uncapped it. Outside, green lights like Japanese lanterns were coming on, outlining the bridges, and orange lights outlining the expressways east. Pierce opened the windows and inhaled a tepid and brackish breeze. May, the merry month of May.

On the long radiator that ran beneath the window a copy of the proposal he had written up for his new, now rejected course opened its pages one by one. Pierce picked it up and began to read, champing his teeth, which were as numb as for dental work.

The course was to have been a complement to History 101, its contents standing in relation to the contents of his history course as dreams stand to waking. History 101 would be a requirement for it. Better yet, History 101 should be taken simultaneously with it.

The first sentence of the proposal was this: "Why do people believe that Gypsies can tell fortunes?" And the last sentence was this: "There is more than one history of the world."

Pierce sat cross-legged on the bed, tugging at the vodka, the pages of the proposal spread out around him. At his present height (heart small and hard, ticking loudly in his breast) he felt no self-pity. He felt spurned but potent, Manfred in the Alps, Prometheus on the rock.

He thought: there's more than one university in the world, more than one job on offer. There is more than one fish in the sea.

The closet doors stood open, and he could see the sleeves of her coats and sweaters, the tips of her shoes; in the drawers of the bureau were underthings, jewels, passport, a Florentine ring that had ceased to be capacious enough to bother wearing. He supposed he was to hold these things as hostages, or in trusteeship indefinitely. He supposed if he waited long enough she would at least return for them.

Change the locks, change the phone. He would do more than that. He would do as he had been done by. They can take nothing further from me, he thought, nothing.

In the morning though he felt only spurned, not potent; shipwrecked and at sea.

Spofford and he ate a simple meal, taken mostly from Spofford's vegetable patch, and when it was finished and the dishes washed up, Pierce retired to the bedroom, the smaller of the little cabin's two rooms, and lay on the sloping bed which Spofford insisted he take. Spofford took out paper and pen, and by kerosene lantern he wrote (with much pausing for stolid thought) a letter to his Rosalind, while Pierce looked through the introduction to the *Soledades* of Luis de Góngora, composing mentally the beginnings of his review. The Solitudes are the, are perhaps the best-known, least-read poems of the, de Góngora is perhaps the best-known, least-read poet of his age. Despite the enthusiasm of Shelley, and despite the enthusiasm of such poets as Shelley. "Gongoristic" and "Gongorism" are terms we all think we, we all use thinking we, are terms everyone uses, but the poems themselves and their peculiar, their elaborate, their peculiarly elaborate, the poems themselves are. He turned to the First Solitude. In the sweet flowery season.

"How do you spell *idyllic?*" Spofford asked.

Pierce spelled it. Spofford wrote. Pierce read, trying to pick apart the monstrous metaphors that lay in the text like knots of varicolored string, comparing the clever verse translation to the Spanish opposite. Now what, he wondered, could be meant by a "stone, whose light/ Is beautiful, however dark the night," which crowns the unworthy head of a dark beast, whose temples ("it is said") seem the bright chariot of a midnight sun? The moon, evidently; was this beast then Draco? Who knows? There were no helpful footnotes, footnotes would help the uninitiated reader, the absence of footnotes is. He turned the page. The broken-hearted Youth, shipwrecked while fleeing the wicked City, comes upon help and comfort among simple shepherds. The nerve of this Baroque tongue-twister, emblem-braider, gem-cutter, to imagine simple shepherds.

> *O fortunate retreat*
> *At whatsoever hour*
> *A pastoral temple and a floral bower!*

"Listen," Spofford said, leaning back in his creaking chair. Pierce listened, hearing nothing but the constant night; and then, faint but near, like a whisper in his ear, a spooky hollow hoot.

"Owl," said Spofford.

Who?

"Owl," Pierce said. "Nice." He read:

> *Here is no lust for power*
> *Nor thirst for windy fame*
> *Nor envy, to inflame*
> *Like Egypt's aspic race*

Aspic race? Snakes. *Gitano* is what the Spanish called them; that was "Gypsy" of course; Gypsy asps . . .

> *Nor she who, Sphinx-like, wears a human face*
> *Above her bestial loins,*
> *Whose wily voice enjoins*
> *Narcissus' modern seed*
> *To follow Echo, and despise the well.*

Unbidden, she came so suddenly and vividly before Pierce that he drew breath: her bronze hair cut short like a soldier's, her Gypsy skin satiny with oil, just returned from Europe by way of the beaches of Aruba, come to pay him a surprise visit. I've brought back a lady friend, she said. Her face clear, guileless, no customs cop could have had a hunch about her, but for sure she was she *"que en salvas gasta impertinentes/ la pólvera del tiempo más preciso,"* what Góngora could have meant by that he had no idea, she who in impertinent salvos blows away the powder once upon a time doled out more carefully—but that lady from Aruba was white, flaky as frost, bitter in the nostrils, they blew it in impertinent salvos, more where that came from.

> *. . . acaba en mortal fiera*
> *esfinge bachillera . . .*

Sphinx. Below was all the beast's: she sitting (he could see it, it tightened and warmed his breast like coke) in his plush armchair, still in her shirt and platform shoes but nothing else, a little embroidered pillow flung at her feet for him to kneel on and work.

> *ceremonia profana*
> *que la sinceridad burla villana*
> *sobre el corvo cayado.*

Ceremonia profana: rustic simplicity leaning on his shepherd's crook might look upon it with amused disdain. He doubted that. If the burly villain at work on his billet-doux in the next room could have been there, could have looked upon that ceremony . . .

"You want a beer?" Spofford said, rising.

"Um, sure," Pierce said.

"They're not so cold," Spofford said, bringing him a dusty bottle. "But you're a sophisticate, right? You can drink beer English style."

"Sure," Pierce said. "A sophisticate, definitely."

"What's the book?"

Pierce showed him. "Pastorals," he said. "Poems about sophisticates who leave the city for the country."

"Oh yeah? Interesting."

"About how much nicer it is here than there."

Spofford sipped beer, leaning on the doorjamb. "It *is* nice," he said. "You should come and stay."

"Hm," said Pierce. "Don't know if I could make a living."

"Can't you do history anywhere?"

"Well. In a sense."

"Come up here, then. Set up as a historian."

"Open a shop," Pierce said, laughing. He put aside the book and rose. He and Spofford went out the screen door into the moon-bright night. Rover lifted his head and thumped his tail against the boards of the little porch. Spofford took a few steps away from the house to urinate.

So real, so real, Pierce thought; he had forgotten; had forgotten this alteration of real odors, this immense volume of air. Fireflies: he'd forgotten fireflies. I wish, he thought, I wish . . .

"You could write a history of the Faraways," Spofford said, rebuttoning. "There's material."

"Regional history," said Pierce. "That's a good field. Not mine though," he added, thinking of it: a field, bounded by a low-piled stone wall, long grasses and lichened boulders, an old apple tree. Fireflies glimmering in the thistled darkness. Not his field: his field lay farther off, or closer in, beyond anyway, geometrical paths through emblematic arches, statuary, a dark topiary maze, a gray vista to an obelisk.

Open a shop. Once upon a time, when he was a kid, when he first decided or understood that he would become a historian, he had had the vague idea that he would do just that, that historians did that, kept shops, dispensed history somehow to those who needed it.

Turns out not so, he thought, looking at the moon, turns out not so. And yet.

A fortunate retreat, at whatsoever hour: escape made good. For sure, if he fled, she would follow. *Esfinge*, Sphinx *chalkokrotos*, not in her own person of course, she had made herself pretty clear to him on that score; not in her own person, no, but no less vividly for that.

"Listen," Spofford said.

The owl, Athena's wisdom bird or obscene bird of night (these Gongorisms are catching, he thought) asked again its single question.

F O U R

▲

You could be born, Pierce believed, with a talent for history, as you could be born with musical or mathematical talent; and if you were, it would, like those talents, show up early, as in him it had.

It was true, he thought, that lacking the born knack a person might still apply himself, and subject himself to the proper discipline, and through hard work and care do all right in the field without it—a thing which was probably not true of mathematicians or master chess players; but still such a knack existed. Nor was it solely a compendious memory, which Pierce didn't really have; or a taste for the past and a delight in antiquity for its own picturesque sake, a quality Pierce's father, Axel, certainly had, while lacking, to Pierce's mind, anything that could be called a historical sense at all. Of course a vivid imagination was a help, and Pierce had that; as a student he had been able to browse happily amid statistical breakdowns of transalpine shipping in the sixteenth century or analyses of Viking boat-building techniques, because what he always saw proceeding in his mind was a drama, real men and women at real tasks, linked in the web of history of course but not conscious of that, men and women doing and saying, dreaming and playing, at once compelled absolutely to do what they had done (they were all dead, after all) and at the same time free in their moment, free to hope and regret and blame themselves for failure and thank God for success.

But Pierce's knack had shown itself long before that, long before he had very many historical facts to apply it to, an oddity of his brain which seemed so natural to him that he was full-grown before he was really aware of it: for Pierce Moffett, as far back as he could remember, numbers—the nine digits—had each a distinct color; and while he could perceive those colors in, say, telephone numbers or equations, they were most vivid to him when arranged in dates.

Thus, the colors of his numbers became, without his choosing it, the colors of events—the colors of rooms where treaties were signed and swords surrendered, the colors of courts and coats and carriages, of mobs and massed armies, of the very air breathed; every century, every decade within that century, every year, was distinctively colored in his mind, bright panels of an unfolding Sunday comic. Like an infant musical prodigy effortlessly picking out tunes on the family cottage piano, Pierce was able to sort every odd fact that came his way, dates of battles, inventions, discoveries, things he gleaned from grownups' talk, from advertisements, schoolbooks, almanacs, into a scheme within, a scheme that had always been there and only needed filling in.

One had no color, was background only. Two was a deep green, somehow silken. Three was heraldic red, and four battle gray. Five was gold, six white; seven was a China blue, and eight black as antique evening dress. Nine was a dull beige. The nought was again colorless, though a dark vacancy where the one was a light vacancy. It was the first number—the number after the one, in dates after the first millennium A.D.—that determined the century color, and the next number the special color of the year; the last number was accent, glinting here and there in the tapestry. Thus some famous events were more present to his mind than others; 1066 had not much spectacle, but 1215 when the lords in green silken surcoats and gold chains sat down on the greensward with the gold-crowned king was an unforgettable scene. And 1235, when nothing much that he knew of had happened, was even more gorgeous, as was 1253, though that was a very different year.

Like vast canvases by different masters using different palettes, the centuries hung separately in his mind, unmistakable for one another—except that they seemed to be labeled wrongly, or rather Pierce kept forgetting that the label to the right and not to the left referred to the picture he regarded. For the thirteenth century was red only in that designation; the fifteenth was not the beaten gold of 1500–1599 but the gray cloth of 1400–1499. So for a reason of his own Pierce had sometimes fallen into the common schoolboy error of naming his centuries wrongly; and still as an adult when he said "the eighteenth century" he could not help sensing in the term only the very last years of it, when the blue silk frock coats and white wigs of, say, 1776, were going out, being changed for the glossy top hats and black worsted of the 1800s.

He came to understand, of course, that the division of past time into centuries was artificial, that even ages which believed themselves to be altering at the century mark were in fact subject to forces far stronger than a mystical and even inaccurate numeration; but what mattered most in mastering history (as opposed to understanding it) was to have a clear hypothesis, a general picture, an *account:* a story, whose episodes flowed one from another, linked yet distinct, like chapters: the dark-golden fifteen-hundreds yielding to the marmoreal sixteens of reason and classicism, and then the seventeens come blue as Wedgwood, *douceur de vivre,* clear skies; the eighteens black with toil and piety, black as their soot and ink; lastly, the present century, tan as khaki, born from a clutch of brown eggs (1900) right on time. His color scheme in no wise clouded Pierce's mind; he had a sure sense of the confusion and heterogeneity of human acts, varicolored, colorless, unsqueezable into any box, least of all the centuries; his system was a filing system only—but one that he had not invented but had found within himself automatically, his knack, his gift.

Gifts can be frittered away. Child prodigies put aside their violins, bored or repelled. Pierce, laden with scholarships and expectations, left St. Guinefort's—his Kentucky boarding school—and went up North to prestigious, machicolated Noate to study under Frank Walker Barr, a book of whose he had first read when he was eleven or twelve (was it *Time's Body?* or *Mythos and Tyrannos?* He couldn't remember at the interview) and who would become the latest of a series of fathers Pierce would revere, whose friendship he would find awkward, whose gaze he would avoid. He drifted into aestheticism, switched to a major in Renaissance Studies, lost a semester of his junior year in a romantic adventure (suicidal girl, flight to the Coast in a Greyhound, rejection, heartbreak), and although returning chastened, never quite fitted his wheels again to the track.

He had lost, seemingly, his vocation (and felt a certain satisfaction at it, as though it had been baby fat or acne), but it was easy enough to knock around Noate in those years without one, not doing much of anything and living in town as though grown up;

many of his friends, matriculated and not so matriculated, were doing it. It was not solely exculpation in Pierce that he would always think of himself as belonging to a sort of half-generation, born too late or too soon, falling continually between two stools. He had the idea that not many children had been conceived in the year of his own conception, most potential fathers being then off to war, only those with special disabilities (like Pierce's own) being left to breed. He was too young to be a beatnik; later, he would find himself too old, and too strictly reared, to be a success as a hippie. He came to consciousness in a moment of uneasy stasis, between existential and communal, psychoanalytic and psychedelic; and like many who feel themselves naked within, unfilled by notions, and without a plot, he clothed himself in a kind of puritanical dandyism, consisting mostly of an unwillingness to be pleased and black clothes of unidentifiable cut. He stood aloof in these clothes from a world he could not quite think how to criticize, and waited to see what would happen next.

In fact even this minimal pose was not quite brought off. Dandies should be small and neat. Pierce was neither. He had been a large and ill-made child, and his ugliness as a teenager had bordered on the remarkable, six feet by his sixteenth birthday, a face of unsymmetrical hugeness very like Abe Lincoln's, thick upshot hair, thick long-hanging wrists and clumsy splayed hands. Inside this frame there *was* someone small, even delicate, and deeply embarrassed by the ears on Pierce's head, the rug on his chest; and though (like Lincoln's) Pierce's disabilities would begin to shape up into interesting qualities by his thirties and seem to promise an old age of rugged character, even craggy good looks, Pierce would never forget how repellent the small person within had always found him. *Joli laid,* his mother called him; his uncle Sam Oliphant (whom Pierce most resembled) translated this as "pretty ugly," and Pierce agreed. A little big and pretty ugly.

Keeping out of the army played its part in drawing Pierce into graduate school at Noate, and avoiding the more arduous heights of scholarship occupied him there. Later on, when preparing himself to set out upon some standard tome as onto an arid sierra, Pierce would remember with chagrin how clever he had been, at Noate, in circumventing such work, in maintaining everyone's good opinion of him without exactly justifying it, and in giving the impression of having acquired learning he had in fact only fingered lightly. Frank Barr hoped Pierce would do a thesis under his direction, perhaps taking up a theme Barr himself had wanted to pursue but had never been able to—he suggested the spread of Nestorian Christian churches in the Dark Ages, to India, China, black Africa: Marco Polo had come upon surviving congregations in Cathay, and myths of Issa, Jesus, could still be heard by astonished missionaries in the Sudan in the nineteenth century. What had they made out of the Christian story they carried so far, isolated through the centuries from Rome, from Byzantium? Fascinating. But Pierce, though intrigued (Barr could intrigue anyone), quailed before the labor involved, primary sources in six or eight languages, untrodden ground, expeditions in pith helmet and Land Rover for all he knew. He stayed with Renaissance Studies, though always sensing Barr's never-expressed judgment; he discovered a collection of Elizabethan confessional literature at the Noate library (*Seven Sobbes of a Sorrowful Soule for Sinne*) and planned a brief, elegant thesis on these and their relation to certain themes in Shakespeare, particularly *Measure for Measure,* in his proposal making austerity a virtue ("In restricting myself to this seemingly narrow compass," etc., etc., as though to do so had been a hard choice) and getting it accepted by a tolerant old fart in the English department. He also acquired a parrot. Teaching the parrot to talk (*De mortuis nil nisi bunkum* was what he got it to say) took up more of his time than the thesis.

When his course work was completed, he made application, but no junior faculty position was offered to him at Noate.

Taken by surprise—not because he had labored to be hired, for he had not, but he had taken it for granted that this future would be offered him as a matter of course and had never seriously consid-ered the possibility of any other—Pierce packed his books and his black suits and the notes for his thesis with an unsettling sense that his luck had, for the moment, run out, that perhaps nothing, nothing at all, would happen next. The parrot was sent to live with Pierce's father, Axel, in Brooklyn until Pierce settled down, and there it remained, year after year, in the south-facing window of Axel's apartment, whistling, staring, disparaging. Pierce took tem-porary jobs at private schools, worked summers at a bookstore; he plugged, occasionally, at the damned thesis; and at the annual mass meetings of the academic association to which he retained membership he continued, along with hundreds (so it seemed) of fresher faces, to present himself to be looked over by the varsity scouts for whatever faculty positions were available. He felt caught out—lost sweetheart discovered at a slave market—when once in the midst of an immense ballroom "reception" Frank Walker Barr put a hand on his shoulder, and invited him for a drink.

"Specialization," Barr said when they had seated themselves on the cracked leather banquette of a paneled hotel bar, the professor's choice. "That's the great problem for scholars now. More and more about less and less."

"Hm," Pierce said. Barr before him was a series of rough ellipses, slope-shouldered torso, round bald head split by his wide grin, small almost browless eyes behind oval glasses. His hands encircled the pale cone of a dry martini, with an olive in it, which he had ordered with ritual care and was drinking with slow relish.

"Understandable, of course," he went on. "Even inevitable, when so much new material continually surfaces, new methods of investigation are worked out. Computers. Amazing how the past continually enlarges, instead of shrinking with distance." He lifted the glass. There was a gold wedding band imbedded deep in the flesh of his ring finger. "Still," tiny sip completed, "little room now for the generalist. Unfortunate, if that's where your talents lie."

"As yours do," Pierce said, lifting his nearly drained scotch to Barr.

"So," Barr said. "Any nibbles? Offers you're considering?"

Pierce shrugged, raised eyebrows, shook head. "You know," he said, "when I was a kid I sort of thought that when I became a historian, what I would do, what historians did, was practice history— the way a doctor practices medicine. Maybe because the uncle I grew up with was a doctor. Have an office, or a shop . . ."

" 'Keep thy shop,' " Barr said, " 'and thy shop will keep thee.' " He made in his throat the famous Barr chuckle, plummy, chocolaty. "Ben Franklin."

Pierce drank. In the dark of the bar, his old mentor was unreadable. Pierce was fairly sure that Barr's kindly but justly lukewarm *descriptio* (couldn't call it a recommendation) was chiefly what had kept Pierce from moving automatically into a slot at Noate, and thrown him on the open market. "How," he said, something—not the drink—warming his cheeks suddenly, "would *you* do it? Practice history. If there weren't Noate."

Barr considered this a long time. The drink before him seemed to glow faintly, like a votive lamp before a Buddha. "I think," he said, "that I would take some job, some job I was suited for—my father was a tailor, I worked for him—and I would listen, and discover what questions people asked, that history might answer, or help to answer, even if at first they didn't seem to be historical questions; and I'd try to answer them. In a book, I suppose, probably, or maybe not."

"Questions like . . ."

"Questions that come up. I remember there was an old woman who lived over my father's shop. She read cards, told fortunes. She was a Gypsy, my father said, and that's why people went to her. But why, I asked him, do people think Gypsies can tell fortunes? History could answer that. Give an *account,* you see." He set down his finished drink; his grin had begun again to grow, his chuckle to rumble in his throat. "The only trouble would be that damn tendency to generalism. I suppose that the first question I tried to answer would lead me to others, and those to others, and so on; and there being no publish-or-perish sort of pressure, no impetus to stop asking and start answering, I might go on forever. End up with the History of the World. Or *a* history, anyway." He took, with plump fingers, the olive from his glass, and chewed it thoughtfully. "Incomplete, probably, in the end. Unfinished. Oh, yes. But still I think I would consider myself to have been practicing history."

A life of useful labor, a thousand relined overcoats, and yet all history in your heart, an endless dimension, a past as real as if it had been the case, and chock-full of answered questions; an account, added up but unpaid. A large dissatisfaction had sprung up in Pierce, or a nameless desire. He ordered a second drink.

"In any case," Barr said, spreading his hands on the table as Pierce always remembered him doing toward a lecture's end, "it's neither here nor there, is it? Teachers are what we are. Now who did you say you've been talking to?"

The warmth in Pierce's cheeks heated to a blush. "Well," he said. "Barnabas College. Here in the city." As though it were one, an unimportant one, of many. "Looks possible."

"Barnabas," said Barr, mulling. "Barnabas. I know the dean there. A Dr. Sacrobosco. I could write."

"Thank you," Pierce said, only for the tiniest instant thinking that perhaps Barr would blackball him, queer his deal, would harry him now throughout Academe forever for not taking on those damn Nestorian churches. "Thank you."

"We'll talk," Barr said, looking at a large gold wristwatch. "You'll fill me in on what you've been doing. How that thesis is coming. Now." He rose, short legs making him a smaller man standing than he seemed sitting.

"So, by the way," Pierce said, helping Barr into his crumpled mackintosh, "why *do* people think Gypsies can tell fortunes?"

"Oh," Barr said, "the answer's simple enough. Simple enough." He glanced up at Pierce, twinkling donnishly, as he had used to do when he announced that blue books must now be closed, and passed to the front. "There's more than one History of the World, you know," he said. "Isn't there? More than one. One for each of us, maybe. Wouldn't you say so?"

Why do people think that Gypsies can tell fortunes?

The dissatisfaction, or the desire, or the puzzlement, that had awakened somehow in Pierce did not pass. He felt annoyed, nettled, continually; landing the Barnabas job did not end it, did not even seem relevant to it. He found himself waking at dawn with the sense that an answer to some question had to be found, a sense that would diffuse into the day's business and leave him restless at bedtime, a taste in his mind like the taste of too many anxious cigarettes.

What, did Barr own his soul or something, that he could set him off like this? It was unfair, he was a grown-up, a Ph.D. or nearly, he had a job (Barr's doing, all right, Barr's doing), and the whole great city lay before him for his delight, bars, women, entertainments all laid on. He began spending the evenings when he was not grading papers in reading, a habit he had almost broken himself of at Noate. He looked for Barr's books, most of which he knew only by report or review; several of them were out of print, and had to be hunted for in libraries or secondhand bookstores. A simple answer: something to stopper up whatever it was that seemed to be coming unstoppered within him, a last trick question to be disposed of, clear the field finally and for good.

On a bitter cold solstice night, too cold to go abroad, Pierce with the beginnings of a 'flu sat wrapped in a blanket (the heat in his aged building had failed) and turned the pages of Barr's book,

Time's Body, which he had brought home from the far-off Brooklyn Public, and read, fever beginning to crackle in his ears:

> Plutarch records that in the early years of the reign of Tiberius the pilot of a ship rounding the Greek archipelago passed a certain island at dawn on the solstice day and heard his name called from shore: "Thamus! When you come near the Palodes, tell them that the great god Pan is dead!" He thought at first to refuse, being afraid, but when he came opposite the Palodes, he called out the words as he had heard them: "Pan is dead! The great god Pan is dead!" And then there arose from the island a lamenting and wailing, not of one voice but of many mingled, as though the earth itself mourned.

A shiver ran up Pierce's spine beneath the blanket. He had read this story before, and had shivered then too.

> To say [Barr continued] that the great god Pan died in the early years of the reign of Tiberius is in a sense to say nothing at all, or a great deal too much. We know what god was born on a solstice day in those years; we know his after-history; we know in what sense Pan died at the approach of that new god. The shiver of fear or delight we feel still at the story is the shiver Augustine felt at the same story: a world-age is passing, and a man, a pagan, is hearing it pass, and does not know it.
>
> But we know too—and Plutarch knew—that on those islands of the Greek archipelago the cult of the year-god, the god of many names—Osiris, Adonis, Tammuz, Pan—was historically practiced. In all likelihood his murder and resurrection were still celebrated in imperial times, and the ecstatic female cults who each year tore in pieces and then mourned their god in wailing and shrieking and rending their garments, were still extant. Had Plutarch's pilot Thamus blundered into a ritual mourning for Tammuz? What is certain is that if he had passed the same islands the previous year, or any year for the previous five or ten centuries, he would have heard of the same climactic event, and been shuddered by the same wailing; for the year, as those Greeks believed, could not have gone round without it.

Pierce was beginning to feel very strange. A sense like déjà vu had overtaken him; a sense that some mental process was disengaging within him, and re-engaging in a different, but not a new, way.

And yet what have we learned, having learned this? Have we disposed of Plutarch's story, and the awful prophecy it contains, the anecdote of a world's passing? I don't believe it.

Suppose a man finds a five-dollar bill on a certain street corner at a certain time of day.

(Definitely, definitely he had read this before, and yet could not remember how it came out.)

Reason and the laws of probability will tell him that this street corner which has produced for him a chance treasure, is now neither more likely nor less likely than any other street corner in the city to produce another one. It remains a street corner, like others. And yet which of us, on passing our lucky corner at our lucky time of day, would not take a quick look around? A conjunction took place there of ourselves, our desires, and the world; it has acquired meaning; if it produces no more for us, are we not tempted to think we have only used up a magic which it once truly had? We cannot help imposing our desires on the world—even though the world remains impervious to them, and keeps to laws that are not the laws our natures suppose it ought to have.

But history is made by man. Old Vico said that man can only fully understand what he has made; the corollary to that is, that what man has made he *can* understand: it will not, like the physical world, remain impervious to his desire to understand. So if we look at history and find in it huge stories, plots identical to the plots of myth and legend, populated by actual persons who however bear the symbols and even the names of gods and demons, we need be no more alarmed and suspicious than we would be on picking up a hammer, and finding its grip fit for our hand, and its head balanced for our striking. We are understanding what we have made, and its shape is ours; we have made history, we have made its street corners and the five-dollar bills we find on them; the laws that govern it are not the laws of nature, but they are the laws that govern us.

So let us learn, by all means, why the voices wailed that Pan was dead. Let us learn—the answers are simple enough—why Moses had horns, and why the Israelites worshipped a golden calf; why Jesus was a fish, and why a man with a water-jug on his shoulder directed the Apostles—the Twelve—to an upper room. But let us not think that in such explorations we have disposed of or robbed of significance the story these figures tell. The story remains; if it changes, and it does, it is because our human nature is not fixed; there is more than one history of the world. But when we believe that we have proved there is *no* story, that history is nothing but one damned thing after another, that can only be because we have ceased to recognize ourselves.

Moses had horns?

Yes: Pierce could see them, in the darkish photograph of Michelangelo's statue in the encyclopedia, open before him on the window seat, open before him next to this book, *Time's Body*, also open before him, to this page. He was eleven years old; no, twelve. The horns were only buds, a baby ram's, odd on the huge bearded head: but they were there.

There was a story. He was seeing it for the first time, there in the window seat, brown winter mountains and a dead garden disappearing without; he didn't know what the story was, could only imagine it, imagine it unfolding and linking and telling itself vastly and purposefully as thunderheads gathering. A secret story had been going on for centuries, for all time, and it could be known; here was its outline, or part of it, the secrets spilled, or if not the secrets, the secret that there were secrets.

Pierce in his New York slum rolled a cigarette and lit it, but this grown-up action did not stop the feeling that had come over him, that his jumbled and darkened interior was resolving itself into a series of pictures, a series of magic-lantern slides projected all at once, yet each clear, each in some sense the same slide.

When he was very small he had been told the story of the man who was caught in a rainstorm and sought shelter in an old barn. He fell asleep in the hayloft, and when he woke it was deep midnight. He saw, walking on the rafters of the barn, a clowder of cats; they would walk the rafters and meet, and seem to pass a message. Then two cats met on a rafter very near where he lay hidden, and he heard one say to the other: "Tell Dildrum that Doldrum is dead." And so they parted. When the man got home that day, he told his wife what had happened, and what he had heard the cats say: "Tell Dildrum that Doldrum is dead." And on hearing that, their old family cat, dozing by the fire, leaped up with a shriek and cried out: "Then I'm to be king of the cats!" And it shot up the chimney, and was never seen again.

That story had made him shiver and wonder, and ponder for days; not the story that had been told, but the secret story within it that had *not* been told: the story about the cats, the secret story that had been going on all along and that no one knew but they.

That was the feeling he had felt in the window seat, too, having looked up Moses in a dozen places in the old *Britannica,* and finding that picture, and seeing that horned head, unexplained, unmentioned even in the picture's caption. They had been there all along, those horns, though he hadn't known it, and now he did, and there was an explanation for them too that he didn't know but that he could learn. And that was History.

And now Pierce coming on that moment, as though breaking open a box that contained it while searching for something else, could measure by it what he had gained, and what he had lost, in the long time that had elapsed between then and now, between that window in Kentucky and this one.

How was it he had come to lose his vocation?

He couldn't turn back now, of course, and find where the thread had been dropped, and pick it up again; time was only one way, and all that he had learned he couldn't unlearn. And yet. He sat with Barr's book in his lap, and listened to the silent city, and felt an unreasoning grief: something had been stolen from him, he had stolen something from himself, a pearl of great price, that he had forgotten the value of and had thrown away thoughtlessly, and now could never have again.

In that year a kind of strange parade seemed to begin in the city. Pierce didn't at first notice it, or anyway took no notice, though he could sense his students growing restless and inattentive, as if they heard a far-off drum. Now and again he would see, in the corridors or on the steps or in the bookstores where he browsed restlessly, or in the streets of his slum neighborhood, characters who certainly looked as though they were from somewhere else; but Pierce was self-occupied and didn't ponder them. He went through his classes and through the streets like a cartoon character who in the thought-cloud over his head bears only a single question mark. Once in a crowded corridor he became so annoyed with himself that he had to counsel himself aloud sternly just to *drop* it, for God's sake, and calm down: and realized in the next moment, as coeds with books pressed to their breasts turned to stare at him, that he had no idea what it was that he should drop: what it was that he had picked up.

He *hadn't* lost his vocation, he had only grown up; he had desired to grow up and there would have been no way to prevent it even if he hadn't desired it. History, that undiscovered country he had seen far off—yes, it had turned out to be only ordinary, different from his own not in kind but only in mundane details of geography and local custom, lists of which he had had to commit to memory: he knew it, for he had explored that country, of course, just as he had wanted to; he lived there every working day.

His progress had always been outward, away from stories, from marvels; it had been a journey, as he saw it, away from childhood, the same journey outward that the human race had long been on, and which he, Pierce Moffett, was only recapitulating in his own ontogeny, joining up with it, at his maturity, at the place it had by then reached.

When I was a child, I thought as a child and did as a child; but now I am a man, and have put away childish things.

There had been a story in the beginning—in his own childhood and the human race's—that a child could inhabit, an account that could be taken literally, about Adamuneve and Christopher Clumbus and a sun with a face and a moon with one too, a stock of stories never discarded but only outgrown, gratefully, name by face, like an old sunsuit. Stories, outgrown just as grownups had always hinted he *would* outgrow them when with fierce literalness he would try to get one or another outlandish detail certified or explained; stories, their aging fabric giving under his fingers. On a certain Christmas Eve, when an argument had been raging in the children's quarters, Sam Oliphant had taken him and his cousin Hildy, a girl just older than he, upstairs into his big bedroom, and explained carefully about Santa Claus, and the explanation seemed not only true but a sort of relief, like breaking out of an egg; he and Hildy were being admitted into a larger circle of the world. Only don't tell the little kids, Sam said, because they're still young, and it would spoil it for them.

And then further on he had come forth again, from a larger story, about God and Heaven and Hell, the Four Cardinal Virtues and the Seven Glorious Mysteries and the nine choirs of the angels. All in a day, it seemed on looking back: all in a day he had stepped outside it all, with a sigh of relief and a twinge of loss and a nod of resolution that he would not turn back that way now even if he could, and he could not, it was too small to go back into, an intricate clockwork sphere that he would carry within him then like an old-fashioned turnip watch, that he could draw out and look at, in perfect working order, only stopped forever.

And on: passing outward through vast realms of meaning, through the circles of history, not only Christopher Columbus who found out the world was round, not only the Founding Fathers and their awful wisdom, but outward through whole universes of thought, each growing somehow smaller the more he learned about it, until it was too small to live within, and he passed on outward, closing the door behind him.

And came then at last to the furthest outside of all, the limitless one, the real world. About which nothing could be said, because in order to reach it he, he and the human race, whose progress he was joining just at this point, had had to pass through every universe that could be talked about. He had them all within him; he had outgrown them all; naked, he looked outward toward silence and random stars.

He had got something fearfully wrong.

Knowing nothing then of what he would later learn of the techniques of Climacterics, Pierce could not chart his distemper, though in looking back he could see clearly enough what had happened to him: he had simply fallen off his twenty-first-year Plateau, his Third Climacteric. The rough synthesis he had made at Noate, the "existential" pose and the know-nothing knowingness, had come apart as his black clothes had come apart. The sine curve of his life had turned downward like a roller-coaster, plummeting him through his Down Passage Year and into the slough beyond. By the spring of 1967 he was well within it.

When classes ended that June, he went back to Noate, to finish up and annotate his thesis, to get it published and approved (just barely) on the strength of its stylish patterning and minute though sometimes fanciful analysis. It seemed a dead object to him, and the labor he expended on it only increased the sensation, it was *pietra-dura* work or Chinese nesting ivory spheres, but it was done. From Noate's library and cloisters (Barr was on sabbatical) he heard the tinkling and piping of the paraders, as though far off; someone told him that in the Quad there had been, while he cut ivory in the library, a Dow demonstration, or a Tao demonstration, he wasn't sure which.

But the music was loud in the streets of his slum. The city had gathered up its filthy skirts and arisen griping and rheumaticky, and begun altogether to move: the building opposite Pierce's, whose gray face he knew almost as well as he knew his own, had come, while he was gone, to be painted in stars, sunbursts, polka dots; the old stone heads that had hidden like dark dryads under the eaves had had their eyes opened with bright paint and looked out surprised. There were transients everywhere, pilgrims in strange clothes, but Pierce's part of the city in particular resembled a medieval city on a fair day or high holy day, there were *pénitentes* in orange robes and shaven heads chanting and whirling in St. Vitus's dance, there were Gypsies come to town camped in the littered squares, furred feathered and earringed, shaking tambourines and stealing things. There were hawkers and jugglers and smokesellers, there were women in long homespun dresses and brass bangles who squatted on the stoop of his building, suckling their babes; there were madmen and friars of orders gray and ragged beggars asking alms.

Pierce read on. Printing had been invented, and the bookstores were suddenly full of odd wares. There were new newssheets in lurid, smudgy colors, there were almanacs and books of prophecy, there were strange scriptures, ballads, broadsides. Deeply surprised, Pierce began to find among them bright-clad reissues of books that had meant much to him in childhood, a childhood that had been largely spent between the covers of books, one way and another, a childhood he found he was able to taste again by cracking the same books, unseen since antiquity, since his own Age of Gold.

Here for example were Frank Walker Barr's ten- and twenty-year-old books, being reverently brought out in a uniform new paper edition, including the ones Pierce knew, like *Time's Body* and *Mythos and Tyrannos;* someone had had the brilliant idea of covering them all with a single titanic Baroque painting crowded with figures, each volume's cover only a detail, so that when they were all in print and assembled, they would form the whole picture. And here also was Sidney Lanier's *Boy's King Arthur,* with all the original illustrations, as bright as Christmas morning and as cold to his touch; a shabby edgeworn copy had stood long on his boyhood bookshelf, a present from his father. And a book he didn't at first recognize in its new soft covers, only to find inside a book he knew immediately, like a childhood friend unmasked, because it was simply a photocopy of the old one he had read. It was *Bruno's Journey,* a biography of sorts, by the historical novelist Fellowes Kraft, and he remembered nothing of it but that he had once been deeply affected by it; what he would think of it now he had no idea. The page he had opened to was this:

> The immense laughter of Bruno when he understood that Copernicus had inverted the universe—what was it but joy in the confirmation of his knowledge that Mind, in the center of all, contains within it all that it is the center of? If the Earth, the old center, now was seen truly to revolve somewhere halfway between the center and the outside; and the Sun, which before had revolved on a path halfway to the outside, were now the center, then a half-turn like that in a Möbius strip was thrown into the belt of the stars: and what then became of the old circumference? It was, strictly, unimaginable: the Universe exploded into infinitude, a circle of which Mind, the center, was everywhere and the circumference nowhere. The trick mirror of finitude was smashed, Bruno laughed, the starry realms were a jewelled bracelet in the hand.

Copyright 1931. Who was publishing these things newly? How did they know he needed them? Why did he see their spines under the arms and in the tasseled satchels of the effendi, woodsmen, Injuns of the gong-tormented streets? He had the funny feeling that doors long bolted within him were being forced, that in the general amnesty of carnival something jailed in him since puberty was being let out—somewhat by mistake—into the open air, to be welcomed by the cheering mob.

Something: what?

When the weather turned cold the jingling throngs sought shelter, huddling wrapped in aged furs on stoops or in heated public places; Pierce took in the odd stray for a night or a week. Boys with head colds, far from home, boiled brown rice on his stove, girls practiced simple native crafts cross-legged on the floor, shared the bed, moved on. In their endless talk, periodless, a slurry of outlandish possibilities as real to them as the dangerous city and the workaday world around them were unreal, Pierce with elation and trepidation heard the end—not of the world, no, but of the world he had grown up in, the world that everyone, growing up, imagines will never change. Climacterics would one day suggest to him that the world forever grows up and explodes into possibility, revolts against the past, evolves the future, and settles down to grow staid and old, all at exactly the same rate as each person experiencing it does; but Pierce didn't know Climacterics then; he let his hair grow long, and looked out his window at the parade, and thought: *Nothing now will ever be the same again.*

F I V E

▲

Barnabas College, like a fast little yacht, had quickly tacked with the new winds that were blowing, even while old galleons like Noate were wallowing in the breakers. Courses in the history, chemistry, and languages of the old everyday world were semester by semester cut to a minimum (Pierce's History 101 course would, eventually, very nearly reach the present day from time-out-of-mind, even as the 200-level courses, out of his provenance, came to deal chiefly not with the past at all but in possibilities, in the utopias and armageddons all adolescents love). The old standard textbooks were chucked, replaced by decks of slim paperbacks, often the students' own choices, they are after all (said Doctor Sacrobosco) paying the bills. Veteran teachers faced with this fell tongue-tied or turned coats garishly; young ones like Pierce, his students' coeval almost, still had trouble facing children who seemed to have come to Barnabas chiefly to be instructed in a world of their own imagining.

Earl Sacrobosco tried to help him out. "You're not plastic enough," he told Pierce, molding something invisible in his hands. "The kids want to play with these ideas that are new to them. So play with them. Entertain them."

"Entertaining students is not my idea of . . ."

"The notions, Pierce. Entertain the notions."

Sacrobosco himself taught an astronomy course which was, at his students' insistence, coming to include practical training in judicial astrology, so he knew whereof he spoke. Earl was as plastic as they come. Pierce did his best, he could entertain notions, he could and did, but he continued to think of his course as a *history* course, on the model of those he had taken under Frank Walker

Barr at Noate: a history course, however commodious and full of digression. His students apparently wanted something else. They liked the stories he was gleaning from his newly wide reading, and made round sounds of wonder at the notions he put forth, which they entertained indiscriminately, mixing them with their other mental guests in a bash that Pierce found hard to crash. They had come to college not, as Pierce's generation seemed to Pierce to have gone to college, to be disabused of their superstitions, but to find new and different ones to adopt; they seemed not to understand the nature of evidence, and were vague about whether the Middle Ages came before or after the Renaissance; they were resentful of Pierce's careful distinctions, and insulted when he showed himself to be appalled at their ignorance. "But this is a *history* course," he would plead before their truculent faces. "It is about *past time* and what has in fact occurred. Stories told about that past time are no good unless they can account for events that really happened, which we therefore have to learn, which is why we study history in the first place. Now about this other stuff, maybe in Dr. Sacrobosco's course or Mrs. Black's course on the Witch Cult as a Women's Movement . . ." But after class they would crowd around his desk, uncowed, bringing him news of Atlantis, the secrets of the pyramids, the Age of Aquarius.

"What," he asked Earl Sacrobosco, "is the Age of Aquarius?"

Pierce and another young teacher, a woman named Julie who had just come to the school to teach New Age Journalism, were at a small dinner party at the Sacroboscos. Earl had acquired a little pot, ho ho, for him and the youngsters to try out after Mrs. Sacrobosco had gone to bed.

"The Age of Aquarius?" Earl said, his eyebrows wrinkling up and down rapidly (his toupee remained motionless though, always a giveaway). "Well, it's an effect of the precession of the equinoxes. Very simple really. See, the earth turning on its axis"—he pointed his forefingers at each other and revolved them—"doesn't have a regular motion, it has a little bobble in it, it moves sort of like a top when it's running down." The fingers described this eccentricity. "One whole movement, though, takes a long time, about twenty-six thousand years to complete. Now one effect of this is that the direction the axis points in the sky—true north—changes slowly over time; the star pointed to, the North Star, is a different star at the beginning of the cycle and halfway through."

"Hm," said Pierce, visualizing.

"Another effect," Earl went on, "is that the star background shifts vis-à-vis the sun. Just as the relative positions of things in this room change if you waggle your head slowly around." They all did that, and fell to giggling for a while. "So, so," Earl said, "the star background shifts. You can measure this by noting, at a specific day every year, what sign of the zodiac the sun is rising with; and the days you choose are the equinoxes, the days that are the same length as the nights, if you see what I mean. And if you do that over a very long time, centuries, you can see that the sun is very gradually falling back. It's rising, on the equinox, slightly later every century, that is, in a slightly more easterly part of the sign. And you can suppose, well, it will keep on doing that till it has fallen all the way back around. And so it does." He lapsed into thought, brow rising, rug remaining fixed. "So it does."

"Yes?" Pierce said. "And so?"

"So every once in a while, a long while, the sun rises one morning in a new sign. It has slipped right out of one and back into the previous one. Right now it rises on the spring equinox in some early degree of the sign Pisces. But it's always on the move—relative to us, that is, it's really us who are on the move; and pretty soon—well, astronomically speaking pretty soon, a couple hundred years or so—the sun will begin to rise in the sign of Aquarius. Thus the end of the Piscean Age, that started two-thousand-odd years ago, and the beginning of the Age of Aquarius."

Two thousand years ago, the Piscean age, the world shifts from B.C. to A.D. Jesus. And Jesus was a fish.

Oh. "Oh," said Pierce.

"Always *pre*cedes, you see," Earl said dreamily. "*Pre*cedes. Before Pisces was Aries the ram, and before that Taurus the bull, and so on."

Moses had ram's horns, who overthrew the golden bull-calf. And then comes Jesus the fish, two thousand years on, new heaven and new earth, and shepherd Pan flees from the mountainsides. And now the world watched and waited for the man with the water jug.

"The kids," Pierce said, "claim it's starting now."

"Yes, well," Earl said indulgently.

Pierce felt again, intensely, that sensation of a series of magic-lantern slides projected within him, all at once, all overlapping, all the same slide. Had he heard about this before too, and only forgotten it? *Iam redit et Virgo, redeunt Saturnia regna:* yes, sure, the Virgin returns, because if, when Virgil was writing that line two thousand years ago, the sun was entering Pisces, then on the *autumnal* equinox it would rise in one two three four five six yes in Virgo. So Virgil it seems knew about this stuff too. And he, Pierce, had read him and studied him at St. Guinefort's, and hadn't understood. He felt as though if this kept up he would find himself sitting once again before his earliest ABC books, his first catechism, saying Oh I get it, this was the story encoded in these stories, this is the secret that was kept from me.

Tell Dildrum that Doldrum is dead: the great god Pan is dead.

"I thought," Julie said, "that the equinox is March 21."

"So it is, about," said Earl.

"But that's Aries."

"So it was, once. Maybe when the whole system was codified, it was."

"But then all these sun signs and birth signs are wrong." She sounded affronted. Pierce knew she set great store by her own sign and what it implied for her. Around her neck hung an enameled copper scorpion. "They're way off."

"It's adjusted for, in the system," Earl said vaguely. He moved his hand as though tuning a TV. "Adjustments are made."

Pierce shook his head, buffaloed. Some kind of collision seemed to be taking place within him, a collision of just unprecedented magnitude, two vast sedans, both of them his, coming together in slow, slow motion, their noses crumpling, their drivers aghast. "But it's just this little bobble," he said.

"Imagine the effect, though," Earl said, raising the smoldering joint to his lip, "if the earth were stationary. The whole heavens would be shifting. Very important-seeming stuff."

"But they aren't," Pierce said.

Earl grinned. "Well, all that stuff is coming back," he squeaked with held breath. "It's a new age."

Redeunt Saturnia regna: the old gold age that once was is come again. Walking home through the illuminated streets, in bed with Julie, at breakfast, on the toilet, standing abstracted before his students, Pierce came to feel often, like a clutch in his throat or a hum in his ears, that sense of collision he had first felt at Earl's: as though he had come upon some kind of crossroads, no, as though he were himself a crossroads, a place where caravans met, freighted with heavy goods, come from far places, colliding there with others come from different far places, headed elsewhere: pack-trains, merchants carrying jewels sewn in their clothing, dark nomads from nowhere carrying nothing, imperial couriers, spies, lost children. The history he thought he knew, the path called History which he walked every working day—the path that led backward through a maze of battles, migrations, conquests, bankruptcies, revolutions, one damn thing after another, men and women doing and saying, dreaming and playing, till it coiled finally and unknowably upon itself at the side of a cold campfire on some vast and silent veldt—from that path, it seemed, there forked another, just as long and just as mazy, only long since lost; and for some reason now, just now, it had suddenly become visible again, to him as to others, dawn winds rising as night turned pale. It seemed to spring out from the very foot of the napless velveteen armchair (recently rescued from the street) in which late at night Pierce sat thinking.

Down that road, the past did not grow darker with distance, but brighter; that way lay the morning lands, wise forefathers who knew what we have forgotten, radiant cities built by arts now lost.

Nor did that road go curling off to an ending lost amid the beasts: no, though far shorter than the road Pierce called History, it was in fact infinite, because just as its furthest age rolled back to its first days, the whole road completed a circle; the serpent took in its mouth the fast-dwindling tip of its tail. Nowadays history is made of time; but once it was made of something else.

Now that would be a story to tell his kids, wouldn't it, he thought. The story of that history not made of time; that history which is as different from History yet as symmetrical to it as dream is to waking.

As dream is to waking.

He pulled himself from his new armchair with some difficulty and went to the window; he turned out his lights and stood looking out into the never dark city.

There had been a morning once, when he was a child–how old had he been, not more than five or six–when he had awakened from frightening dreams, labyrinthine pursuit and loss, and his mother had tried to explain to him the nature of dreams, and why it is that, though you seem in them to be in mortal danger, you can't be hurt, not really. Dreams, she said, are only stories: except they aren't stories *outside,* like the ones in books, the stories Daddy tells. Dreams are your own stories, *inside.*

Stories inside, each one nested within all the others; as though all the stories we had ever been inside of lay still nested inside of us, back to the beginning, whenever that is or was. Stories are what the history not made of time is made of.

Funny, he thought; funny funny funny. In fact he had begun to feel funny, as though the rotation of the earth could be felt through his naked feet. Maybe he hadn't really lost his vocation, after all; maybe he had just misplaced it, had long ago closed the door by mistake on the one story that could not be outgrown: this story about how there is a story. That old closed door had blown open in the winds that were rising, and there were other doors beyond it, door after door, opening backward endlessly into the colored centuries.

When he had first begun teaching at Barnabas, because of his rather ambiguous degree in Renaissance Studies Pierce had been set to teaching not only history but freshman lit, or Introduction to World Literature, a course that still had compulsory status then. Homer, Sophocles, Dante, Shakespeare, Cervantes all fled past in the first semester, well over most of the students' heads, slow-flapping pterosaurs dimly glimpsed; Pierce supposed that if in later life they met any of those authors, it would be nice to be able to claim they had once before been introduced.

When he got to Dante, whom he had always found a trial, Pierce used to employ a trick he had learned from Dr. Kappel at Noate, who had taught him the equivalent freshman course and had also found Dante unsympathetic. At the beginning of class, as Dr. Kappel had, he would draw a circle on the blackboard.

"The world," he would say.

A hatch mark on the world's edge. "Jerusalem. Beneath Jerusalem is Hell, going down sort of spirally or in a cone shape like this." A spiral to the center of the world circle. "In here are the souls of the damned, as well as many of the fallen angels. In the very center, in a frozen pit, a gigantic figure: the Devil, Satan, Lucifer." A little stick man. "Now." He drew a blip on the far side of the world, opposite Jerusalem. "Over here is a seven-level mountain, Purgatory, standing all alone in the empty southern sea. Here on various levels are more of the dead, lesser sinners whose crimes have been forgiven but not paid for."

With a sweep of chalk, he next drew a circle around the earth circle, and a crescent on it. "Above the earth, circling it, the moon. Above the moon, the sun." More circles, extending outward: "Mercury. Venus. Mars." When he had got seven circles indicated around the circle of the earth, one more: "The stars, all fixed, turning around the earth once in twenty-four hours." He tapped the board with his chalk: "Outside it all, God. With myriads of angels, who keep it all rolling in order around the earth."

Then he would step back, contemplating this picture, and he would ask, "Now what's the first thing we notice about this picture of the universe here, which is the picture Dante presents us with in his poem?"

Silence, usually.

"Oh, come on," Pierce would say. "The very first most evident thing about this picture."

A timid guess, usually from a girl: "It's very religiously inspired. . . ."

"No no no," Pierce would say, grinning, "no, the *very* first thing we notice." And grabbing up his copy of Dante, still grinning, flourishing it at them: "It's *not true!* It's not true. There isn't any hell in the middle of the earth with the Devil stuck in it. False. Not so. There is not a seven-story mountain in the empty southern sea, or an empty southern sea either." He regarded his picture again, pointing out its features. His students had begun to dare to chuckle. "The earth, ladies and gentlemen, is not in the center of the universe, or even of the solar system. Sun, planets, stars going around it: not the case. About God outside it all I give no opinion, but he's difficult to believe in in exactly this form. I would think.

"So." Turning to them again, fun over: "It's not true. This is not a true story and does not take place in the universe we live in. Whatever it is about this book that is important, and I think it *is* important," eyes lowered here reverently for a moment, "it's not that it is informative about the world we live on or in. What we are going to have to discover is how it can be important to us anyway. In other words, why it is a Classic."

And then it was on, easily or at least more easily, into the dark wood, the sages and the lovers, the burning popes, the shit and spew, the dark journey downward and the light journey upward. It was a good trick, and Pierce had perfected it over two or three semesters when, one late autumn day, he turned from the completed picture to ask: "Now what is the first thing we notice about this picture of the universe?" And found himself regarded by a pirate band (with its captives) which made up his Intro to World Lit class, their eyes dully alive, mouths slightly open, at peace and fascinated.

"What," he said, without his wonted vigor, "is the first thing we notice about this picture of the universe?"

They seemed to stir, noticing many things but uncertain which was first; they seemed, some of them, beguiled by his mandala, as though he had drawn it to entrance them. Others seemed asleep, or elsewhere, their abandoned bodies breathing softly. Those who took a hectic interest giggled at a joke or a game different from the one Pierce was playing. And Pierce felt grow within him the horripilating conviction that the distinction he was about to make would not be understood; that he did not, after all, wholly understand it himself any longer.

"It's not true," he said, gently, as to sleepwalkers he was afraid to wake. "It's really really not true."

Making his way out of the building that day, past the squatting groups of beggars and the pamphleteers' tables, Pierce found himself wondering how Frank Walker Barr was getting on with *his* classes these days. Old Barr, kind Barr, gently, tentatively suggesting that there might remain in this cold and clinker-built world some pockets yet of mystery, some outlying villages that had not yet been pacified, perhaps never to be reduced; Barr telling stories, insisting on the worth of stories, always with that saving chuckle—well it was coals to Newcastle now, it was worse than that, time had turned around and brought in a new sign, *these kids believed the stories they were told.*

"Well it makes a lot of sense," Julie said to him. "*Astronomically* there might be a long time to wait; but if we were in the cusp we could feel it, and be influenced by it, and see the signs; and we do—I do." Sitting cross-legged on his bed—their bed—she was coating, with dreamy care, her nails in bright lacquers, attempting a suite of symbols, star, moon, eye, sun, crown. "The cusp might be this blank time, anything can happen, the old age of one world and beginning of another; you're poised right at the change, and all things that were are now going to be different, everything conceivable is just for a second possible, and you see, like coming toward you out of the future, the next people, and you're watching them come forward, beautiful, and you're waiting to hear what they'll say, and wondering if you'll understand them when they speak." She held up her mystic hand to Pierce. "It makes a lot of sense," she said.

They're just going to dream their new world-age into being, Pierce marveled; but how otherwise did new world-ages come to be? You have to be on their side, he thought, you have to be: a pity and a love welled up in him for the children, the ragged ranks on pilgrimage along the only way there was to go, after all, making up the future as they went. And in the thought-cloud over every head a single question mark.

What they needed—what he was coming to need himself, for that matter—was not more stories so much as an *account:* an account, an explanation of why these world-tales, exactly these and not others, should be now abroad again, after long sleep, and why, though they could not on the face of it be true, they could just now seem to be true, or to be coming true. An account; a model; some means by which those who fed on notions as on bread might be able to tell which ones were really news and which were the old dreams still being dreamed, were *stories inside* which the human race had never completely awakened from, or did not know it had awakened from: for those who do not know they have awakened from a dream are condemned to go on dreaming it unaware.

Because the Age of Aquarius, no, it was fatuous, wasn't it? Surely it was not the age but the heart, it wasn't even all hearts, that turned from gold to lead and back to gold again; Moses had horns because of some error in translation from Hebrew to Latin or Latin to English, Jesus was as much Lamb or Lion as he was Fish, and the world turned on a bent tree for reasons of its own, which had nothing to do with us. To start *assenting* to one of these huge stories or another—well, what did you do with all the other stories, for one thing, just as big and just as compelling, that appeared in the fabric of history if the fabric (a shot silk, a changeable taffeta) were looked at in a different light? No, surely Barr had only wanted to suggest that economic and social forces could not by themselves generate the bizarre facts of human history, and that to be unable to experience the titanic shuffling on and off stage of windswept allegories was to miss not only half the fun of history but to exclude yourself from how history, man's long life on earth, has been actually experienced by those who were creating it, which is just as much the historian's subject, after all, as the in-fact material conditions and discoverable actions are.

Let's just not be too hasty: that's all Barr was telling his students, his gray-suited and crew-cut students back at the end of the Age of Reason. Let's recognize—though it surprises and confuses us, it's so—that the facts are not finally extricable from the stories. Outside our stories, outside ourselves, is the historyless, inhuman, utterly *other* physical world; and within our human lives within that world are our stories, our ramparts, without which we would go mad, as a man prevented from dreaming in the end goes mad. Not true, no: only necessary.

But the Age of Reason was a shuttered mansion; what Pierce heard constantly now was how the real world that had seemed so clinker-built to Barr was beginning to come apart under investigation. Relativity. Synchronicity. Uncertainty. Telepathy, clairvoyance, gymnosophists of the East levitating, turning their skins to gold by thought alone. Wishing maybe made it so, for the skilled wisher trained long enough in the right arts, arts so long suppressed by the Holy Office of imperial Reason that they had atrophied, languishing in prison. Strong acids, though, might dissolve those bonds, cleanse the doors of the senses, let the light of far real heavens in. That's what Pierce heard.

So what if Barr was wrong? What if inside and outside were *not* such exclusive categories, nor all the truth on one side of the equation? Because Moses *did* have horns, in some sense; Jesus *was* a fish; if those were only stories inside, like a dream, still they were outside any individual; nor could dreaming make them match the in-fact behavior of the constellations, which apparently they did. How come? How did that come to be? How for that matter had the centuries come in Pierce's mind to be colored panels which nothing he learned about could not be fitted instantly into, and from where came his certainty that the more highly colored and complete his crowded canvases became, the more he grasped history in its fullness? If he really did grasp history in its fullness, then were his colors inside or outside?

What if—made of its stuff after all, made of its not-so-solid atoms and electrons, woven utterly into its space-time continuum, its Ecology (new word found lying on the age's doorstep to be adopted and brought up)—what if man, and man's thought, and man's stories, embodied not only *man*'s truth but truths about *outside* too, truths about how not only the human world but the whole great world as well goes on? What if those old, oft-told, eternally returning, so-compelling stories were compelling because they contained a coded secret about how the physical (or "so-called" physical) world operates, how it came to cast up man, and thus thought, and thus meaning, in the first place?

None of them were true, none of those stories! Not a single one of them. All right. But what if they were *all* true? The universe is a safe, a safe with a combination lock, and the combination of the lock is locked up inside the safe: that chestnut had given him an enormous comfort as an existentialist at Noate, a bitter pleasure. But we are the safe! We are made of dust: all right: then dust can think, dust can know. The combination is, must be, locked inside our hearts, our own pumping blood, our spinning brains and the stories they weave.

Could it be, could it be? How did he know? Almost with disdain, a shrinking as from the touch of something loathly, he had always avoided all systematic knowledge of the physical universe; he had carefully just-barely-not-failed every science course he had been made to take at Noate, and had forgotten their boring and ghastly contents as soon as he closed the last lab door behind him. Astronomy had been one of them. He remembered nothing of it except the fact, congenial to him at the time, that comets (those old omens) were actually nothing but large balls of dirty snow. What he knew of how the investigation into the nature of things was going in his time was confined to what he read in the papers or saw on television; only that, and the notions he was now receiving as though through the charged air, Julie's rumors of terrific revelations about to break that never quite did. Starships from Elsewhere were landing as the moon drew closer to the earth; powerful mages hidden till now in Tibet were about to announce themselves the true governors of the planet; scientists had fallen through self-made gaps in the fabric of space and time and the matter was being hushed up: Pierce would hear, with a shiver of wonder, news that if true would transform the whole account of time and life forevermore—and in the next moment, laughing with relief, would recognize in the news an old story, a story that had been old at the turn of the last millennium, had perhaps been one of those told around the old original campfire where stories had first been heard in the world.

And from where then had come his shiver of wonder?

He shivered; he opened the window to the night, and rested his elbows on the sill. He put his long chin in the cup of his hands, and stood thus looking out, like a gargoyle.

Did the world have a plot? Did it, after all? He had not ever believed himself to have one, no not even in those days when he had lived within stories; but did the world?

They out there believed it did. His students, hungering for stories as a man deprived of sleep hungers to dream. For sure Julie would look at the same street corner at the same time of day for another five-dollar bill; at the same phase of the moon, perhaps, the same five-dollar-yielding turn of the wheel. Julie believed that Gypsies could tell fortunes.

Did the world have a plot? Had it only seemed to lack one because he had forgotten his own?

On a crystal May morning, after everyone else seemed to have departed, he and Julie sat opposite each other at the scarred kitchen table, ready to go: between them now stood a tall glass of water and, in a saucer, two blue-stained cubes of sugar which their upstairs neighbor—gentle-eyed, hirsute—had acquired for them, tickets to Elsewhere. In after years he would sometimes wonder if at that moment he did not pass out through a sort of side door of existence, abandoning forever the main course his life would otherwise have taken; but it didn't matter, for there was to be no going back through to find out, no going back along the unrolling path that soon came to be beneath their feet. Not seemed-to-come-to-be: it was no metaphor, or if it was a metaphor it was one that was so intensely *so* that the tenor and the vehicle of it, not identical, might just as well have been. In fact it became evident sometime during that endless morning that truth itself was a metaphor, no not even a metaphor, only a direction, a direction toward the most revelatory metaphor of all, never ever to be reached. Life is a journey; it is only one journey; there is along it only one road, one dark wood, one hill, one river to cross, one city to come to; one dawn, one evening. Each is only encountered again and again, apprehended, understood, recounted, forgotten, lost, and found again. And at the same time—Pierce standing gasping in the winds of Time felt it with the shocked conviction of a Bruno discovering Copernicus, of the first man in history to perceive it—the universe extends out infinitely in every direction you can look in or think about, at every instant.

Oh I see, he said, *Oh I see, I get it,* listening to the falling into place, one by one, of infinite tumblers that were tiny enough to fit inside the turnings of his own minute chemistries. He learned that day where heaven is, and where hell, and where the seven-story mountain; and he laughed aloud to know the simple truth. He learned the answers to a hundred other questions, and then forgot them, and then forgot the questions too: but for some years after— not often but now and then—he would receive, like a wave that reaches far up a dry shingle and then recedes, a dash of that day's understanding: and for a moment taste its certainty like salt.

S I X

▲

Those were the days when Pierce became a popular teacher at Barnabas; then that he came to seem to his students to have a secret he could impart, a secret that had cost him something in the learning. The stack of books bought, borrowed, and stolen grew tall beside his street-salvaged plush armchair; the exotic goods he plundered there he came freighted with into class, there were not enough minutes in an hour or hours in a semester to unload them all.

Meanwhile the great parade wound on, turning in on itself, darkened by waste and penury; the ones who came irregularly to sit on Pierce's classroom floor and listen to his stories had ever less acquaintance with Western Civilization, they seemed to be beings who had come from far places, who were headed for other far places unimaginable to him, and to be only resting before him momentarily, exhausted and dusty.

Still Pierce worked at his account; while far away in the Midwest, Rosie Rasmussen and her Mike set up housekeeping in a gray Vetville beyond a huge and restless university, and while Spofford sat silent and tense in a Harlem hospital rec room with six others who could not forget a certain far-off beach at dawn, a certain green hill, Pierce read on: he read Barr and he read Vico and he read the *Steganography* of Lois Rose; he read the stories of Grimm and Frobenius, and the *Stories of the Flowers* and the *High History of the Holy Graal* and the *History of the Royal Society,* by Sprat; he read George Santayana (no, no) and Giorgio di Santillana (yes! yes!) and a dozen texts he might have read at Noate and never had; he read *The Golden Bough* and *The Golden Legend* and *The Golden*

Ass of Apuleius. While uptown the fledgling Sphinx, a schoolchild still, went through Effie's pills looking for something she might take, while Beau Brachman on a Colorado mountaintop awaited starships from Elsewhere to appear and touch down, Pierce stood on his rooftop with an illustrated Hyginus in one hand and a flashlight in the other, and discerned for the first time the moon rise into the polluted sky in a sign, the sign of Pisces, two fishes bow-tied at the tail.

One question, Barr had said; one question leads to another, and that one to another, and that one to others, and so on, unfinishably, a life's work. Pierce learned where the four corners of the earth are, for they are not the four points of the compass; he learned why there are nine choirs of angels and not ten or eight, and where Jamshyd's seven-ring'd cup that was lost can every night be found. He didn't learn why people think that Gypsies can tell fortunes, but he learned why there are twenty-four hours in a day, and twelve signs of the zodiac, and twelve Apostles too. It began to seem that there is not any numbered thing in the human story that has its number by chance; if any band of heroes, or measurements of a ship, or days of march, or hills a city was built on, did not add up to a satisfying figure, then time and ingenuity and dreaming would eventually wear away or build up the facts, until it too acquired one of the small set of whole numbers and regular geometrical figures which inhabit the human breast, the combination of the safe.

He began to think that even though magic, and science, and religion did not all *mean the same thing,* they all *meant in the same way.* In fact perhaps Meaning was purely an ingredient of certain items which the world put forth and not of others, perhaps it arose just in the way flavor arises out of a conjunction of spices and herbs and long cooking and a sensitive palate, and yet is not reducible to any of those things; was a name only for the nameless conjunction, the slight clutch in his throat, the hum in his ears, *Oh I see, I get it.*

Whatever it was, he had acquired a taste for it. To the matched set of Barr's speculations and the weirdly compelling tales out of his childhood and the little life of Bruno, still unread, were added books on celestial mechanics and the workings of the senses and the insides of the atom; on the history of Christian iconography and witchcraft and on the learning processes of children. A lane had opened up within these books, a path glimpsed within their bibliographies, and Pierce, though darkling at times, bored and repelled sometimes, was led on, from footnote to text, from glossy paperback filled with notions to shabby leatherback filled only with print, pausing only to gather courage to go on, to shade his eyes and see, if he could see, what pioneers had been before him along this way, if any had; and picking up as he went the oddest facts and bright bits of this and that.

And then, all unexpectedly, he took a turning he recognized; on a certain day he topped a certain sudden hill and, astonished, raised his eyes to a view he was familiar with, the frontiers of a country he knew.

A country he knew; a country he had once known a lot about, though he hadn't thought of it in years. A country on whose frontiers he had at one time seemed often to stand, through long summer evenings when the false geography of Kentucky's northern hills, to which he had been unaccountably exiled, would melt, and that more real country come to be, not a long walk away; the country to which he truly belonged.

Spring had come, the new world's first, and summer was returning the nomads to the streets—until it was stolen, Pierce had watched on his TV the masses of them, the children's crusade strung out through the streets of cities, or pressing up against the obdurate front of some public building; watched them ridden over as by a car of Kali wreathed in skulls and tear-gas smoke.

Little Barnabas, in spite of or perhaps because of its trimming, had been marched over as by an Oriental migration or Iberian transhumance, almost without resistance, and now Pierce was spending the hottest day of summer session locked in his office while the children laughed and sang and painted the halls, clamoring for peace. He listened for the sounds of breaking glass and sirens and ate Saltine crackers, a box of which he had found in a desk drawer; he read Huizinga's *Waning of the Middle Ages,* which he thought he had been assigned to read once at Noate, had even once passed a test on, but did not remember having actually read:

> The people force their way in at daybreak into the great Hall where the feast was to take place, "some to look on, others to regale themselves, others to pilfer or to steal victuals or other things." The members of Parlement and of the University, the provost of the merchants and the aldermen, after having succeeded with great diffi-

culty in entering the hall, find the tables assigned to them occupied by all sorts of artisans. An attempt is made to remove them, "but when they had succeeded in driving away one or two, six or eight sat down on the other side."

There it was, sirens, both the moaning kind and the imperative Klaxon. The kids within began to break the windows, and the kids without, barricading the steps, cheered exultantly, defiantly: Pierce could hear them, though he could see nothing through the blind window of his office, which faced onto an airshaft. He flipped the pages of the little book.

... many an expelled prince, roaming from court to court, without means, but full of projects and still decked with the splendour of the marvellous East whence he had fled—the king of Armenia, the king of Cyprus, before long the emperor of Constantinople. It is not surprising that the people of Paris should have believed in the tale of the Gipsies, who presented themselves in 1427, "a duke and a count and ten men, all on horseback," while others, to the number 120, had to stay outside the town. They came from Egypt, they said; the Pope had ordered them, by way of penance for their apostasy, to wander about for seven years, without sleeping in a bed; there had been 1,200 of them, but their king, their queen, and all the others had died on the way; as a mitigation, the Pope had ordered that every bishop and abbot was to give them ten pounds tournois. The people of Paris came in great numbers to see them, and have their fortunes told by women who eased them of their money "by magic arts or in other ways."

Louder just for an instant than the clamor of the New Age around him, Pierce felt the sensation of an answer, so suddenly that it took him a moment to think just what question it was the answer to. He searched the passage again:

They came from Egypt, they said

Oh. Oh yes: oh yes of course. Egypt.

A simple answer; Barr had said it was. A simple answer, one he had even sort of known in fact, only he hadn't known this one essential piece of information, but now he had it, now he knew.

How do you like that.

Egypt: but the country they had brought their magic arts from would probably not have been Egypt, would it, no it would not have been, not in the story Pierce had once known. It would have been a country like Egypt, a country near Egypt perhaps, but not Egypt at all.

How do you like that: now how do you like that.

The pages of the little book fluttered closed in Pierce's hands; the high-pitched chanting of the students was being drowned out by insistent bullhorn commands. Then there came a mingled groan and wail of horror, and the thud thud of tear-gas canisters fired. Pierce was to be liberated.

Elsewhere, ahold of a simple answer, before the bitter fumes reached his hall, Pierce only sat and stared, thinking: *Now how do you like that.*

Pierce had been an only child, nine years old, when his mother had left his father forever in Brooklyn (for reasons which became obvious to Pierce over the years but which had not been clear to him then at all) and brought him to Kentucky to live with her brother Sam, whose wife had died, and Sam's four children, in a ramshackle compound aloof above the single brief street of a mining town. Sam was a doctor down in town, at a little Catholic mission hospital which treated the miners' lungs, and couched their child-brides, and wormed their children. Sam's own children—and that would include Pierce—didn't attend the squalid local school; they were given lessons at home in the morning by the priest's sister and housekeeper, Miss Martha.

Not Joe Boyd, though, Sam's oldest son. When Pierce came to live there, Joe Boyd was already too old to be compelled to go to school with Miss Martha any longer, too old and mean to be compelled to do anything at all he chose not to do. He was a fox-faced boy who rolled the sleeves of his short-sleeved shirts above the lean muscles of his arms; he was supposed to be taking a course of reading with Sam, but he was coming to love only cars. He frightened Pierce.

And Hildy, the year after Pierce arrived, left Miss Martha's tutelage too, to go attend Queen of the Angels School in the far mountains of Sharon, five days a week, gruel for breakfast and patched sheets and litanies. The fact that years later she became a nun herself, of the tart, disparaging, at bottom selfless and brave kind, never kept Hildy from relishing and retelling the horrors of that red brick mansion, the rose of Sharon, the lily of the valley.

So classes from then on were for Pierce, and quiet, private Roberta called Bird, and then Warren the baby, a shapeless lump to Pierce when he arrived, who only later grew a stolid, intelligent character. They sang for Miss Martha, recited for Miss Martha, they listened to Miss Martha remember their sainted mother Opal Boyd, they fled Miss Martha at noon into games Miss Martha would never hear of, and could not have imagined. Pierce's mother, Winnie, when she came, tried to get them all together to teach them French in the afternoons a couple of days a week, but they soon wore her down and out. From noon to morning, from May to October, they were free.

Such was the family Pierce was to make his way in; in their isolation they were like some antique family of gentry, in the special-ness of their circumstances like foreigners living within a pale. It was only the Oliphant children who were taught by the priest's sister; only the Oliphants (as far as Pierce knew) who every month received from the state library in far-off, blue grass-green Lexing-ton, a box of books. Opal, Sam's wife (herself once a schoolteacher, and formerly her children's indulgent tutor, they cherished her memory fiercely) had found out this was possible to do, to request that boxes of the state's books be sent to this bookless fastness, and Winnie continued it: every month the read books were packed up and shipped back, and on receipt another box would be sent, more or less filling the vague requests on the Oliphants' list (Mother West-wind, more horse stories, "something about masonry," any-thing of Trollope's) and picked up at the post office, and opened in excitement and disappointment mixed, Christmas every month. Pierce remembering his confusion and contempt before this bizarre system— bizarre to a child who had had the vast, the virtually illimitable reaches of the Brooklyn Public to wander in, his father went every two weeks and Pierce had always gone with him and could have any book he pointed at—Pierce remembering those battered library boxes wondered if perhaps it had been they, those librarians or whoever they were who had filled them, who by sending him some book full of antiquated notions and quaint orthography had first suggested to him the existence of that shadow country, that far old country that was sort of Egypt but not Egypt, no not Egypt at all, a country with a different history, whose name was spelled too with a small but crucial difference: it was not Egypt but Ægypt.

On an impossible city night, too hot to sleep, too hot and loud with sirens and music and the parade endlessly passing, Pierce stood at his window with a handmade cigarette between his fingers, and that country once again seemingly before him, still there in the past: Ægypt.

Why do we believe Gypsies can tell fortunes? Because they came not really from Egypt, but from Ægypt, the country where all magic arts were known. And still carry with them, in however degraded a form, the skills their ancestors had. Pierce laughed aloud to think of it.

And why were they wandering the earth, and why do they still wander? Because Ægypt has Fallen. It exists no longer. Whatever country occupies its geography now, Ægypt is gone, has been gone since the last of its cities, in the farthest East, failed and fell. Then its wise men and women went forth carrying with them their knowledge, to remember their country and yet never speak of it, to take on the dress and habits of the countries they went out into, to have adventures, to heal (for they were great doctors), and to pass on their secrets, so that they would not be lost.

And so these Gypsies ('Gyptians! Sure, the same word) were probably not really from there, only pretending to be, for those who were really from there were vowed to silence and secrecy.

Which is why it had been so hard for Pierce to discover them, hidden in history, in the upside-down adventures they had got themselves involved in down the centuries since then. Seen from the outside, dressed in mufti so to speak in the dense pages of the encyclopedia, in Miss Martha's history textbook, they blended into the background, their stories could be misread; seen from the outside, they didn't seem to be mages, or sworn knights of Ægypt.

Seen from the outside, neither had he and his cousins seemed to be: in old snapshots they were just scruffy kids in a degraded landscape, eastern Kentucky, coal trains chugging endlessly past their mountaintop, their mountaintop not different from any other mountaintop, not obviously quartered and labeled by secret geometries. Of course not. You had to be inside to know; you had to be told. And they too were sworn to secrecy.

The Invisible College.

Why, Pierce wondered, if they were all alone there and never out of one another's company, had they always been making up clubs, associations, brotherhoods, pledging their faith to one another? When he had first come from Brooklyn to live among them he had had to wait long for initiation into Joe Boyd's Retriever's Club; Joe Boyd, the eldest of his cousins, its permanent president. The Invisible College was Pierce's own invention, to counter that exclusion; wittily, with careful vengeance, he had not excluded Joe Boyd from membership, but instead had elected him president— his presidency, his membership, the very existence of the Invisible College however being kept a secret from him, a secret to which all the other Invisibles (all the kids but Joe) were pledged forever.

His own invention? No, the Invisibles had always been; Pierce had only learned, from hints in books, of their immemorial existence; they were knights older than Arthur's; Arthur's had in fact, perhaps, probably, been only a chapter of theirs, as all the wise and good and brave were in some sense chapters. Who else through the ages had been members? It was difficult to know for sure, but Pierce when asked by his cousins seemed able to decide, from a certain response he himself (general secretary after all to his own chapter) had to them. Gene Autry, almost certainly, knew much that his moon face concealed. Sherlock Holmes and Sir Flinders Petrie. Ike? He thought not, though considering the question raised a problem he had never been able to solve with certainty: it was possible, of course, to be of that College without anyone else knowing it, without the fact ever coming to light, not for centuries; but was it possible to be one of the Invisibles *without ever knowing it yourself?* His cleverness about Joe Boyd's membership seemed to prove (especially to Hildy, legalistic and logical of mind and somewhat skeptical about Pierce's College anyway) that it was.

Well, perhaps it was. It wasn't for him to decide, as it might have been if he had in fact made it all up; but he had not, he had only entered into it, as into an empire, and was himself as surprised to find out its shape and its stories as his cousins were: it wasn't make-believe but History. Once the initial discovery had been made— that there was this country, had once been this country, which was somehow the country where the pyramids were and where the Sphinx was but not exactly that country—then it was a matter of decoding what further facts came to his attention, to discover whether they descended from de Mille's Technicolor country of pharaohs and suntanned slaves and Jews, or from the other shadow

country: Ægypt: the country of those wise knights, country of
forest and mountain and seacoast and a city full of temples where an
endless story began.

An endless story: a story that continued in him and in his
cousins, a story that continued in Pierce's discovering it and elabo-
rating it in the meetings of the Invisible College at night after they
were all supposed to be asleep, arguing questions which that story
raised, questions his cousins put to him in the dark. Would they still
be in this story even when they were grown up? Of course they
would; it was a story about grownups. Would they ever go to
Ægypt themselves, and how? They might, if the story ever came to
an end. For in the end of the story (as Pierce heard it or imagined
it) all the exiles would return, to the city in the farthest East,
gathering there from every clime and time, coming upon each other
in surprise—You! Not *you,* too!—and reconstituted at last, to tell
over the story of their adventures. And why not they, then, he and
his cousins, and maybe Sam and Aunt Winnie, Pierce's mother, and
yes Axel his father too, going by boat or train or plane secretly to

"Adocentyn," Pierce said aloud.

Looking out his slum window he felt a funny gust, like wind in
his hair. He hadn't heard the name of that city spoken for years,
years. When he went away to St. Guinefort's the game had come to
a sudden end. There were no more stories. He had outgrown them,
put them away, his younger cousins dared not ask him—newly
serious in a school tie and a crew cut—to continue it. Did they ever
think of it now, he wondered. Adocentyn.

Now how by the way had he come up with such a name?
Where had he stolen it from, what book had yielded it up for him
to adopt into his imaginary country? It sounded to his grown-up ear
as totally invented as a name could be, as outlandish as a name
heard in a dream, a name that, in the dream, means something it
doesn't mean at all when you wake.

He wondered if he could find out where he had got it. If some
index to some book (what book?) might yield it up. If there were
other stories like the Gypsies, stories that he would discover had
also proceeded from his own shadow-Egypt, Ægypt. There might
be. Must be: after all, he had got the stories he had told from
somewhere. From History, he had told his cousins; since the time
he had stopped thinking about it all, he had begun to assume that
he had simply made it all up out of his own big head, but perhaps

he hadn't. That is, for sure his Ægypt was imaginary; only perhaps it hadn't been he who had invented it.

If he could return there, and find out; somehow turn back that way, and return.

"Pierce?" Julie's voice, from within the dark bedroom where the fan whirred. "You still up?"

"Yup."

"Watcha doing?"

"Thinking."

Not that it would be easy to find again; no, it was just the sort of country that, once left, is not easy to return to. The effort seemed immense and futile, as though it weren't he but the world itself in its socket that would have to be turned against the thread.

"It's the dope," Julie said sleepily. "Come to bed."

Adocentyn, Pierce thought. O Ægypt.

A breeze was rising now at last, as dawn approached, a wind from the sea; Pierce inhaled its brackish coolness gratefully. He *would* turn back: go on by turning back. Perhaps, like Hansel, he had dropped crumbs along the way he had come; perhaps those crumbs had not all been eaten.

Set out, then, Pierce thought. Set out.

His cigarette had burned down to a brown fragment, and he pitched it into the street, a brief meteor. On the fire escapes of the building opposite him, people had made up beds, hung with colored cloths and lit with candles. Down the street, a fire hydrant was open, and gushed into the gutter, washing out beer cans, condoms, matchbooks, newssheets. Wind chimes, camel bells, dogs barking, a tambourine idly shaken. The sweltering caravanserai all awake.

If he thought there was no story in history, just one damned thing after another, Barr had said, it was only because he had ceased to recognize himself. He *had* ceased to recognize himself. And yet every story that he had once been inside of lay still inside him, larger inside smaller, dream inside waking, all there to be recovered, just as a dream is recovered when you wake, from its latest moments backward to its earlier.

He began by looking into Egypt: poking into the ruins, lugging home from the Brooklyn Public big folios, sniffing at indexes, settling down to browse. In none of them was what he was looking for. The topic was vast, of course, and Egyptology took up long shelves at the library, having its own Old, Middle, and New Kingdoms: antique multivolume studies from whose ancient silt poked up etched plates, and then newer mythographical analyses clinker-built and obdurate as pyramids, and lastly decadent popular works chock-full of color photos—in none of them was the country he sought. He felt like someone who had set out for the Memphis of crocodiles and moonlit temples and wound up in Tennessee.

Why do we believe that Gypsies can tell fortunes? Because we thought once they were Egyptians, even though they aren't, and it was natural to suppose they would inherit, in whatever faint degree, the occult wisdom which everybody knows the Egyptians possessed. And why on our dollar bills do we put Egypt's pyramid, surmounted by its mystic eye? Because from ancient Egypt issues the secret language of spiritual freedom, illumination, knowledge, the geometries by which can be cast the New Order of the Ages.

But it isn't so! These real Egyptians Pierce was reading about had been the most hard-headed, materialistic, literal-minded bureaucrats of the spirit he had ever encountered. So far from being able to imagine spiritual freedom, spiritual journeys, they had concocted the disgusting procedures of embalming because of their certainty that only the physical body, preserved like a fruitcake in its box, could withstand the dissolutions of death. The more Pierce grappled with their mythologies, oppressive in their endless elaboration, the more he came to understand that they meant exactly what they said: these tedious stories weren't allegories of consciousness to be interpreted by the wise, though even Plato had thought that to be so; they weren't magic emblems, they weren't art, they were science. The Egyptians just thought the world worked this way, operated by these characters, acting out this grotesque dream. Pierce concluded that the ideal condition, for an ancient Egyptian, was to be dead; short of that, to be immobile, asleep and dreaming.

None of it was what Pierce had meant, not at all. He just about decided that he *must* have made it all up, for the noble history he had known could not have been suggested by this stuff; just about decided.

Then, along another road, unfrocked, in trouble, fleeing, Giordano Bruno appeared, like the White Rabbit—or rather reappeared, for Fellowes Kraft's little book had risen to the top of the stack like a thought to the tip of Pierce's tongue; and Pierce went where it pointed—which was not toward Egypt at all but back toward where Pierce had started out from, the Renaissance; not Pharaoh's age but Shakespeare's, whose near contemporary Bruno was. And by and by, astonished and wondering, he found himself once again at frontiers he recognized.

Oh I remember. I see. Now how do you like that . . .

He began to abandon—by degrees, and without ever quite admitting it to himself—the attempt to construct an account, a vade-mecum for his kids on their pilgrimage; anyway that account had grown suddenly too huge to be squeezed into the compass of an ordinary daylit history course, it needed a course no a college of its own. He went on teaching, but his path had forked; he followed Bruno, and was led down long avenues under emblematic arches, past columned temples; he lost his way amid the suburbs of a Baroque city both unfinished and ruined; found a geometric pleasure-ground; entered a dark and endless topiary maze.

But Pierce, pioneer, knew a thing about mazes, had picked up along his way one crumb of information about mazes: in any maze, of yew or of stone, of zoomorphic topiary or made of glass or of time, put out your hand and *follow the left-hand wall* wherever it leads. Just keep to the left-hand wall.

Pierce put out his hand, and followed; and traveling so (in his street-salvaged plush armchair, the books piled beside him) began to find that what he followed, what he had entered into, what at every turning grew that much clearer to him (*Oh I see*) were the lineaments of his old question answered. And when at length, in another world, the Sphinx in her mother's white bathroom put the same question to him, he had his account: the whole bizarre, unlikely, even hilarious story. He had his account, though how much of it *she* ever actually listened to, how much of it sank into her busy brain, he was not sure. He knew why it is that people believe Gypsies can tell fortunes; he knew why that pyramid and that mystic eye appear on every dollar bill, and from what country the New Order of the Ages issued. It was the same country as the country from which Gypsies came, and it was not Egypt.

Not Egypt but Ægypt: for there is more than one history of the world.

In the heavy August morning, Pierce walked down from Spofford's cabin along the dirt road which led to the asphalt highway which wound beside the Blackbury River and through Fair Prospect. Full of breakfast and ready to rededicate himself, he would still not have minded a day's grace before he had to head on

to Conurbana; it had been years since he had been in country of this
kind—he and the Sphinx, carless, had mostly spent their summers
air-conditioned in the city—and he felt his childhood returned to
him as he walked: not so much in concrete memories, though many
of those too, as in a series of past selves whose young being he
could taste in the breaths of air he drew. It was the day and the
country, though there was little here but summer and verdure to
remind him of the shaggy and tunneled hills of the Cumberland
Gap; it was enough, seemingly.

Maybe, he thought, maybe it is given only to wanderers, to the
displaced, to remember in this way, when suddenly they find themselves in air like the air of the country they have left. Maybe if you
live all your life in one place, and grow up as the same year turns in
the same way again and again, then things don't get left permanently
behind, preserved untouched like pressed flowers which bloom
again whole and unchanged when immersed in the old water. If that
was so, then it must be for his cousins as it was for him, for all of
them were now displaced; Hildy in foreign parts, Joe Boyd in (last
Pierce heard) California, Bird in a midwestern city, Warren selling
cars in Canada. Funny if all on one day, this day, they were each to
happen on a stretch of dusty road like this one, or an old book, or a
pattern of raindrops or sunlight, or simply a chance disposition of
internal chemistries, that brought each of them back in this sudden
and complete way that he was just now brought back: because if
they did, they would be brought back all to the same place. A family
reunion all unknown to them dispersed across the continent. The
Invisible College meets again.

The same folks as yesterday, or different but similar ones, sat
before the little store, and greeted him mildly as he went through
the squeaking screen door into the sweet-smelling interior. He
dropped Spofford's letter to his Rosie into the mail slot, and got out
a dime and his letter from Peter Ramus College.

Half an hour later he was outside again, stunned, not knowing
whether to rage or laugh aloud. He studied in the sunlight the letter
that had brought him here, stranded him here, tempted him this far:
it *looked* real enough, his own name was on it, not seeming slugged
into a form; he could feel on its reverse the marks of struck letters,
the signature at the bottom was ink—no, now looked at carefully it
did seem to be a stamp of some kind. Anyway it was false, generated

by some witless computer at academic HQ even while the History Department was making other choices altogether.

The position he had been invited to apply for was already filled, and had been filled before he left the city; even before he had received this ghost letter.

This conclusion hadn't been easy to come to. The computer itself was "down" for the day, and his file, wisps of electromagnetism held in oblivion, unavailable. Departmental secretaries, the dean's office, were all unwilling to imagine such a dumb possibility, and even when Pierce was forced to posit it, unbelieving himself, they seemed ready to shift the blame to him. Why hadn't he checked before coming?

Why hadn't he checked? Why hadn't he checked? Pierce wandered out along the highway, letter still in his hand. Had it come to that, we all have to check now to make sure our business is real and not electronic leg-pulling in the dark? His own fault that he had trusted mail. Sirs I have yours of the 15th, may I act on it or is this some kind of joke.

Maybe he could sue. He did laugh, standing on the narrow bridge over the river, a derisive snort, and shook his head to clear it of that future, which he hadn't really understood would leave him without one by evaporating. It was too late now in the year to apply for much else.

Is that really that, then? he thought, looking down into the brown slow river. Was he really now disburdened of history as an occupation?

Maybe the old bookstore would take him back. He really had a lot longer to live. What was he to do?

Get into sheep. He laughed again, blank-minded, it just really didn't bear thinking of, there was only one conclusion thinking could have. He could not go back to Barnabas; he could not humble himself before Earl Sacrobosco. Never.

He turned to head back to Spofford's, unseeing, and was nearly struck by a car, a station wagon of the largest kind, full of dogs, children, and baggage, which just then came barreling over the bridge behind him, barely room for it there, and out along the river, leaving a stain of oil smoke on the day.

SEVEN

▲

The play was of Cæsar, stabbed in the Capitol; down the white toga draped over his velvets and silk hose coursed the red blood drawn by the conspirators as they stabbed again and again, their knives sinking in to the hilt and the blood gushing awesomely. And as he bled and staggered, there was time for great Cæsar to make a long speech, about envy that would always pull down eagles who would soar—brute envy, he said, and made a complicated pun on Brutus and brutish and brute beasts he had sheltered in his bosom like the Grecian boy and the fox; like that boy he would say no word further, no, though his vitals were gnawed. He said many more words, and some of the audience groaned aloud with pity and wonder, and a few of them laughed that he didn't die yet; and then he covered his face with the bloody toga and measured his length on the boards: the stage shuddered at his fall.

That was he too, in fresh gay clothes, in the jig that followed, flinging Brutus's wife by her arms neatly. And this was he now in Stratford's common inn, drinking amid the conspirators, a little hoarse, and sweating in the close heat of August. Will, standing on the bench outside and looking in through the open window, watched him turn a coin across the backs of his fingers, and back again, and again.

—And from that Brutus is named Britain, he said. I have it from a famous learned man, a Doctor Dee, my friend.

—It is not, then, said Jenkins the new schoolmaster. It is not that Brutus.

—Did not, said the actor, flipping his coin, did not that Cæsar come here to this isle? And did he not build the Tower of London and win famous victories? Do you deny this, sir?

It was hard to tell if the actor was angry or amused; his eyes flashed and grew large; his finger pointed like a sword; but ever the coin moved calmly across the knuckles of his other hand, back and forth.

—And Brutus was Cæsar's son, adopted by him. Ergo.

—It was not that Brutus, said Master Jenkins. Jenkins was standing, drinking nothing, hands behind his back as though he were not here in this low room at all. Will watched him; next school term he would be under him, and should learn all he could of the man.

—It was Brut of Troy, who lived before Rome at all. After Troy fell to the Greeks, Brut came to this isle as Æneas came to found Rome. So we are not British but Bruttish.

—Bruttish indeed, said Cæsar, and played his death speech.

How many times, Will thought. How many times has Cæsar died since he died, before how many thousand eyes. He leaned his elbows on the sill, all his senses bent inward, listening. Cæsar made a sudden comic pause, an exaggerated halt, pretending to catch sight of him just then.

—Who is that imp in the window? Why does he stare at me?

—John Shakespeare's boy.

—What injury have I done him that he should stare at me? He has the Devil's own red hair. He frightens me.

The way he drew his hand up by his face, claw-fingers outward, eyebrows and underlids lifted, was Fright. Will laughed with the others, and Cæsar took offense, turning huge and dignified: grave hands splayed on the table, brows turning down.

—Let us, he said, have a merry song.

He began a round, lugubriously, but so low and slow it was impossible to join in: he was a sad man now, a sad sad man who wanted to sing. Will shook with laughter and amazement. With a word, a gesture, he could make a person, a whole person one knew but hadn't known one knew; as though he had them all within him and didn't know which one would peep out next for a moment.

—You, lad. In the window. Can you sing this song?

—I know it, Will said.

—Well, sing, then. Here's for your red hair.

By some snap of fingers he spun the coin toward Will without seeming to fling it; Will let it fall short, and sang. The lark and the nightingale. He had a true high strong treble and he knew it; no harm either to let Master Jenkins hear it; if he liked singing as much as Master Simon Hunt the last schoolmaster did, it would go easy for Will again this term. Prest the rose against his breast, tear stood in his eyen round. They were all silent listening to the boy in the window; and Cæsar, Master James Burbage of the Earl of Leicester's Men, had drawn all his different persons within him and was paying close attention, a rapt and measuring look on his face, like a draper taking new-fulled woolen cloth in his fingers, or a brewmaster watching clear brown ale drawn from a new cask.

Rosie closed the book, her fingers at the page; Sam had just then scampered up to her, leaving behind her ball, which followed her for a bounce or two, one of those red and white striped balls with blue and stars on its northern hemisphere. Sam half-hid behind Rosie's chaise-longue, looking toward the veranda door. "He's coming," she said.

Rosie laughed. "Is he?"

Sam watched fascinated as the door opened and her great granduncle Boney Rasmussen came out with slow steps, watching where he went.

"Mrs. Pisky made some iced tea," he said. He propped open the door with a chair and went back inside.

"See?" said Sam.

"Yes," Rosie said. "Iced tea, that's nice." She hugged her daughter. Sam found Boney a figure awesome and wonderful, like a large animal, maybe a monster, whose movements had to be monitored with care, between whom and oneself it was better, at the beginning of any interview anyway, to interpose something, her mother preferably.

"Oh, Boney, that's so nice of you, but you should have called, I'd have come to get it."

He brought out a tray, needing both hands for it, which is why he had propped open the door. He set it down on the big wicker table and offered it with a hand: there was a tall glass and a small one, and sugar and lemon, and a dish of wafers.

"I bet the small glass is for you," Rosie said to Sam, pushing her forward. Boney turned away, looking out the wide screens of the veranda, offhand. He had a very clear sense of how he struck

Sam, and was careful—it touched Rosie terribly to see it—not to impose himself on her. Sam sidled up to take her glass. "Nice afternoon," Boney said to no one. "Might rain."

He was really quite remarkably ugly. His dark bald head was pied with brown spots and had a polished, greenish patina like old leather, like a lizard's hide. His hands seemed to be within wrinkled loose gloves of the same material, yellow-nailed, and they ticked restlessly always as though in time to his pulse. Rosie didn't know exactly how old he was, but he seemed to be as old as it was possible to be and still walk around. In fact he walked around a lot, and even rode an old bicycle around the paths and drives of Arcady. One of those oldsters, Rosie thought, who keep on, though slow; patient with a world that has thickened into something molasseslike and continually difficult. It was probably more painful to watch than to do: Boney bicycling, Boney doing a little gardening, Boney climbing stairs.

He turned his thick blue-tinted glasses on her. "What's that you're reading?"

Rosie showed him *Bitten Apples*. "It's fun," she said. "Is all this true, though, about Shakespeare running off to be a boy actor?"

Boney smiled. His false teeth were as old as most people's real ones; the porcelain was wearing thin in spots, showing a glitter of gold beneath. "I never ask," he said, "what's true in those. He did a lot of research."

"You knew him, right?"

"Sandy Kraft? Oh yes. Oh, Sandy and I were good friends, yes."

"Sandy?"

"That's what he was known as."

Rosie turned to the inside back flap of the paper cover. There was a picture of Fellowes Kraft, an ageless, gentle-eyed man in an open shirt, cheek resting on his fist, a shock of light hair falling over his forehead. Thirty years ago? Forty? The book was copyright 1941, but the picture might be older. "Hm," she said. "He lived in Stonykill."

"Near there. That house, you know the one. He bought it in the late thirties. It's owned by the Foundation now. Sandy was with the Foundation for a while. Off and on. We have the copyrights too, they still bring in a little, you'd be surprised." He clasped his shaky hands behind his back and looked out at the day. "He was a nice man, and I miss him."

"Does he have any family still here?"

"Oh no." Boney grinned again. "Sandy wasn't the marrying kind, if you know what I mean."

"Oh?" Rosie said. "Oh."

"What we used to call a confirmed bachelor."

"But that's what you are, Boney."

"Well." He cast a sly look at Rosie. "Depending on how you say it, it means different things. Don't go spreading rumors about me."

Rosie laughed. That antique sort of delicacy. Boney, she knew, himself had a long-ago secret, a secret sorrow that was never to be talked of; something that might have been, should have been, an awful scandal, but wasn't. Nowadays there were no secret scandals. They were all right out there for everybody to ponder, and talk about, and give advice on. She looked out at the broad driveway. Under the maples her station wagon was parked, stuffed to the roof with belongings she was as yet unwilling to unpack. Boney had taken her in instantly, no questions asked, as though she were merely coming for a long visit; and Mrs. Pisky, his housekeeper for the last millennium or so, took her cue from Boney. Well, Mrs. P., Rosie and Sam are going to be staying for a while, what do you think, the west bedroom has a bathroom and there's the little boudoir too. Oh Mr. Rasmussen they haven't been aired out or anything, I'll do a load of wash, isn't it nice to have young ones around. Whatever griefs, Rosie thought, the old reticences had once caused or hidden, they could be restful too, if you just didn't have an explanation, if you just wanted to get away and couldn't say why for a while. Mrs. Pisky might be a hypocrite, for sure she had a quick eye for the things Rosie brought into the house, a mess of a life as yet unpurged, rolling-papers in the jewelry box and Sam confused and not as clean as she might be—food for Mrs. Pisky's thought, no doubt; but Boney, Rosie felt sure, not only said nothing but as far as was consistent with affection thought nothing either.

Arcady. What on earth would she have done, she thought humbly, if she hadn't had Arcady to come to, great dull brown Arcady with its big flagged veranda and its wicker chaise-longue where she could lie with a book in the sweet coolness, as she had as a child, a library book into whose pages crept the summer outside

and the far hills; what would she have done? How did people bear
it, who had no place to go, when something dreadful had to be
done and they weren't ready yet to do it?

"You notice," Boney said, seeing her turn back to *Bitten
Apples,* "how he uses little dashes instead of quote marks, when
people talk."

"Yeah. I think that's sort of confusing."

"Well I think so too. Hard to read. But now do you know why
he does that? He explained it to me once. He said he just couldn't
bring himself to claim that all these historical figures really said,
quote quote, what he has them say. They never really said these
things, he told me; not really. And the little dashes make it not seem
so much like people are really talking. Sandy said: It's more like
you're dreaming of what they must have said, if they did the things
they did." He looked down slowly, unmoving, at Sam, who had
approached him just as slowly. "That's all," he said gravely. He and
Sam looked at each other, her blond head bent up, his lizard's head
bent down. "Hello, Sam."

Rosie received the bundle of her daughter in her lap with a
grunt, Sam fleeing from Boney's intimacy. She turned the pages of
Bitten Apples, which had fluttered closed, to find her place again.

Boney, his hand on the screen door to go out, paused. "Rosie,"
he said. "May I ask you something?"

"Sure."

"Do you think you'll be needing to talk to a lawyer?"

"Oh. Oh, Boney . . ."

"I only ask because."

"I don't know, I don't think so, yet."

"Tell me if you do," Boney said, "and I'll call Allan Butterman.
That's all."

With a small smile, he went out the door, and down the wide
shallow steps as though they were steep. Sam, watching him go, got
up all of a sudden and went after him, slipping out the door before
it could close on its old slow pneumatic closure, and going down
the steps which were steep to her too; Boney noticed her following,
but took no notice.

And the wide afternoon still remained; long, long till lawyers,
please, please. Young Will went home along Henley Street, past the
shambles and the market cross, up to his father's door, his heart

beating hard, with an invitation to be one of the Earl of Leicester's Boys from Master James Burbage to lay before his father.

There was no one in the leather-odorous glover's shop on the first floor. Will mounted to the chamber above, hearing voices speaking in low tones. The room was dim, shutters half-closed, and with the August day still sparkling in his eyes Will could not at first make out who stood there behind his father's chair.

His father wiped his eyes with his sleeve; he seemed to have been weeping. Again. In the far doorway his mother stood, hands beneath her apron, her thoughts unguessable but troubled. The man behind his father's chair, tall, lank-haired, was his teacher of last year, Master Simon Hunt.

—Will, Will. His father gathered the boy toward him with a two-handed gesture. Will, my own son. We have just now spoken of you.

They were all looking at him; in the old smoked darkness all their eyes seemed to him to be alight. Will felt a tremor of apprehension that chilled the sweat on the back of his neck. He did not go to his father.

—Will, here is Master Hunt. We have prayed long together. For you, for all of us. Will, Master Hunt undertakes a journey tomorrow.

Will said nothing. Often lately he had found Hunt the schoolmaster here with his father, his father in tears; Hunt and he talked of the old religion in low voices, and of the sad state of the world now, and how nothing ever would go right until true religion came again into this land. Hunt had taken him, Will, aside too, and talked closely and intently to him, and Will in a paralysis of strangeness had listened, and nodded when that seemed required, understanding little enough of what was said to him but feeling Hunt's intensity almost as a physical touch that he wanted to shake off.

—I'm going over the sea, Will, said Master Hunt. To see other lands, and to serve God. Is not that a fine thing?

—Where do you go? Will said.

—To the Low Countries. To a famous college there, where there are learned and pious men. Brave men too. Knights of God.

Why were they speaking to him in this way, as though he were a baby, a child to be won over to something? Only his mother had not spoken. She held herself stiffly at the door, half in and half out of the room, in the way she did when her husband reprimanded or beat her children, not daring to intercede for them and yet unwilling to be party to their punishment either. They waited, Hunt waited, for him to speak, but he had nothing to say, except for his own news, which was not now to be said: that he knew.

—Come, boy, come.

Tears were gathering in his father's voice. Will reluctantly went to him; Hunt was nodding solemnly, as though yes, this were the next thing to be done. His father took him in his arms, patting his shoulder.

—I will tell you what. I have decided—Master Hunt and I have decided, with God's help—that you should go away with him tomorrow. Beyond the sea. Listen to me, listen.

For Will had begun to draw away. His father would not release him. A horror was growing in his heart: they meant to deliver him to Hunt, an endless schooling, Hunt's voice and touch always. No.

—Oh, son, oh, son. You have a good wit, a good wit, a better wit than I. Think of it, think. There is learning there, holy learning you cannot have here, listen, Will, that is a treasure to search world's ends for. Listen. You are a good boy, a good boy.

Closed in his father's arms, Will had grown weirdly calm; a cunning almost seeming not to belong to him, a whisper in his ear, made him still; and when his father felt it he released him. And held him then before him by the shoulders, smiling at Will with his mouth while his wet eyes searched his face.

—Good lad. Brave lad. Will you not speak?

—I will do as you like. Father.

The tears welled in his father's eyes. Will counseled himself: say yes, yes, only yes. His mother drew up her apron over her face.

—There was secrecy required, Hunt said. It had to be so. We could not tell you till the last. For fear of the powers of this world.

—Yes.

He knelt by Will and looked into his face.

—An adventure, boy. Going secret by dawn's light. I will be knight, and you my page, and we will fight every devil the world shows us. For the world is full of them now.

—Yes.

His smile was somehow worse than his solemn face. Will's face smiled into it.

—Oh, there will be singing there. There will be singing there as

you have never heard, and plays, and churches full of splendors
made for God's sake. As wonderful as in any book. Not like this
darkened land where they hate beauty and figured song. And truth,
Will. Truth to learn.

Will took a step back from him.

—At dawn? he said.

—Yes, said Hunt. I go now to make all ready. Bring little, now.
Everything will be provided.

He rose, anxious and intent again, his common face, and sat at
the table, where Will now saw there was money being counted out
and a leather pouch. Hunt and his father put their heads together.

—There will be lodging in London, Hunt said. My careful
friend there. He is apprised of this. But the wherry thence to
Greenwich must be hired. . . .

They turned again as one to watch him when Will stepped
farther away.

—I'll go prepare, he said.

—Do, said Hunt, with a wink. I'll return about the middle of
night. You won't sleep?

—No.

—See to him, see to him, John Shakespeare said to his wife.
See to him.

But he was gone up the stairs to his garret room, and had
latched the door before his mother could reach it.

A fissure had opened in the world, huge, and he had found
himself all in a moment on its edge. On the opposite side were his
father, and Hunt, asking him to leap in; and his mother, asking him
to come to her. But he could not. He could feel nothing but his
sudden danger, he could only think fast and calmly how he could
abandon them and save himself; and his mind whirred like the gears
of a clock about to strike.

—Will? his mother said softly; Will didn't answer. From a
secret niche in the wall he drew out paper, he had a fondness for
paper and saved clean scraps of it when he found them; and a little
horn of ink. His hands shook steadily with the beat of his heart, and
only by an act of will he steadied them. He propped the paper on
the sill of the tiny window, and by its light he began to write; he
spoiled one sheet, and began another, more calmly, the words flying
to his mind's tongue as though his father really were speaking them:

or if not his own father, then some father, a believable father, a father whose voice he could hear.

Just after dark, he took the bundle of shirts and hose his mother had made up, and the little purse of coin his father gave him, and the new kid gloves he had made himself, all up to his room: to think and pray there, he said, and wait for Master Hunt. And when he thought his brother and sister were well asleep, and his father below at his wine, he went out the window and down the side of the house by a means he had long perfected for getting out on just such a summer night as this one was.

Master James Burbage was in a great hurry to get out of town. A member of his company had got into a brawl with a local boy over some wench or some piece of money, and the swain had got the worst of it and might die. Burbage, furious with his man, had however no intention of waiting to see local justice done, and himself fined or worse, and at ten o'clock was seeing to the strapping-down of the last of his stage properties on the wagon, to leave by moonlight, when the boy startled him into crying out by sidling up and tugging at his sleeve.

Did he believe the note the boy gave him? Signed, and attested by a Master Simon Hunt. Trusting he will treat with my son the said William in good faith and honestly and train him up in the trade, business and arts of player in my lord of Leicester's company. My beloved son whose person and fortune I entrust to the said Master Burbage and the said. There was no mention of any fees; Burbage had never and would never meet this man John Shakespeare; in the dark, the redhead's face was a mask, a mask saying *I have done what was asked of me and here I am ready*. No, Master Burbage did not believe it, not for a moment, any more than he believed the boy's face. But he thought a magistrate would, if it came to that; or would anyway forgive Burbage for having believed it; and he was in a very great hurry; and the imp had an angel's voice.

—Get up then! he said, giving Will a boost that was nothing to the flight he had given to the boy's full heart. Get up on the seat. No—not on the seat, then—get down in there. Well down. Good. Now, young Master Shakespeare, gone for a player, you will keep to that place until we are past Clopton Bridge, and farther on than that too. No g'yup! G'yup!

And the little wagon train, with Master Burbage riding post and the rest perched about the wagons or riding two to a horse or walking behind trading songs and speeches (and a leathern bottle too) went out of Stratford over Clopton Bridge and south on the road to London; and Will down in the wagon turned a property crown in his hands and listened, his ears seeming to grow huge as bells, to the talk outside and the night, his heart unwilling to cease beating hard and loud.

The note he had left for his father to find said that he had gone for a sailor to Bristol, there to take ship for the New World and make his fortune on the sea, or die in the attempt.

"Telephone," said Mrs. Pisky, putting her head out the veranda window. "Telephone for you."

Rosie closed the book, her finger at her place. Trying for a certain calm deliberateness she got off the chaise. "Okay," she said; she sighed, what a bother, but really it was to breathe out the sudden darkness that swarmed in her—and just then over the lawn and the veranda too, what was it, oh: the heavy clouds that had brooded so long in the next county had come at last overhead. A wind was rising too. Rosie followed Mrs. Pisky through the fast-darkening house to the phone.

"Hello."

"Hello, Rosie."

"Hi, Mike."

A lengthy pause, and Rosie knew that from now on, not forever maybe but for as long as made no difference, all their conversations would begin with one.

"First of all," Mike said. "First of all you've left Sam's night-time diapers here. Three boxes of them."

"Oh."

"Do you want to come get them?"

"I think I've still got a couple around. In the travel bag."

Another silence. The "first of all" had staked a claim that Rosie was satisfied to let him prosecute. If he had a list, she would respond to each item as it came up.

"I've also found," he said, patient archaeologist working the midden she had left, "what looks like the rear-view mirror of the wagon."

"Oh. Yes. I was going to epoxy it on, but I couldn't find any epoxy."

"Epoxy?"

"That's what Gene did, only maybe he didn't use enough. I thought we had some in the toolbox, but we don't."

He laughed. "Well, it's not doing you much good here."

She refused to answer that. It wasn't part of the list. She waited for more. She heard him sigh, in a prefatory, brass-tacks sort of way. "Do you want to tell me," he said, "what your plans are, if any?"

"Well," she said. She glanced up; Mrs. Pisky was busy, or not busy, with something in the butler's pantry off the dining room. Rosie could see her large pendulous ear.

"Do you want to try to tell me . . ."

"Well there's nothing just right now to say, Mike," she said softly. "I mean not just right now this afternoon." There was a sort of huff, that maybe stood for head patiently shaken, or even patience tried. "I mean . . ." You were warned and none of this is any kind of goddamn surprise: that's what she meant. Mike's capacity always to begin the old conversations, the old negotiations, afresh from square one was inexhaustible, probably it came from having to do it in therapy. He seemed to thrive on it, as Rosie withered, became tangled and speechless, unable to finish sentences.

"You mean?" He waited. She seemed to see him shift the phone to his other ear, settle down. She knew this so well, Mike growing quiet and large and patient, waiting, exuding what Rosie called the Cloud of Power. And as she saw it it dissipated, she knew herself to be outside and beyond it, that being outside and beyond it was her reason for being here in Arcady now and not in Stonykill.

"I mean I don't have anything to say."

"Mm-hm."

She realized her middle finger had gone numb inside the book she had been gripping tightly. She released it. There was a long soft roll of thunder like a groan of relief. She put the book down, it fluttered closed, she put her hand on it just as the title page was falling.

"Well, so what are you up to?" he said. Start fresh, new tack.

"Reading."

"What."

"A book."

Beneath the title was the quotation from which the title was taken: *These are the youths that thunder at a playhouse, and fight for bitten apples.* From *Henry VIII.*

"Rosie, I think I really deserve just a little bit of openness. I think you don't feel I can imagine what you're feeling, but . . ."

"Oh, Michael, don't, just talk normal, please." During his silence at that she made a decision. "I just don't have anything to say now for a while. I don't have anything to say that I can say. I mean it. If you really have to talk all about it *right now* then well you can call Allan Butterman."

"Who?"

"Allan Butterman. He's a lawyer."

The house had grown dark as night. There was a more authoritative roll of thunder; in the pantry Mrs. Pisky clucked and turned on the light. "His number's in the phone book, I suppose." Great volumes of warm wet air were blundering through the rooms; Mrs. Pisky bustled quickly around the dining room, closing the windows whose light summer drapes were tossing like startled hands. "Listen, Mike, it's starting to rain, I have to go find Sam. Goodbye."

She hung up.

She glanced at her watch. The lawyer's office would be closed, she'd call first thing in the morning before Mike did. If he did.

It's all right, it's all right, she counseled herself, feeling calm except for the dreadful lump in her throat. It's all right; because only the I-feel-you-think stuff, the big gasbag words, could pass between them now any longer without hurting; every common word carried too much terrible weight to be spoken, diaper, wagon, house, toolbox. Sam. We.

So he could talk to Allan Butterman, who wouldn't mind.

She went out to the veranda. Furry gray clouds moved fast over the valley; the trees were pulled at and lost leaves as though it were autumn. Across the lawn Sam hurried, her hair windblown over her stricken face, and Boney shuffling behind her pulling her wagon. Dry insect-riddled leaves rose in a whirlwind around them.

Blow it all away, Rosie prayed; blow away summer, bring the hard clear weather. She had had enough summer. She wanted a fire, she wanted to sleep under blankets, she wanted to walk in sweaters under leafless trees, clear and cold inside and out.

EIGHT

▲

The storm did not come then; neither did it pass. After the darkening wind and a few inconclusive drops it seemed to pause, leaving the evening sky clear; it lay still visible on the horizon, though, muttering lowly from time to time, probably raining (they at Spofford's party said to one another) on someone else's party, somewhere else. The dense hot air was charged with its nearness, and when the moon arose, to toasts and laughter, immense and as amber as whiskey, her light gilded the scalloped hem of its clouds.

Pierce and Spofford drove down to the party from the cabin in Spofford's aged truck. Pierce's feet were amid the toolboxes and oily rags, and Spofford drove with one arm across the steering wheel, the other propped on the window sill, holding on the roof. Gravel roads, the old truck's smell, night air on his face, had Pierce thinking of Kentucky, of long-ago summer Saturday nights, out sparkin', of freedom and expectation: as though this road were an extension of one he had once been on, one that he had left years ago and had suddenly rejoined at this juncture, who would have thought it led here, who would have thought.

They turned onto an unkempt paved road, jouncing mightily, and in not too long a time drew up at a shuttered roadside stand. By the headlights Pierce saw that it sold, or had once sold, a long list of summer foods. They parked there amid other vehicles, old trucks like Spofford's and newer ones and ones fitted out to special uses, and a bright little red convertible and a vast station wagon. Spofford pulled off the brown Indian-patterned blanket that covered the truck's seat, rolled it and put it under his arm; he hooked with his forefinger from the back a huge jug of red wine, slung it over his shoulder, and led Pierce to a path that ran behind the roadside stand and descended through a pine woods toward a triangle of gold and black water. There were others on the path, darkish shapes or moonstruck and white, carrying hampers, shepherding children.

"Is that Spofford?" said a big woman in a tentlike dress, cigarette between her lips.

"Hello, Val."

"Good night for it," Val said.

"The best."

"Moon's in Scorpio," Val said.

"Is that so."

"Just be careful," Val chuckled, and they debouched into a peopled clearing, firelight, greeting voices and dogs barking.

It was Spofford's party only in that the stretch of waterside where it went on was his, a little pleasure-ground his parents had used to operate in the summer, the stand, a few picnic tables and a scattering of stone fireplaces like a druid ring, a brief wooden pier and a pair of outhouses, Jacks and Jills. Spofford brought the jug of wine, but did no hosting, was only a little seigneurial as he and Pierce strolled down amid the people, saying hi and passing remarks. The tables were piled with meats and fruits, bottles and cheeses and bowls of this and that, enough for multitudes it seemed, each of them there his own host to all. Fires had been lit in some of the dolmens, and woodsmoke mingled with the night air; a thin piping could be heard, curling through the pines' hushing.

Hands in his pockets, nodding to left and right as Spofford did, Pierce walked with Spofford down to the water's edge. The moon above the massy trees on the far shore seemed to be a hole cut out of a jet sky to let the light of a far cool heaven through. Out on the water as they stood there, one, two, three figures broke the surface suddenly, as though they had been sleeping on the river's bottom and had just awakened; laughing and naked, they climbed the ladder onto the pier and stood in the moonlight drying themselves: three women, a dark, a light, a rosé; three graces.

"Well, she's here," Spofford said quietly, turning away.

"Oh?" said Pierce, not turning away. The dark one twined her thick hair in her hands to squeeze the water out; the blond steadied herself with a hand on the dark one's shoulder, drying her feet. The third pointed to Pierce, and they all three looked up, and seemed to laugh; their voices carried to him over the water, but not their words. Pierce, hands still in his pockets, smiled and stood. Just then there was a heavy padding behind him, and a naked man ran past him and flung himself into the water, praying hands outstretched and long hair flying, as though drowning himself in tribute: it was he they had laughed at.

He was followed by a blond child, rushing in to his knees with a shriek and then stopping in surprise; then an older child who raced on past him and went under. A large woman, their mother it might be, drawing off her smock, her great breasts rolling with her stride, followed them in, churning the gold-barred water into silver foam.

Pierce turned away, a fullness in his breast and the grin still on his face. Adamites. How had they escaped the curse?

"You couldn't *buy* this, in the city," he said to Spofford, who poured red wine for him black in the moonlight. "Couldn't buy it. This amenity."

"Yeah, well," Spofford said. "It's not for sale." He handed Pierce a thick crackling joint from which ropy smoke arose. "You want something to eat?"

Roasted corn and tomatoes sweet as berries, the harvest was coming in; crumbling bread from someone's oven, blackened weenies, nine kinds of slaw and salad, his paper plate sogged and bent beneath it. "What do you suppose this is?" he asked a woman filling her plate next to him, prodding a cakelike thing. "I dunno," she said. "Beige food."

He carried his plate to a suitable rock for sitting, in view of all; on the rock next to him sat the piper, his thin uncertain music coming from a set of bound reed pipes, and himself looking Pan-like in a mild-mannered way, bow mouth pursed to blow and a boyish beard. A sleepy child sat with his head in the piper's lap.

"Syrinx," said Pierce when the piper stopped to shake spit from his instrument.

"What say?"

"The pipes," Pierce said. "Syrinx is their name. She was a girl, a nymph, that the god Pan loved. And chased." He paused to swallow. "She was chaste, I mean she tried to get away, and just as he reached her some other god or goddess took pity on her and changed her into a bunch of reeds. At the last moment."

"You don't say."

"Yup. And Pan made his pipes from the reeds. Syrinx. Same word as 'syringe' by the way—a hollow reed. And he blows her to this day."

"So who calls the tune?" the piper asked. He tried a note. "You can't play much on it."

"You can play," Pierce said, "the Music of the Spheres. In fact."

"Maybe after a few lessons." The curl of his mouth and his light, husky voice made it seem he was about to laugh, as though he and Pierce shared a secret joke. "I was trying for 'Three Blind Mice.' "

Pierce laughed, thinking of octaves and ogdoads, Pythagoras and Orpheus's lyre. He could go on. It was the smoke; he rarely smoked these days, it only made him paradoxical and cryptic, he had found, whatever clarity it seemed to create within him, which made him doubt the clarity. The piper looked at him as though trying to make him out, or remember who he was, still smiling that smile of pleasant complicity. "I'm a stranger here," Pierce said. "Name's Pierce Moffett. I came with Spofford."

"My name's Beau." He offered no hand, though his smile broadened.

"I'm not supposed to be here," Pierce said.

"Oh yes?" Something about Pierce or his explanation tickled the piper more and more.

"I was headed somewhere else entirely. I was buswrecked. So."

"So you're a crasher. Just broke right on in."

"Right."

"Not hurt, though?"

"Hm?"

"Hi, Rosie," Beau called into the darkness. "Come talk." Pierce looked into the crowd of people passing. A dark girl walking away, beer in her hand, glanced back at him just then and caught his eye, and smiled as though she knew him, and went on.

"Well," said Beau, fingering the stops of his pipe, "if you're here, I guess you put yourself in the way of it. Right? One way or another."

"Well, that's so," Pierce said. He set down his plate, and instantly there was a dog to investigate it, who found nothing of interest. "That's so, I suppose, in a way," he said, rising.

The child in Beau's lap lifted his head, wanting more music.

Beau played. Pierce wandered away after the smile he had seen, which had disappeared amid the partygoers. Syrinx. Now what would an item like that go for around here, that was a real hot item, special this month. Only he would have to show his wares in order to sell them, and showing them gave them away. What would you pay to know where, why that pipe, what that pipe's intervals can be made to picture or echo. . . . She sat on a log down by the shore, a little apart it seemed; when she twisted her long hair in her hands, he knew her. He heard someone passing say to her:

"Hey, is Mike coming, do you know?"

She shrugged, shook her head, Mike wasn't coming; or no, she didn't know; or she refused the question. Or all three. She seemed briefly embarrassed, and drank thirstily.

"Hello, Rosie," Pierce said, standing over her. "How's Mike?" It was the smoke, the damned smoke and drink making him devilish.

"Fine," she said automatically, looking up and smiling again; her teeth were brightly white, large and uneven, long canines and one front one chipped. "I forget you," she said.

"Well hell," he said, sitting beside her, "hell of a note."

"Are you in The Woods? I don't know everybody there."

"In the woods?"

"Well," she said, looking helpless.

"That was an imposition," Pierce said. "A joke. You don't know me from Adam." And how will we know, when we get to Paradise, which man there is Adam, without being told? Special this week.

She seemed to take no offense, only looked at him curiously, waiting for more. She had the long-nosed, plump-cheeked look of an Egyptian cat sculpture; the summer dress she had pulled on was pretty and childish. "No," he said, "really. I'm a friend of Spofford's. I came along with him."

"Oh."

"We knew each other in the city. I'm visiting. I'm sort of thinking of throwing in with him here, though. Getting into sheep." He laughed, and she did too, it seemed like a punch line; at that moment Spofford himself appeared out on the little pier, with others, doffing his clothes.

"So you know all these people?" she asked.

"Not a bit," he said. "I thought you would."

"It's not exactly my crowd."

"But Spofford."

"Oh, well, yes." Spofford was naked now, except for his broad straw hat; he was being challenged by the others; horseplay was threatened, but Spofford drew apart, holding them off.

"Best-looking man here," Pierce said. "*I* think."

"*Do* you."

"Far as I can tell."

"What about the guy I saw you talking to before?"

"Cute," Pierce said. "Not my type, though."

They watched Spofford whisk off his straw hat and skim it down the pier; then he poised himself, looking in fact (Pierce noticed) very striking, and dived.

"Mm," Pierce said. "I like that."

She giggled, watching him watch, holding her glass in both hands; she looked into it, and found it empty. Louder music was beginning, thud thud thud of a portable stereo, there were glad cries and encouragements for this. Pierce drew from his pocket a slim silver flask—a gift of his father's, someone else's initials were on it, it was worn plate but Axel had thought it just the thing for his son—and uncapped it.

"I don't usually drink hard stuff," she said.

"Oh?" he said, poised to pour.

"It's not good for me." She moved her glass beneath the spout, and Pierce poured scotch, he had filled the flask and put it in his bag when he left the city, you never know, clever of him.

"So how did you say I know you?" she asked, lifting her cup to stop him pouring, as priests had always done when he poured wine for them at Mass.

"You don't, yet." He capped the flask, taking nothing. He suddenly wanted to be clear-headed. Among the Adamites there was no shame in nakedness; no sin for the saved. He felt goat-footed among them, uninvited but himself also, for other reasons, un-ashamed. "I never saw you before tonight." He indicated the water. "Rising from the Deep."

"Oh yes?" she said, returning his look. The music chugged and rang, and her head moved to it, laughter in her eyes. "You liked that too?"

They both laughed then, heads close together; her eyes—maybe it was the moon, which had come overhead and gone small and white but brighter than ever—her eyes glittered with moisture but didn't seem soft; it was as though they were coated thinly and finely with ice or crystal.

The music was both new and old, supplemented by a gang of instruments the people produced, rattles and bangers and cowbells and bongos. The dancing was eclectic too, with overtones of country clodhopping and Shaker ecstasies; everyone joined, or nearly everyone, Pierce sat it out mostly, in the city these days the dancing was done chiefly by semiprofessionals, wiry boys dashed with sweat and glitter you wouldn't want to compete with—Pierce had no skill in it anyway, and for this happy corybanting he had no taste; even in the days of the great parade he had not been good at melding with the throng and going with the flow. A fogey. And it was of that parade that he was reminded here, by the bouncing folk and the homemade rhythms, as if a contingent or spur of it had split off back then and wound up here and kept on turning in happy ignorance of what elsewhere had become of their fellows; still piping, still corybanting, going naked but raising kids and vegetables and baking bread and breaking it with others in the old new hospitality. Couldn't be so, not really; it was the smoke (the old taste of it was in his mouth, sweetish and burnt, he had never been able to describe it, artichokes and woodsmoke and buttered popcorn) and the sense he had of having stumbled in among them, city dirt in his pores and city vices in his heart.

Flirting. Only flirting. He could see Spofford nowhere in the maze of dancers or on the now-still water. Rosie turned and shuffled with the rest, impossible to tell if she had a partner, or if anybody did. The advantage to a watcher of this sort of dancing was that, since there were no rules of movement, it revealed character; there was no way to be good at it except to have a natural sense of rhythm and the knack of displaying it. Rosie moved dreamily and privately, erect, long hair aswing. She seemed to be unassimilated to the rout, though part of it, as though she had gone native amid a primitive tribe who, less graceful than she, knew better than she why they were doing this dance.

At a change of music she came over to him, a little flushed, her high evident only in the brightness of her eyes. "Don't you wanna dance?"

"I don't dance much," Pierce said. "But save me the waltz."

"You still have that teeny bottle?"

He uncapped it; she had lost her glass, and drank from the flask; so did he, then she again. She looked around herself. "There's one thing about your friends," she said. "They can be a little cliquish. No offense."

"They seem very hospitable to me."

"Well, sure. To you."

"Honest," said Pierce, rising, "I just got here." And for her information: "I'll probably be leaving tomorrow. Or the next day. Soon, anyway. For good." He began to walk down toward the water; she followed. Where had Spofford vanished to? Out on the water a rowboat turned lazily, full of children being rowed around. Another rowboat was tied to the pier.

"No," she said. "You were throwing in with Spofford. Getting into sheep." She handed him the flask. "How come you keep changing your story?"

"I live in New York," he said. "Have for years."

"You think so?" Brightly.

"So listen," he said. "If it's not your crowd, and it's cliquish, why did you come?"

"Oh, to swim. And dance. Just look around."

"For somebody in particular?"

"No," she said, regarding him as frankly as her strange crystallized eyes allowed, "nobody in *particular.*"

Pierce drank. "Would you," he said courteously, "be interested in going for a row? In the moonlight?"

"Can you row?" And then, like a kid: "*I* can. I'm good at it."

"Well, good," Pierce said, taking her elbow. "We can spell each other." Another punch line, the smoke could transform any remark into one, he laughed at that and at the rowboat he was untying (the pointy end he remembered went first with the operator facing backward) and, also, at a warm certainty just then hatching within him. He took off shoes and socks and left them on the pier, rolled his pants to his knees and pushed off, clambering in himself with not quite the grace he had hoped for.

He maneuvered the old boat out into the moonlight, gradually putting back into his muscles skills he had learned long ago on the Little Sandy River and its cricks and branches; once again that old road seemed to lead here, knock of oarlocks and gulp of soft night water on the bows. "So," he said. "The Blackberry River."

"Oh, this isn't the river really," she said. She was straddling her seat, moving her feet to keep them out of the seepage at the bottom. "Just a backwater. The real river's over there." She pointed, thought, drew her finger along the bank. "Over *there*."

He looked over her shoulder, but could see no exit. "Shall we go see?"

"If I can find the channel. More port," she said. "No, more port. That way."

Pierce pulled, catching a crab and nearly tumbling backward into the bows; she laughed and asked if he was sure he knew how to do this, reminding him of his claim to know in the same disbelieving tone she had taken toward his stories of who he was and where he had come from. He ignored it, and composed himself, looking over his shoulder at what seemed an impassable thicket of tangled trees. The current tugged gently at the boat, and more by its effects than by her directions they slid into a tunnel made of moonlight and willows.

Pierce shipped one oar, it was too narrow here to row, and the current knew the way. He kept them from the tangled feet of trees and tall bullrushes with the other oar, stilled and feeling enormously privileged. How had he deserved this, this beauty, how did they; she, who lived always within having distance of it, with it for hers, with these willows drowning their long hair, these water-lilies floating in their sleep? How could it not make you both good and happy?

She trailed one hand in the water. "Warmer than the air," she said. "How can that be."

"A swim?" he said, his heart all in a moment in his throat.

"Well lookee here," she said, hand in the single patch pocket of her dress. "I have found a number here in my pocket." She held it up to him, between a V of fingers like a Lucky in an old ad. "Do you have a match?"

In its flare she looked at him, her face changed or revealed further by matchlight; questioning or for some reason uncertain, afraid even. The match went out.

"There," she said, pointing.

They entered onto the river, a wide avenue black and bordered with immense trees; an avenue of humid sky matched it above. The current turned them idly toward the mystery of the bank; Pierce unshipped his oars and dipped them. As faint as though proceeding from the blurred and goldish constellations, the tinkle and murmur of the party's music.

"You're going to get stuck," Rosie said calmly.

He pulled his right oar, but the boat struck something projecting from the bank, and swung around. It was a little wooden landing stage, and the boat lay up there now ready to be tied, like an old horse who has led a new rider back to its stable.

Okay. All right. The little pier led to stairs, though nothing could be seen at the top of them. "Explore?" he said. "Go ashore and forage."

"Oooh."

But he had thrown the painter around a piling in two quick loops, that boating trick at least he remembered. He rose to help her out.

"What if somebody lives here."

"Friendly natives."

"Maybe a dog."

Her hand was small and moist, and he felt, hand on her back to put her ashore, the cotton of her dress slide against the silk of her skin. Beside her, he offered the flask again. They listened to the silence.

"Don't be a scaredy-cat," she said, taking his arm. Slowly, in care for their bare feet uncertain of the ground beneath, they went up the stairs—logs only, forced into the soft earth, and a big root commandeered—beneath pines that warned them away in awed whispers.

"A house."

A cottage; a big screened porch and a chimney, a swayed rooftree outlined against a moonlit open distance. The pine-needle-strewn path led up to it. It was dark.

"Who's doing that in the dark," she whispered.

"What."

"The piano."

He could hear nothing.

"The piano," she said. "Wake up."

There was no piano. They walked around the house; it was a strange composite, its patent moonlight side was stucco and had two stubby pillars supporting an entablature over the door and two arched windows. The big screened porch in back was an after-thought. Beyond what seemed in the moonlight to be velvet lawns and topiary but may have been only meadow was a tall house, many-chimneyed, on a wooded rise.

"Their cottage."

"Probably." The big house was dark too. Why were they whispering? Their tour took them back to the dark side, the screened porch. It needed repair: here by the door a hole big enough for a hand. Pierce put a hand through, and as though he were practiced at this, a yegg, a spy, slid open the bolt.

It was not, any of it, any choice of his, except the choice to do all that was offered. If he had been led by some shining psychopomp into a fabulous otherwhere, Elysium's fountains and mountains, he could not have felt more removed from his daily self, less responsible. Drink this. Eat this. And she went ahead of him through the door, taking slow steps, wondering.

The place had been long uninhabited. Two broken wicker chairs were all the porch held. Rosie tried the door into the house; it was locked. But the large window beside it, when Pierce pushed it up, gaped open, making a shocked noise like an indrawn breath. He stepped over the low sill.

Odor of mothballs and mice, moldered wallpaper and dead summers past. When, where had he once before broken into a locked place that smelled so, a place where old summers had been left? There was a rolled rug like a cadaver in one corner, but nothing else. Moonlight lay in cool rhomboids on the floor.

"What if it's not safe." Her voice was loud in the vacant indoors. She turned to face him, slashed with window light, and with a single step he was with her.

She met him with no surprise but with what eagerness he couldn't tell; he fed not greedily but wholly on her anyway, as though drinking water; when he was filled, momentarily, and drew away, she parted from him with a little drunken bob like a bee-visited blossom; and, her hand falling from his breast where she had pressed him but not pressed him away, she walked off. "This is the living room," she said.

There was another room after that, where a card table cocked a bad leg back as though favoring it, and a black stove had pulled its long arm half out of the hole in the wall. Kitchen. Bathroom. "Oh look," she said. "Secret."

A door in the bathroom led to a further room. Another addition? There was no other way into it, it seemed, except through the bathroom. An iron bedstead stood askew there, stunned, caught out, a thin buttoned mattress sprawled across its springs. Pierce from the door watched Rosie approach it with slow steps. Then she looked back at him, sharply he thought, as though he had surprised her here, startled her—and then he had come up behind her and encircled her.

She suffered him, hands idly, unseriously tugging at his hands, head fallen back against his shoulder. He gathered up her dress and their two left hands went together between her legs; her hair was short, thick, like the nap of a velvet. She turned to face him then, and he freed her for that, but when he did so she slid from him and walked away, saying something he didn't understand.

"What?"

". . . if the dancing's all over, and I have to get up early tomorrow." Her dress had curtained her again, though she hadn't tidied it. "I'm always the last one dancing." She looked at him idly, as though he were her guest here and the visit was growing protracted. He had a mad thought that she knew this room, had long known it; and, for it was in some way the same thought, that he could do anything at all to her here, anything, and would meet with no resistance but this strange inattention. It was not he she was wandering from.

"I know I shouldn't," she said, pushing back her hair, "I know I shouldn't, but if you still have that little bottle, I'd like another sip. If I may."

He was to ignore that. He knew it; he was to refuse in fact to listen further to anything she said; that was why she said it. The hair rose on the back of his neck, the hairs too along his arms.

"Sure," he said, unpocketing the flask. "Sure, here you go, only let's go. Enough of the haunted house."

"Scared?" she said, and laughed, and came and took his arm; he gave her the bottle, and she tipped it up as they went back through the house. "I live in a house like this sometimes," she said. He helped her through the window. "I mean on the river, a cottage, it's nice, I like the water *so much*. There's your bottle back. I think the little stopper on a chain is the cute part."

Arm in arm, gay companions again, they went back to the boat. Pierce, his heart and loins confused and turgid, didn't know whether he had cheated himself, or failed her, or escaped harmless, only that he had come down from an upper floor he hadn't known he was mounting to. It was the shock of finding himself heedlessly stepping up onto the topmost stair that had raised the hair on his nape, that had made him think to go back.

She standing in the corner by the iron bed, stoned, dreaming, in two.

Hands and head at odds, making jokes, he pulled clumsily out onto the water. The moon was going down, and the river was darker; against the current he fought the wretched boat back into the gurgling channel, and she was no help. She had got the giggles now, and found his exertions hilarious; she razzed him as he struggled, oars caught in grasping weed, sweat tickling in his eyebrows. "Come on now," he said, growing afraid he might be lost, "let's keep our heads, let's keep our heads," but that was a punch line too. She stopped giggling only when, at last, they entered onto the backwater and he pulled for the firelit shore.

"Well!" she said cheerily, disembarking. "Thanks for the lil boatride." She gave him a hand. "It was nice meeting you. You're very interesting."

"Nice to meet *you*," he said.

"I'm sure I'll see you around."

"Sure," he said. "At the county fair."

"I like the fair."

"Is that a fact."

Not all the drink and smoke had melted the strange ice behind which her eyes had grown vague. She stepped lightly away from him up the beach, the hem of her sundress swinging; Pierce put his hands back in his pockets and turned to the water, whose gold had faded. One fat man in an inner tube floated there, paddling softly.

Now what on earth, Pierce thought. A sudden draft of hereness and nowness. Where was Spofford? He was coming toward him from the woods on the opposite side of the campground; in the light of a fireplace where trash was burned and, doubtless, the last marshmallows toasted, he waved to Pierce.

The piper had gone, and most of the others. Pierce was struck suddenly by a thought: These people now all have to drive cars to get home. How do they manage? How will she?

"Good party," said Spofford. He was consuming a piece of cake, one hand held below it like a paten for the crumbs.

"Fun," said Pierce.

" 'Bout done?" Spofford asked.

"I'm with you. Whenever you want."

Spofford seemed thoughtful, though he smiled. He tossed crumbs into the fire and dusted his hands. "Good party," he said again, with satisfaction. He looked around his premises, assured himself that there were enough of those careful guests left whose pleasure it is to tidy up, and said, "Let's go."

If she has an accident, it will be partly my fault, Pierce thought. He almost thought to reproach Spofford: You ought to watch out better for her. You don't know what danger she puts herself in.

Oh lord.

Spofford threw the brown blanket into the truck. "Did you meet people?" he asked. "I didn't mean to just throw you to the lions there."

"Oh, sure."

"I should have taken you around."

"I got on."

"Nice people. Mostly." He grinned sidelong at Pierce, starting the truck. "And old Mike didn't show up, it seems."

"No?" said Pierce, feeling foolish. What had he been up to, what? Putting his gross foot through the fabric of relationships he didn't begin to understand, in a country, his friend's country, that he had just come into, a guest. Where he didn't really belong at all.

The truck jounced out onto the darkling highway, Spofford whistling softly between his teeth. When they had gone a long time in silence, Pierce said, "I guess I ought to be getting back."

"Oh yeah?"

"Duty. The Future."

"Whatever you say."

Night, wind, the sweep of the truck's headlights. The moon was gone. Pierce hugged himself, weary, amazed. He seemed suddenly to have been gone from home for an age.

"Hey," Spofford said, and took his foot from the accelerator. In the roadway stood a deer, a doe, motionless on delicate stilts. The truck coasted to a halt, and the doe, as though deciding at length to take fright, remembering to be shy, dived away with neat assurance into the tangled wood. A big raindrop spattered on the windshield, and then another.

"Here comes that storm," Spofford said.

*   *   *

When Pierce awoke in Spofford's bed on the far side of the night the rain had ceased; at some point Spofford must have got up and opened the windows without waking him, for they were open now. The night was clear, or clearing; Pierce could see a single star in the window's corner.

It was a noise like the approach of a tiny high-speed drill that had awakened him. For a long moment he gathered the world around him, listening to Spofford snoring softly in his sleeping bag in the next room; waiting for the mosquito at his ear to settle and be slapped; living still in the long rich dream he had been dreaming, allegory of the lumps in Spofford's bed and the insect orchestra outside.

What had it been all about now. . . .

Standing with an old man looking over a far country at dawn or at evening, a country so far it was made of time not space. Standing, yes, at a cave's mouth with that old man who had a star on his forehead. Standing, being shown that country, why, how had they come there. Pierce struggled to keep the softly closing doors open, the doors into the further-back parts of the dream, years-long parts, the doors closing blindly, why must they, why.

Oh yes. Oh I remember

Years-long, his education at the hands of difficult masters . . . Or was it only the one master, the old man, in different disguises? The savage unwittingness bred out of him by tasks he could still sense, could taste but not remember, puzzles to solve and paradoxes to resolve, oh I see, I get it, but whatever had they been, duality, identity, metaphor and simile. Journeys, or illusions of journeys, for it seemed, had seemed, had kept on being proved or revealed to him that he had not ever left the confines of the deep-down place where this schooling had gone on, not till now; not till he was taken by the hand and led up, up a long earth-damp tunnel following the old man's lantern, and out the cave's mouth, to be shown the way into the far lands; clear air real at last, dawn winds ruffling his hair and the master's robe as they stood together there to part forever. He knew his task; he knew his arms and his enemies. And he saw, by the old man's clear sad eyes, that oh he would do his best, he would, but that he would forget it all, everything he had learned, his task, his education, who he was and where he had come from, everything; would remember, when he had traveled far, nothing but how far he had traveled; would remember only and vaguely that he was a stranger here in this sad country, in these sad streets, in this sad dark cell where he waited for the girl to bring him sandwiches and milk and

Oh yes! Pierce came fully awake, remembering.

A tray of sandwiches and milk brought him as usual by the smiling girl, the child who had been so kind, teasingly kind, as though she were not really sorry for him at all; the tray brought him as usual, as it had been for years, the only break in his work, what work, his years-long education down here, that cot, this lamp, those books—only today there was a letter propped against the glass, a letter. A letter! He didn't have to open it, just the sight of it was enough, he remembered suddenly everything: who he was, how he had come there, oh yes! Yes! The whole latter part of the dream, the aged master, the task, the words of power learned, the far country seen, that was all his sudden memory as he picked up the letter, a blank bond envelope glowing like milk glass; memory, washing him like clean water.

Oh yes, oh God what a relief to remember and not lose it. Pierce lay still on Spofford's bed feeling with deep gratitude his possession of his dream, a sensual pleasure like the scratching of an itch or being washed in clean water. Amazing, amazing. Why, what is it, how can flesh and blood come up with such stuff, how can flesh feel it. My lord life is strange. How is that Meaning comes to be? How? How does life cast it up, shape it, exude it; how does Meaning come to have physical, tangible effects, to be felt with a shock, to cause grief or longing, come to be sought for like food; pure Meaning having nothing to do with the clothes of persons or events in which it is dressed and yet not ever divorceable from some set of such clothes? A star in his forehead. A star.

The mosquito with an enormous racket came close to his ear again, and settled, instantly ceasing its noise. Pierce waited with awful cunning for it to get comfy. After a long moment, when its delicate proboscis was inserted, itch-fluid flowing, Pierce could locate it exactly; and with a swift box to his ear he slew it. He grunted with relief, rolling his trophy into a pellet between his fingers, his ear ringing from the blow. A bug in his ear. There were stories of people driven mad by unextractable bugs lodged in the ear canal.

He stretched across the bed's terrain and tasted the cool air passing unhindered through the little house and as though through his body too. He had a sudden percipience, a pearl seemingly distilled from the clear waters of his dream, of how he could go about getting out of hock to Barnabas College and perhaps make a future for himself that was not a cell. Yes. Simple. Not easy, but simple. It would take nothing but cunning, and years of work; but some of those years of work had already been put in, under that lamp, among those books

Dawn was coming. The window was a pale square of greenish light, a fretwork of dark leaves and a white moth fluttering for egress. Pierce threw off the sheet and rose, wide awake; he went to the window to free the moth that beat against the screen.

The task had been to forget, of course; what he had seen in his master's eyes was not reproach but pity; the task had been to forget, to become clothed in forgetfulness as in robes and armor, robes over armor, layer upon layer, so that he could come to pass disguised into this sad city. The very journey and the far country to cross had been forgetfulness.

A hiatus in his work. A long hiatus. But he remembered now.

He leaned his elbows on the windowsill, looking out, face in his hands like a gargoyle. In the street, dogs barked; wind chimes, camel bells, a tambourine idly shaken. The stifling caravanserai all awake.

She had known all along, of course, who had been keeper or jailer or both; no wonder she had smiled, no wonder she had shown him solicitude but no pity. He could almost hear her laughter behind him.

For now the world began to move beneath him once again, dawn winds rising as night turned pale. The tents were struck, the caravans stirred, the drivers cried out and wielded whips: camels, hooting and complaining, rose up, on two legs, on four legs, their tall packs swaying and jingling, exotic goods borne out of the colored centuries. Set out, set out: past the old gate that led to the East the striated sands went on levelly toward the horizon, toward the goldgreen sky whereon blazed a single star before sunrise. Steely-white ovoids with a high unworldly hum were ascending two four six from beyond the arid pinkish mountains, catching the light of the unrisen sun: starships, archons jealous and watchful. Beyond those mountains the fertile plains, the city and the sea. The task lay ahead, stretching so far as to be made of time not space, time's body, and yet not uncrossably far; and a country he knew, after all, or had once known, a country he had crossed before.

Pierce set out, walking backward into oblivion, deep asleep in the Faraways; and he didn't wake again until Spofford began breaking up kindling for their breakfast fire, and the smell of burning applewood filled the cabin and the chilly morning.

II
LUCRUM

O N E

▲

"So you're off today?" Spofford asked him.

"I guess. Yes."

"Okay. Get some grits first." He warmed his hands at the stove. "Cold," he said. "Summer's about over."

Outside, mist clouded a clear morning, rising quickly out of the valley and the river. Pierce thrust his hands into his pockets and pressed his arms to his sides; even in the city, he thought, this morning would be fresh, the streets rain-washed, the air new.

"There's a morning bus from the Jambs," Spofford said. "I'm not sure when, but we'll catch it." He grinned. "If you're sure now you don't want to stay for good." He stopped breaking eggs into a bowl and studied Pierce, who stood silent and abstracted in the doorway of the room. "You sleep okay?"

"Huh? Oh. Sure. Strange dreams." He had begun to shiver. "I forget what, now, mostly. I remembered, when I woke up in the night. But now I forget again."

A plan. A plan, a pearl of purpose distilled from whatever the dream had been: that much he retained. He turned it in his mind's fingers. Well: all right. It was real. It even warmed him somewhat, like the huge red wool shirt Spofford tossed him to put on; warmed him and made him grin. The first thing to do, when he got back, was to call Julie Rosengarten. Who would, no doubt, be astonished to hear from him. And now what again was the name of that agency she had gone to work for? Something highfalutin, from a classical tag, he had kidded her about it; *per ardua ad* oh yes: Astra Literary Agency.

The rocky road to stardom. All right. Okay. Keep thy shop, old

Barr had said, chuckling in the warm security of tenure at Noate; keep thy shop and thy shop will keep thee. Okay. There was more than one way to make a living at this, and this was the only way he had of making a living.

"Yup," he said, sitting down to Spofford's eggs, he was ravenously hungry for some reason. "Onward. Duty. The Future."

"I hope you'll be back," Spofford said. "Now that you know the way."

For some reason Pierce was visited with a quick vision of Spofford's Rosie rising from the deep. He cleared his throat of toast crumbs that had suddenly caught there, and looked busily around the little room; there was nothing there of his to collect and pack, for he had unpacked nothing.

"Have to keep up with your friends," Spofford said. "At least I do. I miss that educated conversation, hey, you know there's not a lot of that around here."

"I'm sure I'll be back," Pierce said. "Sometime."

"You will," Spofford said. He poured smoking coffee. "You'll be back. I'll see to it."

Late, her wagon still ridiculously packed with her life, Rosie drove into Blackbury Jambs for her appointment with Allan Butterman. She had lost some time dressing, starting out with skirts and jackets but unable to find a combination unwrinkled, decent, and seasonal; had decided then (never having gone to a lawyer's office before) that no, this was not like a job interview but more like a visit to the dentist, you should dress for comfort, and over a plaid shirt, fresh and tart-smelling new flannel, had put on yesterday's overalls. Mrs. Pisky, holding Sam's hand, and Sam, had waved goodbye from the porch as though Mommy would never return. Bye-bye. Bye-bye.

Town had, just for this crisp morning, lost its summer somnolence and was busy with traffic. Rosie noticed Spofford's truck, but not Spofford; she nearly tangled with the New York bus just pulling out from before the candy store, which was its stop, as she was somewhat blindly trying to pull in. Slam of brakes, the brakes were good, and something heavy toppled over in the rear of the wagon.

The bus drove around her, with a huffy snort of exhaust, and away; Rosie waved apologetically, and a passenger obscure behind the green glass waved back. She took *Bitten Apples* from the seat

and with it under her arm went down Bridges Street to the Ball
Building. When she was a child she had thought—it had seemed
obvious to her—that this red-stone nineteenth-century block, four
stories high and the grandest in town, was called the Ball Building
(its name arching over the central doors) because of the stone balls
that topped its corner finials. Her dentist had had his office here.
His name had been Drill. He thought that was funny; Rosie only
thought it was proper, like the Ball Building. The big town, the big
strange-smelling halls of the big Ball Building: she hadn't finished
putting that town together with this small one.

Allan Butterman's secretary looked startled to see her. "Oh,
I'm so sorry," she said. "Mr. Butterman had to go to a funeral this
morning. He forgot. He came in, and had to rush right home to
change."

"Oh, hey, that's okay."

"He should be back in a couple of hours."

"Fine, that's okay. I'll just come back. I'm not really in any big
hurry or anything." The faint smell in the lawyer's office of antisep-
tics and medicaments drifting in from the doctors and dentists
around him had Rosie thinking of the fantasy she used to have on
being taken to Dr. Drill, that she would find him out, sick, on
vacation, dead. It had never happened. As she went back out into the
warming day she noticed her throat was dry and her heart fast.

Two hours. Okay. Some shopping or something. In limbo, she
wandered down to the bridge and started out on it, looking south
toward Butterman's on its rock; too far to see, even in this clear
light.

It all seemed an immense trouble suddenly, a hornet's nest she
had perhaps been saved from stirring up by Allan's surprise funeral;
and maybe she should take that as a sign; maybe she should forget
about the Law, and go home. But when she thought about home it
was of Arcady she thought, and not of the fieldstone-faced ranch
house in Stonykill. So another of her minds seemed anyway to be
still made up, below this mind that wavered.

He would ask her (she supposed, she couldn't imagine his not
asking, certainly he would have to know) why she wanted to start
these proceedings. Well I don't want to start anything, she thought
of answering; what I want is to stop something. But that wasn't an
answer.

She had no reasons, in fact. The thing was that she seemed no longer to have any reasons to be married.

It seemed clear to her that nothing, not her growing dislike (no stronger word would do) for Mike, not his flings and his needs, not her restlessness, nothing could be reason for divorce if there were reasons to be married. She supposed that in the old days, the Old Days, her parents' days or before, there needed to be no reasons, to be married in the first place was enough reason to stay married; but now—a cursory survey of her own friends' histories, of TV, the papers, showed nothing but evidence—now those who were still married stayed married only by a constant effort of imagining why they were married; a daily effort, since in any one day you could become unmarried. It was logical to think that a union based purely on choice, on willed election, would be stronger than one based (like her parents') on mere social assumptions and taboos: but in fact the elective marriages could just evaporate, overnight, in a moment of inattention. And leave nothing behind, no reason.

She thought of Sam.

People stay together for the children. Her parents had done so. Yet now there were uncounted thousands—a majority for all she knew—of children in daycare centers and kindergartens who came from Broken Homes. Surely with so many people working at it, a way would be worked out, eventually, soon, for children to be raised by separated parents so that they didn't suffer. Maybe anyway they had never suffered as much from Broken Homes as people said.

She knew for sure—a cold and dreadful certainty far away and finished—that Sam could not be hurt by Rosie's parting from Mike as much as Rosie had been hurt by her mother's staying with her father: by that awful death-haunted house, no home to break.

She would have been better off without him.

She would have been better off without him: it wasn't the first time she had thought those words, but the first time in the context of her own motherhood. They startled her there. She wasn't making any comparisons: no. No. She turned away from the bridge, brushed by a dark wing of that old grief as it fled past and backward. She went up along High Street a block to the Donut Hole, and sat in a cool booth; she ordered coffee and a jelly doughnut and opened *Bitten Apples* to the bobby pin that marked her place. Two hours to wait.

Part Two was set in London, and Rosie had been liking it; Kraft seemed to like it too, the book seemed to expand and stretch, as though his fingers had been itching to get to this good stuff. Paragraphs grew longer, there were lists and catalogues of funny and bizarre sights, foods, habits, customs. The town was a continuous show, or so it was described, not only the Lord Mayor's show and the guild processions and the Inns of Court plays but the true playhouses now being built and the innyards converted to playhouses like the Red Bull, playing farces and tragedies and Chronicles, the patrons noisy and attentive and critical and as good a show as the play, or the Theatre, where the Earl of Leicester's Men played. But in Southwark there were still the bear pits, where Old Braw and Tattered Raf and the Precious Boy crunched the mastiffs' heads like apples, everyone knew their names and went to see them, tinkers' boys and great ladies and visiting grandees from other lands, they were tended by their loving masters and healed of their awful wounds and lived to break the backs of other dogs—Rosie felt sorry for the dogs, but few then did, apparently. There were white swans on the river and traitors' heads on London Bridge pecked at by kites: there were conspiracies, and plots, and attempts on the Queen's life by witchcraft that horrified everyone—a poppet was found in Lincoln's Inn Fields made in the Queen's image and stuck full of pins, and the Queen's friend and astrologer Doctor Dee had to be called in to see about it, it was nothing, he said, a toy, the Queen would live long and in good health; and she showed herself to the people on her barge just so that they could see she was all right, and kept Christmas at Richmond.

It was all so highly colored, Rosie thought, like a cartoon; and it was hard not to think they thought of it that way back then as well, in their outlandish clothes of every rainbow color and a few she could only imagine, saffron and mulberry and lawn and gooseturd. When they died they left these impossible outfits to their servants, who couldn't wear them and so sold them to the actors: the boards of the innyard theaters were bare and the sun shone (or didn't shine) for lights, but there the characters strutted rich in silks and embroideries that said King and Lord and Princess: no matter whether it was ancient Rome or Harry the Fifth's time or faraway Italy they wore the same dead lords' outfits, so long as they were gorgeous enough. Young Will (as Kraft kept calling him), thrust in among all this, learned to dance and sing (in the theaters they seemed to dance, "leap," and sing as much as they acted—the dancing sounded more like tumbling, Rosie wondered what it could have looked like, was it silly or graceful?) and made friends among the court- and street-wise kids of Leicester's Boys. Inducted by stages into their company, tricks played on him, initiations to pass. Tough boys to quell. Show them you're not afraid. Master Burbage stepping into the fray and the fussy black-robed chorus-master, now what's all this, what's all this.

Will was tried out at first for women's parts, the hard ones to fill—for there were of course no female actors at all; Rosie remembered that she had once learned that. Two oranges in his bodice. Kisses and catcalls. There came to be a strange, even dark, kind of sexual tension in the story that Rosie wondered if she was only reading into it because of what Boney had said to her about Fellowes Kraft: it was as though there were other initiations not told of, a kind of corruption touching the hubbub, just touching: at great men's houses where the boys played there were sinister young lords with long curls and earrings in their ears, drunk and heavy-eyed, someone spewing in the corner. With the spring the plague came to London: Will's special friend, who played Phyllis and Clorinda and Semiramide, but who had fought no-holds-barred for Will in the boys' brawls, died, holding Will's hand. Pale and delirious and babbling bits of verse and love songs. Will grew up a little. The young lords went to their estates or to France, the players' carts went to the provinces to escape the plague; the Earl of Leicester's Boys followed the court and the Queen on progress.

The Queen! The book seemed to be empty of women except for her, as though she drew all the feminine to herself, one woman in the realm but what a woman. Kraft seemed to get a little tongue-tied and dazzle-eyed around her, and so did everybody in the story. Robin of Leicester danced attendance, he and the Queen had been lovers for years (but what did they *do,* Rosie wondered) and if anyone knew her heart of hearts it was smooth careful Robin: but no one did. To Wanstead in May Leicester brought his boys to perform a masque written by his nephew Sir Philip Sidney, perfect gentle knight in silk as blue as his clear child's eyes. *The Lady of May.* That was Elizabeth herself, who was the masque's chief actor and only object, though she had no lines written for her; she needed none. In the soft chartreuse gardens she and her company come upon a nymph, stepping from between the lilacs and doing reverence: *Do not think, sweet and gallant Lady, that I debase myself thus much to you because of your gay apparel ... Nor because a certain gentleman hereby seeks to do you all the honor he can in his house ... I would look for reverence at your hands, if I did not see something in your face that made me yield to you....* And the Queen answered her prettily and graciously *impromptu* with a sharp wit that almost unsettled the boy-nymph, and reddened his cheeks beneath his rouge.

Will, grown tall and earnest-looking, played the pedant Rhombus, a stock comedy character he was good at: pedants and scholars with mouthfuls of inkhorn terms he alone of the boys could commit easily to memory. Let me delicidate the very intrinsical maribone of the matter. Well-spoken, Doctor, I see you have your degree *Magister artis.* I do, if it please your Majesty (sweeping a low bow, with a hand to the crick in his old pedant's back), I have it *honorificabilitudinitatibus.* The Queen laughed aloud at that, a word he had used to rattle out to make Simon Hunt laugh at Stratford School; and after the play she reviewed the Boys, and stopped before Will, a head higher almost than his fellows, a red-haired head.

Uh-oh, Rosie thought, she's going to make a prophecy.

The Queen's head rose up out of her rich dress small and white and lined, the face of a maiden long imprisoned in a fairy castle; her red hair was dressed in jewels as complex as curls, and a stiff white ruff of lace rose up behind to frame her wide-eyed, domed, long-nosed face. So she was a peacock too, a white peacock all displayed. Will before this fabulous monster could not look away; her bird's eye looked sharply into his, green as emeralds.

Two things the Queen loved were red hair and jewels. She brushed Will's hair with her ringed hand, and her white mask smiled.

Honorificabili-tudini-tatibus, she said.

When cool weather came the Earl of Leicester's Men returned from their tour of the North and took up their stand again at the playhouse James Burbage had built out beyond the reach of the London magistrates. It was a playhouse like no other in England at that time, and Burbage loved it and lavished money on it as on a wife (his wife had more than once noted so to him); in fact it was not a playhouse at all, not a bear pit or an adapted innyard or a hall fitted out with a stage and some doors and some seats for gentlemen—no, it was not a playhouse but a Theatre, as the Romans had named their circular buildings, and so it was called: the Theatre, the only one in England.

—We shall have those vessels, this year, Master Burbage said.

He stood feet wide apart on the stage, looking out over the empty pit and the ranks of galleries for the penny custom. Behind him the boys' company rehearsed a new piece. Above him the heavens looked down, painted in gold on the night-blue canopy, the zodiac and its resident planets, the sun, the moon.

—What vessels? Will asked him.

The boy—hardly a boy any longer—sat on the stage's edge, dangling his long skinny legs. He had the playbook in his hand, but he had no part in the new play. There was no comic pedant or poet in it, only heroes and their loves. The new fashion. Stern and antique.

—Brazen vessels, Burbage said. Brazen vessels, made—made in a certain fashion—made and placed under the ambries here, and there: I know not just how: and so they echo or swell the voice, catch it and cast it back.

Will looked around the Theatre, trying to imagine this.

—Vitruvius saith, Burbage intoned, that the true antique Roman theatre had such vessels. Placed here and there by careful art. So says my learned friend Doctor Dee. Who has read Vitruvy and all those authors. Whom you should read and study, boy. A player need not be *ignoramus*.

He looked down at the boy. What was he to do with him. If his coming into the Boys had been regular, well, his going out of it when the time came might be regular too. Master Burbage in his haste had not considered that part of it. If a boy had good parts, and grew up lissome, sweet, small, and of the right voice, he might easily at adolescence graduate to women's parts in the men's company, and thence to a full share in the company; if he did not, well, he could be returned to his family, his contract finished, let him try another trade.

Somewhere, tucked in among bills and receipts in Burbage's lead box, was that ridiculous paper of Will's. He had better burn that.

For Will had not grown lissome and small: he had grown like a weed. His knees great knobs holding calf and thigh together like a poor piece of furniture. His red hair had gone dull and thin, a big bulge of forehead swelling out from it, Burbage wondered if he had water on the brain, for sure he had grown vague and silent and almost idiotic in the last year. And that voice: that sweet, piercing voice was broken: broken and showing coarse squawks and toneless tones like hay stuffing.

What if he had clipped him. Clipped his little stones in time as the Italians do. Burbage shuddered to think of it.

—We shall have them, he said. If the antique theatre had such marvels, this age should show them too. Now. Doctor Dee will know about this. We must get from him his book of Vitruvius, or have him look in it, and draw for us a picture and a plan of them, so they can be cast. Leave that, leave that.

Will looked up from his playbook. The one thing he had to make him a player, Burbage thought, was the memory. Verse caught in his brain like sheep's wool on briars, he could gather it at will. He would have all the parts in the new piece tomorrow. So. If anyone fell ill.

—Listen, he said. He took money from his purse. I want you to go down to Mortlake, to Doctor Dee's house there; go down by water. Are you listening? To Mortlake. Between the church and the river his house is, ask the way at the church.

Will had tossed down the playbook and stood, nearly tripping himself on his big feet.

—Yes, he said. Mortlake, between the river and the church.

—Give him, Burbage said, my duty. Say to him, say . . .

—About the brazen vessels. I will. I understand.

—Good lad. Now brush yourself and clean your nails. Find a clean shirt. That is a learned man, and the Queen's friend. Hear? Don't dawdle.

Will took the coin, and turned to go.

—Will.

The boy looked back. That way he had come to have, that not a thing mattered to him, that he was hereby only by some accident, with his big head and loose bones, it had nothing to do with him: all that belied by his great watchful eyes. What to do, what to do.

—Ask Doctor Dee, Burbage said. He is a wise man, lad, and could help you. Tell him to look into your nativity, and see what he can see. Tell him the expense is mine. Tell him that.

Will turned to go without answering.

Down by water all alone! He was not to dawdle, but it was impossible not to dawdle, down Bishopsgate street and through the city wall at Bishopsgate, past the inns on Fenchurch street where plays were cried. At Leadenhall street he turned right and into the Cheapside throngs; carriages—only come to share the narrow streets with chairs and drays and people in these last few years—pushed through them arrogantly, the coachmen up behind lashing the horses forward. Several rich carriages were standing outside the huge new emporium built by Thomas Gresham for his own glory and the realm's: the Exchange, newly dubbed "Royal" by Her Majesty, a whole world's worth of markets under a pillared roof. Inside—and through 'Change was a shortcut riverward that Will knew—inside the merchants fat and lean in sad gowns of stuff did important business in grains, hides, corn, leather, and wine in the cloistered shops of the ground floor, while above, in the Pawn, the jewelers, instrument-makers, bookbinders, the glovers and hatters and haberdashers, the armorers and druggists and clockmakers did their business and sold their wares. At the doors, though, and along the walls and streets beyond, smaller merchants without shops carried on their trade too, carrying it on their backs, crying oysters, apples, cherries ripe and cockles new, brooms good brooms, samphire gathered from the cliffs of Dover, even water, sold by the tankard.

Will bought a pippin, and ate it on his way down Cheapside toward Paul's, past the shops of the goldsmiths where the swells and the foreign gentlemen went in and out, and the nips and foists and cutpurses too who preyed on them. By the time Paul's yard was reached the crowds were thick with beggars, old soldiers limbless or eyeless, counterfeit-cranks pretending to loathsome diseases who pawed or tried to paw you, only bought off with alms; at the cathedral doors the poor like a flock of importunate geese set up a clacking with their clap-dishes whenever anyone likely-looking passed within. Paul's had lost its wooden steeple to lightning long before, and was anyway as much public concourse as church—though divine worship did go on daily; the beruffed boy choristers (oh Will pitied them, with glee in his heart) sang out by thoughtless rote into the vast spaces.

Will, cutting through the church from the north-side door to the south-side across the nave, stopped to read the notices posted up on the pillars: men offering themselves for hire, dancing-masters and fencing-masters offering lessons, teachers of Italian and French and doctors and astrologers advertising their services. He read an apothecary's broadside:

These Oiles, Waters, extractions or Essences, Saltes, and other Compositions; are at Paules Wharfe ready made to be sold, by IOHN CLERKSON, practisioner in the arte of Distillation; who will also be ready for a reasonable stipend to instruct any that are desirous to learne the secrets of the same in a fewe dayes &c.

And look what he offered: *essentia perlarum,* was that essence of pearls?, and *balsamum sulphuris,* and *saccharum plumbi* or sugar of lead, the *vitrum antimonii,* that was the antimonial cup; *sal cranii humani* (Will shuddered to translate this, salt of human skull, what could it be); and more ordinary stuff too, "divers and sundrie vernishes, strange and terrible Fireworks."

An aged bawd who mistook his idling over this fascinating notice came close and made to speak to him; Will, startled, moved quickly away, stumbling over his feet, and a knot of lawyers watching for clients at their accustomed pillar laughed together, perhaps at him. Quickly he went out, back into the sun.

There was another world there: Paul's churchyard was London's book market, and in stalls sheltered amid the buttresses, under the sign of the Hart or the Compasses or the Dolphin, books were offered that Will could not buy but could look at: Holinshed's chronicles in enormous folios, *Joyfull News Brought Out of the Newe Worlde.* And amid and among the stalls went the ballad-and-broadside sellers, with news of their own: Spanish plots and double murders, rules for love and rules for chess, stories new-brought out of the Italian, all true, all true.

Past Blackfriars then the traffic was all for the water, the greatest thoroughfare of London. Will was chivied down the water stairs with all the others, to contest with them there for the watermen's services, and only made his way onto one after being shouldered aside by an alderman and his servant for the first boat to stop; and then down the river. Clouds scudding fast beyond the crowded steeples outpaced the fast river traffic, the eelboats and wherries and other light craft bobbing with bellied sails and the towering merchantmen. Will hugged his knees in his cramped space aboard the boat, and listened and saw and tasted the whole September day, seeming to have all of it inscribed on his heart for good.

Late now, and hurrying, he climbed the water stairs at Mortlake and asked the woman washing for Doctor Dee's house, and asked again at the church, and again at a gate leading into a garden, where a woman leaned, smiling, her cheeks blushed like September apples and so plump they narrowed her smiling eyes.

—Doctor Dee is it. And who might you be.

—I am sent by Master James Burbage of the Theatre in Shoreditch.

—A player.

—I am that.

She studied him, amused and good-natured, and at last opened the gate she leaned against.

—The doctor is in the garden, she said. This is his house. And this is his wife.

She curtseyed slightly, mockingly. Will bowed.

—Go quietly in, she said. He is busy there, with I know not what. But then he ever is. Busy. With I know not what.

Will went where she pointed, into a well-kept garden now pillaged and gone yellow with autumn. There were knots of herbs and a carp pool and two, no three sundials of different kinds; and in the center something that didn't belong to a garden. A sort of small house or tent, rigged up on poles with heavy cloths hung around it, and on the front of it a panel, painted black, in which there was a glass, a lens, a small round lens that caught the sun.

The curtains fluttered and bellied, and out from the little house came stooping a long man, made longer by a long sad-colored robe and a long narrow beard going gray. He glanced at Will and raised his eyebrows, but took no further note of him; he took from his clothes a little round cap, and with it he covered the glass eye in the black panel. Then he went back within.

Will stood, shifting from foot to foot.

When he came back out, Doctor Dee wore a pair of black-rimmed spectacles with claw-ends that fitted to his ears; they made his round wide eyes even more surprised, even more round, than they had been. He motioned to Will.

—Come here.

Will went to him, and the doctor took his shoulder. He led him to stand in front of the tent house, facing the blinkered glass; then he bethought himself, and moved Will back some feet from it.

—Master Burbage, sir, sends you his duty, and . . .

—Now what you must do, said the doctor, holding up a long finger in warning, is to stand perfectly still. Bat not a single eyelash till I tell you so. Do you hear?

Will nodded. He was growing alarmed. Was he to be charmed?
Best to do what he was told. Doctor Dee went back to the black house,
stood by it, and again warned Will with a skinny finger.

—Still. Still as the dead. Now.

He snatched off the little cap that covered the glass eye, and
seemed to count or pray under his breath. Will, motionless, stared
at the glass eye as though from it, as from a basilisk's, killing rays
might shoot. Then the doctor covered it again; he breathed deeply,
and disappeared within.

Will stood frozen, hearing his heartbeats, tears gathering in his
unwinked eyes.

At last Doctor Dee came out again, and seemed to see Will for the
first time.

—I beg your pardon, sir! You may move, move, leap and
dance.

He carried something, something flat like a plate, wrapped in
black velvet.

—Come, he said. Come along, and tell me what my friend
Burbage wants of me.

The house Doctor Dee led him into seemed to be more than one
house, several thrown into one, with doors broken through walls
and passages made to lead from barn to kitchen to still-room to
washhouse; Will followed along after the doctor's billowing robe
and slipslop slippers, into a large long room, windowed on both
sides with small mullioned windows, and stuffed full of more things,
in greater disorder, than any room he had ever been in or dreamed
of.

It was a wizard's den for sure. What made it so wasn't only the
brass armillary sphere, bones of the whole heavens in small, which
any wizard might have; it wasn't only the two parchment-colored
globes standing together like different thoughts about the world, or
the astronomer's staff marked in degrees, which Will couldn't understand the use of but which was surely more marvelous than any
lignum vitae. It wasn't exactly the clutter of objects rare and
common, the yellow-toothed skull (*sal cranii humani*), and the gems,
prisms, crystals, and bits of colored glass gathered together in earthen-
ware pots or scattered on tabletops or hung in windows to color the
daylight; or the manuscripts tied up with string or the slips of paper
written on in three or four different languages and tacked up here
and there as though to remind Doctor Dee of secrets he had concocted

but might otherwise forget; it was all these things, and the convex glass on the wall that reflected it all, and the black cat that sniffed at the remains of a plate of supper there (pigeon's bones and a rind of cheese), and even the feather duster protruding like a shabby bird from the pocket of a coat hung on a nail. Most of all it was the books: more books than he had ever seen gathered in one place together, books in tall cases, books piled in corners, books leaning wearily together on shelves, books bound and unbound in this room and in the passage beyond and rising to the ceiling on shelves in the next room; open books laid atop other open books on tables and in the seats of chairs. In the houses of his Arden relatives, Will had seen many books, dozens together, locked up in cupboards, silent. These hundreds—thousands it might be—he could almost hear them whispering together, whispering to each other of their contents.

Doctor Dee, hearing Will's footsteps slow and halt, came back from the passage.

—Are you a lover of books?

Will couldn't answer that.

—There are books here a player might study, he said. I have Aeschylus. Euripides. Do you read Greek? No. Well, here are histories too, Leland and Polydore Vergil. I have bought Holinshed's new chronicle, but it has not yet been brought me. Plutarch, Englished by North. Those are fine tales.

—Have you read them all? Will asked, not quite in a whisper.

Doctor Dee lowered his strange spectacles and smiled at him.

—If you like, he said, you may come back, and look into them. Read what ones you like. There are many who come here to find this or that. Tales. History. Knowledge.

For a moment he waited for the boy to say something, a *thankee sir* at least for politeness's sake, but Will only stared.

—Come along then, he said, and tell me what my friend Burbage wants of me. Come.

He led Will out of the room and down a twist of corridors and into an odorous still-room where there were jugs and bottles, retorts and cucurbites like great fat birds, corked jars full and empty; he pushed the boy before him through a door and a heavy curtain into a darkened shuttered room in which a single candle burned.

—Come, he said. Your business, sir.

As best he could Will stammered out what it was that Burbage wanted to know, about the brazen vessels, which after all he hadn't really understood; Doctor Dee nodded and hummed in his throat, going on with his work, which must, Will thought, be magic for sure.

—And cast back, throw back the voice, over, under . . .

—Mm. Mm-hm.

He had taken out from the folded velvet a square of thin metal, blackish, which he took carefully by its edges. He slipped it into a small basin full of fluid, where it sank, turning brown, then reddish brown. Doctor Dee studied it carefully. Black streaks began to appear on its surface, a dapple of marks coming forth, making shapes.

—Ah, said the doctor.

With a tiny pair of tongs he lifted out the square of metal, turning it this way and that, letting the fluid run off it. Then he took it and the stub of candle to the end of his workbench, and slipped the candle under a little pot on a tripod.

—Mercurius, he said. Smiling, he pressed his finger to his lips.

When the mercury in his pot was hot enough, he held the metal square over it, at an angle, fumigating it, peering at it now and then with satisfaction. At last he pushed open the shutters, daylight flooded the little chamber, he held out the metal plate to Will.

Will took it and looked. On its surface, as on an engraver's plate, but far clearer, there was a picture: a boy, solemn, rigid, standing in a garden, a sundial behind him. Himself.

Himself, these clothes he wore, this old hat on his head; his face. Will was looking into a mirror: a mirror he had looked into a quarter of an hour ago, and still stood looking into. Forever.

Doctor Dee saw him speechless, and with two fingers took the picture from him by an edge.

—A toy, he said, and tossed it into an open box there of other stained plates. There are greater things. There are even greater toys.

He put his arm around Will's shoulder.

—Now, he said. We will look into Vitruvius. And into your nativity too, is that not it? And see what we can see.

"What's the book?" said a large shadow that had come between Rosie and the window light.

"Hi," she said to Spofford's bulk above her. "Pretty crazy. This sort of magician character just took a photograph of Shakespeare."

"No kidding."

They looked at each other for a silent space, smiling.

"What are you in town for?" Rosie said.

"Brought my friend Pierce in to catch the bus. Picked up some stuff. And you? Mind if I sit down?"

"Well sort of. Yes and no. Oh heck sit down."

He slid carefully into the booth opposite her, watching her lowered face. "What's up?"

She huffed out a sigh, cupping her cheek in her hand and staring down at her book as though still reading it. Then she closed it. "I'm going to see a lawyer this morning," she said. "Allan Butterman, up the street."

Spofford said nothing, and the wary smile he had retained from his greeting didn't alter, but he seemed to expand in the seat; his long legs stretched out under the table and a brown arm hooked over the booth's back.

"There's something I want to say," Rosie said, folding her hands as in prayer. "I like you a lot. A lot. You've been great. Swell."

"But."

"I don't want you to think I'm doing this *for you*. 'Cause I'm not."

"Nope."

"I'm not doing it for you or anyone. I'm just doing it. The whole *idea* is that I'm doing it alone, it's something that *makes* me alone. Whatever happens later on." She drummed her fingers on the table between them. "That's why I sort of didn't want you to sit down. Why I sort of don't want you to say anything about it."

She meant she refused to have him as a reason. If other and larger things, more desperate things, could not be reasons, then Spofford, a good thing, could not be one. It was only fair: to her and everyone.

"I won't," he said. He crossed his arms before him. There was a pale fish tattooed on the back of his left hand; sometimes it was invisible. "The black dog's day is not yet."

"What?"

"That's from a story. Seems this lord had a black dog, a good-for-nothing hound, ate him out of house and home, didn't do anything but lay in the doorway to trip over, useless. Wouldn't hunt, couldn't track. People kept telling the lord to get rid of the dog, and he says, 'Uh-uh. The black dog's day is not yet.' "

"Where did you get this story?" Rosie said laughing. Spofford—

it was a thing she liked about him—was always showing himself to be full of surprising nooks and crannies where odd items like that were stored.

"Well," Spofford said, "that story, I would guess, comes from Dickens or from Scott, one. My folks had two humongous sets of these books. Works. Dickens, and Scott. It's about all the books they did have. And I don't say I read them all, but I read a lot of both. I got them sort of spelling each other, you know, so I can't always remember whose stories are which. I would say that story is Wally Scott. And if it wasn't Wally Scott it was Chuck Dickens. Who would know, probably, is my friend Pierce."

"And that's the whole story?"

"Heck no. The black dog has his day. Saves the guy's life. *That's* the end."

"Every dog has his day."

Spofford said nothing further, only grinned so that the dead tooth showed in his mouth, so insolently self-satisfied that she had to look away not to grin back.

"So by the way," she said, gathering up purse, book, and change from the table purposefully, ready to go and changing the subject, "how did your friend—Pierce?—how did your friend Pierce enjoy his visit?"

"He liked it," Spofford said, not rising with her. "He'll be back."

He *had* liked it. He would think of it often, in different ways and in different contexts; he had already begun to think of it in the frigid airless bus passing away. And—on city streets, still violent with summer, foul with loathsome summer; in his tower apartment, grown too large now as the suit of a wasted starveling; or when steeling himself for the task he now knew lay ahead—he would sometimes feel those scenes he had visited lying just behind him, a pool of golden light, so close that he was uncertain just how he had traveled from there to here: to here where he supposed he must now be for good, or as nearly for good as made no difference.

T W O

▲

"Sorry, sorry, sorry," said Allan Butterman, tearing into the office where Rosie had been put. "You were waiting for hours, right? I am really terribly sorry."

He detached from his arm a black band that was pinned there, and dabbed at his face with a large and handsome handkerchief. In a vested black suit and tie, he looked chic, his somehow French features (sharp nose, black eyes and glossy hair, white smooth skin) emphasized, his plump cheeks supported by the starched tall collar. "Oh god," he said; he sighed greatly, and stuffed the handkerchief into his pocket.

"Was it somebody you knew real well?" Rosie said carefully.

"Oh no," Allan said. "Oh no. No. Just an old old client. Old as Methusaleh. Very very old client of the firm. Oh god it's really just too bad." He bit the knuckle of his forefinger, staring out at the river and the day; he sighed again, and composed himself.

"Now," he said. "First of all, how are you, would you like a cup of coffee? I'm Allan Butterman, Allan Butterman *Junior*, I'm not really sure your uncle has entirely understood that it's me who's been answering his letters and so on lately, my father passed away about two years ago. So." He smiled wanly at Rosie.

"Did Boney tell you?"

"He sort of hinted. A divorce. Or at least a separation."

"That's right."

Allan huffed out his breath, shook his head, stared down at his desktop. He seemed to be keeping one step ahead of awful grief, and Rosie was almost afraid of embarking on details for fear of delivering him up to it. "I'm already separated. I mean I left anyway."

He nodded slowly, regarding her, the lines of his brow contorted. "Kids?" he asked.

"One. A three-year-old girl."

"Oh god."

"It's sort of been in the works for a long time," Rosie said, to comfort him.

"Yes?" Allan said. "When did you guys decide?"

"Well," Rosie said. "He didn't, really. I sort of did."

"He's not in on this?"

"Not exactly. Not yet."

"When did you tell him you intended to seek this?"

"Well, day before yesterday."

Allan spun in his swivel chair. He put the tips of his fingers together, and regarded the day again, but as though it could give him no joy. He laughed, shortly, bitterly. "Well," he said. "I'll tell you what. I don't actually really handle divorces much. Mr. Rasmussen said you had a problem, and I said of course, come in, let's see what we can do. But actually there might be other guys who would do a better job for you than me.

"Okay. Having said that. Even if I were to handle this eventually for you, I would ask you right now just to think very seriously about it, and see whether you've thought it all through. Marriage is real easy and cheap to get into, and real complicated and expensive to get out of. I don't suppose you and, and . . ."

"Mike."

"Mike, you and Mike had any kind of marriage contract or prenuptial agreement about this?"

"No." She'd read about people doing that; it had seemed the kind of grotesque idea only other people thought of, like getting married in an airplane, or buying a common burial plot. Now she wondered. An escape clause: fingers secretly crossed, I take it all back. "No."

"Okay," Allan said. "Let me explain this. It used to be, not long ago, even when I first went into practice, that for two people to get a divorce one of them had to have done some pretty serious wrong to the other. Adultery. Habitual drunkenness. Drug addiction. Mental cruelty, which was no joke then, and had to be really established. Okay? That meant that if two people just didn't want to

stay together anymore, no particular reason, then they had to arrange for one of them to lie in court about the reason—and for the
other not to contest the lie. And if the court suspected that that
kind of collusion was going on, the divorce didn't get granted. It
was a very nasty business all around, husbands wives attorneys all
lying through their teeth.

"Okay. Nowadays, just since recently actually, we have what's
called the 'no-fault' divorce. The laws have finally caught up with
the fact that most divorces aren't really due to anybody's fault, and
shouldn't be adversary proceedings. So now, in this state, you can
get a divorce on the grounds of 'irretrievable breakdown of the
marriage and irreconcilable differences between the parties,' or i
and i as it's called. Irretrievable, irreconcilable."

The huge words made Rosie swallow. "Well, it's not really
anybody's fault," she said. "Really."

Allan had picked up a long yellow pencil and now held it
balanced between his fingers like a drumstick, bouncing its eraser
on his desktop. "Really?" he said. "You know what it seems to me,
Rosie? It seems to me that maybe you haven't really tried everything
to work this out with, with . . ."

"Mike."

"You seem to be sort of jumping into it, if you don't mind my
saying so. I mean maybe therapy . . ."

"Mike's a therapist."

"Oh ho. Shoemaker's children, huh."

"What?"

"What I'm saying," Allan said, "is that I think you should wait.
I think you should try other solutions, other than divorce I mean.
Take a vacation. Rest. Get away from each other for a few weeks.
See how it looks to you then." His drum-taps altered. "To tell you
the straight truth, Rosie, I would not be willing myself to initiate
proceedings for you at this point."

Whatever way it was that Rosie looked at him then, whatever
her face said, caused him to gesture at her defensively with his
pencil, as though sketching, and to say, "Now wait a minute, wait a
minute, all I'm saying is this: I'm going on vacation *myself* for a
couple-three weeks, starting tomorrow, I'd have gone today if it
wasn't for, oh well, anyway: let us, you and I, make an appointment
to get together exactly three weeks from today. And see. And just
see what's become of everything in that time.

"You never know," he said.

A strange sickening letdown had begun within Rosie; it could not be that she had urged herself to this to have it all come to nothing, to one more exhortation to patience: could not be. She crossed her arms, feeling truculent.

Allan tossed down his pencil. "Don't get me wrong," he said. "I'm not saying your problems are trivial or anything, or that in three weeks you might not still want to pursue this. But the thing is, in the no-fault divorce we've been talking about—even if you decide divorce is the only way for you—this no-fault divorce requires that both parties be in agreement about it. You can't get it by yourself."

"No?"

"No. In a no-fault divorce, you're going to the court and saying *We agree that our marriage has failed.* If one of you *doesn't* agree, well then."

"Then what."

"Then you would have to go back to the old method. You'd have to *sue* for divorce, and you'd have to have grounds."

"Uh-huh," Rosie said.

"A reason," Allan said. "You'd have to have a reason to get a divorce; a good reason." Subject to his dark and mournful gaze, Rosie lowered her eyes. "Do you feel you have grounds?"

Rosie nodded.

"What grounds?" Allan asked.

"Adultery," she said.

Earl Sacrobosco was tickled, really tickled (his words) at Pierce's recapitulation, which was total and just in time for the semester's beginning. He had never really doubted it, he said, and had never ceased including Pierce in his plans for the year; he rubbed his hands and grinned as though he had personally brought Pierce back alive to the hard chair before his desk.

The deal offered Pierce in the spring had been somewhat sweetened by an exiguous raise, but it was saccharine to Pierce, the extra would be going chiefly back into the Barnabas coffers, remaking his loans had burdened him with a higher rate of interest. There was a penalty too to be paid for his quick arrogance in the spring: a speech had to be made, Earl would not have minded a prolonged one, about Pierce's reason for a change of heart. Well, he had come to see (he said) that he had dismissed too quickly a position and a college he had invested many good years in; he had had time to think (humble jailbird before his parole board) and a maturer eye could perceive that, though the road ahead might be a long one and the journey couldn't be hurried, Barnabas deserved Pierce's commitment. All this said as briefly as was consistent with true repentance, while ashes fell in Pierce's heart. He didn't need to say what his real reasons for returning were; Earl was aware, and communicated his awareness, that Pierce had simply nowhere else to go.

It was further agreed (Earl clearing his throat and getting down to business) that in place of the ambitious course of Pierce's own devising which had been rejected by the Curriculum Committee, Pierce could take on two additional units of Elements of Communication, which was reading and writing for analphabetic freshmen.

"Getting back to basics," Earl said. He had discarded the rug he had long worn, and looked better for it, though it was evident why he had worn it: his bald pate was the sort that grows a dirty fuzz all over, with a dark smudge at the front like an Ash Wednesday penitent's. "Personally, I was very interested in the course," he said, clicking the mechanism of a ballpoint and releasing it. "It did seem pretty graduate-level, though. And I'm afraid that I agree with the committee that there just wouldn't be the call for it."

"It was an experiment," Pierce said. His long arms hung between his knees, he wrung his hands, he wanted to get out.

"We've already got a reputation to fight of being a fad school that gives a useless degree. Enrollment's down, transfers are up. We've got to have solid food here."

"Readin', writin', and 'rithmetic," Pierce said.

"All that stuff is coming back," Earl said. "It's a new age."

That same afternoon (his heart somewhat in his mouth, he had spoken to her only coldly, briefly, infrequently since the time she had so heartlessly ditched him, long ago, lifetimes ago) Pierce called the number of the Astra Literary Agency and asked for Julie Rosengarten.

Strange, he thought, how an old name can take up such room in your throat, he had not been certain for a moment if all of it would come out.

"I'm afraid she's on vacation," said a voice like Julie's. "For almost three weeks."

Doing well, then, or very badly. "Well my name is Pierce Moffett, and Julie and I . . ."

"Oh god, Pierce."

"Julie?"

"Honestly, I'm on vacation. Oh god. I was honestly literally just walking out the door to catch the train."

"Huh, well . . ."

"My finger was on the button of the machine. Honestly."

She was awed by a fateful moment: he knew how she looked just now, it was a face he had seen often.

"I don't want to hold you up," he said. "But I have something I want to talk to you about."

"Yes!"

"A book idea."

"Yes? God, Pierce, if I hadn't just crazily picked up the phone."

"Well, when you get back."

"Yes. Yes yes yes. Pierce. I knew we'd talk again, talk for real. I *knew* it. There's so much, so much to say."

"Yeah, well."

"Three weeks. Three weeks to the *day*. Lunch." She named a restaurant he knew, one they had used to frequent but whose name he had himself not thought of in a long time, still open apparently; did Julie still go there? "I can't wait to hear this idea. You know I always thought you could do a book."

Had she? "It's a good one. You know some of it already, in fact."

"Really? I can't *wait*. Pierce, I'll miss my train."

"Have a nice time."

"I'm sorry, sorry. . . ."

"Go."

He cradled the receiver, and sat down on the broad bed; he put his hands on his knees and watched within the strange currents set up there by the sound of her voice, the old inflections.

Three weeks. He should have something firm, on paper, he supposed; a pitch, a proposal, for her to take away with her, and sell. He supposed there was no reason not to start on that right now.

There was, then, he thought cockily (his heart though still strangely full and his hands still on his knees), there was some use you can put these old lovers to. For sure she owed him one.

He ought to get up now, and roll out the elaborate electric typewriter, powder blue, which the Sphinx had once taken in trade from an anxious customer and given to Pierce for Christmas (see how useful, how helpful?) and place beside it a pile of blank bond paper. He ought to get out his old proposal for the course Barnabas College had not wanted to offer, and study it.

Mystery 101. How history hungers for the shape of myth; how the plots and characters of fable and romance come to inhabit real courts and counting-houses and cathedrals; how old sciences die, and bequeath their myths and magic to their successors; how the heroes of legend pass away, fall asleep, are resurrected, and enter ordinary daylit history, persisting as a dream persists into waking life, altering and transforming it even when the dream itself has been forgotten or repressed.

More, though. To be a book, a real book, it would have to contain not only the mystery but the detective, not only the dream but he who dreams it. To be a book, it would have to have a plot; it would have to be very different from what's usually called history, it couldn't be a simple addition of facts, or any kind of arithmetic at all, no it would almost have to be a sort of calculus, a differential calculus of self and history, inside and outside; it would require one to *play* history in the same way that chess masters play chess, not laboriously working out the consequences of possible moves, but perceiving as by a sixth sense the powers of the pieces to be or to do: a thing that can't be done by logic or training or application, no, it's an ability you have to be born with. It's a knack. A gift.

She *did* know the idea, she did, though not in the intelligible form it had at length achieved in his mind. She had been there when the first inklings of it had broken in on him, and in the time after she left him he had become almost as obsessed with it as with her: sometimes indeed they had not seemed like different things. And the sound of her voice just now had opened like a key the box of those days.

And those days then too would have to be a part of his book, wouldn't they? The days when he had become a popular teacher at Barnabas, the days when he stood at his slum window en route to the most revelatory metaphor—he would have to recover those days as well as the enterprise that had filled them.

He got up, at length, and did bring out the huge typewriter. He rolled a sheet of paper within it, and sat for a time before it. He rolled and lit a cigarette, and put it out. He got up; he changed his shirt; he turned up the laboring air-conditioner, and stood looking long out the window at the burnt and brownish evening.

Set out, set out. He wished it were already fall, season of wisdom and work. He wished he had not so carelessly hurt his head and heart when younger with abuse of substances, Thomistic notion. He sat again, and took out and discarded the piece of paper he had put into the machine, it seemed somehow already stale; he inserted another, and sat before it hands on his knees, the typewriter seeming to have somehow grown in the meantime even a little larger than it had been before.

"I don't understand about history," Rosie said to Boney. She was washing and he was drying their dinner dishes; it was Mrs. Pisky's day off, when she went to visit her sister in Cascadia.

"Yes?" Boney said.

"How much of it do they really know?"

"How much of what?"

"History." She held up to the light a cleaned plate, so old and fine the light shone dimly through it. "I mean this book by Fellowes Kraft. He knows tiny details of things, and he just tosses them out, like of *course*. I know it's a novel, but still." She realized she didn't know quite what she was talking about. "Still."

"Every history is a kind of story," Boney said. "You couldn't really understand it if it weren't. If it were just everything that happened."

"But do they know everything that happened?" Of course they didn't: not even historians: that was obvious. They just made up a story out of what they did know. Just the way Fellowes Kraft did. Only historians never said what parts they made up. "In this book, there's a character who's like a magician," she said.

"I remember," said Boney. He took off his blue-tinted glasses, and wiped them with the dishtowel, and put them on again.

"Not only," Rosie said, "not only does he take a photograph of Shakespeare—he never could have, right?—he also reads his horoscope. And then he has him look into like a crystal ball. To see what he can see."

"Yes," Boney said. He had stopped drying dishes.

"A crystal ball," Rosie said. "And old Will looks in it."

"Yes."

"And doesn't really see anything, even though he sort of pretends to. To please the old man, who he's sort of scared of. He tells him that someone will come along who *can* see things in this glass. That's the message he pretends to get.

"Now first of all," Rosie said. "Nobody knows anything much about Shakespeare. As I remember. Especially his childhood."

"I think that's right," said Boney.

"And then a magician. With a crystal ball. I mean."

"Well," Boney said. "As a matter of fact, that person is very real. Oh yes. Very real. Doctor John Dee. He really lived, in the place where he's described in that book as living, and he really did do the things he's described as doing. He did. He was an adviser to Queen Elizabeth, and perhaps a sort of consulting physician as well. He was a mathematician and an astrologer, when those two things weren't very different. He had what was likely the largest library in England at the time. And he was also, really, what he is in that book: a magician."

"A photograph?" Rosie said. "Of Shakespeare?"

"Well," said Boney.

"It's as if," Rosie said, "he every once in a while, for the fun of it, pretends that the world used to be different than it is, and things could happen that can't anymore."

"Hm."

"But it wasn't. They couldn't."

Carefully, Boney hung up his dishtowel, thinking; then, finger to his lips, he left the kitchen. Rosie turned off the taps and, wiping her hands on the seat of her overalls, followed him.

"Sandy knew so much," Boney was saying, going purposefully through the long dark dining room. "He knew so much. It used to amuse him to put things in his books that he knew everyone would think he had made up, but which he hadn't made up at all. And he liked to have things—real things—in his books, alongside all the imaginary things; I mean, he liked to have, in his possession, a real silver dish from the time he wrote of, and describe it in his book along with all the imaginary silver dishes: a real one hidden among the imaginary ones. Or a jewel, or a weapon. If he could have a thing that his characters really had once owned or used, it pleased him even more. He spent a lot of his time looking for such things.

"And he found them, too."

They had gone into the sitting room, where the lights were not lit, and the dark rug and groups of thick furniture retained the long twilight. Boney went toward a commode made of varied woods, atop which were photographs in silver frames, faces Rosie didn't know, faces long ago.

"Doctor Dee was a real man," Boney said, trying with his shaky hand to turn a tiny key in the keyhole of the commode's drawer. "As real as Shakespeare. He really did have showstones he looked into, and mirrors and jewels. And later on, a few years after your story, someone *did* come along who could see things for him in a crystal ball: who could see angels, and have conversations with them. Yes. A medium. It's all true." He tugged at the drawer, and at last got it open.

Rosie had begun to feel a little odd. It's all true. As though the actors in a play were to drop their roles, and then turn out to be in fact the characters they played, and turn to face their audience for real. She watched Boney take from the drawer something in a velvet bag.

"One of the glasses he used," Boney said, "a sort of polished mirror of obsidian, is in the British Museum. Sandy and I used to plot how we could steal it. There were others, now lost I guess. And there's the one in the book you're reading."

He had loosened the drawstring at the top of the bag, and let fall into his hand a sphere of smoky quartz the color of moleskin, pure as a tiny planet or a ball of gray evening. He held it up for Rosie to see.

"There were angels in this glass," he said. "Dozens of them. Doctor Dee talked with them. And all their names began with A."

THREE

▲

Nine choirs of angels fill up the universe, each choir meshing with the higher and lower ones like immense gears of different ratios, their meshing making for hierarchy throughout creation, making distinction, difference, this, that, and the other. Titanic Seraphim unfold around the throne of God, unable to look away; reaching behind themselves, they take the hands of Cherubim, mighty many-winged armed ones, who stand behind the Thrones that stand upon the sphere of the fixed stars, turning it as they walk, like a treadmill. Powers are the spokes of the wheel reaching down through the Dominations who wheel the planets, the sun, and the moon, and who are (Doctor Dee thought) at the same time those planets themselves; and Virtues extend invisible from those circles downward through the earth like bones, to make it live and work. On earth, Principalities, watching over the empires and nations, and Archangels, over the Church; and Angels last, in countless milliards, one for every soul, one perhaps for every living being, down to the atomies that a lens could show wriggling in a spoonful of garden dirt.

Angels, linked in sequence like the weave of a garment, hand to hand, mouth to ear, eye to eye to eye, ascending and descending forever on the world's business with a sort of taffeta rustle that can be heard, if you stand silent enough, in the most silent places of the earth, or in the depths of a coiled shell.

They are there; they are there, and if God were to withdraw them the universe would not only come to a halt and die, it would very probably disappear altogether with a single indrawn breath.

They were there, Doctor Dee knew it, and they could be seen, those who were momentarily resting from their labors; they could

be waited on, like great lords at court, in the corridors and ante-
rooms of Being; as they passed their attention could be caught, they
could be spoken to. Doctor Dee was sure that it was so; and yet not
once, in any of the many glasses, mirrors, showstones, and jewels
which he owned and stared into, had he ever glimpsed one of the
angels he knew must be answerable to them. Sometimes, leaning
close and standing stock still, he had thought he heard, far off and
unintelligible to him, the chitter of their voices, as it might be mice,
and laughter infinitely small. But he had never seen one.

There was little else in spiritual practice that he had not done,
or could not do if he chose.

In the Elemental realm he knew medicine, of course, and arithmetic, not only Geometry but Perspective and Music and Megethologia
and Stratarithmetria as well. He was a handler of mirrors, a worker
in light, master of Catoptrics and several arts of shadow, reversal,
inversion, and projection. He knew the *Steganographia* of Abbot
Trithemius (in his youth he had copied out by hand a huge manuscript of it) and could do all that art of codes, ciphers, curtailed
writing, casting messages afar at will, and so on—insofar as it
operated here below; the old abbot also knew how to summon
angels to a glass, and wrote their language, or so he said, but his
prescriptions hadn't aided Doctor Dee to reach them. He could
astonish—he had astonished—his neighbors, and his fellow students, and his Queen, with what he could do, from making an eagle
for Jove to fly in a play at Oxford to curing a wound by treating the
weapon that caused it; he had astonished himself, for that matter, as
once when, in stirring a jar of mutable airs, he had let loose a crowd
of tiny elementals, which pursued him then like angry hornets, till
with them shrieking at his heels and head he had leapt into the
Thames to escape.

In the Celestial world he was more learned still. He had made
armillary spheres with Mercator, he had letters from Tycho Brahe
praising his *Propædeumata aphoristica,* wherein he had calculated
that twenty-five thousand possible conjunctions influenced the life
of man—a daunting figure, and Doctor Dee would end by refusing to
cast nativities at all. He could not, however, refuse to cast the
Queen's: it was he who had chosen by his arts the very day for
Elizabeth's coronation, which had poured down rain (he hadn't
foreseen that) but which no one could say was not a fortunate day.
He had cast the nativity of the King of Spain too (Saturn lying cold

and heavy on his liver and lights, he would be great but never happy) and the King of Spain had given him in return a mirror of black obsidian brought a thousand miles from Mexico, behind whose dazzling doubling surface John Dee was certain angels would be forced to pause: but he could get no spiritual creature in it, though he uncovered it and looked in it now and then for years.

He was a tall, long-boned, long-faced man with wide, always-surprised eyes made wider by the round spectacles which he had ground himself; his pointed beard would go white as milk before he was sixty. He was passionate, forgetful, restless, and good; certain of his own pious purposes; certain that the vast knowledge—vaster than the knowledge contained in all the folios and manuscripts of his library, the largest in England—the vast knowledge contained in God's holy angels as in vessels could be obtained by man: that it could be drunk: and that if it were, then neither the man who drank it nor the world would be the same thereafter.

And so he practiced his arts, and he schooled a generation of Englishmen (Philip Sidney learned mathematics at Doctor Dee's house in Mortlake, Hawkins and Frobisher came to look at his maps); he went back and forth to court, and when on the Continent he kept his eyes and ears open, and wrote to Walsingham of what he saw; he made his mirrors and his elixirs, and raised his children, and dug in his vegetable garden. And pressed, always, in his mind and in his study, against that barrier beyond which the angels conversed among themselves.

One means by which he thought he might get through was to go by way of the doors open in the souls of others.

He came to be able, after long study, to discern those doors, though he could not have set down in any clear way what signs he went by. A kind of cast in an inward eye. An impression Doctor Dee would receive that someone he came across—a child he was tutoring, a young curate come to borrow books—was standing slightly elsewhere from where he appeared to be standing, or in a faint breeze that no one else felt. Through no virtue or choice of his own, it seemed, only by a sort of accident of birth (though Doctor Dee doubted it was an accident at all) a man possessed a door, like a strawberry mark; or was possessed by one, as by a falling sickness. With great circumspection (for however well he himself knew the difference between his enterprise and vile conjuring, it was a distinction that not everyone could—or would—make) Doctor Dee sought out the strange ones, and sounded them, and sat them before his stones and mirrors to see what they could see.

They knew, in London, that edgy company of nativity-casters, philtre-makers, smokesellers and University roarers, that Doctor Dee in Mortlake would repay well an introduction to such a one, if he really was such a one, which Doctor Dee would know in a moment: whoever could be cozened by that company, Doctor Dee could not be. And yet he well knew—it troubled him—that it was not only the pious, not only the honest, through whom a way could come to be pierced. Nor that, just because a man might try to cheat him with false skrying, the same man could do no true skrying as well.

Like his Queen—who didn't always like to be reminded of it, except by her wise wizard, who had traced her line and his own all the way back to Arthur—John Dee was a Welshman; like his Queen he knew well that burden of feeling the Welsh call *hiraeth,* something neither hope nor regret, neither revelation nor memory, but a compound of all of these, a yearning that could fill the heart as with warm rain. He was fifty-six years old that night in March when a certain young man from the Welsh marches was brought to his house in Mortlake. The wizard had waited by then ten years for him, though it wasn't anyone quite like him that he had expected: nor did the doctor know that in the weeks and months, the years to come, he would be bound (bound by the blessed Archangels themselves) more intimately and singularly to his skryer than even to the wife he cherished.

He had, in the first place, no name, this young man; or he had more than one, which seemed to him like the same thing. The name he had grown up with was a fiction, the result of his being raised the ward of a man whose bastard he may or may not have been, and having no other origins that he knew of. He had discarded that name, and the name he used now was merely that and not his own at all: Talbot, a hero's name, though not chosen for that reason, chosen nearly at random from a church monument because he needed a new one. It was as Mr. Talbot that he was known to Clerkson and Charles Sled and those men in London whom he lived among and sat in taverns with, Edward Talbot of no particular place, living with one or another friend until a quarrel or a new friend of better hope appeared; it was as Edward Talbot that Clerkson introduced him to Doctor Dee.

He had no ears, either: what he had were two scarred, docked humps at his ear holes, and he wore always a close-fitting black cap to cover them, which gave him a scholarly look, or anyway an antique look, like a doctor of Queen Mary's days. The loss of his ears had happened in a town whose name he wouldn't remember, for a crime (it was coining, or something worse, or quite different) which he had been mistakenly charged with, the result of slander and the ignorance of vulgar people, he would not rehearse the true story though—his own version of the story—not even to himself. All of that had happened after his time at Oxford, where he had earned no degree, and which he had left because of another story that he wouldn't or couldn't tell in a way that anyone else could understand; even years later Doctor Dee could not have told it over, though he had heard bits and fragments of it often. He was twenty-seven years old on that night in March, clouds flying fast as pinnaces over the moon's face, when Clerkson brought him over river to Mortlake.

He had a book, which he couldn't read, which was the reason for his coming; and he had a friend, or an enemy, who had long accompanied him, whose breath he knew but whose name he did not know.

—How do you come to have it? Doctor Dee asked him when the book was put before him.

Mr. Talbot's long white fingers plucked at the complex knots with which he had tied up his bundle.

—Well, I will tell you, he said. I will tell you that whole tale. How I come to have it: I'll tell you.

Clerkson's hands reached impatiently for the strings of the bundle, but Talbot waved them away; he said no more, though, only his hands trembled as he pulled aside the old cloths the book was wrapped in.

Doctor Dee stood, moving aside his cup of wine so that the book could be opened.

It was a manuscript on thick parchment, narrow and sewn up with heavy greased black thread. There was no cover or binding. The characters it was written in started immediately at the top of the first page without any heading, as though this were perhaps not the first page at all. Doctor Dee picked up the lamp and bent close over the page. Mr. Talbot turned the heavy worm-holed leaf. The second page was the same: a solid block of characters from top to bottom.

—It is in a cipher, the doctor said. I can read a cipher, if it hides a language that I know.

—A cipher, Mr. Talbot said. Yes.

He looked down again at the page. So long had he stared at these pages that they were as familiar to him as any pages of any grammar he had ever memorized, and yet because he could extract no meaning from them, none, they kept all their strangeness. To look at them was to feel himself in a compact with mystery, at once excluded and privileged; it was the same sense he had used to have as a child, looking into books before he had his letters: knowing those marks to be meaningful, charged with meaning, and not knowing what they meant.

He moved aside so that the doctor could sit before the book.

—How, Dee asked him again, do you come to have this?

—I was in a manner led to it, Mr. Talbot said.

—In what manner? the doctor asked. He had picked up a stylus and begun touching different letters of the book.

—Led, said Mr. Talbot. And the whole story, the marvelous story, filled him suddenly brimful, and he, encompassed in it, living in it, couldn't begin to think how to tell it.

—Do you, he said at last (lapsing into Latin to cast what he could not relate into a sort of discourse), do you have any knowledge of the things a man of wisdom might learn through, through congress with spirits? Certain spirits, do you know of this kind . . .

Doctor Dee raised his eyes to him slowly. He answered in Latin.

—If you mean the working of things by what the vulgar call magic, no, I know nothing of that.

Mr. Clerkson sat forward in his chair. A smile was on his wolfish shaven face: it was for this he had brought Mr. Talbot here.

—I have asked, Doctor Dee said, in prayers, for knowledge of things. Through God's angels.

He regarded Mr. Talbot for a time; then he said, in English:

—But tell me what you had to tell: Led.

—There was talk, Mr. Talbot said with a glance at Clerkson, about a dead man, and a conjuration; that the dead man was made to speak, or an evil spirit to speak through him; but all that is false, and no man who wished to learn wisdom could learn it in that way.

He had a dreadful impulse to touch his ears, tug down his cap; he resisted it.

—They think that if a man seeks treasure he wants only coin to spend, he went on. There are other treasures. There is knowledge. There are lawful means to learn where treasure lies, true treasure.

The second offense, the justice had told him, got not the pillory but death. . . . How had that evil story come out of his mouth, and not the story he had started out to tell? For a moment he could think of nothing else. He watched Doctor Dee trace down the letters of the page to which his book was opened. He picked up the cup of wine he had been given but hadn't touched, and drank.

—A spirit led me to that book, he said. It was in old Glastonbury that I found it.

Doctor Dee's stylus stopped on the page, and he looked up again at Talbot.

—In Glastonbury?

Mr. Talbot nodded, and drank again, and though his heart had begun to tick quick and hard he blinked slowly and calmly at Doctor Dee's stare.

—Yes, he said. In a monk's grave at Glastonbury. A spirit that I knew spoke to me, and told me; told me where to dig. . . .

—Did you dig? At Glastonbury?

—Only a little.

Surprised by the old man's fierce response, he began to spin out a circumstantial tale that hid more than it told. The part about Glastonbury was anyway the part he knew he would find it hardest to tell, though the spirit that had been repeating the story over and over to him was quite insistent about it. All that Mr. Talbot really wanted to tell, what was in his mouth to tell and confusing anything else that passed through it, was the end of the story: the meaning: the fact that he had been vouchsafed the book (and a stone jar too, a stone jar full of powder whose use he guessed at, that he had in his pocket) just so it could be given to this man, brought here on this night and offered to him. He knew it to be so.

But he could not say so. A kind of shyness came over him, and with the story not told at all he could suddenly say nothing more.

—No no no, said Mr. Clerkson. He means only that he brought it for you. A gift. Found in that holy place.

He dared put out his hand and push the book an inch closer to where the doctor sat.

—My thanks, then, said Doctor Dee. If it be a gift.

—What Mr. Talbot desired, Clerkson said, was to learn somewhat from your worship in spiritual practice. As he has said often to me he knows himself to be apt in it. He . . .

Without looking away from Doctor Dee, Mr. Talbot spoke to him:

—I have no need of you to interpret me.

—Mr. Clerkson, said Doctor Dee, rising. Will you go with me? There are the volumes you asked after, in the next room. I would speak to you a moment.

Clerkson, still smiling, went with the doctor, passing back to his friend only a quizzical look that might mean anything. Mr. Talbot took the curved forelimbs of the chair he sat in in his long hands, and felt their smooth solidity. He looked about him at the place he had come to: at the books rising to the ceilings on swaybacked shelves, piled in corners and on tables in unsteady columns; at the optical instruments and the globes and the great hourglass, which just now wore a velvet hat of Doctor Dee's. He took breath hugely, and rested his head on the chair's back. He was where he had wanted to be, and he could stay.

Doctor Dee came back alone. Mr. Talbot felt his round-eyed gaze, felt its warmth like the warmth of the sea-coal fire burning in the grate. The doctor closed the door behind him—Mr. Talbot heard it latch–then he went to a cabinet, and took from it a velvet bag, whose drawstring he loosed. He let fall from it into his hand a sphere of crystal the color of moleskin, pure as a tiny planet or a ball of gray evening.

—Have you looked into a glass before? he asked.

Mr. Talbot shook his head.

—A boy I know, said Doctor Dee, saw somewhat in this stone. He was a player, and perhaps he lied to me, but he said that there are creatures who are answerable to this stone, only it was not he to whom they would speak; that he to whom the stone belonged was to come later.

He took a metal frame, like a claw, and set the stone within it.

—Perhaps, he said, if you look, you will see the face of that one who led you to the book.

He could not have spoken more gently, more meekly; yet Mr. Talbot heard or chose to hear a command: *Come, look into this glass.* And hearing a command, a command that would brook no denial, he chose to think that all which would come of his going now to look into it, to kneel before it and look, was not his fault but the fault of him who with a long white hand showed him the glass in its frame: and of those who beckoned to him already from within it.

He had not known that he was groaning aloud.

When Doctor Dee took his shoulder, everything in the glass— the ship, the child, the powers, the depths—closed up one after another as though he hurtled backward away from them through curtains rapidly drawn: backward through the window, through the showstone in the armed child's hand, through the row of strong young men in green whose names all began with A (seeming startled and windblown just for a moment, looking on one another, before a hand—it was the skryer's own—drew a bright curtain over them and they too were gone), and he fell backward into the upper chamber at Mortlake and the night: the real globe of smoky quartz came into view, and his own hand before it was the curtain drawn over it; he was groaning, and Doctor Dee was helping him to his feet and to a chair.

Doctor Dee looked down upon him as he might upon some rare and strange creature whom he had just captured, or just released.

—I felt faint, Mr. Talbot said. Just for that moment.

—Was there anything more spoken to you, Doctor Dee said, gently but urgently. Was there anything more said.

For a long moment Mr. Talbot said nothing, feeling his heart return into his bosom. When he had had time to think what he should say, what it would be best to say (he could not remember if anything had been spoken to him) he said:

—There will be help given here. There will not be any answer withheld from you. They promised that to me. I'm sure of it.

—Now God his grace to us be praised, said Doctor Dee almost under his breath. Given sight *in chrystallo*. I have written it all down.

A warming shudder covered Mr. Talbot head to toe; he turned his eyes to the stone in its frame on the table, so far from him now, so small, the stone in which there were depths like the depths inside himself. Annael Annachor Anilos Agobel. If he opened his mouth now the names of a hundred more, a hundred thousand more, would come trooping out.

He opened his mouth, a huge yawn filled him up, stretching his jaws and crossing his eyes. He laughed, and Doctor Dee laughed too, as at a child overtaken with weariness.

When he had been given some supper, and put exhausted to bed upstairs, and Clerkson had been sent home with his gift of books, Doctor Dee wiped and put on his spectacles, and trimmed his lamp, and sat again before the book that Mr. Talbot had brought.

He knew a dozen codes, some of them of as great antiquity as this book appeared to be. He read several of the old secret monkish manuscript hands; he knew the oghams of old Wales. His friend the great magician Cardanus used the trellis code: a page of writing to be read down the first line of letters and up the next and down the next, revealing the true message hidden in a false message read in the usual way, in lines left to right: it seemed to Doctor Dee a childish trick, and easily broken.

All codes, all that he had been presented with, could in the end be broken. There was only one kind that could never be: a kind of code he had conceived of while studying the great book of Abbot Trithemius, the *Steganographia,* which Christopher Plantin had found for him in Antwerp long ago. A code impossible to break was one which did not transpose letters into other letters or into numbers, did not transpose words or sentences into other words or sentences, but which transposed one kind of thing—the thing to be secretly spoken of—into another kind of thing entirely. Translate your intentions into a speaking bird, and let the bird speak of your intentions; encode your message in a book on automata, and the automaton when built will trace the message with a clockwork hand. Write (it was what Abbot Trithemius had done) a book on how to call down angels, and if you do so correctly, you will instruct the angels how to write the Abbot's book themselves, in a tongue of their own, which when used will translate into works, miracles, sciences, peace on earth.

In a more practical way, this was how Doctor Dee often encoded: he kept a huge number of stock phrases in various languages, which would be substituted for the key words of the secret message. The word "bad" could be enciphered by "Pallas is blessed of charm" or "You are admired of women, Astarte," or "A god of grace enthroned." If the same phrase were in Greek, it meant a different thing: "crown" perhaps, or "stealthily." Whole fictions could be constructed out of these phrases, they were designed to fit together with standard couplings to yield long tedious and half-intelligible allegorical fantasies that actually meant something brief and fatal: *The Duke dies at midnight.* In fact the great trouble of the method was that the encoding was always so much longer than the message.

Late at night, unraveling such a one, Doctor Dee would sometimes think: All creation is a huge, ornate, imaginary, and unintended fiction; if it could be deciphered it would yield a single shocking word.

This night, with this book, he began with the first page, trying to find a simple anagram for these barbaric dense marks. He found none. He used the twenty-four letters of the alphabet, translated these into numbers, the numbers he arranged as a horoscope of zodiacal signs and houses; the horoscope he translated into days and hours, and these numbers into letters in Greek. The wind died down; the moon set behind gathered clouds. In one of the one hundred and fifty cipher alphabets the Welsh bards knew, different trees stood for the letters; in another, different birds; in another, famous castles. A black rook calls to the nightingale in the hawthorn tree below the fortress of Seolae. It began to rain. Doctor Dee tossed into the fire each fruitless line of inquiry as it turned to nonsense. Dawn came; Doctor Dee wrote out in his scribble hand (he had four different hands he wrote in, besides a mirror hand) one meaning for the first line of Mr. Talbot's book:

IF EVER SOM POWR WITH 3 WISHES TO GRANT

Which made little sense to him. But if he went backward—backward through the forest where the rooks called in the hawthorns along the track below the fortress, backward through the ogham and the Greek and the stars and the letters and the numbers, the same line could be read this way:

THERE WERE ANGELS IN yͤ GLAS 246 MANY OF THEM

and that made his heart pause for an instant, and fill again with a richer blood.

There *were* angels in the glass; his wish was to be granted.

He rose from his stool; gray morning almost not distinguishable from night filled the mullioned windows. He knew, knew for certain, that he stood poised on this night at the beginning of a huge enterprise, one that he was not entirely sure he had the strength for, one that would not end with his own death, but still would require his lifelong aid for its completion; and at the same time he knew that in another sense, another deciphering, he was plumb in the middle. He blew out the lamp, and went up to bed.

FOUR

▲

"Egypt," Julie Rosengarten said dreamily.

"Egypt," Pierce said. "The riddle of the Sphinx. Pyramid power."

"Tarot."

"The speaking statue of Memnon."

"Eternal life," said Julie.

"Only that country isn't Egypt," Pierce said. "Not Egypt but this country, like this." With a felt-tipped pen he wrote it out on the napkin brought with his whiskey:

ÆGYPT

"I remember this," Julie said, looking down at this glyph. "I sort of remember this."

"It's the story I want to tell," Pierce said. "A story I somehow stumbled into when I was a kid, when almost everyone else had forgotten it; a story that's just coming to light again—an amazing story. And it's got a great twist to it, too."

"I sort of remember," Julie said.

"Anyway it's *one* story," Pierce said. "If this were a novel it would be the 'frame story,' isn't that what they call it, but it would have an even bigger story inside it. About history. About truth."

Julie bent over the typed pages of his proposal, reading it or rather scanning it symbolically. Her freckled and vacation-browned breasts went white farther within the bodice of her summer dress; her hair had gone dark-honey color. " 'Where are the four corners of the earth?' " she read. " 'What is the music of the spheres, and how is it made? Why do people think that Gypsies can tell fortunes?' " She lifted her eyes to him, they too had gone light and honeylike. "Weren't you going with a Gypsy for a while? How did that work out?"

"Part Gypsy. For a while." Hey, why do people say four corners of the earth, Pierce, how can a ball have corners? Why do people say they're in seventh heaven, what's wrong with the other six? Why are there seven days in a week, and not six or nine? Why is that, Pierce? "It didn't work out."

Julie lowered her eyes again to the papers.

They had embraced, Julie and he, tightly, at the door of the restaurant, both arriving there at the same moment, nearly colliding in fact. There was a cold stone in Pierce's breast, there had been one all morning, for he remembered the finality, even cruelty, of his last words to her in person. They hadn't seemed to sink in, back then; and they had not apparently persisted in her breast as they had in his. One advantage, maybe, of a real belief in Fate is that it takes the sting out of all past hurts, errors, shames; all that has been. Going through changes: that was as much as Julie would admit to having been doing, and all she would ever charge others with. A kind of new old purblind politeness that was weirdly endearing. Pierce drank of his whiskey deeply.

"See," he said, "when I was a kid I thought or imagined that there was a country—Ægypt—which was like Egypt but different from it, underlying it or sort of superimposed on it. It was a real place to me, as real as America. . . ."

"Oh right," Julie said. "Gypsies."

"You remember," Pierce said. "You were there. You were my guide, some ways."

"God we used to talk."

"And the 'frame story,'" Pierce said. "It's about my country; how I came to find out that it wasn't me who made it up really at all; how that country came to be. Ægypt." He touched the word he had written. "Because I did find out. I did."

She put down the proposal, to give all her attention to him, and rested her cheek in a dimpled hand.

It was in the spring after Julie Rosengarten left him, first for the West Side and then for the Coast and Mexico not to be seen again for years—a spring somehow flavored differently from any spring before it or since—that Pierce picked up Fellowes Kraft's little life of Bruno, and began to read it from the first page, as he had not done in more than twenty years. . . .

"Remind me again," Julie asked him, "who Bruno was."

"Giordano Bruno," Pierce answered, crossing his hands on the placemat before him, which showed scenes of Italy, the dome of Peter's, the tower at Pisa. "Giordano Bruno, 1546 to 1600. The first thinker of modern times, really, to postulate infinite space as a physical reality. He thought that not only was the sun in the center of the solar system, but that other stars were suns too, and also had planets going around them, as far and far farther than the eye could see—infinitely, in fact; infinitely."

"Huh."

"He was burned at the stake as a heretic," Pierce said, "and since he had promoted the new Copernican picture of the heavens he's always been regarded as a martyr to science, a precursor of Galileo, a sort of speculative astronomer. But what he really was, was something much stranger. The universe he saw wasn't the one we see. For one thing, he thought that all those infinite stars and planets were alive: animals, he calls them. And they went around in their circles because they wanted to. Anyway . . ."

Anyway Kraft's book had proved to be on the whole pretty ordinary, all taken from secondary sources fleshed out with a tourist's impressions of the scenes of Bruno's frantic life: the monastery in Naples from which he fled, the universities and courts he haunted, looking for patronage, Venice where he was arrested, Rome where he died. The couple of hundred pages had neither the exactness of fiction nor the vividness of history. But midway through it Kraft divulged, or stumbled across in passing, or handed out without quite saying so, the key not only to Bruno but to the mystery Pierce pursued.

What was it, Kraft was wondering, that compelled Bruno and Bruno alone to break out of the closed world of Aquinas and Dante, and find an infinite universe outside? It could not (Kraft thought) have been the discovery of Copernicus alone, for Copernicus posited no such frightening thing as infinite space populated infinitely; his sun-centered world was still bounded, as bounded by a sphere of fixed stars as Aristotle's had been. Bruno always insisted that Copernicus hadn't understood his own discoveries.

No (Kraft wrote), the impulse must have come from elsewhere. Where? Well, Bruno seems to have looked into almost every book extant in his century, though certainly he didn't finish all the ones he opened. He was versed in the most esoteric of studies. He sought regeneration for himself and his church at the ancientest and most hidden of wells. Could he not have found a way out of the crystal spheres of Aristotle in the teachings of old Hermes the Thrice-great?

Pierce read this, and stopped. Hermes? Was this the same Thrice-great Hermes that Milton outwatch'd the Bear with? Wasn't he a mythical sage of some kind in classical literature? Pierce had no clear memory. What teachings were these?

Hermes teaches (Kraft went on) that the seven spheres of the stars enclose the soul of man like a prison, his *heimarmene*, his Fate. But man is a brother to those strong dæmons who rule the spheres; he is a power like them, though he has forgotten this. There is a means, great Hermes says, to ascend up through those seven, unfooled by their angry shows of resistance, passing each one by means of a secret word which they cannot refuse; exacting, in fact, from each of them a gift, the gift of arising to the next sphere; until, at last, in the eighth sphere, the ogdoadic sphere, the released soul perceives Infinity and sings hymns of praise to God.

Thus Hermes (Kraft wrote, Pierce read) and what if Bruno, having taken to heart this ancientest and most sacred of myths, and opening Copernicus's book one starry night in Paris, in London, suddenly put the two together: and felt within his buzzing brain the puzzle solved? For if the sun is at the center and not the earth, then there are no crystal spheres to hold us in; we have only and always fooled ourselves, we men, kept ourselves within the spheres which our own flawed and insufficient senses perceived, but which *were never there at all*. The way to ascend through the spheres that hem us in was to know that we had already so ascended, and were on our way, in motion unstoppably. No wonder Bruno felt a titanic dawn approaching, no wonder he felt compelled to cry it across Europe, no wonder he laughed aloud. Mind, at the center of all, contains within it all that it is the center of, a circle whose circumference is nowhere, stretching out infinitely in every direction he could look in or think about, at every instant. Dare you say men are as gods? the shocked inquisitors in Rome would ask him. Can they change the stars in their courses? They can, Bruno answers; they can; they have already.

Here Pierce had put down the book for a moment, surfeited and laughing himself, wondering what his twelve-year-old self could ever have made of all that; and when he raised it again, he found a footnote.

Whether or not (the footnote read) this understanding which we have ascribed to Bruno is the true secret teaching intended to be discerned in the writings of Hermes Trismegistus (Oh hm, Pierce thought, that name) we leave to others to pursue. The interested reader might begin with Mead, who writes: *Along this ray of the Trismegistic tradition we may allow ourselves to be drawn backwards in time towards the holy of holies of the Wisdom of Ancient Egypt.*

"And there it was," Pierce said. "There it was."

"Trizma-what?" asked Julie.

"Just listen," Pierce said. "Here it comes."

The book of Mead's to which Kraft directed him (and perhaps his young self once too, who knew) was unfindable: *Thrice-greatest Hermes,* by G.R.S. Mead (London and Benares; the Theosophical Publishing House, 1906; three volumes). Looking for it, though, led Pierce to some strange places, the shops and shows of cranks and mystics he had not realized were quite so numerous, places he could not wholly bring himself to enter and yet could not deny must have some connection to the place he sought. Certain at least that he had not made it all up, he withdrew from their imaginings as from a private ritual; he turned away into better-lit places. And he was getting warm. History of ideas, *History of Magic and Experimental Science, Journal of the Warburg and Courtauld Institutes,* which he had thumbed in graduate school.

He was definitely getting warm. There were others on the path suddenly, greater scholars than he; they were finding things out, they were publishing. Gratefully Pierce turned away from Bruno's *Opera omnia latine* which he had glimpsed far down a stack at the Brooklyn Public, and into the shallow waters of Secondary Sources: and at length the University of Chicago mailed to him (he had been awaiting it more eagerly than he ever had any golden decoding ring of Captain Midnight's) a book by an English lady who—Pierce knew it even before he tore the brown paper from the volume—had trekked his lost land from mountain to sea, and returned; returned, at the head of a caravan of strange goods, maps, artifacts, plunder.

"And this," Pierce said, feeling just for a moment like the helpless narrator of that old endless campfire joke, "this is the story that she told." He drank again, and asked: "Do you know the word 'hermetic'?"

"You mean like hermetically sealed?"

"That, and also hermetic, occult, secret, esoteric."

"Oh yes sure."

"Okay," said Pierce, "this is the story:

"Sometime in the 1460s, a Greek monk brought to Florence a collection of manuscripts in Greek which caused a lot of excitement there. What they purported to be were Greek versions of ancient Egyptian writings—religious speculations, philosophy, magical recipes—that had been composed by an ancient sage or priest of Egypt, Hermes Trismegistus: Hermes the Three Times Very Great, you could translate it. Hermes is the Greek god, of course; the Greeks had made an equivalence between their Hermes, god of language, and the Egyptian god Thoth or Theuth, who invented writing. From various classical sources they had—Cicero, Lactantius, Plato—the Renaissance scholars who first got a look at these new manuscripts could find out that the author was a cousin of Atlas, the brother of Prometheus (the Renaissance believed that these were real ancient people) and that he was not a god but a man, a man of great antiquity, who lived before Plato and Pythagoras and maybe even before Moses; and that these writings were therefore as old as any in the history of mankind.

"A terrific stir was started in Florence by the arrival of these Egyptian writings. They'd been rumored to exist, even in the Middle Ages: Hermes Trismegistus was one of those shadowy ancients who had a medieval reputation as a great wizard, along with Solomon and Virgil, and various Black Books and treatises were ascribed to him—but here was the real original thing. Here was Egyptian knowledge older than the Romans and the Greeks, older maybe than Moses—in fact there would be speculation that Moses, raised an Egyptian prince, got his secret wisdom from this very source.

"See, what you have to remember in thinking about the Renaissance is that they were always looking *back.* All their scholarship, all their learning, was bent toward re-creating as best they could the past in the present, because the past had necessarily been better, wiser, less decayed than the present. And so the older an old manuscript was, the older the knowledge it contained, the better it must turn out to be, once it had been cleansed of the accretions and errors of later times: the closer to the old Golden Age.

"So can you see how exciting this must have been? Here was the oldest knowledge in the *world,* and what do you know? It sounded like Genesis; it sounded like Plato. Hermes must have been divinely inspired to foreshadow Christian truth. Plato himself must have drunk at this source. In dialogues between Hermes and his pupil Asclepius and his son Tat you can see not only a philosophy of ideas like Plato's but a philosophy of light like Plotinus and even an incarnated Word like the Christian *logos*, Son of God, creative principle. Hermes practically became a Christian saint. A rage for Egypt and Egyptian stuff began that runs right through the Renaissance.

"More, though. These Egyptian dialogues are intensely spiritual, pious, abstract; they talk a lot about escaping the power of the stars, about discovering the soul's power to be like God, but there's almost no real practical advice about that stuff. Where there *was* practical advice, though, was in those old magic books the Middle Ages had transmitted and ascribed to Hermes; and who knew, maybe they were the practical side of the abstract principles. Corrupted, of course, and terribly dangerous to use, but still containing the power of the good ancient Egyptian magic of Hermes. So Hermes was responsible for serious people taking up the practice of magic in a big way."

"Wow," Julie said. "Huh." Her eyes had begun to shine in a way he remembered; her finger idly wiped the sugar from the rim of her daiquiri. He had her now.

"And the new science too," Pierce said. "If man is brother to dæmons, and capable of anything, what's to stop him working in the world, doing amazing things? If the whole plentitude of Nature can be ordered and reflected in the knowing mind of man, like Bruno believed? I think Bruno *did* get encouragement from Hermes to take up the Copernican system, not because the idea was evidentially more convincing, but because it was more marvelous, more wonderful, the true secret Egyptian view come back again."

"Well," Julie said, "everybody knows the Egyptians knew the earth went around the sun. They kept it secret, but they knew."

Pierce stopped in his spate, mouth open. Julie's eyes were still ashine with intelligence and attention. "So go on," she said, and licked her finger.

"Well but remember," Pierce said. "Remember now, there was almost nothing really known then about the culture and beliefs of ancient Egypt. Even before the Roman era the understanding of hieroglyphics had disappeared; they wouldn't be understood again until the nineteenth century. Nobody in the Renaissance knew what was written on obelisks, or what the pyramids were for, or anything. Now, in the light of these intensely spiritual, semi-Platonic magical writings, they began studying. Hieroglyphics: they must be some sort of mystic code, picture-story of the ascent of the soul, aids to contemplation, maybe hypervalent, like Rorschach blots or Tarot cards. . . ."

"Sure," Julie said.

"And pyramids, obelisks, temples—they ought to contain encoded Egyptian science, geometry older than Euclid, secret proportions and magical properties maybe now able to be unlocked. . . ."

"Sure."

"But it's not so!" Pierce cried, displaying his palms. A diner at the next table cast a cool eye in his direction, lovers' spat probably, don't show them you noticed. "It's not so! That's the most wonderful and amazing and strange thing. These writings which the Renaissance ascribed to the god-king-priest Hermes Trismegistus, and from which they got their whole picture of ancient Egypt, weren't really ancient at all. They certainly weren't written by one man. *They weren't even Egyptian.*

"Whoever wrote the writings which came to Florence in the 1460s didn't know a thing—anyway knew very little—about real Egyptian religion. Scholars today have a hard time finding even a trace in them of the real corpus of Egyptian myth or thought.

"Not even a trace.

"What they *really* are, these writings, as far as we can tell now, are the scriptures of a late Hellenistic mystery cult, a gnostic cult of the second or third century A.D. A.D.," he emphasized. "There were lots of them flourishing in Alexandria around then, among Hellenized Egyptians and Egyptian Greeks; Alexandria then must have been sort of like California now, cults, everybody into something. So if these scriptures contain stuff that foreshadows Christianity, it's no surprise; if they sound like Plato or Pythagoras or Plotinus, it's not because they influenced Plato and them, but the other way around. Platonism was just very much in the air just then.

"So. The Renaissance made this titanic mistake. There were lots of reasons for it. Church fathers like Augustine and Lactantius in the postclassical period had talked about Hermes Trismegistus as though he were a real person, and so did Roger Bacon and Aquinas in the Middle Ages. There was no extrinsic evidence to show that the writings were fake, or not what they purported to be. There *was,* however, a lot of *internal* evidence; and by the middle of the seventeenth century the writings had been shown to be late Greek (there's a mention in one manuscript of the Olympic games, for one thing), but the enthusiasts didn't pay any attention; through the seventeenth and even eighteenth centuries they went right on believing in the Egypt of Hermes. The body of esoteric Egyptianism grew huge. Even in the nineteenth century—*after* Champollion, *after* Wallis Budge, after the real actual Egypt came to light—people like Mead and the Theosophists and Aleister Crowley and the mystics and magicians were still trying to believe in it."

"Aleister Crowley!" Julie's eyes widened further.

"And all because of this crazy error, because of these pseudo-Egyptian scriptures! Because of the Hermetic writings—see, there's that word, hermetic, magical, secret, sealed like an alchemist's jar—because of those writings, Egypt came to mean all things mystical, encoded, profound; ancient wisdom lost; old age of gold now perhaps able to be recovered, to enlighten degenerate moderns. That's the tradition; that's what came down to us, in a thousand books, a thousand references. It's the tradition that continues in the founding of the Freemasons, for instance, who always make a big deal out of their connection to Egypt, and through the Masons it comes to the Founding Fathers, some of whom were Masons, and so the pyramid and the eye of Egypt get onto the Great Seal of the United States and onto the dollar bill. And in the same way, the Sphinx and the temples and the wise priests get into *The Magic Flute,* which Mozart based on the pseudo-Egyptian lore of his Masonic lodge.

"And somehow—I don't know exactly how—somehow it all descends to me. Somehow this intensely magical, other-worldly, imaginary country comes to me, is revealed to me, in Kentucky, through books of different kinds, through the goddamn air, somehow. But at the same time I knew about the actual historical Egypt too, about which real knowledge has been accumulating through the centuries; I knew about mummies and King Tut and Ra and Isis and Osiris and the Nile rising and all those slaves hauling blocks of stone. So what it seemed like to me was that there were two different countries, somehow near each other or at right angles to each other. Egypt. And Ægypt.

"And I was right! There *are* two different countries. The one I dreamt and thought about, it has a history too, as Egypt does, a history just as long but different; and different monuments, or the same monuments with completely different meanings; and a literature, and a location. You can trace the story of Egypt back, and back, and at a certain point (or at several different points) it will divide. And you can follow either one: the regular history-book one, Egypt, or the other, the dream one. The Hermetic one. Not Egypt but Ægypt. Because there is more than one history of the world."

He finished his drink. A waiter had appeared beside them, had been beside them for some little time, perhaps listening to Pierce's peroration. Julie at length drew her eyes from Pierce and looked up at the waiter. "We'd better order, huh?"

"That's the story I want to tell," Pierce said. "But it's just one story, and not the tenth part of it. Not the tenth part."

"Eggs Florentine, I guess," Julie said. "No potatoes."

"Magic cities," Pierce said. "Cities of the Sun. Why was Louis the Fourteenth the Sun King? Because of Hermes."

"Tea," Julie said. "With lemon."

"And there are other stories," Pierce said. "Other stories just as good. Angels, for instance. That's a story I want to tell. Why are there nine choirs of the angels, do you think, and not seven or ten? Where do the little bodiless cherubs on Valentine cards come from? And why 'cherub'?" He looked at the waiter, ordered (his stomach was a dark pit), and showed him the glass he had emptied. "Another," he said. "If I may."

A certain light seemed to have been withdrawn from Julie's eyes. He was going too fast for her, overloading. How could it be communicated, how? If you had not had one history, one Renaissance drilled into you, the plain one, then how could you feel astonishment to discover this other one, the fancy? "And a dozen others I could tell," he said. "A dozen others." Rich, inexpressibly rich, the false histories and systems of thought that had been opened for him to look into by the wise scholars he had come to know, as rich as strange, incomprehensible even, stories somehow once conceived in and understood by minds that purported to be like his, yet couched in books whose thousands of folio pages, surreal illustrations in weird perspective, geometric charts and diagrams and mnemonic verses, seemed to be trying to describe some different planet altogether. Martin del Rio, Jesuit of Spain, had written a book of a million words, about nothing but angels.

Pierce snapped out his napkin and drew it across his lap. Lost

planet found, fanfares and wind-tossed drapery, it was the surprise
he wanted most and felt least able to express: the surprise not only
of having found it, but of having found it to be, however faintly,
familiar.

"It's as though," he said, "as though there had once upon a
time been a wholly different world, which worked in a way we can't
imagine; a complete world, with all its own histories, physical laws,
sciences to describe it, etymologies, correspondences. And then
came a big change in all of them, a big change, bound up with
printing, and the discoveries of Copernicus and Kepler, and the
Cartesian and Baconian ideals of mechanistic and experimental
science. The new sciences were hugely successful; bit by bit they
scrubbed away all the persisting structures of the old science; they
even scrubbed away the actually very strange and magical way the
world appeared to men like Kepler and Newton and Bruno. The
whole old world we once inhabited is like a dream, a dream we
forgot on waking, even though, as dreams do, it lingered on into
all-awake thinking; and even now it lingers on, all around our
world, in our thought, so that every day in little ways, little odd
ways, we think like prescientific men, magicians, Pythagoreans,
Rosicrucians, without knowing we do so."

"So yes okay but Pierce . . ."

"So what I'm proposing," he went on, holding her off with a
raised palm, "is a kind of archaeology of everyday life; a sort of
scavenger hunt or paper chase, tracing backward these old persis-
tences. Discovering them, though, first of all; discovering old mythical religious ahistorical accounts of the world in their modern
versions, and then tracing the elements that compose them back to
their earlier appearances, to their sources, to their first forms, if
those can be found, the same way I did for my Egypt, Ægypt; back
to the door into dream they issued from, the Gate of Horn."

"Horn," Julie murmured, "horn, why horn I wonder."

"And you know what?" Pierce said. "More and more often I'm
learning that when you do trace them back, these false histories and
magic accounts of the world, and follow them to the crossroads, so
to speak, to where they take off on their own from the regular
history of Western civilization, then you always keep coming to the
same juncture: somewhere between 1400 and 1700. Not the notions
themselves, no, they're mostly much older; but the forms in which
they come down to us. Because at that time, I'm not certain why

though I've got some ideas, right at that time when what we recognize as modern science was coming into being, there was also an enormous revival and codification of all kinds of Ancient Wisdom and magical and traditional pictures of the world. Not only Hermes and Ægypt, but Orpheus and Zoroaster and Jewish Kabala too, and Lullism—don't ask—and the wildest neo-Platonists, like Proclus and Iamblichus, who was also a big Egyptianizer. Alchemy, all reimagined and hugely inflated by Paracelsus that nut; and astrology given a big impetus by new modes of computation; and angel-magic, and telepathy, and Atlantis . . ."

"Atlantis," Julie breathed.

"It was like that hour before waking when your dreams are clearest and most memorable. A moment when all the histories and sciences of this old other world were put into their most complete and striking form, and seemed the most hopeful and convincing: just when it was all about to be suppressed and smashed and forgotten forever . . ."

"Not forever," Julie said. "Never forever."

"Well so completely that a person, me, could go to Noate University, and get a degree in Renaissance Studies, and get only the teeniest glimpse of the tip of the drowned mountain. *Even though the greatest thinkers of the Renaissance, the very ones who were inventing science, thought that the great project of their age was rescuing all that lost knowledge!* Not coming up with new modes of feeling, new sciences, new machines, but Recovery! Memory! The power contained in ancient theologies, old magic systems, Noah's science, Adam's language! Ægypt!"

The diners at the next table were once again turned to them. Pierce drew back into his chair, which he had been leaving, and Julie leaned forward to hear him. "Ægypt," he said softly.

"And what kind of stuff," Julie said, "could they do?"

"What do you mean?"

"I mean what could they *do*, these magicians?"

Pierce blinked. "Do," he said. "Well now see this wasn't at all the boiling-pot medieval stuff, conjuring, which was all based on the power of the Devil and the dead. The Renaissance magus mostly *thought:* he acquired power just by being attuned to the wholeness of the universe, and his own innate knowledge of it."

"Power," Julie said.

"Well power," Pierce said. "So they *supposed*. I mean they did do alchemy. They made talismans of the planets, to draw into their minds and souls the planetary energies. They looked into crystal balls, and thought they saw angels. Bruno dreamt up a dozen elaborate mnemonic systems, for memorizing everything in the world, *containing* everything somehow. But a Renaissance magician's power wasn't used to enrich himself, or curse people. It was used simply to *know.* It was a *system of science,* with the same goals as the other kind of science, the kind *we* call science. . . ."

"Only we've forgotten what they did. What they could do. All that got suppressed, right?"

"We've forgotten this whole *story,*" Pierce said. "All we retain are details, impressions, bits and pieces scattered through our mental universe, like parts of a huge machine that's been smashed, and can never be put back together again. Gypsies. Angels. Moses's horns. The Age of Aquarius. That's my *point,* that's what I . . ."

"But well just tell me a second," Julie said. "I mean all your little stories about history are interesting, and all. But tell me now. Tell me why it is you want to do this book. What your reason is for wanting to do it."

Pierce thought he saw a snare in Julie's look, but didn't know what it was. "Well, for its own sake," he said cagily. "Because I just think it's a fascinating story, a kind of intellectual mystery story. I'm not sure you have to have any kind of practical reason. I mean History . . ."

" 'Cause I don't see this as a history book at all," Julie said.

"Well, a book *about* history."

"Or a book about history either. I think what you're really writing is a book about magic. About the great lost tradition of magic. And that's a book I know I can sell."

"Well no but see . . ."

"You talked about a lost world-view," Julie said, and with an impulsive gesture took his wrist in her hand. "And bits and pieces of a smashed machine, that can never be put back together again. Well I don't believe it can't be put back together again."

"There *are* scholars, historians who are trying," Pierce said, "trying. . . ."

"And you know what I believe?" She had leaned close to him, her summer-light eyes all soft fire. "I believe that machine worked. And you know what else? I think you believe it worked too."

FIVE

▲

"Nonononono," said Pierce.

"Pierce you know I think it's just so amazing that you've brought this idea to me now, I think it's just so *right*. The time. The world. You." She raised her arm, and waved, smiling, as to a friend; her bracelets of wood and lacquer clashed. "See, that old tradition is so important to me. I believe in it. I believe in it. You know I do."

"You seemed to, once." What had he done. He took a paper pouch of tobacco from his pocket, and began to make a cigarette, a habit that had initially intrigued, and ended by annoying, the woman opposite him.

"I feel it much more strongly now. There are things that have happened—well, never mind, someday I'll tell you, but I might not even *be* here if, well anyway I *know*. I know those old ways of knowledge don't die or get outdated. They might go underground. But there will always come a time when people are ready to understand them again, and the tradition is rediscovered. Isn't that really what you're saying? The Renaissance was one time. Now is another."

"Now," Pierce said.

"Well yes! You can see it all around. Pierce you used to talk about nothing else. You were *fascinated* by it. Synchronicity. Recurrences. Act theory. The Age of Aquarius. And why? Why?"

"Why," Pierce said.

"Because! Because it's time! The cycle has turned, and . . ."

"History doesn't repeat itself, Julie. It doesn't. It's only one way."

"No but like you said," Julie said. "It's rediscovered, this tradition, but in a new way; you remake it, in your own terms, and that remaking of it changes the way you understand the whole history of it. Right? That's what taking it up again *means.*"

Pierce paused, his half-made smoke lifted to his tongue.

"To take it up like we're taking it up right now, this kind of knowledge, like *you*'re taking it up, means understanding it newly."

"Hm," he said. Noncommittally he sealed and lit the cigarette. "Hm."

"Because don't you think regular science, the kind you said won out over the older kind, don't you think it's sort of run itself into the ground? Doesn't the old, other stuff seem right now actually more modern?"

"In what ways more modern?"

"Well you tell *me.* I mean it just *took in* more, didn't it, things that the regular kind of science leaves out. Telepathy. Intuition. Other ways of perceiving. Didn't you say that Bruno and so on believed the earth was alive? Well it is."

"Ecology," said Pierce, the notion just then occurring to him. "Bruno's planets, those living beings: our earth was one too, he thought, constantly in process. One big animal, and Man a part of it. A Biosphere."

"Yes!" Julie said. "Yes, and what else, what else?"

"Well the Monad," Pierce said. "The idea that the universe is one thing—that everything in it is intimately connected, interpenetrated by everything else. A dance of energy. Modern physics talks that way. It's why the Renaissance magicians thought the magic that they did could work: why the casting of a talisman could reverberate in the interior of a planet."

"Yes!"

"The union of observer and observed," Pierce said, warming. "The idea that the observer, his mind-set—they might have said his spiritual intention—can alter what's observed."

"Influences," Julie said, waving away Pierce's smoke. "Affinities."

"A sense of the marvelous, of possibilities. Electricity wouldn't have baffled those guys. Or X rays, or radio. The magicians believed in causative action at a distance, but the rationalist scientists of the time threw it out; then they had a hard time with it when Newton proposed it again as basic to the universe. Newton called it gravity. The magicians liked to call it Love."

"Love," Julie said, and a sudden sparkle bloomed in her eyes,

Pierce had always marveled at how swiftly it could come. "See?" she said.

"You'd have to be so *careful* though," Pierce said, "careful to distinguish. . . ."

"Oh sure, sure," Julie said, and her red thumbnail furled and released the corners of his few pages. "We have to talk, we have to think. To shape this thing, and focus it. But I know there are people, lots of people now, who want to hear this news. I know it." The waiter's hand placed on the table, in neutral ground between them, the check. Julie's hand covered it. "And I tell you, Pierce. That book I can sell. The history book, just history, I don't know."

She allowed his thoughtful silence a long moment's room, and then—"Listen, Pierce," she said softly, almost shyly, "I know this sounds really dumb, but I have to go now and eat another lunch."

"Huh?"

"Well I don't think I'll really eat. But it's so crazy, so much of this business is done at lunch. And I've been away for three weeks now, and so I have to make up for it. Two lunches a day. Why is that, books and lunch."

"I don't know."

"We never really got to talk." She regarded him, cheek in hand, and seemed to remember an old smile she had once kept for him. "I thought about you so much, these last few weeks. Lots of stuff. I wondered: did you ever come up with that third wish?"

"No," he said. It had been with her that he had first begun working out the constraints and possibilities of three wishes. He didn't want to say that she herself, her person, had been the tentative subject of the third, what time she had been off in California; the subject, in more than one casting. "No. Not finally."

"Maybe now," she said. "You're learning all these new powers."

"Not for me," he said. "What should I do, practice conjuring?" He tossed his napkin onto the table, rising. "You've got to remember the one great drawback of practical magic, Jewel. It didn't work." She was rising too, but he forestalled her. "Sit, sit for a sec while I, and then we'll go. One sec."

She sat, becalmed, before her cold cup, her hand on the typed pages.

She really hadn't been suggesting that his book ought to teach magic procedures. No. The meaning, the world-view behind them,

the soul-sense they made: that's what she meant. The practices
themselves—that was much too dangerous. She knew more than
one person who had been hurt that way: or who had hurt others.

Pierce would laugh to hear her say that.

What a strange guy. She had used to ask him what good does it
do you, Pierce, working out these wishes, protecting yourself every
which way, if you don't believe you can make wishes?

And he would say: Believing in it doesn't make it so, Jewel.

Old Pierce, she thought with a welling of pity. He thinks he's
so sharp, so unfooled: like a color-blind person, undeceived by
color. What he could never see is that those powers he had been just
talking about weren't wandering around in the world free like
mutts waiting to be adopted; they were the creations of souls,
created between souls, they were creation itself, and bringing themselves into being was the use they had. If you can create such power
in your life, then it's your duty to create it. If you are somehow
granted it, it's not for no reason. That's what evolution is.

One day he'll learn, she thought, if not in this lifetime, the
next, or the next. It's the task set for him, even if he doesn't know
it: he who knows so much else.

There *was* a reason she was here, no longer Pierce's lover but
with her hands on Pierce's work. The world *is* changing, evolving in
a new and accelerated way, and its evolution too is up to people,
people bringing the future into being.

Evolution. She felt a soft surge as of sea foam through her
veins.

All that summer she had heard about these noises off the
Atlantic coast, a series of great booms like sonic booms but not
sonic booms. The TV had reported them but could give no explanation. No one knew what they were. The little group that Julie was
one of, a group which kept in touch coast to coast as much by an
interlock of thought and feeling as by phone and letter, had all
come to think that what this might be—just might be—was the
signal that Atlantis was rising: the time had come ripe at last. At
Montauk Julie had stood sunburned on a headland in the salt
breeze, growing certain that it was about to be: that the blazing tip
of its pyramid would any moment break the rolling sea's surface,
then its towers and ramparts too, shedding green water, she knew it,
she just *knew* it.

She felt it still, that certainty, just as she still felt the burn on

her shoulders and the sweet tone of her muscles. She should tell
him: and tell him too that her certainty itself was part of what was
calling that drowned world back: like calling to like. She should.

"Okay," Pierce said beside her, hands in his pockets and a
guilty impatient air about him that she had used to know. "Okay."

"Okay," she said. And she placed on the bill a card of gold-
colored plastic.

She took a cab; Pierce walked home, the September sun in his
face and Julie's new business card in his pocket (midnight blue,
with the stars of Scorpio picked out on it in silver). In the fading
elation of his two scotches he could not tell if he was downcast or
triumphant.

The return of the magus, bearing in his hands the old potent
physics out of the past, secret doctrines decoded, the numbers of
the pyramid, was that in the end what he had to sell? Then he
would sell it. There *had* been a time when he had thought of
nothing else, when he had stood on his rooftop watching the grimy
spheres of heaven revolve around him, *Oh I see, I get it:* but to hear
those notions in another's mouth, unqualified, fitted to a different
kind of consciousness, made them sound at once loony and banal,
too much and not enough.

And yet were they not brave, those old mages, knights of
Ægypt, were they not heroes? Wrong as they may have been in
almost everything they thought they knew for sure, they *were* heroes, the more Pierce had read about them the more they had come
to be his own heroes. An Agrippa, a Bruno, a Cardanus about to
take up the wand, open the book of Hermes, incise strange geometries on a sheet of virgin wax: they may have thought they were only
tapping into the ancientest wisdom, only cleansing corrupt sciences
and restoring them to purity: but what they were postulating was a
new heaven and a new earth, and it *was* one like our own.

There were ten thousand dæmons in Bruno's heavens: but for
all its occult influences, for all its affinities and sympathies, the
magician's universe worked the way it did not because God or the
Devil was interfering in it, but simply because that was the way it
was. It was an immense, even a limitless universe, a nexus of spirit
and matter in which the magus's perceptions and aspirations were
bound up, it was far more full of possibility than the small, en-
closed, God-and-Devil-animated world of orthodoxy, and it was
natural. The true magus didn't need to believe in witchcraft, or in
miracles in favor of believers, because his universe was not only

large enough to contain reasons for any astonishing thing that happened, but so full of forces, world spirits, angels (themselves objects as natural as stones or roses) that anything was possible, any effect of desire or will working in the world.

So despite how wrong the magicians might have been about any given feature of it, and they could be wildly wrong and amazingly gullible, the *size* of their world, and the fact that not only did they not know all that it contained but knew—with joy—that it was *impossible* to know all that it contained, makes their minds like ours.

And not so incomprehensible then after all, or so inexpressible either.

Well then.

He was just then passing beneath one of the stone lions who guard the public library, and he sat there on the step and took a notebook from his pocket. The sun was dazzling. He wrote: "Travel backward to a lost land heard of in childhood; find it to be incomprehensible, rich, strange; then discover it is the place from which you set out."

Oh god you would have to be so careful though, so careful. Time *doesn't* return, turn full circle, and bring back what is past; what turns full circle is the *notion* that time will turn full circle, and bring back the past. That was the secret Pierce knew, the one he must tell. Time turned not in a circle but a spiral, sleeping and waking; any Golden Age perceived to have dawned again, or sad decline repeating itself, or new millennium come, creates in the very perception all the past Golden Ages, or declines, or rebirths, or millennia that it seems to be repeating, *Oh I remember, I remember:* we ascend upward through the spheres that seem to hem us in.

Wake up, his book must say, you can do nothing unless you wake up. Like Bruno shouting that the sun was rising: wake up.

Bruno himself should be the book's hero, in fact; Bruno with his cocksure announcing, Bruno with his infinitudes and his planets swimming through space like great placid beasts, alive alive-oh; Bruno with his endless impossible systems for remembering and thus mastering everything in the whole wide world—an enterprise that might after all turn out to be not so different from Pierce's own. "Mind, at the center of all, containing within itself all that it is the center of"—yes! Just as Pierce himself had felt the brains within him tightly packed with all that he had ever perceived, like a

Kodachrome movie reeled up tightly, and all colored too, for if the mind is not colored, then nothing is.

So could he not do that, then? Could he not entertain the notions that Julie thought would sell, the notions that brought that sudden sparkle to her eyes; could he not do that, and be paid to do it, while at the same time engaged on a different enterprise, the same he had been engaged on for so long: to grasp as in a hand the truth of stories patently false, to recover as a dream is recovered the dream-logic of history, because he had himself long dreamed it, and was now awake?

Could he? He could and would. If fools fell for the stories he would retail, let fools fall for them; for himself, he was *smart,* and if he did not know the way to say one thing which had the effect of another, a much more qualified, even a contradictory thing, then his long Catholic upbringing, his expensive education at St. Guinefort's and at Noate, had gone for nothing. We thank You O Lord (he blasphemed, exulting) that You have concealed these things from the simple, and revealed them to the wise.

They couldn't make Bruno give up his large world, in the end, and take their small one instead: and so in the summer of 1600, that white-numbered year, they took him from his cell in the Castel Sant' Angelo, and, dressed in white penitent's robe and seated backward on a donkey, he was led to the Campo dei Fiori, the Field of Flowers (Pierce imagined a meadow filled with June blooms) and there they tied him to a stake, and burned him.

But Pierce would not be burned: no, even if he aimed for the same powers, the same infinite grasp and freedom that Bruno had aimed for. That was the difference between then and now: Pierce would not be burned.

"So," said Allan Butterman to Rosie, inviting her with a hand to sit, elegant again in soft tweeds and a shirt blue as the October day. "So now."

"So," Rosie said. She swiveled slightly in her comfy chair, feeling quite at home here on her third visit. "It seems like it's okay, and he doesn't mind."

"Doesn't mind?"

"Well we had some talks. And he didn't really want to talk about anything legal. But I wanted to get it decided and over with. And he said he thought we should talk a lot more, and anyway he didn't like the idea of 'no fault' when it was me who walked out. So I explained to him what you said. What our options are."

Heart beating hard and throat dry, stuttering somewhat from overrehearsal, she had made her speech, explaining to Mike that if he didn't want to participate in a no-fault divorce she intended to sue him for divorce on the grounds of adultery. The awful weightiness of this, which seemed at the same time as weightless and illusory as some big scene in a movie, had ended discussion for the day; Mike, saying he was unsure of his ability to control his response, left the Donut Hole, neutral ground where at a deserted hour they had met.

It was a little like playing Rock, Scissors, and Paper, this countering of Mike's psychotherapeutic strategies with her new legal ones; sometimes when the hands came down she won, sometimes he, but at least she didn't always lose.

She had left it at that for a few weeks, feeling like a gambler who has put up a big stake and waits for the other side of the table to see it or fold; she pondered this scary and exhilarating sensation, the sensation of having power, of being out on a limb that was strong enough to hold her. When she thought she had waited enough, she made this appointment with Allan Butterman, and then called Mike to get an answer: Allan, she said, would have to know how he was to proceed.

And Mike had been reasonable. He had, apparently, lost interest in tormenting her about it all, as though he weren't up for the game; he had seemed—as since their separation she had felt him more and more often to be—distracted, not altogether there, to be on the point of turning away saying *Yes yes* half over his shoulder, his eyes elsewhere. Rosie supposed she knew the cause, though it surprised her.

"This same woman?" Allan said.

"The same one," Rosie said. "I thought it was just going to be a fling. It looks like it's more than that. It looks like he's kinda swept away. But really he's always been sort of a dope about women." That had used to be one of Rosie's real strengths, that Mike had been a dope about women, that she had known it and he had not. She swiveled thoughtfully in her swivel chair. "I wonder if he's still in his Down Passage Year."

"His what?"

"That's in Climacterics," Rosie said. "It's sort of a new science

Mike's inventing. I can't tell you a real lot about it, because I don't understand it really, and also because I'm not supposed to talk too much about it, it's basically a simple idea and he's afraid if the wrong person hears about it they'll steal it."

Allan stared at her, seeming to be pondering something other than Climacterics.

"It's about how life is divided up into these seven-year periods," Rosie went on, at least wanting to reassure Allan she wasn't talking nonsense. "Every seventh year you sort of hit a plateau, where you're pretty sure of yourself and have a good hold on things. Then gradually you descend, like on a curve, through a Down Passage Year; then you bottom out, and there's an Up Passage Year, and finally you plateau again, seven years later. Psychologically."

"Uh-huh," Allan said.

"It really sort of works," Rosie said. "You can draw it on a curve." It did sort of work; it described Mike's own life better than it did any other life he had applied it to, but Rosie remembered seeing her own ups and downs reflected pretty truly in the chart Mike had drawn for her shortly after he had worked out The Method, as he always called it, with those audible capitals. She remembered his excitement, passion even, and her own wondering assent, a winter's night years ago. . . . With a wholly unexpected heave, like a freak flood, she filled up suddenly with grief, and covered her eyes, a sob caught in her throat.

"Oh god," Allan said. "Oh don't."

She looked at her lawyer; his face was a shocked mask of pity. Her own rush of feeling receded before his. "Wow," she said, and snorted. "Sorry, sorry, where did that come from."

"No no," Allan said. "No, oh god it's just so rotten."

She laughed, fragments of her broken sob caught in it. "It's okay," she said. "You got a hankie?"

He proffered a box. "Go ahead," he said. "Go ahead and cry. That schmuck."

"Allan," she said, blowing her nose. "Really I'm okay. Calm down. What's next to do."

"This is exactly why I don't do divorces," Allan said, massaging his brow. "I just really can't take it."

"What now," Rosie said. "What now."

Allan cleared his throat vigorously, and drew out a long yellow pad, and one of the new sharpened pencils he always had (never dull or short, what did he do with used ones?) and tugged at his ear. "Okay," he said. "Okay. What we have to try to do is come to an agreement now, you and Mike and his attorney and I, about various matters pertaining to your life with Mike, and try to make it as mutually acceptable as possible, and simple enough that even the judge can understand it.

"So let's see. Let's make a list. First is custody, of, of . . ."

"Sam. Samantha. I'll get custody."

"Uh-huh." He didn't write. "And Mike?"

"I'm sure Mike won't want custody. We haven't really made it clear though."

"Uh-huh."

"I mean it's clear to *me*."

Allan favored her with a smile, a smile of almost professional approval, and wrote. "Well and you've got to be clear too about visiting rights, support, some kind of decision-making process about in*sur*ance, and *school*ing, and who informs who about when the kid goes to the *den*tist, the *hospital.* . . ."

"Okay."

"As long as you're still talking," Allan said. "If attorneys do it, it costs more, and maybe you get an agreement nobody likes but the attorneys."

"Okay. Okay." Her heart had filled. Sam.

"Support?" Allan said. "Are you working now?"

"I was," Rosie said. "Teaching art, at the Sun School."

"Oh yes."

"But it looks like they don't need me now." It looked like the little alternative school, housed in a small made-over mill in Stonykill, was going out of business, declining into mess and recriminations.

"If you can," Allan said, "it might be best to stay unemployed. Till after the decree." He drew a line across his pad. "Okay. Property to divide . . ."

"Not really anything," Rosie said. "A house, but the hospital paid the down payment and holds the mortgage, so. And then stuff. Just stuff."

"Stuff," said Allan, nodding. "Stuff." The way he had of speaking, that seemed to weight all his words with a huge burden of feeling: Rosie thought it must be a trick of some kind, or an effect he wasn't really conscious of. But then again maybe not, maybe he did feel the woes and pains of his clients as deeply as he seemed to: maybe, like a practiced weightlifter, he was able to support a larger burden than most people. A cowlick had sprung up from his plastered black hair, and his eyes were sad again. Rosie found herself liking him a lot. "I don't care about it," she said. "I don't really want any of it."

"Sure," Allan said. "You know, back when I *did* do a lot of divorces, everybody always said, 'I don't want any of it, let her have it, let him have it.' And you know what all the awful arguments, all the pain was always about? Stuff."

"Are you married?" Rosie asked.

"I used to sit here and listen to people grieving about a car, a TV, jewelry, a goddamn set of porch furniture, and I would think, how petty can people be, can't they rise above all that? Didn't their love mean more to them than these materialistic details? It took me some time to figure out that love is *in* the details. It's in the books and records and the stereo and the convertible. Love is always in the details. And that's where the pain is too." His eyes, sadder even, were on her, and his white hands folded before him. "*Not* married," he said. "It's a long story."

"I've been wondering something," Rosie said, beginning once again to swivel in her chair. "You know the old castle down in the middle of the river, on the island?"

"Butterman's."

"Was that you who built it, your family I mean?"

"Well sort of. Some distant connection. I've never worked it all out."

"I hear I own it. That the family owns it."

"I think that's right."

She smiled. "Not part of the settlement," she said, and Allan laughed, the first time she had seen him do so. "What I've always wanted to do," she said, "was go and go in. I never have."

"Neither have I."

"You want to, sometime?" She stretched out in her chair. "You being the family lawyer, and all."

He strummed his pencil on the leather drumtop of his desk. "I wanted to give you one funny piece of advice," he said. "You know that even if this no-fault approach works out, it's going to be about a year from the trial date before your divorce is final."

"Oh my god really?"

"Six months after the trial, you get a judgment nisi. *Nisi* is Latin for 'unless.' Unless something untoward comes up. Then there's a 'nisi period'—six more months, for you guys to think about it, and decide maybe you don't want it—"

"Hm."

"Or more importantly when you can file objections to the settlement. Objections saying that the other party acted fraudulently, or that new facts have come to light. Say, new facts relating to making a correct decision about custody."

Rosie said nothing.

"People don't always know how they feel at first," Allan said gently. "They can change their minds. And if they *do* change their minds, and if they *do* want to do something other than what they agreed to do at first, then they're going to be looking for grounds on which to make an objection. And they have a whole year to look. Okay?"

Rosie began to understand; she lowered her eyes, feeling reproached.

"All I want to say," Allan said, even more gently, "is that if uncomplicated custody is what you want, and what you can get now, then my advice to you is to be a model single parent until those final papers come. If you need to know what one is, I'll spell it out. And if you can't be a model single parent—if you can't be—then Rosie you ought to be a damn careful one."

Before she left town that day, Rosie stopped at the library, to return her latest Fellowes Kraft novel, and take out another. The one she returned was *The Court of Silk and Blood;* the one she chose, without much thought, was called *A Passage at Arms,* and had a seascape, galleons and a compass rose, on the cover. Afternoon was late when she drove out of the Jambs, autumn afternoon closing suddenly.

The things, she thought: the cars and house and stuff, all that to deal with. No marriage could be over till that was done. Hm.

She thought that probably Mike would find the stuff a big problem, but Mike was a Capricorn, a holder-on to things, and their disposition would always strike him as requiring a lot of thought. Rosie, however much of her soul she might hide in a pair of dangle earrings or a box made of inlaid woods, only and always avoided

stuff: life, it sometimes seemed to her, was an obstacle race, full of stuff to be leaped, skirted, lost and left behind. In her own natal chart (still in its manila envelope, now somewhat crushed, on the seat beside her) the second house—Lucrum, "like lucrative," Val said, "money, possessions, jobs, stuff like that"—was empty of compelling planets.

The sun set, leaving a glassy lavender and peach twilight in the cloudless West. In the mountains above Rosie's station wagon, deer walked, fattening on the apples of old orchards; down on the river, fallen leaves floated south, gathering in colored rugs at eddies and backwaters and on the shore of the little pleasure-ground that Spofford owned. At nightfall, a flock of migrating starlings return- ing to the towers of Butterman's made a banner in the air above the castle that snapped, as though in the wind, before the birds settled to rest.

By lamplight Rosie read *A Passage at Arms,* about buccaneers on the Spanish Main. That magician character who took Shake- speare's picture in *Bitten Apples,* the one whose crystal ball Boney had shown her, appeared in it, lending maps to Sir Francis Drake, plotting with the Queen against the Spanish. Rosie wondered whether really all of Kraft's books were sections out of the one story, cut out and offered individually, as a landscape painter might cut up a big view into little ones framed separately. The English won out over the Spanish, but the Spanish king, brooding spiderlike in his magic palace, planned revenge. Rosie took it back (late and foxed with autumn rain, Sam had left it outdoors) and chose another.

She would read them all, in the end; she would read them in Allan Butterman's waiting room and in waiting rooms at the court- house and the accountant's office (the affairs of her dissolving family were an impenetrable mess). She would read them standing on lines at the bank and the Registry of Motor Vehicles. She would read Sam to sleep with them, who at bedtime cared more to hear the peaceful sound of her mother's voice making grown-up sense than any story Sam herself would be required to grasp. She would put them down when her eyelids trembled to close, often past midnight, and pick them up when she woke, way too early to rise, before Mrs. Pisky or even Sam was afoot.

Yet Rosie was not, actually, a great reader. Cumulatively, she had not read a lot in her life; in normal times a thick book, a long tale, held no special attraction. Only at certain times, as though it

were an old fever contracted in childhood and breaking out periodically, did she fall into books; and when she fell in she fell all in. It
was escape: she was quite clear about that. Often she had known
just what it was she was escaping from—though during her first
year married to Mike, the year of John Galsworthy, she hadn't
known; and she hadn't at all understood the first outbreak, in some
ways the severest, the year her family moved to the Midwest and
Rosie worked her way steadily and blurrily through not only the
collected Nancy Drew but all of Mr. Moto and the Biography shelf
of a branch library too, reading lives that did not strike her as
materially different from fictions, learning facts she would never
altogether forget or ever remember exactly about Amelia Earhart,
W. C. Handy, Edward Payson Terhune, Pearl Mesta, Woodrow
Wilson, and a host of others. That year she walked continually in
her life carrying another life, the one inside books, the one that
engaged her the more intimately; her living was divided in two,
reading and not reading, as completely and necessarily as it was
divided into sleeping and being awake.

No more than about waking life did it occur to Rosie to pass
critical judgments on what she read. It engaged her or it didn't;
when it engaged her she could not have said why. Never, in her
intense period of reading mystery stories, did it occur to her to try
to figure out what the author was up to, what the solution was; she
thought once, looking back, that she hadn't really grasped initially
that these stories which she liked were mysteries, that each one
would have a solution; if she had read one that didn't, she would
not necessarily have felt cheated. What she really liked about them,
she thought, was the same thing she liked about biographies: they
went only one way.

There was a kind of novel that didn't, and made Rosie feel
uneasy: a kind of novel that it seemed you could only go about
halfway or two-thirds into before you somehow started coming back
out. All the incidents and characters that appeared in the first half
of the book, the ones that created the story, would reappear (sometimes even in approximately reverse order) to complete the story, as
though the book's second half or last third were a mirror image of
the first, with the ending exactly like the beginning except that it
was an ending. It wasn't that such books didn't resemble life; Rosie
didn't know if they did or didn't; but if they did, then it might be
that life too had a mirror half, that its direction all one way was

illusory, and Rosie didn't know this to be so only because she hadn't entered on the later, the cursory wrap-up part of her own life.

Once when she had picked up a novel at a tag sale she had found pasted on the fly leaf a yellowed newspaper review of it. The review seemed to like the book but complained of its somewhat mechanical plot. When Rosie read it she found it to be one of those with a mirror final third. So what she had been perceiving all along (she realized with surprise) was *plot*—a thing she might have said novels have and biographies do not, without knowing just what she meant by saying that. And now she knew.

And still she didn't know to what extent lives resembled novels by having plots, by having symmetries, falling into two parts, the long way in, the quicker way back out again. Certainly there was something mechanical about this picture; but there was no way— yet—to know whether life was in fact mechanical and symmetrical, or not. For sure when she sat with a Kraft novel in her lap, waiting in offices to further her divorce from Mike, it didn't seem an academic question; she thought she might very well be just halfway through her own story (if it had a halfway mark) and that so far from ditching her husband she was only establishing the conditions of his later and ineluctable appearances in the story. Which was his story too after all.

Kraft wasn't much help. Despite the forward tumble of history always proceeding in his books, proceeding (with an almost audible roar and mutter) from far past toward nearer past, all one way, the stories themselves which he told often had the mirror-shape of a plot. *Bitten Apples* had such a shape: right in the center of it that magician or scientist drew the diagram of young Will's horoscope, and put his planets in, and told him that he would not, unless he chose to fly in the heavens' face, make his living as a player upon the stage. And from there, scene by scene, the book walked back out through itself with great neatness. Rosie guessed that it would (saying "Oh no" aloud in comic dismay at breakfast so that Boney raised his bent head to see what she groaned at) as soon as Simon Hunt—Will's old teacher in Stratford, who snuck off to be a priest—appeared again before Will in London.

Now it was Hunt who was at bay, Hunt hunted, a Jesuit, a price on his head. Will, though tempted (only for a shameful second) to turn him in, saves the frightened priest, hiding him at one critical moment in full view of Walsingham's patrol: on stage, playing a farcical monk in an anti-Papist play, dragged down to hell by devils.

Good scene for a movie, Rosie thought.

And at the end Will was on tour of the provinces, and coming once again to Stratford by the Avon; at seventeen feeling old, and worldly-wise, and done with playing. The last long scene with his chastened father—as exactly distant, almost to the number of pages, from the end of the book as the very first interview was from the beginning. Come home, Will. Forgive me: forgive me.

And yet—Rosie wondered how it was done—there was not in this perfect symmetry of scenes the oppression she had felt in other books; it was all somehow encouraging. Maybe it was only her own knowledge, acquired outside these pages, of the further history which none of them who were inside the book could know: not John Shakespeare, not James Burbage (saying goodbye to Will by the property-wagon in Stratford innyard, brushing away a kindly tear but thinking himself well rid of the tall young man), not Will Shakespeare himself, turning back up the High Street for home.

It was time to settle down; time to take up his father's trade: a clean trade, however unexciting, that could support a man's age.

That could support—Will felt his heart rise, though his big sober feet fell in good order in the High Street—that could support a wife, and sons. A dark-eyed wife of Stratford town.

And if he worked steadily, he might one day erase from the town's long memory his adventure in London, and earn for himself the name of good citizen, credit to the town of Stratford—even, maybe, Gentleman.

Will went up to his father's door, his hand on the butt of an imaginary Gentleman's sword, slung at his side. In the innyard, Burbage's players set up the stage for the old play of Cæsar, stabbed in the Capitol.

Oh, corny, corny, Rosie thought almost laughing with pleasure, for there at the bottom of the last page, in large capitals, was not "The End" but

THE BEGINNING.

SIX

▲

One lamb had died; it lay, a wet lump, near its mother, who nuzzled it dazedly. Farther down the shed, a ewe had died delivering: beside her, a living lamb attempted to suck. Spofford lifted his lantern, in whose light his breath clouded, and carefully numbered them, so weary he almost could not keep count. The rest were all right. So: one dead lamb, its mother full of milk; and one motherless lamb. But the living ewe wouldn't give suck to the orphan; some instinct, smell, something, prevented it. So the orphan lamb would starve, unless Spofford began now to feed it by hand.

Or he could try an older method, that he had heard of from someone, who, he forgot who; he had in his mind the dim image of an old shepherd who had learned it from an older, and so on back through the years. Well all right.

He opened his knife, and working swiftly and almost automatically as though he had done this many times before, he took the thin wet skin from the dead lamb, pulling and cutting it free. When he had it, he took up the orphaned lamb, and after bundling it in the pitiful rag of its cousin's skin, he laid it by the dead lamb's mother.

The mother examined it, insofar as she could; she nuzzled it, and found it to be her own. At the disguised lamb's insistence, she let it suck: let it live.

How do you like that, Spofford marveled, bloody to the wrists of his sheepskin coat. Now how do you

"like that," he said aloud, waking.

It wasn't night in February, lambing time, but morning in December. It had snowed in the night, the first snowfall of the year;

a white light filled the loft of his cabin, so that he knew without raising his head that it had snowed.

Boy (he thought, stirring) sometimes they can be so convincing. So convincing.

He sat up, and scratched his head with both hands. His sheep-skin coat hung, clean, on a peg. He laughed aloud: that was a great trick with the lamb. He wondered if it would work. He hadn't—as far as he remembered—ever heard of it, though as a boy he had once hand-fed an orphaned lamb. For sure the aged shepherd whom, in the dream, he had remembered telling about it (apple-cheeked, with stump of pipe and lamb's-wool hair) was nobody he knew in waking life, a complete fiction.

Over breakfast he decided he would ask one or two sheepmen he knew in the county whether that switcheroo was a possibility. Whether it was a well-known old trick.

And if it was?

Washing up, he made a further decision. This seemed a day charged with significance: that dream, this snow-light, certain deeps seeming just for today to be open and plumbable within him. So when his chores were done he would go over to the Lodge to visit Val, a thing he had been intending to do for a long time. While he picked his teeth with a trout's bone he kept just for that purpose, he outlined in his mind what questions he would ask: what advice it was he was after, and on what matters.

Val's Faraway Lodge, in Shadowland, was closed for the winter season. Val always described this closing as though it were she herself who was being shut up for three months: "I'm closing on Thanksgiving," she would say. "I'll be closed till Easter." And in a sense Val too *was* closed. As soon as snow of any consequence began to fall, she stopped driving; her Beetle (into which big Val fit neatly, like a big clown into a tiny car in the circus) became a shapeless white hummock in her driveway, and only when it had lost its snowman suit in spring did she start it up again. Meanwhile she (and her old mother, who lived at the Lodge as well) depended on the phone, on the thoughtfulness of those passing her way, and on a certain talent for hibernation, a trick of living on the summer's pleasures, occupations, gossip, and news as on a store of accumu-lated fat. Even her store of physical fat seemed somewhat to shrink as the days grew longer toward the equinox.

The Lodge is a white frame low two-story building on the

Shadow River, almost unfindable down two dirt roads, its sign and its furnishings pretty well unchanged for thirty years. What Spofford often wondered, what he had never thought of a tactful way of finding out, was how long it was since the Lodge had ceased to be a whorehouse. That it had been one in living memory he had deduced from several hints dropped by local folk, from the general layout of the place (the bar and restaurant in front, connecting to the sitting room of the apartment behind, and several small rooms now unrented upstairs and in a wing shadowed by pines), and also from the character of Val's mother, Nanna, whom, now in retirement and functioning chiefly (according to Val) as Val's cross to bear, Spofford could easily imagine as a country madam: even though he had never known (not in this country) a country madam. She was nowadays given over to special communications with God and telling whoppers about her past that caused Val to snort and speak rudely to her. The two of them had never lived apart.

"It'll melt by tomorrow," Spofford said. "But I brought this stuff anyway. Put it in the larder." There were staples and delicacies and the carton of Kents she had asked for and a string bag of oranges.

"Was anything plowed?" Val said. She had only a vague idea of the realities of winter, but she liked to talk about it. "No? And you came out here with this stuff? Oh god you big brave brute!"

Spofford laughed. "It's not enough snow to fill the tire treads, Val."

She grinned at him, seeing through this piece of modesty, and showed the stuff to her mother. "Look, Ma. What do you think."

"He's a good boy," said her mother, beside her on the bed. "God will give him something special."

"Get God to do that," Val said. "Get God to fix a ticket for him."

"Don't you mock."

The two of them were sharing Val's bed before the big TV, which was on, showing a soap Val followed; she and her mother, wrapped in a quilt against the cold, pillows propped behind them and a coffeepot nearby, weren't exactly still in bed, or exactly up either; they were late and long risers. On the bed, with the *TV Guide* and the *Faraway Crier* and some gossip magazines, was a tray of dog's breakfast, and a dog, a little Pekingese with exactly the hair and the winning expression of the cartoon kid for whom he was named. He yapped and panted at Spofford.

"So anyway," Val said, and laughed her low infectious laugh; she had a way of laughing that way, at nothing, periodically, as though a party were always going on around her. "Your chart, right? You came for your chart."

"Kind of," Spofford said.

"It's not done."

"Well."

"It's almost done. You want to see? Dennis! Get your *foot* out of the food. Oh god look what he's done." She gathered up the dustmop dog, and pulled her big chenille gown around her; she rose, cocking up the cigarette in the corner of her mouth and squinting her eye against the rising smoke. "Come see."

There was a card table set up in the corner of the sitting room, with a lamp beside it, where Val worked. In between two fat Chinese sages of soapstone were her ephemerides, tables, and guides. A mug of colored pencils, red plastic ruler, compass, and protractor gave an impression of schoolchild's homework, but Val wasn't playing. She was respected in the Faraways; she made a good part of her living from the casting of horoscopes; there were those who wouldn't make a move without her encouragement. She bet that as many sought help here as in any minister's study in the county, and confessed to her their fears, and even wept in her big lap.

She put down Dennis, who shook himself carefully head to stump of tail; she drew out Spofford's chart from under a calculator and some sheets of typing paper scribbled over with figures. "The math kills me," she said. "It just kills me." She sat to study what she had done, motioning Spofford to sit too, in that chintz-covered maple chair, and drew an ashtray to her side.

Val well knew that there were a thousand ways to do what she had done, and endless further computations that could be made, if you had the patience and the skill to make them; but they were not useful to her. She worked her numbers only until she began to grasp a natal chart in the inward way or with the inward sense which was what made her good at this. And when that engagement happened her math began to be fruitful, the planets in their houses began to make sense, began to turn their faces on or away from each other, exalted, dignified, dejected, or confused; the little paper universe began to tick and tock, and Val could begin to work.

That was called "rectification of the chart." The reason for such rectification was obvious to Val: if all the babies who were born in a single hour in all the hospitals of a single city, all therefore under identical astral influences, would have fates and fortunes subtly or radically different from one another (and surely they would), then each soul on earth was subtly or radically different from every other, and that difference could not be apprehended in the mere accurate placement of planetary symbols in a scheme of houses. And in any case, as far as Val could tell there was no end to how accurate you could be, and with every advance in accuracy everything could change, a person's planets could slip from one sign or house into another, oppositions could be negated, squares turn into meaningless rhomboids.

No, what mattered always more than accuracy, more than math, was *apprehension:* the growing conviction that you had it right, that it made sense. Oh look here, Mercury is inconjunct with Saturn in the seventh house, of *course;* and your mother must have had her moon in Gemini, of *course* she did. When the twelve houses became to Val's mind's eye not wedges of an abstract pie but *houses*—and not anyone's houses but this soul's houses, houses that, ramshackle or sleekly marbled or grim and machicolated, could be no one else's—then, and only then, did she begin to speak.

"Houses," she said to Spofford. "There are twelve houses in a horoscope, and dwelling in them are planets. Twelve compartments of life, twelve different kinds of things life has in it, that's the houses; and seven kinds of pressures or forces or influences on those things, that's the planets. See? Now, depending on when and where you were born, and just what stars were coming up over the horizon just then, we arrange these houses one to twelve, counterclockwise from here, where you get born."

"Hm," Spofford said.

"The trick is," Val said, "that this chart is made of time, and so are these houses; and we have to turn them into places to be in.

"The first three houses, from here to here, are the first quaternary: the first fourth, see, because there are four sets of three in twelve, right? The first quaternary is dawn. And spring. And birth. Okay?" She fingered another cigarette from within her crumpled pack, and lit it. "Okay. The first house is called *Vita:* that's Latin, you shmoe, you wouldn't know it. *Vita:* Life. The House of Life. Little Spofford gets born, and begins his journey."

She went on, pointing out to Spofford where his planets lay, in which houses, and whether they were comfortable there, or even exalted, or quite the reverse, and what it all might portend for Spofford's fate, and for his happiness, and for his Growth. He listened happily, intrigued and satisfied to hear himself articulated into parts in this way, his inchoate self set up in neat geometries, and the general dun color of his soul (as he perceived it usually) broken by the prism of his chart into a spectrum of clear hues, some broad bands, some narrow ones.

"What's this?" he asked; a line from Saturn in its own twelfth house—*Carcer,* the Prison—connected to Venus, just opposite in the sixth house.

"Opposition," Val said. "Challenge. Saturn in the twelfth house can mean isolation. Self-discipline. Aloneness, gloomy hermit stuff. Uh-uh. Opposed to Venus in *Valetudo,* the sixth house, which is the house of service sort of; there, she means bringing harmony to other people's lives. Sometimes by intervention, getting your two cents in and helping out. Okay?"

Spofford looked down at this tussle. "So who wins?"

"Who knows? That's the challenge." She dispersed smoke with a wave of her hand from before her. *"But.* There's more. See: here's Mars right next door in the seventh house, that's *Uxor,* the Wife; and old Mars is trine with Saturn over here, and when two planets in opposition have a third planet that's sextile to one and trine to the other, that's called an Easy Opposition. Easy because no matter how hard the opposition, it's balanced by the big weight of the third planet.

"Mars in *Uxor!* Means maybe a romance started on an impulse, that you just never get out of. One of those with a lot of yelling, you know? Or it could make for real strong partners in a marriage, buddies to the end.

"That's up to you."

Done with what she knew so far, Val crossed her hands on the table before her.

"Well," said Spofford.

"Well."

"Basically," he said, tugging down his cap, "what I hoped to find out about was the future."

"Yeah?"

"About a certain woman. My chances. How it looks from here."

"What certain woman? Hey, take it easy. I don't want to know her name. But astrally. What's her sign?"

"I can never remember. I think Pisces."

"Pisces and Aries aren't all that great, first off," Val said. "But there's so many factors."

"Not all that great?"

"Fire and water," Val said. "Remember. And Aries is the youngest sign. Pisces is the oldest."

Spofford regarded the chart which Val had turned toward him. He seemed to be able to discern in it anyway all that he needed for the moment to know. Saturn, the pull of melancholy, his small house; a gray sad stone, like the gray sad stone he seemed to feel so often in his own breast. Solitude.

But Venus, Saturn's soft-smiling opposite number . . . An old soul, Rosie had said to him once, a jolly old soul, in an old old water sign. He'd already intervened: he would fight for her too, if fighting could help. And Mars, fiery, his own planet, inhabited the house of taking wives (Spofford's scarred forefinger touched the sign, ♂); and had not he, Spofford, been a warrior? Maybe he could get some help here, if it came to it. Like the GI Bill.

Shine on, then, he thought; shine on. "It don't look bad," he said, rising. "It looks all right."

When he was gone, Val sat for a time with her hands folded before her, and then with her chin resting in the cup of one hand, and then with both hands laced behind her head.

Rosie Mucho had better be careful, she thought. That guy has set his cap for her. He's got a moon in Taurus, too, a whim of iron. Rosie had better be ready for that.

She turned in her chair. Behind her on the bookshelves were several old-fashioned letter files, the kind with orange backs and black-and-white spatterdash spines, little brass clips to close them with, and leather tabs on their sides to draw them out by. She chose one of these, opened it, and after a little search amid its contents drew out a twelve-part pie chart like the unfinished one she had been explicating for Spofford, only all different, different domiciles housing different guests differently disposed. She placed it next to Spofford's, and cradling her brow with one hand and drumming with the fingers of the other, she studied both together.

Pisces: Love and Death. That's how Val thought of the sign. Chopin was a Pisces. Only here was a commonsense ascendant, Taurus with Venus in the House of Life.

Well, she was a good girl, and probably a survivor, but a little crazy; more crazy than she probably knew. Moon in Scorpio: Scorpio is Sex and Death.

She had better be careful.

The snow continued, growing heavier, through that day and the night; the big plows came out toward morning, sailing ghostlike behind their bright lights, their blades casting aside long wakes of snow. Next day when the sun shone at last the world had been neatly packed up in it; Spofford's sheep were not so round, or so white, or so soft, as the hills and woods seen from the kitchen windows of Arcady where Rosie stood waiting.

"Pst," said the tall radiator.

"Pst," said Sam, half in and half out of her snowsuit but ready enough to go that Rosie needed only to encase her upper half and put her out the door. The snowsuit's arms and hood hung down like a pelt Sam was shedding.

"Psst," said the radiator.

"Pssst," said Sam, and laughed.

"*There* he is," said Rosie, gratefully, "right on time."

"I wanna see."

Rosie lifted her up to see a little red car turn in at the gate, fishtailing somewhat in the heedless snowplow's leavings piled there in the driveway.

"I hope they're careful," Rosie said to Sam, pulling up the Siamese twin of her snowsuit and tucking Sam into it.

"It's slipry."

"Yep."

"Daddy can drive."

"He can?"

"You could come too."

"Not this morning. I'll see you later."

Rosie hurried Sam through the house to the vestibule and swung open the heavy front door. In the drive the little red car idled, trembling as though with cold, and breathing whitely from its tailpipe. Mike made his way toward the house carefully, holding out gloved hands for balance.

"Hi."

"Hi. Okay? Hi, hi Sam. Hey." He gathered up the wrapped bundle of his daughter and squeezed her; Rosie, embracing herself, cold in the open doorway, waited for their colloquy. Sam had news. Mike listened.

"So what's up today?" Rosie said at last. "What's the schedule?"

"I don't know," Mike said, looking not at Rosie but at Sam, whose fingers were in his mustache. "Maybe build a snowman, huh? Or a snow fort."

"Okay!" Sam said, wriggling to get down. "Or a snow *car!* Or a snow *hops* pittal."

"Hey, but not *here,*" Mike said. He put her down. "We'll go home and make one."

"Hey," Rosie said to him, warningly.

"Okay."

She gave Mike a zippered case. "Blankie. Bottle for later. *Don't* give her milk in it while she naps; dentist says. Book. Stuff."

"Okay," Mike said. "Ready?"

Sam, standing between them, looked from one to the other, still new at this choice.

" 'Bye, Sam. See you later."

"Come on, Sam. Mommie's cold in the doorway. Let's let her go inside."

Sam still would make no voluntary move to go, so Mike at last with a cheerful Whee! picked her up again and carried her off like a pirate, almost taking a header on the snowy path. The little car harrumphed. Mike climbed into the driver's side, pushing Sam in before him, must be a little crowded in there Rosie thought, but she knew Sam liked that car.

Rosie waved. Bye-bye. She smiled. She waved again, a grownup's wave, for the car, no hard feelings. She went inside and shut the door. The last segment of caught winter air went off down the hall.

Boney stood at the hall's end, hands behind his back.

"It's sort of okay," Rosie said. "Sort of like having a good babysitter. Free." She hadn't uncrossed her arms, they still hugged her. "He never spent this much time with her before. Never tried this hard to please her."

Boney nodded, slowly, as though considering this. He wore an old old turtleneck sweater, its stretched neck-opening far too wide for his own skinny turtle's neck which protruded from it. "Did you have anything planned for this morning?" he said.

"No."

"Well," he said, pondering. "I'd like to have your advice about something. Talk something over."

"Sure, sure."

"What say?"

"I said *sure,*" Rosie said, releasing herself and coming to Boney's side, no need to make him shout. "Sure. What kind of something?"

"If you're sure you've got nothing else to occupy you," Boney said, watching her closely.

"I haven't got anything else," Rosie said smiling, taking the arm he offered her and squeezing it gently. "You know I don't."

"Well," he said, "this might be a good opportunity then. We'll just go down along to my office there."

Every time, every time Mike went off with Sam, Rosie felt it, this cloud of guilt and loss that was absurd and unusable, a cloud she refused to stand under and yet couldn't get rid of—it was like that dream she had used repeatedly to have in the first months of Sam's life, that somebody with a right to judge had decided that Sam wasn't hers, or that Rosie wasn't competent to raise her and would have to give her up: the same sense of guilt and loss, the awful shriving off of her adulthood, and at the same time that feeling of being once again free and alone, like a child—a sneaky sense of freedom and solitary possibility that was no substitute for Sam, but was there anyway. Now either this cloud came from that dream, or both this cloud and that dream came from the same place, and what was that? Guilt, guilt over not wanting to grow up, could that be it; not wanting in your own secret kid's heart to be double or triple but only and forever single—and then loss, too, loss of everything dear to you, everything earned in growing up.

Everything, everything dear to you but yourself.

"Here we are," Boney said, opening narrow double doors and showing her in.

Rosie had never been in what was called the office, though Boney had often been spoken of, when she was a child, as being there, occupied there, not to be disturbed there; she had used to picture him denned and brooding like a dark mage, but supposed now, hearing again in memory those injunctions, that Boney had probably been taking a nap.

And in fact in the corner there was a buttoned leather chaise-longue with an afghan thrown over it which looked pretty cozy.

"The office," Boney said.

It had once been and was still mostly a library; handsome bookcases of some light wood reached up to a coffered ceiling all around the room, even in between the deep tall windows that looked out to the garden; and they were all full, though not entirely with books, there were letter files and what seemed to be shoe boxes, and piles of old newspapers and magazines on the shelves as well.

"Mike comes every week, does he?" Boney asked, moving a pile of mail from the seat of a leather swivel chair.

"Yup." She glimpsed what he might be driving at. "I mean just temporarily. Really, really, you know, I don't intend to hang on here the rest of your life. It's just until . . ."

Until what?

"Don't get me wrong," Boney said, having laboriously cleared himself a seat, and taken it. "You're more than welcome. I was only wondering—if you are pretty sure you're not taking up again with Mike—how you're fixed for money."

Rosie sat down on the chaise-longue.

"The little school," Boney said. "That wasn't really steady."

"No."

"What I was going to suggest—well, let's start from the beginning." He leaned back in the chair, it creaked stiffly, seeming as old and in need of oiling as Boney. "You understand about the Rasmussen Foundation."

"Well, I know there is such a thing. I mean I don't really know how it works."

"It's just the family money, what's left of it, that was put into a nonprofit corporation, and used for funding worthwhile sorts of things. Things my brother or I were interested in or that the community needed." He grinned his ivory-toothed grin, and gestured toward a trio of steel filing cabinets that stood incongruously against the wood paneling. "That's our business nowadays, you see," he said. "Giving away money, instead of making it."

"Whom do you give it to?" Rosie asked, wondering for a moment if he intended to offer her a grant, and how he would justify that.

"Oh, people apply," Boney said. "You'd be surprised, the requests we get. Most of it goes to the same people every year, continuing grants: the Blackbury Jambs Library, the wildlife sanctuary, the Parr Home. The Woods."

He glanced up at her, the wrinkles rising along his spotted pate.

"There's a board of directors," he went on. "They meet once a year, and approve the grants. But it's me who sends them the proposals. They pretty much approve what I send them. If they're all in the proper form, and all."

"You're not going to give me one, are you," Rosie said laughing. "For being a good guy and a help to the community?"

"Well, no," Boney said. "I hadn't thought of that, exactly. What I was coming to was that in the last couple of years the proposals just haven't been getting to the board." He slowly laced his hands together. "And there's other business that's not getting done, that ought to be done."

"You need help? If you need help . . ."

"I was going to offer you a job."

Boney at his big desk, hands folded in his lap, head almost lower than his shoulders, was dark against the tall windows and the snow. It struck Rosie for the first time with clarity that Boney was certainly, and not long from now, going to die.

"I should help out," she said. "Just for room and board. I would. I'd be happy to." A lump had begun to form in her throat.

"No, no," Boney said. "There's too much work. A full-time job. Think it over."

Rosie thrust her cold hands in between her knees. There was, of course, nothing to think over.

"I hope," Boney said softly, "you're not insulted. Working for wages for the family. I do it, Rosie. It's sort of all that's left."

Now tears gathered swiftly in her eyes. "Sure I'm insulted," she said. "Sure. Say, listen, isn't it really freezing in here? Do you ever start up that fireplace?"

It was clad in green serpentine, and a brass screen in the shape of a peacock stood before it. There was a brass basket of kindling and logs, and a set of brass tools, and a box of long matches. "I never do," Boney said, rising effortfully and going to look at the fireplace as though it had just then opened up in the wall. "Mrs.

Pisky doesn't like to see them lit. Sparks on the rug. Smoke in the drapes."

Rosie had knelt before it and moved aside the peacock. She pulled open the flue. "What do you think?" she asked.

"Okay," Boney said doubtfully. "If you'll take the blame."

"I will," Rosie said. "How about some paper?"

Boney turned back to his desk, and after sorting briefly through the mail, brought her most of it. "One thing, when you're thinking it over," he said, "that I thought might interest you. You remember I told you that Sandy Kraft once worked for the Foundation."

"I think you said so. What did he do?"

"Oh, research. Various things. In the old days."

"Uh-huh," Rosie said.

"Anyway. Now his copyrights are owned by the Foundation. And every now and then we get some interest in them. The reprint rights. And I thought, since you seemed so interested in them yourself."

"Uh-huh." She set fire to the mail and kindling and wood with one of the long matches. The chimney drew nicely. "I see."

"And more," Boney said. "More than that." He stroked his bald head. "His house. It belongs now to the Foundation, and nobody has been in it since he died. To see what's there." Rosie couldn't see his eyes behind the fire reflected in his blue glasses. "I can't do it."

"Uh-huh."

"So. Think it over, why don't you, and if you think . . ."

"Boney," she said. "I'm on."

"Oh," he said. "Well, we'll have to talk about hours, and salary and all. . . ."

"Yeah, sure," Rosie said. "I mean yes, of course we will, sure. But I'm on." She smiled at him reassuringly.

"Hmp," said Boney, looking down at her where she knelt on the hearth, pleased or a little disconcerted by her swift decisiveness. "Well. Okay." He put his hands in his pockets. "Good."

He turned away to the bookshelves behind her. Rosie began to notice things in the room she hadn't noticed before. The steel filing cabinets seemed somewhat to be bulging, just able to contain their contents. There were several cardboard boxes in the corners, which seemed to be full of waste paper, or maybe unanswered mail, neglected proposals.

The Woods, huh. Mike had hinted that The Woods was in some financial difficulties. She warmed slightly to think she might have some power over them. If only an expediting power. Or a delaying one.

"This," Boney said, returning with a book he had taken from the shelf. "You might be interested in this."

It was called *Sit Down, Sorrow,* and it was by Fellowes Kraft.

"A limited edition," Boney said. "A memoir. Just a couple hundred copies printed by a small press. You might learn something there."

"Well," Rosie said. "Wow." There were a few photographs tipped in. The deckle edges of the fat paper it was printed on were crumbling in tiny splinters. Rosie opened it and glanced at a page.

> I am sometimes asked how one can keep at his fingertips all the details not only of historical event but of dress and food and custom and architecture and commerce that are needed to make a historical novel convincing. Well, I suppose enough notebooks and *aides-memoire* of various kinds can be used, but in my case, even though I don't have a particularly capacious brain, I carry all that I need within, for I have these many years practiced a system of mnemonics that has proved capable of retaining an almost limitless number of facts in an ordered way, and which works in what strikes many people as a very curious manner indeed.

"It's too cold now," Boney said, and it took Rosie a moment to understand that he was still talking about Fellowes Kraft's house. "It's too cold now, with the heat off and the electricity. But in the spring."

"Sure," Rosie said. What was that expression in *Bitten Apples,* that they used for the old Queen? In her crazy white makeup and red wig and jewels and rings ... A fabulous monster. That's what Boney is, she thought, watching him warm his old claws at the fire she had made. A fabulous monster.

"In the spring," he said, seeming to have fallen partly asleep. "In the spring. You'll go in, and see."

"Each of the twelve signs," Val said to Beau Brachman, squatting uncomfortably on Beau's floor and dying for a smoke, "each of the twelve can be sort of summed up or reduced to a single word."

"One word?" said Beau, cheek in hand and smiling.

"Well, one *verb,* I mean, with I. Like 'I do' or 'I can.' Every sign has one, that sort of sums up that sign."

"Uh-huh," Beau said. "Like . . ."

"Like I'm about to *tell* you," Val said.

She had been brought into the Jambs on this sloppy January day by Rosie Mucho, who had left Val to make her visits while Rosie did business with Allan Butterman, her own and Boney's; later she and Val were to go together to the Volcano in Cascadia and consume plates of South Seas tidbits and drink Mai Tais in the bead-curtained lounge, while Rosie caught Val up on her troubles and triumphs.

"Aries," she said. "The first sign. Aries says *I am.* The first sign, right, the youngest of all. Then Taurus, Taurus says *I want.* Material desires, see, very big with Taurus. Get the idea? Gemini, Gemini says . . ." She suddenly looked at Beau sideways and raised an admonishing finger. "You're not *listening,*" she sang out warningly.

"I hear you, Val," Beau said. "I hear you."

"I know you think this stuff is bullshit."

"No, I just think . . ."

"You think the whole thing is a big prison. That's what you told Mama."

"I *know* it's a big prison. Destinies. Stars. Signs. Houses. Little words and verbs. All that you're saying, Val, with all of that stuff, is *This is the way you're stuck.* But you're *not* stuck. There's a word for all of this stuff you work with: *Heimarmene.* A Greek word. It means fate or destiny, but it means prison too. And the thing is not only to understand where you're at—what your sign is and your destiny right now—but to break through it too, break through the spheres that bind you in." He had gotten excited enough to rise from his crosslegged ease. "I have *all* those twelve signs in me, Val. I have all those verbs. All those seven planets, or eight or nine. They're all mine. If I want to be a Taurus, I will be. Or a Leo or a Scorpio. I don't have to work through all twelve in endless lifetimes. That's what *they* want." He gestured upward. "But it's not so."

"They?" Val asked.

Still smiling, Beau slowly put his forefinger to his lips. Silence.

"You nut," Val said, marveling. She laughed aloud. "You crazy nut."

"Oh listen," Beau said, struck by a sudden thought. "Are you by any chance going to the bank today? The one on Bridges Street, is that yours? Because can you make a deposit for us? We're holding all these January checks we just got. . . ."

"Capricorn," Val said, aiming a gunlike finger at him. *"I have."*

There were heavy footsteps just then on the stairs outside, and someone tried the door. Beau and Val listened curiously as the someone tried to insert a key, and failed; swore; peered in through the tiny and winter-fogged window in the door, shading it with his hand.

"Come in," Beau at length called out. "It's not locked."

Some further fumbling, and a large man in a long salt-and-pepper overcoat stood on the welcome mat, wet and distracted, looking from one to the other of them. There was something about him (Val thought) of an unfinished Gary Merrill type. Not bad. A Sagittarius, she almost instantly concluded. A Sagittarius, definitely.

"Sorry," he said. "I thought it was empty. I was told it was empty."

"Nope," said Beau.

"Is this the one for rent?"

"The apartment? No." He showed it with a hand. "It's mine."

"Is this Twenty-one Maple?"

"No. This is the even side. This is Eighteen. Twenty-one is right opposite."

"Oh. Sorry. Very sorry."

Beau and he looked quizzically at each other for a time, each trying to remember where and when he had met the other, and failing. Then Pierce Moffett turned and left.

"A Sadge," Val said, reaching by instinct for her Kents, and putting them back again in her bag, no smoking at Beau's. "I bet a dollar."

"And what's his verb?" Beau said, still trying to place the intruder.

"His verb? Lemme think. Sagittarius. Scorpio is *I desire,* and then Sagittarius . . . Sagittarius is *I see.* That's it. *I see."* She drew the bowstring of an imaginary bow, and aimed along the arrow. "Get it? *I see."*

The upstairs apartment at Number 21 across the street was empty, as promised, and the key which Pierce had been given by the lady at the real estate office did open the door. He stood dripping onto the linoleum of the kitchen, which the key had let him into, and looked down the length of the place, which was disposed in railroad fashion, like his old slum apartment had been. Beyond the bleak but large kitchen was a minute sitting room, with a nice tall arched window. Beyond that was the largest room by far, wainscoted strangely in painted wood and with a ceiling of stamped tin: it would, he supposed, have to function as bedroom and study in one.

Peculiar. Inconvenient. But possible.

Beyond the windows of the large room, through a glass door, was a sun porch, running the width of the apartment: a narrow sun porch with casement windows. And beyond that the Blackberry River and the Faraways, for the apartment faced outward that way.

Here in the kitchen he would make and eat his meals; there, he would sit to read. Beyond, in there, he would sleep and work; and once a month, at a desk there, he would write a check for the absurdly small sum they were asking for this place.

And beyond, out there, he would sail the porch. Just as he had once used to sail a narrow second-story porch of the Oliphant house in Kentucky long ago. Vigilant; calm; his hand on his wheel; sailing at treetop level a sun porch windowed like a dirigible's gondola, or the bridge of a steamship headed east.

SEVEN

▲

The reasons why Pierce in the end really did leave Barnabas College and the city and go to live in Blackbury Jambs in the Faraway Hills were the same reasons for leaving he had once given to Spofford: love and money.

Love and money, both striking at once, on the same day, like Danaë's golden shower: so that though it took him some months to actually accomplish the move, it would always be clear to him on what day he had begun to move, or to be moved.

It was an oddity of Pierce's love life that he had never courted any woman he had ever been deeply attached to: had never first noticed, and then considered, and then flirted with, considered further, wooed, made slow progress toward, and won. His big affairs—he could count them on one hand and have fingers over—had each begun with a sudden collision, a single night or day in which the whole of the succeeding affair was contained in small, all its liberties, sympathies, pains only needing to be unfolded from then out. It wasn't exactly love at first sight, for usually the initial collision was followed by a period of suspension, even indifference, with Pierce enjoying his conquest or his good luck and checking off another course in the banquet of life, more where that came from. But the collision had deflected him; he ran parallel to her then, and she (axiomatically) to him. They were in for a penny that first night, but Pierce at any rate was in for a pound as well.

Pierce, awake too early on an ashen December morning and reviewing his history with the torpid clarity of hangover, could not think of an important exception. It had happened so with every one.

It had happened so (Pierce shifted beneath the covers of his messy bed, which he could not seem to leave) with Penny Pound, the girl with the smoky eyes and the thin scars on her wrists with whom he had fled to sunny California just at the beginning of his sixth semester at Noate. She'd had to be back in her dorm at eleven that first night, and he had headed dutifully that way with her after a postmovie coffee shared in the communal kitchen of his rooming house in town; and on a street corner halfway between his place and the dorm they had stopped to kiss; and as though turning through a revolving door without going out (though ending in a new place nonetheless) had almost wordlessly turned back. Pierce next day had not felt noticeably different than he had the day before; he got her back into her dorm and saw nothing of her for a week. And then when they met again it was all as it would be; they were inseparable, her huge and unresolvable griefs were his, her young body and her old hands; if some wise elder (his own elder self, except that his own elder self had never learned it) had advised caution and circumspection, he wouldn't have understood the advice. True, the first time she said she loved him (at Sam's house, he had taken her there for a long weekend, they lay *en deshabille* in the old schoolroom while two doors away his mother placidly pasted trading stamps into a book) he had been unable to respond—but only because he was awed by the words, which it was his assumption could only ever truly be said once, and for good. Once they were said, running off with her was mere practical necessity; in those days of universities standing *in loco parentis* (nowadays they didn't even know that lingo) the two of them were barred from cohabiting, from coitus too if they could be caught at it, and she was the first woman he had both loved and lain with, so there was nothing for it but to cash in their just-paid-for class-admittance cards like chips—his had been paid for with a scholarship, no matter, by an oversight he was allowed to liquidate them anyway—and use the money to flee; and though when he staggered from the bus at a rest stop into the unreal sunshine of Albuquerque he did for an awful moment think What have I done, he didn't ever, then or later, certainly not on the long bus ride back east alone, back into winter and the string of lies he had left behind him, ever really think he had much choice in the matter.

Well, he had been very young, and so had she; it was hardly an unusual story, was it? He might be forgiven, he thought, considering; considering his upbringing, considering the tenderest part of his adolescence constrained within the halls and gyms and endless males of St. Guinefort's; might be forgiven his surprise and lack of cunning on finding himself loved and laid at once. Certainly he had suffered for it, atrociously, extravagantly, he had almost slit his own wrists, not out of romantic disillusion but simply because he couldn't bear to stand a moment longer in the storm of loss she had left him in, he bareheaded and unable to conceive how she could behave in such a way.

Yet he couldn't blame only that thoughtless child for the extravagance of his grief, as wholly surprising as the suddenness of love; nor could he blame on youth alone an obtuse innocence that had persisted long beyond youth.

What was it then? Was it growing up a single child with impossible, queer, chivalric Axel in Brooklyn, was it the isolation of the Oliphant compound in Kentucky? Who had taught him, who had shaped his heart in this strange way? Somehow, somewhen it had been communicated to him that there *was* a door you passed through, and rarely, only if potent stars conspired together; a door opening to a heart, a body, both made in heaven or in some fire just as refining. And then there you were; it was a *hortus conclusus;* he had no more been taught that there was a way back out again than he had been taught that the way in—which he had discovered all by himself with such astonishment, such horrid joy—was a beaten path. A beaten path.

He laughed shortly, and coughed on bitter spittle. He laced his hands together on his breast and looked up into the large and ornate mirror that hung above, cantilevered from the wall in such a way that it reflected the bed: reflected, just now, himself to himself.

Those who do not remember their own histories, he thought, are condemned to repeat them.

By the time he had met Julie Rosengarten, he had shed that ignorance, or rather had not shed it but at least had clothed it decently; he could well think of that one night with her (one really kind of strangely wonderful night) as no collision but a mere ding in the then-thickening sexual traffic of adulthood and swinging Manhattan. She hadn't heard from him for six weeks, but six weeks after their second date they were wearing each other's sweaters, they had a dog in common, and Pierce was thinking how to bring up the subject of a Mixed Marriage to his mother and Sam. A year later he was still hanging on, obtusely, innocently, for good and all, while Julie conducted a flamboyant affair with the upstairs neighbor, which she just couldn't get Pierce to notice. In the final division of property the dog, after a moment's hesitation, chose to go with Julie.

Farce plot. My wife. My best friend. My dog.

Women, he could only conclude, extrapolating from his own experience up to this December day, were naturally polygamous, whatever the common wisdom said to the contrary; able to love deeply and forever for a while, to go off suddenly and spectacularly in all directions like one of those immense fireworks that eject a globe of stars as solid as can be, which hangs in the colored night for an eternity, a brief eternity, the length of an awed exhalation from the spectators, and then goes out as though it had never been. And men (take himself, for a single example) were naturally monogamous, bound by the literal meaning of the promises they made and the actual endurance of the forever those promises contained. *En ciel un dieu, en terre une déesse,* as the old Provençal poets put it. How the stories had got around, so superficially convincing, so widespread, that matters were otherwise, he didn't know. He could suppose a cabal; or, what was more likely, that in an older world, a world he didn't live in, those stories had been true; and only now, now that the world was as it was and not as it had been, were women able to unmask and unfold and be as their natures dictated. The Pill and all that. Who the hell knew. In any case, should he not by now have learned that it was so, and learned to act on it, no matter what his history, no matter what dim antiquity his character had been forged in or out of what medieval materials? And if he found himself suddenly (all in a night, all in one snowy night) wandering in the pages of an erotic novel, a piece of pornography of the best modern kind, he with a heart and vitals shaped for some other age, some other book entirely, didn't it behoove him to learn the ropes there before he just leaped right out of his skin?

Just be a little careful, he had told himself that night, lying beside her sleepless and astonished; just for God's sake be a little careful this time. But it did no good. A whole winter intervened, and when she returned from Europe he was hers, had of course all along been hers; the high life they entered into only veneered his uxoriousness with a knowing air, while ravening lewdness intensified his monogamy, and gave it secret rein. Maybe, maybe, if he'd had to knock, and woo, finagle and cajole—but when all portals, all, all, were flung open to him, the rest was already as it would be, foregone, including his lying here now staring up at his mirrored self staring back down at him, hands folded on his breast, big feet protruding from the bedclothes, big face vacant. Foregone.

Like the Bourbons, he had forgotten nothing and learned nothing; and he was here again where he had been. His history repeated itself, and if the first time was tragedy, and the second time farce (as Marx said, in the other context, the context from which Pierce helplessly drew these bitter clichés) then what did that make the third time, and the fourth?

Day was full, as full as it would grow today, and the radiators hissed furiously. Pierce flung off the bedclothes, but didn't arise; he lay contemplating (he couldn't do otherwise, the ormolu mirror was carefully pitched so as to be unavoidable) his long nakedness. Big hands, big feet: in his case the common computation worked out correctly.

You know what? she'd said to him that first night, said to him with her look both sly and frank. *You know what? You got a nice cock.*

A cold wave surged in his blood, memory of desire and certainty of loss; Pierce watched it come and pass, like some kind of attack, vertigo or angina.

This isn't funny, he thought. I'm not that young anymore. I can't take it. This time around was like a disease, a disease he couldn't shake off, one of those childhood diseases that the young and strong survive, a few days in bed, but that cripple the grownup.

Stay me with flagons, comfort me with apples, for I am sick of love. Sick sick sick.

I will take vows, he thought, that's all; I will take fucking vows. If, after two marriages (of course they were marriages in fact only, just as some marriages are marriages in name only—but of course there exactly it was) and a sex life that seemed to him as varied and violently satisfying as any normal man's had any right to be, there was still in him this innocence he should long ago have shed but had not, an innocence that would just go on doing him this dreadful harm, then the best thing he could do would be to choose solitude.

"Take vows," he said aloud to the man above him, pale lean and ready for autopsy (look nurse this man has no uh-oh valve on

his heart, his penis is completely detached from his brain). Just give
it up. Thanks but no thanks.

He didn't have to be about love; he was a man not a novel. He
supposed there must be other pleasures life held, other goals beyond
or different from the enormous blisses of encompassing sexual
thralldom. They seemed to rise, far off, on an expanding horizon,
though he couldn't concretely imagine them. Fame. Orderliness.
Quietude. Money, goods, a connoisseurship of—well of the world
and the self somehow; the pleasures of solitude, not solitude he fell
into or was forced into as into a cell whose bars he could only shake
in impotent grief, but solitude elected, embraced. He had a poi-
gnant vision of himself, a different person in another place: self-
sufficient, a confirmed bachelor, a careful pleasant gent no one can
quite figure out—an eccentric, keeps to himself, has that beautiful
house full of nice things. And he an *objet de vertu* in his own right,
seen walking into town for the Sunday papers, dressed dandily and
peculiarly, plus-fours and a knobby walking-stick, a dog beside
him. Salt moisture burned in Pierce's eyes. A faithful dog.

Something to wish for: something else to wish for, something
different from what could be reflected in a mirror above a broad
bed . . . If he could wish now, he would wish for something to wish
for.

A bell rang with tearing urgency just then, flinging Pierce out
of bed and into a startled posture of defense, a ready crouch. The
phone. No not the phone. The doorman. The doorbell. It was the
doorbell, who on earth, he grabbed up a terrycloth robe and belted
it around him. The doorbell burped again, a reminder, someone was
still there.

"Yes?" He could see nothing through the foggy peephole.

"Pierce," she said. "It's me. Can I come in?"

The adrenaline that had been pumped throughout him all in an
instant by the bell was washed away in an instant by a new fluid, a
cold stinging one that drowned his heart and was in the tips of his
fingers and toes even before his hand had reached the lock to open
it. Still he could marvel at how fast it went. Now how did flesh and
nerves manage such speed.

She slipped in through the door as soon as there was a crack
wide enough, as though she were pursued; she wore a fur coat he
had never seen before, frosted on the shoulders with snow.

"Well hello," he said, the last vowel swallowed with the thick spittle that had gathered in his mouth.

She went to the center of the room and stood gripping herself, chin thrust into her coat and her eyes not on him. Then she rooted in a deep pocket, drew out an envelope, and turning to him, held it out.

"There," she said. "There."

He could almost hear her heart beating from where he stood. He took the envelope, fat and creased by what it contained.

"That's it," she said, turning away, still hugging herself. "That's it, that's it, that's it."

The envelope was full of money. Large bills, fifties and hundreds, some twenties more worn and traveled.

"Do you have a cigarette?" she asked. She sat down on the bed, pressed her face into her hands and rubbed her forehead, eyes, and cheeks. Then she looked up at him and grinned. "You look pretty funny," she said.

"What," he said.

"It's all there," she said. "Everything I owed you. Everything I said we'd earn. I told you. I told you I would."

"How," he said.

"Pierce, don't ask, okay. That's it, that's all. I'm done, done for good and ever." She shuddered hugely; then, patiently, as to a child one isn't sure will understand: "Pierce, honey, now do you have a cigarette?"

"Yes, sure." He had bought a pack of factory-mades last night in his drunkenness. He searched among the clothes scattered squalidly over the floor. Here. Now a match. He tucked the envelope under his arm and went through his pants.

"You still hate me?" she said softly behind him.

"I never did." His hands trembled so that he could hardly insert them into the pockets, the change and keys within tinkled. "Here."

She had begun to uncoil; she looked around the place slowly, he could see in her eyes her thoughts reassembling it for herself. She lit the cigarette. "So what have you been up to?" she said.

"You have to tell me," he said. "A little something."

"No," she said. "Listen. If we're going to be friends, I want to be friends, if we're going to be friends you can't ask. If you ask I won't answer. I just won't and I won't be friends." She softened.

"Maybe when it's an old story." She looked up at him; he thought something gaunt, something old, had come into her face, maybe something that had been there before she fled but that he had forgotten, remembering mostly an older, that is a younger face. Or perhaps it was only the December morning. "Okay?" she said. "What's the matter?"

Pierce had begun to laugh.

"What's so funny?"

"Nothing's funny. Nothing." His breast heaved with chuckles and his knees shook. "Chemicals. Laugh-chemicals. I don't know." He drew the envelope out from under his arm and tossed it onto the bed beside her. "I don't want this," he said. "I don't need this."

"Are you kidding," she said. She lowered her eyes. "I was just going to leave it. In the mailbox. But I couldn't force it in the little slot, I lost my key somewhere, I wasn't even sure you were still here." She flicked her cigarette with a painted thumbnail. "I know you need it."

"I," he began to say, but then took her clue. There are needs and needs. He had meant that it was not this that he needed. She had only meant it was all he was to get.

"Tell me something," he said. "Have you come back?"

She shook her head slowly.

"What are you going to do?"

She shrugged one shoulder. "I just got back to town," she said. "I'll stay with Effie for a while. Look for a place."

Far, far back within him he heard his own voice, the voice that had only ten minutes ago been speaking to him of abnegation, of solitude: but all around that voice, and far larger, a machinery had begun to assemble, a machinery of cunning and desire that didn't even seem to belong to him but which took over him, churning out stratagems, watching his step, planning his moves. He went to the refrigerator, listening, and from the freezer took out a bottle of vodka. A glass. "Don't look, don't look," he said, shielding his pouring from her. "I find myself not quite the thing, this morning, is all."

She laughed. "Hey. One for me too."

He brought her a snifter, an inch of icy fluid in the bottom. "All we got," he said.

She sipped, and shuddered in heavy spasms. "Ugh, wow, good stuff. Good stuff."

"Welcome back," he said, courtly, and toasted her.

"Thanks, Pierce," she said. "Are we still buddies?" And, imitating Axel's needful, thrusting style, it had long been a joke between Pierce and her: "We're buddies, aren't we? Aren't we, aren't we, Pierce?"

He laughed, his trembling stilled by drink. "Sure. Forever."

She swallowed the rest of the vodka, and slowly, relaxing, lay back on the bed. Her coat opened, revealing a short dress and glossy stockings. She had grown thin. He studied her thighs and the points of her pelvis with pity and attention. She hasn't taken the best care of herself, he thought, feeling a connoisseur's twinge of loss and waste and desire. Not the best care.

"Oh, boy," she said. "I'm beat."

"Rest," he said. "Sleep, if you want."

"Listen," she said. "Thanks for keeping my stuff. Not sending it to the Salvation Army or whatever. I want to come get things, if I can. You know. My things."

"Sure."

"When I have a place."

"Sure." He couldn't bear this much longer. "Soon, though," he said. "If you can. Because." He turned away again, it was still winter outside the window. "Because I've been thinking of getting out of here."

There was a silence from her behind him.

"Moving away," he said.

"Oh yeah? And going where?"

"Oh, I don't know." He turned back to her; he could feel his face saying Driven out, what does it matter where, there's a whole meaningless world out there to wander in. "Out of the city, anyway. Maybe to the Faraway Hills. I visited there this summer. I liked it there."

"Gee. A big change."

"Yeah, well." He felt suddenly an intense pity for himself, as though what he had just said, what he had just then thought of saying, were really true. She only lay, looking up into the mirror above the bed. She wiped a dot of makeup from the wick of her eye. "It wouldn't be soon, anyway, actually, I mean not instantly."

"I'd like to take this mirror," she said. "If I can."

"No."

She sat up slowly, smiling but wary. "It's mine," she said. "Isn't it?"

"It was a gift," he said. "From me. To us."

She pulled her fur around her. "The country, huh. You'd have to learn to drive a car."

"I guess."

Her smile broadened. "Well I think it's great," she said. "I think you're brave." From the envelope on the bed she extracted a ten, but in doing so she loosed the packed bills within; they cascaded across the bed. She showed him the bill. "Taxi fare," she said. "Got to go."

"No, wait," he said. He thought wildly of explaining: If you take the mirror I'll have nothing of you, a thousand images of you are in it; no one else should ever be in it but you and me, don't you see? Isn't that fair, isn't that reasonable? "Wait a sec. Let me shower and get dressed. We'll go out, get some breakfast. There must be a few stories you can tell me."

"I can't now," she said. "Soon though. We'll get together." She took a step toward the closet, tempted, but changed her mind. "We'll get together." She gestured toward the bed, or the money. "You can buy me dinner, we'll have fun; I got a few stories."

"Champagne?" he said. "And . . ."

"I told you," she said, her eyes holding his, there was a long story in *them* for sure. "I'm done with all that. For good and all." She laughed, and came to him, reaching up for his embrace; he caught her up, she turned her face away and pressed her cheek to his. He smelled the cold air still trapped in her fur, the heavy warmth of her perfume; snow melted in torrents within him and his heart spoke a thousand things into her ringed ear, all of them silent. The phone rang joltingly, they both jumped.

"Gee, busy morning," she said, extracting herself.

The phone insisted. Pierce followed her toward the door. "Call," he said. "Call soon. I didn't change the number!" The phone shrieked in rage. Pierce at last turned and ran to it, hearing behind him his door click closed.

"Hello!"

A pause, the confused pause of a wrong number.

"Hello?" Pierce said again, this time in his own voice.

"Oh. Pierce?"

"Yes." He had a strange conviction that the woman who spoke was that woman in the country, the river cabin, the boat ride, Rosie.

"Pierce, it's Julie. Did I wake you?"

"Oh. Hi. Hi. Yes, sort of, well I was awake but . . ."

"Listen," Julie said. "I've got some news for you." She paused. "Are you sitting down?"

"No. Yes. All right." He carried the phone to the bed, and sat there amid the money.

"We sold it," Julie said.

"What."

"Good God Pierce we sold your damn book for Christ's sake!"

"Oh. Oh. Good lord. Really?"

"It's not terrific money."

"No. Oh well."

She named a figure of money that Pierce had no way of knowing was exiguous or generous. "Cockerel, though," she said.

"What?"

"Cockerel Books. Wake up! And listen, listen. They want to do a trade *and* a mass market, so even though the advance isn't huge, it could end up earning lots if it catches on."

Silence.

"Pierce. Do you want to talk about it? You don't have to do it. We could take it elsewhere." An impatience had crept into her tone.

"No, hey, listen, let's talk, let's talk right away, but I'll do what you think best."

"They want some editorial control."

"What?"

"I mean they think the book could do *real well* if it could be *slightly* tailored to a particular audience."

"Crackpots."

"Now now." She laughed. "Not that at all. But they did mention some titles that have been big hits lately. *Phaeton's Car. Worlds in Division. Dawn of the Druids.* Books like that."

"Hm."

"They think yours might be like those."

"You mean a tissue of lies?"

"Hey now."

Not a tissue of lies, no; but it would have to be subtly degraded, almost certainly, in a way that material presented to a classroom, however simplified or schematized or highly colored, did not need to be: he would have to commit not only *suppressio veri*, but *suggestio falsi* as well. He saw with sudden clarity how the book he proposed to write would appear to a historian's (Barr's?) eyes; how it would have to contain pages that would seem simply fictitious, as fictitious as those pages of disposable novels which are mere transcripts of ordinary (but wholly imaginary) conversation, peppered with real proper names unsubtly altered. All right. Okay.

"All right," he said. "Okay. Let's talk."

"One other thing," she said. "They don't like your title."

"No?"

"They think it would be misleading. And hard to file, too."

"All right. Okay." Pierce felt, in a general way, shot from a gun; it was hard to know, with the scenery changing so rapidly, what he was supposed to balk at, if at anything. "We have to talk."

"I thought dinner," Julie said, more softly than she had said any of her news. "Champagne. Oh Pierce." A pause charged (Pierce could feel it through the earpiece, he could see her shining face) with clairvoyance of destiny. "I knew it," she said. "I knew it."

When he had stood for a long time beneath a thundering shower, Pierce counted his money, the bills on the bed and what Julie had named to him, and made a few inconclusive calculations. He swept up the cash into its envelope, stripped the sheets, and after donning a T-shirt and a mohair suit (all his clothes were soiled) he filled a laundry bag.

"Good lord," he said aloud, ceasing his gathering to stare into the iron day. "Good lord."

He put his feet into rubber sandals, and fumbled change out of an ashtray; he went out and down, stopping at his mailbox and taking out a small handful of mail.

Didn't like the title. It was of course the only title the book could have. He supposed that a red herring though could be interposed meanwhile: *The Invisible College,* how about. *The Pneumatics. The Safe-Crackers.*

The King of the Cats.

When he had got the wash churning queasily in a soapy sea beyond the porthole window of the machine, he looked at what mail he had, something from Florida, some trash, some booksellers' catalogues, a letter in a minute and legible hand from the Faraway Hills.

"Pierce," it said. "Long time no hear from. Thot you would like a word from out here. Its a quiet month my grandfather called tying down time. Everything is getting put away, tied down, nailed up etc for Winter. This will be my first whole Winter in this cabin. I put in 1 bag beans 1 bag rice 50 lbs spuds 1 bottle brandy powdered milk lamps shotgun etc just in case. Sheep are fine + send their regards. By the way I have heard that down in Blackbury Jambs there is a nice apt. that will be for rent soon. People I know are leaving in Feb for the coast. 2nd floor, nice view sun porch fridge etc. Just thot I would throw that in. Be nice to have you in the county."

It was signed, "All best, Spofford," and there was a postscript: "The Muchos have filed."

Pierce read the whole of this letter twice, and then sat in thought with it in his lap until his clothes had to be moved from machine to machine; and then, as he sat watching his empty pants and shirts signaling to him wildly as they were flung around, he realized with a slow-breaking and astonishing certainty that today, this day, was his birthday. He was thirty-four years old.

Pierce Moffett, even back in those days when he had stood on his rooftop on the giddy edge of assenting that the cosmos was in some sense a story—that the universe was a cosmos—still would not have supposed that the story was in any concrete way *his* story, or believed that his own individual fate might be discernible in the harmonies he began to hear, the geometries he began to see. In fact it had come as a surprise to him to learn that most people who take an interest in auguries, clairvoyances, and astral prophecy do so not in search of some general illumination about the nature of life and thought and time, but in hopes of finding guides in them for action, Cliff's Notes to the plots of their own lives. Julie Rosengarten, for instance, had always read them so. But Pierce—if, one morning as he walked the city, a safe had fallen on Pierce out of an upper story, cutting off his tale for no apprehensible reason and without the least foreshadowing, he would not, so to speak, have taken it amiss. A profound conviction that his fate was far more subject to accident, blunder, and luck than to any logic, cosmic or mundane, a conviction which long predated his occult studies, had also survived them easily.

On the other hand, sometimes the omens can call out so clearly that even such a one as Pierce has to take notice.

That very day, the day of his birthday (his birthday!) he did make a vow; a vow that he would never have thought himself capable of, but made with all the small strength left him by the morning; a vow of abnegation that was the least he could offer up in exchange for what had so suddenly been showered on him. That's it, that's it, that is *it:* from now on he would dedicate himself to furthering only his own fortunes, and would not fritter away in the hopeless pursuit of love any more of the gifts apparently reserved for him.

A week later, with a vengefulness delicious and vivifying, made more vivifying by the tinge of fear that colored it (for he didn't really trust his future to remain in sight for long), he returned unsigned to Earl Sacrobosco his contract for the spring semester. He needed time to work on a special project, he said, that would require some difficult research, the right hand of scholarship as teaching was the left; and since sabbaticals were not on offer for the untenured help, he must regretfully etc.

There.

He wrote to Spofford in the Faraways, stating a January date when he might take another jaunt thither, and asking him to telephone the next time he found himself near an instrument, call collect, reverse the charges.

And at Christmas he bought as usual a small bottle of gin and an even smaller bottle of vermouth, and went across the black bridge to Brooklyn, to visit his father Axel: and to break, if he could think of a way to do it that was both clear and not hurtful, the news to him.

E I G H T

▲

Twenty years before, Axel Moffett had won a good amount of money on one of the high-rolling TV quiz shows then popular. His field was Western Civilization, and he had the advantage of knowing and loving deeply all the hoary anecdotes and Great Moments and imaginary Turning Points and romantic incidents in the supposed lives of the supposed heroes of that civilization, from Alexander and Boadicea to Napoleon and Garibaldi; Pierce, schooled in a more scientific history, would have done far less well. There were no essay questions asked, and Axel, though shaky on exact dates, could almost anticipate, as soon as any question was begun, which of the relatively small number of great stories was being fished for. To an uninstructed audience, though, his knowledge must have seemed unimaginably wide; it had seemed so, for that matter, to Pierce, fourteen years old, watching his black-and-white and strangely reduced father answer firmly what Austrian had briefly been emperor of Mexico (Axel had loved the movie, poor poor Carlotta, and Brian Aherne's soft and hopeless eyes). Around the TV in Kentucky, they all cheered, except Pierce's mother, who only shook her head smiling, as though it were only another unfathomable oddity of her husband's, only another to be forgiven and forgotten.

He got about halfway up the pyramid of cash on offer before being stopped; the producers decided that he was too queer a fish to be allowed the highest prizes (though he had amused for a while, with his antique courtliness and his way of answering with blazing eyes and a loud of-course tone, as though he were being challenged). It wasn't a question of rigging—Axel could not have been rigged, and ever after could reenact his horror and shame on discovering that others on that very program had been; it was a simple matter of asking him for a fact so obscure, so out-of-the-way, so disconnected from the Great Themes that a specialist would not have known it (and it was tried out on some). To the masses, of course, it seemed no more of a crusher than many others Axel had answered easily or anyway sweated out (What song did the sirens sing? What name did Achilles take when he hid among the women?) but Axel hearing it could only stand stupefied in his glass box without the vaguest guess, until the clock ran out.

What was odd was that Pierce had known the answer to that question.

He had listened to it asked—in the TV lounge at St. Guinefort's Academy this last time—and had heard the tick-tock music begin which marked the time in which an answer had to be given, syncopated with a distant Ping-Pong game elsewhere in the school hall. He had heard, unbelieving, the answer worth thousands unfold in his own mind while Axel stared. The music stopped; there was a moment's grace, but it did Axel no good. From his card the host read out the answer, the same answer that had unfolded within Pierce; the studio audience mourned, Pierce's schoolmates turned from the screen to look at him, some jeering, some curious, some groaning over the lost bucks. Pierce sat silent. Axel was led away after being commiserated with by the gleeful host, his stricken head held high, a look on his face, all lost save honor, that Pierce would never forget: if he had seen his father led to the block it could not have made a more heartrending memory.

He never told his father that he had known the answer.

The money Axel had by that time won seemed anyway a vast treasure; in retrospect it would appear almost trivial, as so many dollar figures of those days would, but it had been enough then to buy the pretty if shabby building off Park Slope in which Axel lived, and to which Pierce had been born. Axel had thus become a landlord, which he hated, but the building would support him without a lot of labor in the often mismanaged and sometimes dreadful years that lay ahead for him. Even now when its rent-controlled tenantry hardly paid the taxes and the most minimal of maintenance, it was somewhere for Axel to lay his head. That was how he put it to Pierce: "At least," tears often blooming in his eyes, "at least somewhere to lay my head."

This Christmas afternoon Pierce found him standing in the

entranceway of the building, like a homeless bum taking shelter there (the comparison was Axel's). "The bell's broken," he said, fumbling with the key, "and Gravely's gone to his people on the island. I didn't want you standing out here ringing, thinking I was gone, though where I'd be I don't know." Gravely was the super, a black man of great kindliness, even sweetness, who had been there since Pierce was a child; Axel revered Gravely, and Gravely called Axel Mr. Moffett; stooped, gracious, slow, and wise, he was one of the almost fictional characters that entered Axel's life as though from the old movies he loved, and who had passed out of real life everywhere else, if indeed they had ever inhabited it. Pierce feared for Axel when Gravely was dead.

"Where I'd be I don't know," Axel said again as they climbed the stairs. "Where I'd be—I don't know. Oh Pierce. The homeless on a night like this. The homeless man on this night of all nights. This night of all nights in the year."

Pierce's uncle Sam had described Axel once as "a little theatri-cal." To nine-year-old Pierce (newly come to live with Sam) this didn't communicate much, but after pondering it Pierce thought that maybe what Sam referred to was Axel's habit of repeating, over and over and almost to himself, a phrase that momentarily struck him, like an actor rehearsing it, trying it this way and that way, pressing emotion or levity into it until it made him laugh or cry. Later on, other meanings of Sam's description seemed more obvi-ously intended, but still it was probably true what Sam also said, that Axel had missed the boat by not going into acting or Holy Orders, one.

They were greeted as Axel opened his door by a harsh shriek of Latin: *"De mortuis nil* squawk wheep!" Then: "Shut up, shut up."

"Amazing," Pierce said laughing, "how many parrots learn to say 'shut up.' I wonder why that is."

"When," said Axel with a look of exhausted patience, "are you going to take that thing *away. Out.* Out of my *life."*

"Well," Pierce said, "that's sort of something I came to an-nounce, in a way." He pulled the small bottles from their snow-soggy paper bag. Because of his past history, Axel kept no liquor in the house; he drank only beer and a little wine in taverns. But at birthdays and Christmas he must have a martini, two martinis, to remind him of a more festive time, happier days. He was already at work with pitcher, ice, stirring rod.

"People drink them now *on the rocks,*" he said. "Horrible, horrible. That's not a *martini.* Though I think the little sliver of lemon is a good idea. A twist. A *twist* of lemon. Really, Pierce, he should be returned to the jungle. It isn't kind. He looks so *shabby.* He should be flitting through the jungle, the Amazon. Like a green thought in a green shade. He makes me feel like an old maid, something Victorian and dowdy. *Dowdy.* When when *when* are you going to take him away." He was laughing now. *"Liberate* me from this enslavement to a *bird."* He stirred. "Like a green thought in a green shade. Like a green thought: in a green shade. *Libera me domine."*

Pierce sat on the colorless sofa, contemplating his bird and his old home. It had acquired a patina of Axel that had obliterated almost all that had remained in it of his own life and his mother's here, even though very little had changed. The walls hadn't been chocolate brown when he was a boy, but he didn't think Axel had painted them so; they had just grown so. This sofa had once been a blue one he could remember; the framed etchings of cathedrals and the Cameron photograph of William Morris had once been pictures he had looked long at. There was even a lost pattern on the rug that belonged to his memories. It was all buried here, like an earlier Troy, beneath the tidy dirtiness, the rummage-sale and salvage acquisitions, the old-man smell.

"Libera me domine," Axel said again as he brought the pitcher and two glasses. Pierce had to strip the twists from the lemon, Axel's plump white tapering fingers were no good at such tasks, "nerveless" as he said; and rub the glasses with them, and then pour and present. It was like a hasty tea ceremony. Axel enjoyed it enormously.

"You see the glasses," he said. They were tall and etched, with fluted green stems. "Venetian. Well not really Venetian, but *like* Venetian. Victorian copies, I suppose, maybe, possibly." They struck Pierce as Woolworth's, but he knew little about such things. "Off the truck, of course. The boys brought them to me. Here, Axel, you kinda like this fancy stuff, why don't you take these, heck we'd just break 'em. They *know,* you see. They can't really appreciate the things themselves, but they know there's something there, something they don't grasp. Beauty. Books: they always bring me the books. Hey, Axel, what's this, I found this. And it was Rabelais in French, a little quarto volume, only one of a set, and I said, "Yes, Teddy, this *is* a great classic"—kindly, grave, careful of simpler

sensibilities—"and it's in French, of a very old-fashioned kind. . . .
You read that stuff? he said, and I said, Yes, I can make it out, I
know the lingo. . . . Well, they tease me, they're just honest hard-
handed kids. Merry, merry Christmas, you know your coming here
means a lot to me, a lot. Pierce. It means a lot." He sighed. "Just
hard-handed good simple boys. Rowdy. Rowdy." He chuckled at a
private memory.

"Are you guys making any money?" Pierce asked. He always
felt loutish cutting across his father's enthusiasms with questions
like that, but he couldn't seem to help it. He mistrusted this salvage
business Axel had got involved with, a gang of Brooklynites who
after work and on weekends stripped abandoned houses and tene-
ments of copper and lead piping and whatever else of value they
could find, under contract to the demolition men. They had a
headquarters in an old firehouse they rented from the city, a place
to get away from their wives and drink beer prodigiously; they were
pledged to one another and to an older man called the Chief, a one-
time Navy chief Pierce gathered, who ran the operation—so Axel's
stories suggested—in a manner somewhere between a scout camp
and a gang of Villon thieves, though Axel insisted there was nothing
illegal about it. Axel kept the books; just how much of the fun he
joined in he didn't quite say.

"Money, well, money," he answered. "It takes money to make
money." Suddenly he took umbrage. "Money! What are we talking
about *money* for on a day like this! On this day of all days in the
year!"

"Squawp wheek!" said Pierce's parrot. Pierce had often noticed how a sudden rise in the noise level made a parrot talk. Axel
rose heavily, glass in his hand; the bird sidled along its perch toward
him, turning its baggy eyes alternately on him. There was a fixed
expression on Axel's face and Pierce wondered if he meant to
strangle the bird. But he only stood before it, and after a moment
began absently stroking its chin with the back of his forefinger. "I
got a card from Winnie," he said.

"Yes?" Pierce said. "So did I. She sounds good."

Axel sighed hugely. "I went to midnight Mass last night. At
Saint Basil's. You remember we always went. Winnie sang. She sang
so purely." He leaned against the mantelpiece, head low, shoulders
drooping. "I mentioned you both, in my intentions. My wife. My
son."

Pierce too lowered his eyes for a moment, and said, "You still go, huh. Pretty crowded still?"

"The Mass of the Angels," Axel said. Axel managed to combine a basic atheism with a certain amount of emotional churchgoing and a special devotion to the Virgin. "The music. *Gloria in excelsis Deo.* Winnie could always just touch the high notes, so, so . . . just *touch.*"

"Well, she sounds good," Pierce said. "Rested. Getting a good rest. The card was pretty funny, though. I think it must have been Dora's choice."

"I mentioned you both," Axel said again. "In my intentions. I did. You're all I have now, Pierce. All I have."

Pierce twisted the Venetian glass in his hand. His remark had not deflected the train of reminiscence charged with guilt and loss that came with the finishing of the first martini and the embarking on the second; but he hadn't expected it to. It was as much a part of Christmas here as a gloomy forecast of declining powers and the deep desire Still to Do Some Good were a part of birthdays, which Axel also took with great seriousness; as he took his marriage vows, and his fatherhood, and his failure at these, or what he took to be his failure. Pierce was never able to reassure him; it was hard, given the depth of Axel's feelings, to tell him to forget it, it didn't matter much, or to suggest to him when Axel approached with grave chivalry the memory of his wife that Winnie (Pierce felt pretty sure) rarely thought of the matter one way or the other. It had always been Sam (and Dora now that Sam was dead) who had remembered Axel, remembered to send cards, remembered that Axel had a part in Pierce and a duty toward him too. Winnie had mostly wanted to rest.

His mother's capacity for rest had been great—Pierce rarely remembered her except as sitting placidly, sweet face vacant, hands loosely folded in her lap—but it had never been enough. Restlessness, in every sense, was for her like one of those obscure and chronic Victorian maladies that show few symptoms but whose prevention or mitigation is a lifetime's work. It had only broken out seriously a few times that Pierce knew of: presumably when she had married Axel, perhaps when she had left him to go live with her brother Sam when Sam's wife died; and after Sam's death, when it had taken over her badly enough that she'd had to go away, to a rest home, to recover her restfulness.

She'd met Dora there. Dora had spent years caring for a
widowed elder brother (as she supposed Winnie had done too,
though it had been as much the other way around), a brother whom
she was visiting almost daily in his final senility at the rest home. His
death left Dora nothing to do, a condition she feared as much as
Winnie longed for rest; and so she had taken up Winnie's life, with
all the fascinating stories and collateral relatives it seemed to contain, including Pierce and Axel, and now she managed it and
Winnie from a string of bungalows she had bought in Florida with
her own and Winnie's insurance proceeds. There Winnie seemed
truly to have come to rest at last.

"Pisanello," Axel said, taking the card he and his son had both
got from Florida, and holding it out to Pierce. "*Quattrocento,* yes? I
don't think though that they should imitate the gold leaf by these
gold sprinkles. That seems very tasteless to me. Can't they leave well
enough alone? Must they gild the lily?"

"Paint the lily," Pierce said.

"Paint the lily, and gild refined gold? Gild refined gold, and
paint the lily? Now pour again, Pierce, will you? Please."

Before they struck out onto the slushy streets toward the old
and famous (and in Pierce's view now sadly declining) Brooklyn
restaurant where long ago the Moffett family had gone for special
treats and which now served Axel's and Pierce's Christmas dinner,
there was an exchange of gifts: for Axel, as every year, a trifle of
clothing or decoration ennobled by the famous name of a wood-
paneled Madison Avenue shop, or by an English brand name or
royal arms; for Pierce, lately, something off the truck. A book,
this year.

"You remember it, of course," he said, even as Pierce was
tearing the wrapper. "Oh god I remember how you loved it. You'd
ask to see the pictures, the beautiful pictures. . . ." Axel imitated
round-eyed child wonder.

"Oh," Pierce said. "Hm."

"Not a first edition," said Axel.

"No, well," said Pierce.

"I read it to you."

It was Sidney Lanier's retelling of the Arthurian legends, in the
old deluxe Scribner's edition with pictures by N. C. Wyeth, all
ultramarine skies and white silver armor. He did remember it. He
owned a glossy paperback reproduction of it, in fact, but he didn't

remember that he had *especially* loved it, as he had other books, and opening this musty hardback brought no special pang; pictures and text suggested something remote, untouching and untouched, clear but not his: everything that Pierce thought Axel meant by the word *pure,* which Axel used in a way all his own, to express something that moved him deeply and Pierce not at all.

"Hey, thanks," he said, "sure, I remember." He didn't want to meet Axel's eyes for fear they might be full of tears. He could well imagine that, when he was a child and Axel had read him these stories, Axel had mistaken Pierce's silence and his amazement before his father's deep emotion for deep emotion on Pierce's own part; but what Pierce truly remembered with great vividness of his bedtime stories was not these knights at all, but Axel's acting out, in minute detail, episodes from the Flash Gordon serial. Ming the Merciless, the Mud Men of Mars, all of it, the best bits of dialogue said over and over, punctuated by Axel's self-appreciative laughter and Pierce's delight; his father's eyes flashing histrionically, his chubby face transmuting from heroic resolve to threatened purity to demonic malice and back again. That's what Pierce remembered.

And yet (he turned to the last picture, the effulgent chapel, the mystery within) he did remember a night when this book was the bedtime reading. He remembered it, though it was possible that Axel, who believed that he remembered every detail of Pierce's life with him, had forgotten it. It was the night before the day when Pierce and Winnie left for Kentucky.

Pierce in his pajamas, teeth brushed, prayers said, lay with the covers up to his chin, in the corner formed by the two walls against which his little bed was pressed (the more tightly the better, to prevent the midnight egress of whatever might be underneath). Axel, awesomely grave and gentle—as he had been all day, only gripping Pierce's hand and turning away to sob now and then through the day's walks and treats (Winnie left alone at home to pack)—took down from the shelf the *Boy's King Arthur.*

"This book," Axel said. "Do you want a story from this book? The book of knights?"

Pierce nodded, whatever was required of him, only let him get alive through the ritual of these days weird and solemn as a midnight Mass. Yes, that book.

Axel, rubbing his forehead, smelling a little of drink and Sensen, opened the volume. "Well, here's a story," he said, "a story of a little boy just like you," which issued as a hollow groan. "Like you, and he was a good boy like you. His name was Percival."

He cleared his throat wetly, and began.

"The father of Sir Percival was that king hight Pellinore who fought so terrible a battle with King Arthur. King Arthur drove him from town to town and from place to place until, at last, he was driven away from the habitations of men and into the forests like a wild beast. And that was a very great hardship for the lady who had been queen; and likewise, it was greatly to the peril of the young child Percival.

"Now Percival was extraordinarily beautiful and his mother loved him above all her other sons. Wherefore she feared lest the young child should die of those hardships.

"So one day King Pellinore said: 'Dear love, I am now in no wise prepared for to defend thee and this little one.' " Axel stopped at these words, swallowing and staring for a moment; Pierce, stilled by strangeness, only waited. At length Axel went on: " 'Wherefore for a while I shall put ye away from me so that ye may remain in secret hiding until such time as the child shall have grown in years and stature to the estate of manhood and may so defend himself.

" 'Now of all my one-time possessions I have only two left me. One of these is a lonely castle in this forest (unto which I am now betaking my way), and the other is a solitary tower, at a great distance from this, and in a very desolate part of the world where there are many mountains. Unto that place I shall send ye.

" 'And if this child groweth in that lonely place to manhood, and if he be weak in body or timid in spirit, thou shalt make of him a clerk of holy orders. But if when he groweth, he shall prove to be strong and lusty of frame and high of spirit, and shall desire to undertake deeds of knighthood, thou then shalt not stay him from his desires, but shall let him go forth into the world as he shall have a mind to do.' "

He stopped reading, and squeezed shut his eyes against the tears. "You'll be a good boy, won't you," he said. "You'll be a good boy, and take care of your mother, like a good knight."

Pierce in his corner nodded.

"And so it was," Axel said, finding his place with difficulty, "and so it was that King Pellinore betook himself to that lonely castle where King Arthur found him and fought with him; and Percival's mother betook herself to that dwelling-place in the mountains of which King Pellinore had spoken—which was a single tower that reached up into the sky, like unto a finger of stone. There she abided with Percival for sixteen years, and in all that time Percival knew naught of the world nor of what sort it was, but grew altogether wild and was entirely innocent like to a little child.

"Oh my dear son." Axel bent toward Pierce as though to bury his head in his son's lap, but did not; he gripped his own forehead with his hand. "You'll grow up to be strong, won't you, yes, and manly, and innocent; and if you want to do deeds of knighthood, oh don't let them stop you, don't. Oh don't."

He threw up his suffering head. "Don't let them make you hate me," he said. "Your father. Don't let them make you hate your father." The histrionic abjuring, the careful gravity, had broken; Pierce, awed, saw an adult person in grief like a child. "And you'll come back," he sobbed. "You'll come back, won't you one day, you'll come back." Pierce said nothing. He didn't know if that house in Kentucky was truly a finger of stone in a solitude of mountains, nor whether he ever would come back to this lonely castle; but he knew that he was not being sent away. He knew that his mother was taking him away, running away with him, and that he was not beautiful at all.

He had come back, after all. But now he was to leave again.

At dinner he made his announcements, beginning with the sale of his book, for a figure he inflated somewhat. Axel responded with awed congratulations; there was no higher vocation he knew of than to write; he himself, for all his wide and random learning, found it enormously difficult to express himself on paper, or to compose so much as a letter. Then came the decision to leave Barnabas. That drew mixed reviews; teaching ranked only just below authorship on Axel's scale. Pierce assured him that, if he ever had to go back, Barnabas would be only too eager to take him back, and that anyway there were other schools, in other places.

"Other places," Axel said. "Oh, well. Other *places,* yes."

The decision to leave New York entirely fell heavily. Axel was shocked and dismayed, his rubber face falling dreadfully. At first he chose to regard it as a bizarre speculation merely, a wild thought of his son's, which gentle contempt would help cause to pass; it was ludicrous, if he were embarking on a book, to forgo the greatest libraries, galleries, archives in America and languish in the sticks (here Axel gave impressions of the country drawn perhaps from Marjorie Main pictures, goat-bearded yokels astonished by book-larnin'). But Pierce as gently insisted. And at last Axel grew quiet.

"It's not as though I see you all that much," he said. "Now I won't see you at all."

"That's not so," Pierce said. "Hell, it's not much more trouble to get from there to here as to get here from Manhattan. In real time and effort. I'll be back. Often. To use those libraries. We won't lose touch."

Axel remained uncomforted. "Oh no, Pierce, no. Oh where's that waiter, Moselblümchen. Tomorrow to fresh fields and pastures new. Pour, pour."

There is a way in which even the most self-preoccupied of eccentrics can know themselves to be eccentrics, know that a set of commonplace connections between themselves and the world has been severed, or was never made. Axel knew it. He knew that his channels of communication were dim, and clogged with static, and he mourned his isolation. His son's return to the city as an adult who found Axel interesting and amusing, and not as a child who was puzzled and embarrassed by him, had been an unexpected gift for Axel, unexpected and precious. He had exploited it hard, bending Pierce's ear in long rambling phone calls, insisting on afternoons for museum visits and organ recitals, undeterred by strings of refusals. Pierce meant a lot to him: he said so frequently; less as a son—for all his seriousness about the role, he found a paternal attitude impossible to sustain for long—than as an understanding, or at least patient, friend.

Pierce tried to be patient. He tried to make room for Axel in his life, a life into which Axel fit only with difficulty. He found an exasperated fascination in the fact that this strange man—a whole head shorter than himself, barrel-shaped, with delicate tapering hands and feet he was proud of—was his father; he didn't remember him being this sort of person at all when he was a child. The two of them together on an outing like this reminded Pierce sometimes of that mild little boy and the insect-winged cigar-smoking fairy godfather who used to accompany him in the funny papers, what was his name again, McFeeley, Gilhooley, he never remembered to ask Axel. Axel would know, for sure.

"Take me with you," Axel pleaded, mostly in jest. "On your back like old Anchises."

"You can visit. I'm sure I'll have a spare room. Or anyway a sun porch."

"A *sun porch!* A sun porch. And how do you get to this place, and back? There are buses, I suppose. Buses." .

"There are buses. And I'll eventually get a car, I guess."

"A *car!*"

Pierce's single attempt at fiction in his grown-up life had been a portrait of his father. He'd wanted to call it "The Man Who Loved Western Civilization," and he worked for some time over it, but his transcriptions of Axel's table talk rang false, they made Axel sound like a pompous autodidact and a phony, they were empty of Axel's passion and engagement. And the lurid details of his life, when written down, sounded unbelievable, totally fictional—just as they did when Axel, pure of heart and nearly incapable of a deliberate falsehood, related them to Pierce.

Pierce had to suppose it was a real world Axel lived in, for all that it was not Pierce's. For a time after Pierce and Winnie had gone off to live in Kentucky and before the TV money put Axel back on his small feet again, there had been some years of near-destitution, on the streets, on the bum; and there had been times since, too, when Axel had charitably visited or awkwardly slipped for a while back into a halfworld populated by tough but kindhearted ex-Navy chiefs, by nonagenarian Broadway actresses expiring among their souvenirs in low hotels, by scholarly Jews in dusty bookshops who perceived Axel's true qualities beneath the shabby clothes; by worker-priests he admired, manly and clean, and smarmy Salvation Army hypocrites to whose tender mercies (Axel's words) he had once been subjected.

"Tender mercies," Axel would repeat, with a touch of Ming. "Tender mercies."

For all Pierce knew, all of them, and the plots they acted out, were just as Axel described them. For all he knew, the men of the salvage operation Axel was now involved in really did run their hands through their hair and shuffle their feet shyly, as Axel described them doing; perhaps they really did say things like, "When a feller's down he needs a friend to pick him up," and in general act like characters out of *Boys' Town* not much grown up. Anyway Axel was far less innocent about his city than the dreamy scenarios he spoke in sometimes suggested; less innocent in certain ways than Pierce. He could still shock his son with what went on after hours in the back rooms of working-class bars frequented by cops and firemen. Pierce had learned a lot from Axel in recent years, and not only within their shared interest in Western Civ; well outside it, too.

And so, though Axel's long and impassioned wooing of him had been often irritating; and though it was in general impossible to have actual conversation with someone whose stream of consciousness scoured the banks and overflowed the channels of any temporary subject; and though all of Pierce's friends and lovers had found Axel pretty well unbearable for anything longer than a brief visit, still Axel held Pierce's attention. On the whole he genuinely liked his father, which he found, sometimes, strangest of all. When late at night, "exalted" as Axel said by wine, weaving distractedly through the Brooklyn streets he knew and loved, Axel would sing Thomas Moore songs in a sweet clear tenor, Pierce even loved him.

"Tomorrow," Axel said, this Christmas full of misgivings, "tomorrow to fresh fields, and pastures new."

"Fresh woods," Pierce said. "It's fresh *woods*."

"Tomorrow to fresh *woods*. And pastures new." They had come along, after dinner, arm in arm, to the Brooklyn Heights embankment, to look out over Manhattan—the final part of their recently evolved Christmas ritual, every part of which had become instantly precious to Axel. Here, usually, they observed poor Hart Crane's apartment, now owned, to Axel's annual disgust, by the Jehovah's Witnesses; usually, Axel expatiated on the skyline, spoiled, he thought, by the two titanic cigarette cartons far downtown, they every year offended him anew. Tonight he seemed not to see them; he had drunk more than usual, Pierce unable to deny him a second bottle. "Oh Pierce. You must promise me. That you won't abandon me."

"Oh, now Axel."

"You mustn't abandon me." With a dreadful hollow tone. And then mitigating it with forced insouciance: "Your old dad." He took Pierce's arm again. "You wouldn't cast off your old dad, would you? Would you? We're buddies, aren't we, Pierce? More than father and son. We're buddies, aren't we?"

"Sure we are. Of course we are. I'm telling you, it's not that far."

"And so the youth arose," Axel said, with a sweep of his arm, "and twitched his mantle blue." He laughed and camped the gesture: "*Twitched* his mantle blue. Tomorrow to fresh woods, and pastures new. Oh see me home, Pierce, just see me home, it's not that far. I beg you."

He *did* love his father; he was a burden but Pierce was not very often truly ashamed or wearied by him; and yet he did wonder, as he rode the train back across the river toward Manhattan, the city's fiery parcels all undone, how much having Axel for a father had to do with that vow he had felt himself compelled to make on the night of his birthday: did wonder (cold hands thrust deep into his peacoat pockets, cold heart just for the moment empty) how much the effects of that strange and unhealing wound which Axel had somehow long ago sustained had descended to him, and how much it might have to do with the wound that Pierce had begun to know was open and unhealed within himself.

Well. Tomorrow to fresh woods, and pastures new.

And so in the spring Spofford came down from the Faraway Hills in his old truck, and he and Pierce loaded it with the contents of Pierce's apartment, except for three dozen cartons of books sent separately. Spofford's truck was an open pickup, and they both looked anxiously at the sky as they loaded, but the day stayed fine. They hung in the elevator the brown rugs the super insisted they use, and in this padded cell, two busy madmen, they rose and fell accompanied by Pierce's desk, typewriter, bed, dishes, pictures, bibelots, and an ornate broad mirror heavy as a tombstone, all of it looking misplaced and somehow tawdry and ashamed when taken out into the spring sun.

Pierce had made all his goodbyes, dinner the night before with the Sphinx the most lavish of them. She had got herself, she said, a tiny old-law apartment, one of the few still left in a chic neighborhood uptown where some of her old customers lived; she wasn't yet able to afford electricity, lived by candlelight and ate out, and wanted no telephone. She had begun to make a kind of living going around to thrift shops and rummage sales, acquiring knickknacks, printed souvenir scarves and hand-painted ties, costume jewelry, ephemera, "art drecko" she said, laughing and lighting another cigarette. Her resale prices of these items were inflated to reflect the sureness of her taste and the skill of her hunting; she hawked them to acquaintances, often those same old customers of hers, their desires for such stuff were strong and their wallets were full. A floating antique store.

Maybe (he said, at the brief evening's end, exhausted for some reason but compelled to go on, no doubt for the same reason) he could see this little candlelit place. His own place being in such chaos tonight . . .

No, she didn't think he could. It was a dump really. Maybe when she got it fixed up.

"I'll be gone by then."

"You'll be back. And I'll come visit *you*."

Pierce, imagining her high heels on his front walk, her perfume beside the Blackbury, thought that unlikely. And yet it was probably no more unlikely than that he himself should have done—or come a few quick steps from the verge of doing—what he was about to do: move. He had gone one recent evening full of spring odors on a walk down University Place and around Gramercy Park, peering into the locked park where the grass was green and the tulips opening. He walked the park's perimeter, looking into the tall windows of spacious apartments that bordered it, paneled places he had always coveted. He thought: Maybe if a place like that one, or that one, were mine; a key to this park; enough income to support it—then maybe I'd stay. The Sphinx remote uptown notwithstanding. "Make me an offer," he said to the city. But it made none, and neither did the Sphinx, she only kissed him smokily and without tears and told him to write.

And now he was packed and departing.

Never liked this place anyway, he thought, looking around his bared apartment, bleak-looking with Pierce's life taken out of it, the oblong ghosts of his pictures on the walls, the few good and many strange things that had befallen him here either swept away with other detritus or packed to be taken. He shut the door on it forever, and clumped away down the corridor in his new country boots, carrying the last of his belongings, a tall red kitchen chair. This item crowned the pile in the truck, and with it waggling unsteadily above, he and Spofford rattled out of town, looking, Pierce supposed, like Okies fleeing a drought. And on the next morning Pierce stood on his sun porch watching dark and silver lights come and go in the Blackbury River beyond, his hands thrust into the sleeves of his sweater and an unbidden grin on his face.

Okay, he said, not exactly aloud, speaking to all powers what-

ever that might bear his three wishes in their hands; okay, come
now. Come now, 'cause I've made my own fortune, I've saved
myself, I can make it from here: come now so I can turn you down.
"Come now," he said, "right now," for he did not know how long
this moment or this strength would last.

NINE

▲

At about that hour, Beau Brachman across the street came out onto
his balcony in the sun, the first morning sun strong enough to
tempt him out; and he lay on the little platform he had build there
a prayer rug. Moving with thoughtful care, but feeling inwardly a
little of the glee of a journey undertaken after long confinement, he
mounted the platform and folded his legs beneath him. He placed
his hands on his knees, as on a belvedere or the rail of a ship. He
looked outward, over the roofs of town and the sparkle of the river.

He would go only a short excursion, he thought, being out of
practice; would only go out to see, like the woodchucks also now
newly abroad, like the hawks returning, what had become of the
world since he had last got a clear look at it.

Twenty minutes passed, twenty minutes measured by the clock
in a teapot's belly that stood on a kitchen shelf at Val's Faraway
Lodge, twenty minutes on Boney Rasmussen's self-winding Longines
with the lizard band.

Turning, carefully, on the somewhat unsteady prayer rug, Beau
aloft looked back down at his abandoned self still sitting firmly on
its prayer rug on its balcony. He turned away then, and looked
over the northwestern mountains, which from his balcony facing the
river he had been unable to see: Mount Merrow, clad in birch
woods; Mount Whirligig, with a girt castle on its top; Mount Randa
chiefest of them all. Turning further that way, Beau saw the Monument on its brow, like a unicorn's horn.

Upward. The valleys of the Faraways, seamed with roads and
rivers, all pale in the spring sunlight, the roads still dusty with
winter's sand and salt and the meadows puce and lifeless. A few

cattle abroad: there, he noted without surprise, was Rosie Mucho's great Bison station wagon, lumbering toward town and an appointment with a lawyer or a judge; there, a little more unusual, was Val's Beetle, out and about, nearly meeting Rosie at the Fair Prospect bridge. A dozen other trucks and cars were revealed as up we go, a little red convertible, a rattletrap pickup. Beau lifted his eyes: he was ascending the hills.

Up high here the air was clearer, the center of the sky darkening to cobalt as the pellucid sky above a desert does, and the reticulated mountain ridges were sharply cut and clear to him. Mount Merrow where the rich lived, in glass houses on steep slopes, looking outward; taller Mount Whirligig, in motion now—it was apparent to Beau as he approached it—like a clockwork toy. The castle on its summit came and went, as though it were two-dimensional, invisible when edge-on, visible face-front, visible, invisible. Two-dimensional or not, though, it had a dark within, and Beau sensed a kind of forcing going on in there, a forcing as of a winter bulb: as though a foetus were being painfully articulated in the darkness limb by limb. Beau felt a sharp disgust. What was it? This far from earth, Beau apprehended not sights so much as meanings, imports, symmetries and discordances, and he apprehended them the more intensely the further away he got and the darker the air grew: as though he went progressively blind, and meaning, like a flavor he tasted, grew that much stronger to his senses.

Mount Randa then, its bald brow and its wrinkled face bearded in trees patiently waiting to green. Hawks banked restlessly in the troubled air around the cliffy cheeks. On the slopes Beau could see, making his way up a steep track as of an old tear, a pilgrim, amazed with weariness and longing for the summit: toward which Beau himself now spiralled lazily, hawks falling beneath his flight-path. The summit. And—as the hills bent their gaze on him, as the sky took notice—Beau sped toward the Monument.

What it was, or seemed to be as Beau came closer to it, was a stone pediment, carved with crowded letters; and on the pediment a stone elephant, inelegant and strong, who lifted his trunk and bent his thick neck to squint at Beau approaching; and on the elephant's back an obelisk, cut with hieroglyphs, bird animal and thing. Strong elephant! As Beau circled him, the obelisk swung beneath Beau, a pointer, a gnomon; he hovered there until the Monument was still, and then, with delicious vertigo, he felt himself spilled from his rug. His sure, bare foot, extended, touched the tip of the obelisk; his knee bent, and with all his strength he vaulted upward, elephant and obelisk shifting and straining behind him in compensation, nearly toppling but not toppling. Beau shot a vast distance into the darkening sky.

Stars were visible. And he was visible to them.

His vault had pushed him to escape velocity, and now he traveled with undiminishing speed; but there was not, or did not seem to be, an infinity to travel in. The vastness resolved itself into nested spheres, like the wings and drops of an old-fashioned stage-set, containing him and constraining his flight. There were spheres of air and fire; beyond them the spheres of the seven Archons coming and going like mechanical racehorses in their tracks. Beyond them, arm in arm in arm like paper cutouts, twelve vast figures girdled the topless and bottomless heavens, Æons, six of them below the horizon and six above, the six who had seen him leap. They really looked down on him now: and their eyes were not kind.

Heimarmene. The whizzing gears of heaven. Beau knew well enough that heaven did not stop with them, that beyond them were spheres which they themselves had not heard of and could not imagine, every one lifetimes wide, containing lifetimes of labor and errantry and laughter and tears to cross before the next could be reached. Beau would put each one inside him as he crossed it, growing larger, growing toward his own infinitude, until at last he met his infinitude coming this way to meet him.

As yet, though, he had not even reached the first sphere of fire, where who knew what awaited him. He had ceased to speed outward, and only floated, vertiginous and suddenly heavy.

Afraid? Afraid, too.

There was a name for each of those powers he must pass by, and the spheres they made, the Æons that composed them, the suffering that they occasioned (all one thing); once Beau remembered the name of the first, and had a voice to speak it with, he would begin to cross.

But not now. Already he was falling back, the weight of his heart tugging at him, knocking at his iron ribs.

Knocking. No, it wasn't his heart at all. Beau tumbled backward out of the air, over the mountain, past the obelisk and grinning elephant, head over heels onto his prayer rug, and onto his balcony on Maple Street. Someone was knocking on his door.

"Beau?"

He came in from the balcony to see Rosie Mucho, peeking around the corner of the door, a comic mime of bashful intrusion.

"Beau? You up?"

"Come on in, Rosie."

"Gee, Beau, I'm sorry, were you, were you . . ."

"What is it, Rosie? You want to leave Sam here, right, even though it's not her schedule."

Someday, he thought, someday: he *would* go on, and just not return. Once get beyond the border, and you need never cycle back; instead of returning, you pass on. Realm on realm, forever, every one different.

"It's kind of an emergency," Rosie said. She let herself further in, and Sam red-cheeked from the outdoors came with her, holding her mother's pants leg.

"It's okay," Beau said. "Rest, rest. You want tea?"

"I can't." She came to him and drew him out of Sam's earshot, Sam having stopped to squat before a wary tiger cat curled on the rug. "Here's the thing. I have to go to court, in Cascadia. Mike and me. Can you believe the nerve? It's all his fault we have to go, and just an hour ago he calls to say he can't, he doesn't have a car. I have to give him a *lift.*" Her face showed huge disbelief. "Can you believe it?"

"Easy, easy. You're flying right out of your body. It'll be okay."

She closed her eyes, and took her elbows in her hands; breathed deeply; opened her eyes, as from long sleep, and as though onto a changed world: all to calm herself. "Okay," she said. "It's a little crazy."

Beau with a touch undid her locked arms, and took her in his own, pressing his breast tightly to hers. Tears sprang, absurdly, to Rosie's eyes, brought forth like a reflex action by Beau's hug. After a considered moment, Beau let her go.

"Okay?"

"Okay," she said, abashed and grateful. "Bye."

Sam's curly head, a little tracking station, turned to follow her mother's head as it left Beau, bent to kiss her, rose again to go. "Back soon, Sam. Be good." The tears in Sam's own eyes, which had been rising and sinking for some time, spilled over then, but Rosie was gone down the stairs.

She picked up Mike outside the Donut Hole, honking her horn to get his attention. He had, between the last time Rosie had seen him (in court) and now, shaved off his mustache. She chose to take no notice of this. He climbed into the wagon and pulled the huge door shut; he greeted Rosie, at once shamefaced and pleased with himself.

"The cat that ate the canary," she said.

"I have never," he said, still smirking, "understood what that idiom is supposed to communicate."

"I have to say first," Rosie said, "that I am really annoyed at you for this." She moved the machine around to face the other way, the highway and Cascadia. "I just can't help thinking you do it on purpose."

"I have a purpose," Mike said, turning now more grave. "I do have a purpose. I don't suppose that's what you mean. But you might credit me with some better motive than just trying to annoy you."

Ever since the separation agreement had been arrived at (a pretty simple document whose existence nevertheless embarrassed Rosie profoundly) Mike had set about tinkering with it, altering it and adding to it. He would brood over this or that clause or condition, and (often enough late at night) would call Rosie, and want to talk about it; long rambling not unfriendly calls, about marriage and justice and his feelings. When Rosie refused to talk with him anymore, he got his lawyer to call hers—his lawyer was a little light-boned grey-eyed fierce-faced woman Rosie shrank from, who was apparently willing to go to infinite pains for him; and eventually the niggling had accumulated to such an extent that now the agreement had to be seen again by the judge.

"It was important to me," Mike said, "and I am a person too in this situation, Rosie, which . . ."

"I won't talk about it, Michael. Allan told me not to talk about stuff with you and I'm not going to talk about stuff."

The car turned out from the Jambs onto the highway south, joining the lanes of traffic going to Cascadia, where the county courthouse is.

And yet it was probably true, Rosie thought, that he didn't really do it to annoy her. He was just more into it than she was; his own needs, what he felt was fair to him, took up more of his attention. Allan Butterman told her that hers should take up just as much of her attention, but they didn't. For Rosie merely having to negotiate over the stuff, the money, the rights, made them not worth having; the sharper the negotiation, the less worth having. Surrendering stuff took less negotiating than struggling to keep it, and so if Allan hadn't been there she supposed she would have just surrendered it all, and lived with that.

"Well, how are you then, in a general way?" Mike asked. "If that's okay to bring up."

"All right," she said warily.

"You doing anything?" He was looking not at her but out the window, as though searching for something, the way TV actors in cars do to fill the time while they say their lines.

"You know I'm working for Boney. The Foundation. Full time."

"That's not what I meant," Mike said. "When you were with me you always had a lot of projects. You painted."

"I did not."

"That kind of thing. Maybe you're too busy now."

The motels and restaurants of the Cascadia strip had commenced, the amoebic geometries of their signs and roofs. The Eaterie. The Morpheus Arms. The Volcano.

"Actually," Rosie said, "I've been planning a painting."

"Yes?"

"A big one. A lot of work."

"Yes?"

"It's a picture," she said, improvising, "of Valkyries—is that what you call them, the women warriors who carry away the dead soldiers?"

"Um, yes. Valkyries."

"Well of them. But not in battle. Afterwards. Valkyries disarming. Sitting at the end of day. Taking off their gear."

Mike had begun to grin, eyeing her sidewise, interested.

"Big women," Rosie said. "But not posing. Not dramatic. Just ordinary; hurting a little maybe; bending over, undoing their whatchamacallits, on their shins. Piles of armor around, like football gear."

"Girls' locker room."

"Sort of. But not a joke. Just—realistic." She had not ever

before thought of this subject in fact, had just been handed it, but now could see it with great vividness: the dull glowing Rembrandt colors, a dark nowhere; big glossy bodies of ordinary women, talking, idly checking for bruises, their faces like those in candid snapshots, filled with private thoughts. Who were they?

"I like it," Mike said. "A look into the girls' locker room. Something that's always appealed to me."

"Not like that," Rosie said. "Not what you're thinking."

"No? So what would they be up to?"

"They're just *there*," Rosie said. "They're tired."

Mike went on grinning, at a painting of his own. Rosie felt a small familiar irritation, an impatience at being misread, especially misread by Mike's omnivorous horniness. "So how are you?" she said, turn the tables. "How's Vampira?"

"Rosie."

"So are you guys going to get married, after this is over?"

"It's not really a topic of discussion." He returned to looking out the window, stroking the place where his mustache had been. Poor guy, Rosie thought glancing over at him; caught in the toils of love.

Mike had once told her that when he first took courses in psychology they were still talking about a "latency period" in boys, and Mike had been puzzled because he'd never had a latency period. There had never been a time, he said, when he hadn't wanted to get into the pants of girls, or get girls into his; he'd spent his childhood trying.

Funny in a psychologist, Rosie thought, that unreflective projection of his desires onto the world which Mike was capable of. His desires were sometimes—often—frustrated, and caused him pain (and dealing with the pain was what Mike called Growth, and Maturity); sometimes he would even say he felt at the mercy of his desires, and better off without them; but still he took them as simple givens, and the value they imparted to what he desired as well. He never considered that desire might make him misunderstand its object. He might *say* he considered it, but he didn't.

That was one reason for the silly threesome that Mike had inveigled her into, her and a counselor from The Woods whom Mike had become entranced with: the simple unquestioned value Mike put on it, his big night, as hard to refuse as an eager kid who wants to shovel your walk or rake your leaves.

"It might not work out real well for you," she said, suddenly meaning it. "I mean I know she's your type, that dark tawny weird type . . ."

"Actually she's very sharp," Mike said. He lifted his chin, a quick gesture, to free his neck from his shirt collar, a signal that he was talking seriously of himself and his enterprises. "She's been doing research for me, using the Method. Climacterics. Applying the parameters to sort of random lives. She's turned up some interesting stuff. She's very willing."

That had been the other reason, of course: Rose, her willingness, her abstracted mild acquiescence. Mike just took it for heat, since he wanted it to be heat. But it was spooky.

Her eyes somehow not there, not looking at what was there.

That night had meant nothing to Rosie at the time, or seemed to mean nothing, she had only been surprised at how well it went, and how little aftertaste it left. But in the course of it she had shed something, she saw that now. She had stepped away. She had turned, and begun to walk away. And though maybe she had at first meant only to walk away from Mike and his needs, from her marriage, from Stonykill, she had somehow gone on walking ever since, farther maybe than she ever realized, always away, never toward.

A huge shudder arose unrefusably within her, and shook her shoulders.

"What," Mike said.

"Nothing," she said. "Somebody stepped on my grave."

The Bison achieved the crest of the last low rise of the Faraways, and the strip leading into Cascadia unrolled across the valley, the gas stations and miniature restaurants and car-lots full of cars like a jumble of brightly colored toys; the road that divided them plowed ahead and was lost in the old gray city, from here almost like a *cinquecento* view, the crowded neighborhoods and blackened steeples, the dome of the county courthouse.

If she ever wanted to negotiate hard, Rosie thought, if she needed to, she could hold all that over his head. Call Rose to the stand, and get Allan to force her to tell what Mike and she did together. For Rosie had herself been a Model Single Parent, had been good, had not been much tempted actually. She had done without since that night last summer, the party by the river, the Full Moon Party: when Spofford had slipped her into the shuttered hot-dog stand and laid her on his old brown Navajo blanket, while the party murmured on outside.

Rosie had learned, in her appearances beside Allan Butterman in court and in arbitrations, why Allan seemed always burdened with intense emotions held just in check. In such circumstances Rosie felt herself awash in swiftly changing feelings, unable to avoid or mitigate them: rage when Mike lied, triumph when Allan answered cogently, guilt, embarrassment, loathing, none of which she liked feeling. These hearings did not seem to Rosie like negotiation at all but like some awful dark ritual in a Piranesi prison, a punishment only after which she would be free: you can go if you can stand this, can walk on these hot coals, wash in hot bull's blood. Allan, who surely didn't feel any of this himself, probably just soaked it up from his clients and those he dealt with, excess vapors.

"I don't know how judges can tell," she said to him during a pause (Mike huddling with his lawyer in a corner opposite). "How do they know if what they decide is right?"

"They don't," Allan said, stretching out his legs and crossing his small feet shod in black. "A judge I know confessed to me once that it really bothered him, the fact that he didn't know. Not that I was really surprised to hear it. He was very conscious, he said, that all he knew was what was put before him. The husband and the wife are both on their best behavior; the kid in his Sunday suit. If he was their next-door neighbor he'd be in a better position to know. But he has to make his decision based on what he *does* know, even if what he knows is nowhere near the whole story, or not even the right story, and even though his decision is going to affect all the parties for life."

Rosie felt a sudden awful perception, like a blast of cold wind. She might have been wrong in the decision she had made, so instantaneously, to take Sam. When it might really be Mike who after all and in spite of everything loved her more. A gulf seemed to open for a moment within her, beyond which Allan was hard to hear.

"The only thing that gave this guy comfort," Allan said, "is that he was pretty sure, if he did make a wrong decision, everybody would be back before him again eventually. And again. Until the whole true story finally came out." He glanced over at Rosie. "I wonder," he said.

*   *   *

She tried to insist that Mike get a ride home with his little lawyer, but he argued (did he never get tired?) that he might have to wait for some hours for her to resolve her various courthouse business, and it seemed unreasonable for them not to share the same journey in what had been, until recently, his own station wagon.

Maybe he was tired after all. He climbed into the back of the wagon, pushing aside the torn coloring-books, the galoshes and maps and ice-cream cups, the empty oil cans, and stretched out. His was the sort of body put to sleep by gentle forward motion and an engine's noise. He didn't even wake when Rosie turned off onto a Scenic Overlook and stopped, idling.

My castle, she thought.

It was shapeless and comical this close up, like a bunch of random chimneys, and shabby pale from winter, like the rest of the world. Butterman's. Not *hers* really, of course, not actually, no matter how long it had stood in her soul like a castle in an allegory, standing for all that was hers.

All that was hers.

If she slipped out now, opening the door without waking Mike, she might leap the low barricade there, and make her way down to the river's edge. She might find a boat there, a rowboat left accidentally, overturned on the shore, its oars beside it; and set out in it across the wrinkled river like gray silk, and reach the rocks of Butterman's. And then.

Silly, she thought: as if that pile were far enough away to run and hide in. She would only be found, after a search, and brought back, and made to go on with the life she led or pretended to lead.

She had in fact done no painting for a long time, though it certainly wasn't true she had been too busy. It was that she had somehow grown unconvinced of herself as a painter: not doubting her talent or her skill necessarily but only her reasons for doing it, unsure why she or anybody at all did it, painted. My art, my painting.

It was like the station wagon and the savings bonds and the loan payments Mike wanted to negotiate over: you had to know why you did it in order to bring it off, or get it for your own.

Mike knew. Mike knew what was his, and what he wanted, and what he loved; and if Rosie was sure that what Mike loved was mostly Mike—that he just went on making a simple mistake, like a kitten batting at its own image in a mirror—well, that might be what love really is, an illusion, but an illusion without which life couldn't be carried on, like color vision or three dimensions, and Mike had it, and she had lost it.

No that couldn't be.

It couldn't be: yet she had grown alarmed, hands on the wheel of the wagon, Mike breathing rhythmically behind her.

My painting. She looked within her for the warmth which the odd vision of Valkyries had given her, but it seemed to have gone. Sam, no, not Sam. My job, then. My dog. My car. There seemed to be only a vacuum to which she named these things, a sad frightened wanting without an object, a nothing really, a nothing that sat beside her and ate up everything she put between herself and it.

My dog Nothing.

She put the car in gear, and Mike's breathing altered with the engine's; she carried him sleeping out onto the highway, and entered the stream of cars, homebound for the Faraways as she was herself. In her side-view mirror as she climbed she glimpsed Butterman's castle, receding quickly to the south, and shrinking with distance.

III
FRATRES

ONE

▲

In silvergreen rainy April they went down to Glastonbury on the long straight roads, Mr. Talbot on a swayback borrowed nag, Doctor Dee on his spotted mare, an oiled goatskin mantle on his shoulders and a broad plaited hat like a countryman's on his head, and his son Arthur up behind him. The soft clouds gathered and parted again, the light rain was fresh and almost warm. As they rode Doctor Dee pointed out a flinty wall, an old, old church; he showed them how the Roman roads ran, straight and clear—and how another way went too, older far than that one, through towns and market crosses and churchyards, hidden and lost now but straighter than ever the Romans built. Alongside and beneath this green England there lay another country, made of time, old as this spring was young: time folded like the folded hills, back almost to the Flood, when men here knew no arts, nor speech, nor wore any clothes but skins.

—A thousand years after that Flood, said Doctor Dee, and twenty or thirty after Troy's fall, came that Albanian Brutus here to this septentrional isle.

—Was that Brute of Troy? asked Mr. Talbot.

—It was. And this Brute who had saved Troy from the Greeks (though later they conquered it), he found our forefathers in their ignorance, and yet pretty ready to learn, and of a good wit. And he, Brutus, became their King, the first that ever there was over the whole of this isle.

—And Arthur was of his line, said Arthur Dee, who knew this story, and his own share in it.

—He was. So you can see by his arms: three gold crowns in a

field of azure, that were the arms of Arthur's first kingdom of Logres; these quartered with the arms of Troy, which you may read of in Virgil. And so.

—And the Saxons? asked Mr. Talbot.

—No. They were out of Germany. Arthur was a thorn in the Saxon's eye. He was a Briton, heir of Brutus. And this land, his land, could not be right ruled, not by Saxon or Dane or Frenchman, till Arthur come again: till a Welshman, of our blood, mount the throne again.

—And so he did, said Arthur.

—And so he did, when Harry Tudor took the crown. And his granddaughter now upon the throne, if Arthur could be woman, she were he.

They rode in silence for a while.

—Some there are, said Doctor Dee, who would deny there was any Arthur.

—Let them try that, said Arthur, his cheek pressed against his father's back, sheltering under his father's hat.

—Let them look into Saint Jerome, said his father. Who praised Ethicus his assertion, that the isles of Albion, this one and Ireland, should be called the isles *Brutannicæ* and not *Brittanicæ*. And old Trithemius says that Arthur's empire covered twenty kingdoms.

—But kingdoms were not so large then, said Mr. Talbot.

—So they were not. Yet by the force of arms did this Arthur conquer the isles of Iceland and Grœnland and Estotiland. Which by right should be under our Queen now, all of them in the *mari Brittanico* between Britain and Atlantis up even to the North Pole.

Arthur Dee laughed aloud.

—And so I have told Mr. Hakluyt. And so I have urged Her Majesty.

Arthur Dee laughed again, a triumphant laugh, and hugged his father tighter, which made the doctor laugh too, and the three of them rode on laughing in the sun's face who just then peeped out, only to withdraw again.

Toward evening they passed a house by the side of the road, and an old woman in the doorway, under its dripping eaves, hands beneath her apron. There were daffodils and primroses in her garden; there was woodbine on the wall, and flowers bursting even in the moldy thatch of the roof, as from a meadow. She smiled at the travelers.

—Good day to you, Gammer, said Doctor Dee, leaning a bow from his saddle. How goes it with you.

—The better that your worship choose to ask.

—I see a new bush tied to your stake there.

—Your worship has eyes in his head.

—Can you put up three travelers, and give them supper? One of them a lad.

—I can do that, she said. I can give them white bread and brown, and cheese and new ale; and a bed all to themselves.

—There is a straight line, Mr. Talbot said, from Upton-on-Severn to Glastonbury.

—Yes, said Doctor Dee.

A single rushlight guttered at the bedside. Arthur slept. Doctor Dee and his skryer sat together on the bed's edge, their voices low not to wake the boy.

—This straight line, Mr. Talbot said, cannot be seen but from high in the air. For a time a road will mark it, and then a hedge; a church will sit astride it, or a market cross; and then a road will run its way again. But only from on high can it be seen to run along, true, straight as though scribed across the earth.

—Yes.

—It seemed, Mr. Talbot said, that he bore me up. I thought to swoon. I saw this line from on high.

—A dream, Doctor Dee said.

—It seemed no dream. He bore me on his back. In form he was . . . in form he was like a dog, or a wolf; he had a hairy head, and hairy paws with brown nails on them. But for his shape—I could not well see it, for he seemed dressed in a robe like a monk's robe, of heavy stuff. Which I clung to when he flew.

Mr. Talbot watching Doctor Dee's face saw a thought in it. He said:

—Whether he is a good spirit or not I know not. He has long been near me, not always in that form. I did not summon him. I know him to be the same in different forms because his face is always kind.

Doctor Dee said nothing.

—That line bore us its way, Mr. Talbot went on. As though it were a gutter down which a stone would roll, or a chase into which a hart is run. That straight line. So fast he went along it that the long brown robe he wore snapped behind him like a flag. And then methought I smelled the sea.

The green sea-moors of Somerset, changeful and full of noon light, moved below him (Had it been a dream? Had it been? He touched the stone jar he had, hidden within his coat) and then, coming closer as they dropped toward earth together—he felt his heart sickeningly mount to his throat—a low bare hill and a tower, an abbey and a ruined church. The one he clung to stretched out his hairy hand, and as he pointed here and there, south, east, west, there came to be visible, rising up out of the earth, figures. Figures that lay upon the earth, made of the earth, made of the rise and fold of hills, the creases of sunken roads, the lines of ancient walls, of rivers and streams: a circle of great beings, man, animal, thing, with forests for their hair and glittering outcrops of rock their eyes or teeth; a circle linked, touching, every figure facing west. For a moment one of them would not be there, would turn itself back into farms and fields, and then it would be there again: lamb, lion, sheaf of wheat.

—Yes, said Doctor Dee. Lamb. Lion. Sheaf of wheat. What others?

—I know not. Fishes. A king. I could not see.

Turning in a slow spiral downward like a hunting hawk, the one who bore him fell toward the abbey church. One by one the vast personages retreated into the earth as into sleep, and could no longer be discerned.

—Then he showed me. In the old abbey. The place where I should dig.

—And did you dig then?

Mr. Talbot rubbed his brow, as though to bring up the memory.

—I think I did not. He . . . I swooned. I remember nothing. He bore me away, and I awoke home again.

—Or woke never having left, said Doctor Dee.

Mr. Talbot glanced toward Arthur, and then leaned close to the doctor's ear, to speak urgently.

—If it was a dream, it was a true dream. For I went later on foot that same way. And there was the church, as I had been shown it. There was the place I was to dig, there where two pyramids were. But for the stonecutters at work there, it was the same, all the same. I waited for night to fall. By the moon I dug. I found the chamber, and in it the book.

Doctor Dee said nothing, nor looked at Mr. Talbot. He studied his own hands on his knees. Then he rose, and pinched out the light.

—We will know more tomorrow, he said. We will reach the abbey before noon.

Long after midnight Mr. Talbot awoke, forgetful of where he was, still walking Thames-side with his book under his arm, feeling pursued on a windy night and seeing a dark boat and a boatman skimming toward him over the water's surface. He lay open-eyed, remembering. Arthur's face lay close to his, his long-lashed eyes seeming half open but his spirit far elsewhere, Mr. Talbot could tell it by his breath, so regular it seemed not the boy's own. On his other side, wrapped in his big coat, Doctor Dee slept, deep-rumbling.

A little light came in through the horn of the low small window. The eaves dripped. Mr. Talbot thought of Wales, where once he had run away to hide when he was a boy. He thought how he had hidden in the mountains, and lived alone for many long months; how he had built himself a hut of skins and branches, like brutish men of olden time, and sat within it listening to the rain drip from the leaves. After long thought he had dug a mine into the earth; he had shaped a vessel of clay, and fired it in a fire of wood and coal. He knew what to do next.

He awoke again then, and lay awake till dawn, feeling clear and pure inside more intensely than he had ever before, as though his heart were turning to gold. Had he ever gone to Wales really? He thought about what he had seen and done there, the rain blown across the stone faces of the hills, the mine, the fire. He felt within himself two clear pools, one dark, one light, that he could dip from: this, and that; the one, the other; and there was not anything that could not be made from the mixture.

After the Dissolution of King Harry's time, Glastonbury Abbey and its messuages, its woods, streams, and fields, had been deeded to various lords and gentlemen, sold by them, resold. Whatever of value could be stripped from the church and the buildings was stripped, lead roofs and gutters, ornament, glass; the books and manuscripts were thrown away or burned or sold to booksellers or paper-makers by the cartload. Now dock and dandelion grew in the roofless aisles, violets in the tumbled stone; the campfires of homeless men sheltering within the ruins of chapel and chapter-house blackened the walls. The immense cathedral served the present owners as a kind of quarry; dressed stone could be taken away by whoever paid a fee to the landlord.

—They know not what they do who sell these stones, said Doctor Dee when the little party stood within the abbey precincts. They know not what they do.

He put out his hand to touch a stone eagle, fallen there, a stone book within its talons, bright grass grown up around it.

—Here stood the ancientest church of this isle, he said. Here that holy man of Arimathea came, with that Cup never seen again since those times. Here, only the place is lost, Patrick is buried, and what other great carcasses? Dunstan of Canterbury, in a tomb known only to the monks of this place, and now since they are driven away, known to no one. And Edgar, peaceable, provident king.

—And Arthur, said Arthur.

—In a great sarcophagus, not of lead or of stone but of oak, an oak tree hollowed out, they found him; his shin bone larger than your shin and thigh together. There were giants in the land in those days. His wife with him; a lock of golden hair was in the tomb when it was opened, but a monk touched it, and it turned all to dust.

—Guinevere, said Arthur. He was shivering in the thin rain that had been falling all morning.

—Is it there? Doctor Dee asked Mr. Talbot. There where you dug?

Two obelisks stood by the old track through the abbey, Dod Lane. Mr. Talbot, hugging himself, turned in the huge churchyard.

—I don't know, he said. It seems not the same now. I cannot tell.

—We'll look, said the doctor.

And so all of that afternoon they climbed over grass-grown monuments and poked between fallen stones and climbed down into vaults filled up with rubble and started a badger from his den, while Mr. Talbot, finger to his lips and eyes uncertain, tried to remake the journey or redream the dream that had once brought him here; until, wet and tired, they took shelter in the Mary chapel, under an unfallen piece of roof. They made a camp there, and lit a fire on the stones of the floor, and ate bread and cheese they had brought from the inn.

—I have a journey to go, Doctor Dee told them then. A short

journey. If I do not return before nightfall or soon after, I will not come till morning. Then we will look again.

He rose, and took up his staff and plaited hat; he saw to it that his son's coat was dry inside, and that there was a dry place for him to sleep by the fire, and a cloak to wrap him in; he blessed the boy's head.

—Watch well, he said to Mr. Talbot. Think hard where we shall look.

When he had walked away, picking his way carefully amid the wet stones, Mr. Talbot sat with Arthur by the fire. The boy had grown silent, a little uncertain with his father gone.

—Shall we look? Mr. Talbot said.

—No.

They sat, hands in their sleeves, looking into the feeble fire.

—I'll tell you a secret, Mr. Talbot said.

Arthur's eyes opened wider.

—My name, said Mr. Talbot, is not Talbot.

—What is it then?

Mr. Talbot said nothing more. He put a stick into the fire; the wetness of it sizzled and smoked.

—I know what that book tells, he said then. It tells how the work of making gold is to be done. I know that's what it tells, though I can't read it.

—How is gold made? Arthur asked.

—Gold grows, said Mr. Talbot. Deep deep in mountains, where the earth is oldest, gold is. So you make deep mines to find it. But you must never take away all the gold; you must not, for you will take away the seed of gold, by which it grows. Like fruit, take away that which is ripe; leave the rest to ripen. And it will. Slowly, slowly, the stones of the mountain, the clays of it, grow up to be gold; they become gold.

—Do they?

—In Wales, Mr. Talbot said. In Wales, when I went into the mountains, I knew the gold was growing, all around me, in the earth; deep within. It seemed I could hear it grow.

—Hear it?

—One day, in a thousand years, a thousand thousand, all stone will have grown into gold.

—The world will end by then, said Arthur.

—Perhaps it will. But we can teach the gold to grow faster. If we learn how. We can help, like midwives, to bear the gold from what contains it; we can bring it to birth.

Arthur said nothing to that. The rain had slackened, begun to cease, and the clouds once again to part and change; the sun shone. Glastonbury was not gold but silver.

—I'll go piss, said Mr. Talbot.

He went out past the little fire and into the long green alley of the chapel's nave, and thought a long time. He went down toward the sanctuary along the wall, stopping to look into side-chapels. When he reached the sanctuary and the place where the altar had been, he looked back; he could no longer see the campfire. He took from within his coat a small stone jar, well sealed with wax.

He looked around for a spot. He saw a narrow flight of steps, leading downward beneath a carved arch; when he went down them, he found that the way was blocked with fallen stones, except for a narrow opening just large enough for him to get half his body in, but not to crawl inside. He thought he heard, within, a sound of water, as though there were a well inside. He closed his eyes; he saw the dog-face of a smiling being; he dropped the jar into the space within.

Tomorrow, with Doctor Dee, he would find it there, as he had found his book; and the story could go on.

At the top of the bald high hill called the Tor of Glastonbury there is a tower like a finger of stone, St. Michael's tower. At the foot of the hill, in the valley that lies between the Tor and the hill west of it, Chalice Hill, there is a well, the Holy Well. The road that leads up the Tor passes this well. Doctor Dee, on his way upward, stopped by it. Chambers have been built around it, of heavy stone that shows the tool that worked it, and which Doctor Dee supposed the Romans put there, or even the Druids before them.

They were great and wise men, the Druids, and of the doctor's own race, though in their pride they had denied Christ and striven against His disciples. There were tales of how they had set up the stones that stood in a ring on Salisbury plain, had brought them here out of Ireland through the air, like a flock, and settled them there on the plain. Doctor Dee knew that when blessed Patrick had questioned them, and asked them who made the world, the Druids answered: the Druids made it.

He stepped down into the mossy way which led into the

chambers of the well. At the dark door he put out his hand against the stone, listening for a time to the sound of the waters; then he entered. It was somewhere up on Chalice Hill that the spring arose which fed this well; it arose, so it was said, at the spot where Joseph of Arimathea buried the Cup from which Our Lord drank at His last supper. The Cup, *calix, crater,* from which that hill was named. Unless the chalice the hill was named for was the hill itself, a cup inverted on the earth and pouring out its liquid water-wine here. Doctor Dee looked down at the stones which the water passed over—they were streaked and soaked with red. Blood Well was this place's other name.

He drank there, and prayed, and went on. The road left the shelter of the greening trees, and by stages proceeded around the Tor in a spiral as it went upward. The sky began to clear, and a sharp breeze was on the doctor's cheek. As he rose higher, farther and farther spread out the lowlands in his sight, even as far as to the sea. Above these lowlands rose Cadbury Hill, and Chalice Hill, and Weary-all Hill like a whale lifting a huge back into the air, and this hill he climbed. In ancient times, he knew, they had all been islands, these hills; the lowlands were all under sea. Glastonbury itself had been an island, Avalon, isle of apples. This Tor could be got to by boat; Weary-all was the isle where Joseph first put ashore, where he plunged his staff into the earth. There, the Thorn had sprung up, the Thorn which blossoms at Christmas. Doctor Dee had seen it, the Holy Thorn, all white flowers at Christ's nativity: for he had climbed these hills many times, and described their antiquities, and measured the earth around. Chorography was another art of his: the measurement and description of a portion of earth and its contents and its geometries. Only there was no portion of earth that was like the one he stood on now, no other portion that he knew of.

Breathing strongly, and pressing his own staff into the roadway, he climbed. The road turned. He was approaching the summit; and as he trod the spiral track, the lowlands and the hills around began to awake.

The Lion that Mr. Talbot had seen could not be discerned from the Tor, for he lay on the slope of the hills opposite Somerton; but now the doctor could make out Virgo, toward the east, outlined by the black and silver penstroke of the Cary River—Virgo, like his Queen, with her staff, and the wide panniers of her skirts. East of her, the Scorpion lay curled by the river Brue, the sting in his tail an outcrop of bright stone.

The Centaur next awoke, who was Hercules too, hero and horse in one, made of the Pennard Hills or himself making them or both; West Pennard church steeple the arrow in his bow. And north of him the Goat, and the old fortification they called Ponter's Ball making the Goat's horn. Doctor Dee went on walking sunwise around the cone of the Tor. Figure by figure the Twelve came forth, from the Ram in Wilton and Street with the corn on his back green now that would be golden fleece come harvest time, all around to the two Fishes tied together at the tail: one being the great whale of Wearyall Hill, the other lying in the village of Street, its round eye the old round churchyard there. A huge nativity which no one who did not know it was there could ever see, not even from the top of the Tor, though it might be discerned—it might be—by one who flew overhead, hovered overhead like that hawk, and looked down.

If it had not been a dream, who had carried him?

Doctor Dee had reached the precincts of the tower. In its height the wind hooted, the freshening wind that plucked at the doctor's beard and at the hem of his coat. Now the land lay open all around, and Doctor Dee stood in the center as though at a gnomon and looked out over Logres.

Kingdoms had been smaller then: and yet when the sea had filled the low places and covered the sands between the isles and high places which formed these figures, figures of the starry universe above them, then Arthur and his knights had had kingdom upon kingdom hereabouts, land upon land to travel in. For one kingdom is all kingdoms: a hill, a road, a dark wood; a castle to come to; a perilous bridge to cross.

Avalon was the isle where Arthur was borne away to die or sleep: and yet the same isle was Camelot where he reigned. And Avalon was Perceval's island too, by right from his father King Pelles who had his seat there: so some old books had it. It was the place from which Perceval set out to seek the Grail: that Grail sometimes a cup, sometimes a stone, sometimes a dish, which was not different from the cup that blessed Joseph brought to this septentrional isle, which poured good water still: had poured water into Doctor Dee's hands this very day.

By Michael's tower Doctor Dee sat down, and drew his coat around him. Clouds lifting from the Severn Sea like winged crea-

tures showed him a white bar and a gray line that was his own land
of Wales far to the West, the West into which the Druids had gone
away, bearing the past with them.

There was not one Grail; there were, or will be, or have been,
not one Grail but five, five Grails for five Percevals to find. There
were Grails of earth, water, fire, air: there was a stone, a cup, a
crater or furnace, and the basin borne by Aquarius, who is a sign of
air. And another, the Grail of the quintessence. Unless that Grail be
not truly the whole seven-ringed cup of heaven itself, containing all
things, contained within all things, the cup from which, willy-nilly,
every soul must drink.

He thought: Is the universe one thing? And is the whole of it
contained in every part?

Years ago, long years ago, he had discovered what might be a
sign for the one thing the universe is. He had drawn it with rule and
compass, and for a year he had bent his mind upon it to see if it
would grow, to see if it would begin to draw to itself like a
lodestone more and more of what the world is made of: fire, air,
earth, water; numbers, stars, souls. The more he regarded it, the
more it did so. It became a glyph like the holy glyphs of Ægypt that
contain knowledge otherwise inexpressible, words too long to speak.
He carried his sign with him as a woman carries a child, until one
week in Antwerp (he was a fire of knowledge in that week, a
burning bush) he had committed his sign to a little book, and
belched out all that he knew about it, wrote without knowing what
he wrote, until he was empty.

He had written it; he had had it set in type, and printed.

And it might still be that the sign which he had made was a
sign for the one thing that the universe is. But it was a seal over
secrecies now. It had passed from him, and he no longer knew what
it pictured; he could not understand the book he had written.

He might come to know again and understand. He might,
now. *Not any answer withheld from you.* The hawk that hung in the
middle of the air, looking down, began to fall in a long gyre. The
sun was setting in the sea: Doctor Dee could almost hear it hiss.

To go about Logres, as the sun goes about the year; to search
the circle of creation, and find in a castle that is your own the Grail,
long-sought, long-hungered-for, that belongs to you. In the High
History which Doctor Dee had read in the old language, King
Perceval's name is construed *Par lui fet:* made by himself.

And the cup that he sought, wounded, in the castle of his wounded father, what was it but this cup Aquarius which Doctor Dee looked down on in the star temple laid out in Somersetshire below?

And though it might be only here that such figures of earth (now darkening, and closing great eyes in sleep) had been cut by wizards' hands, still the stars shine everywhere; and so it must be that in every place there is a star temple, impressed upon circles of earth, large or small. And inside every one of them must a Grail be hidden.

Doctor Dee raised his eyes to the heavens, whose stairs were swept of cloud now, and Tell me, he said: Tell me: Is the universe one thing? Is it, after all?

The angels saw him, who manage those skies he put his question to: they saw him, for this ring of earth is a place they often stop by, to gaze into it, as into a mirror, or through it, as through a keyhole. They smiled, hearing his question; and then one by one turned away, to look over their shoulders—for they were disturbed by a noise, a noise as of footfalls far away and faint, the footfalls of someone coming through behind.

T W O

▲

All on an April morning, Pierce Moffett walked out of his apartment and down Maple Street toward town. In the yards along his way householders were digging, planting, freeing shrubs of winter garb and cutting their ragged hair. Some turned to watch Pierce go by, and most greeted him. "Morning!" Pierce said heartily, grinning inwardly to be hailed in this way, it was as though he had suddenly been returned to the common intercourse of earth and man from some stony planet, these nice people couldn't imagine how odd it was for him to be wished a good morning by strangers in the street. He blessed them, blessed their big fannies protruding as they bent over their pots and borders, blessed their hedges and the lemony blossoms of their springing black bushes, now what was that stuff called again, was that forsythia?

There was so much to learn, or to relearn, the names of plants and flowers and the order of their coming forth, the usual greetings to be offered between citizens and the usual replies to them; the streets and alleys of the town, its stores, customs, history. Pierce sighed deeply. *The world is so full of a number of things,* he thought, *that I'm sure we should all be as happy as kings.*

As happy as kings. He had turned from Maple Street down River Street (had the founding families pondered a long time before choosing these simple self-evident names, Maple, River, Hill?) and then down to where River Street meets Bridges Street, and the town's chief buildings faced the fast brown river and the spring sky. There on the corner he went into a small store whose red-and-white tin sign said VARIETIES. He asked for a pouch of his usual cheap tobacco, and noticed that there were magazines here as well

as candy, gum, and cigarettes, a good selection in fact in a tall
wooden rack, including one or two fairly abstruse journals Pierce
had supposed he would now have to subscribe to, but no. Good.
He wandered farther down the dim length of the shop. There was a
brief soda fountain with a real marble top and three or four stools,
he turned one with a hand as he passed and it grumbled as such
stools should. There was a notice posted beside the stacks of today's
newspapers, stating that those who wanted a Sunday *New York
Times* must sign up for one in advance.

Well.

For a long time Pierce had stopped taking that immense wad of
newsprint; he had become convinced that what gave Sunday the
particular character it had for him—a character it retained in all
seasons and every kind of weather, a headachy, dreary, dissipated
quality—was not Jehovah claiming his own day and poisoning it
even for unbelievers, not that at all but a sort of gas leaking out
from that very Sunday *Times,* a gas with the acrid smell of printer's
ink, a narcotizing, sickening gas. And in fact the symptoms seemed
to have been at least partly relieved when he began refusing to buy
it. But out here its effect might be neutralized. How anyway were
Sundays spent here? Maybe he'd have to start going to church.

Still farther along (the shop was longer and more full of a
number of things than it had seemed from the street) there were
counters of stationery and school supplies, pens and pencils, tape,
glue, and stacks of long pads just the yellow of those flowers he had
seen. There were typewriter ribbons too, and small bottles of white
paint for painting out errors; there were erasers, both rhomboid and
cockade style. There were in fact all the tools of his new trade,
everything seeming to be of the best quality and just unwrapped.

"Anything I can help you with, there, sir?" asked the lady at
the front counter, whose cat's-eye glasses were fitted with a beaded
chain that hung down her back, and swung when she turned her
head.

"Oh, just looking." From a row of different-sized account
books, he pulled a tall slim one, its corners and spine bound in
maroon leather or leatherette, and the word RECORD in tall serif
letters impressed on its gray buckram cover. How was it that
antique designs like this continued to be produced? Perhaps only to
keep the accounts of stores like this one. The edges of its pages
were marbled, and it was surprisingly expensive.

He decided to buy it, and to record in it his new life in the country. He was not as certain of his prose as he ought to be now that his living would be depending on it, and he had often heard that keeping a diary was a way of keeping the tools edged. And he might welcome something to do, these long evenings after they rolled up the sidewalks of Blackbury Jambs.

Outside again in the pale sunlight, he looked up and down the street, toward the Shadow River bridge one way (narrow and of stone) and the Blackbury River bridge the other way (wide, black iron). The broad water out beyond sparkled and shivered; it almost seemed to Pierce that he could see, if he half-closed his eyes, the different waters of the two commingling rivers, cold and clear, slow and dull—an illusion, doubtless. Just behind him, when he turned away, was the library.

All right.

It was a sort of shingle-style Romanesque concoction, surely the most inefficient style ever adopted for public buildings; quite a bit of it went to hold up a large and functionless cupola. There was a piece of native slate embedded in the wall of the foyer, with a leaf and possibly an animal track impressed on it. Inside was cool and bright, that cupola in fact let in the sun pleasingly; the oddly shaped wings and galleries had each a function; it was a nice place. Another old woman with a chain to her glasses (they would be important, apparently, to his life here, these women; he had already been served by one at the bank) presided at the central desk. He would ask her for a card. If for nothing but to pick up the odd entertainment: for here close by the door, for those who didn't care or dare to penetrate farther, was a rack of current best-sellers, colorful blocks wrapped in plastic like chocolate boxes.

One among them was the book *Phaeton's Car,* whose huge success Julie thought might presage the success of his own. Pierce pulled it out. A paper strip inside the plastic said it was a ONE WEEK BOOK, not nice for an author to be told that even if it was true.

He knew the book, of course, its contents were mostly containable in its blurbs and its premises were unavoidable on talk shows. Once long ago starships from Elsewhere had landed here, and alien intelligences had dwelt among us; they were responsible not only for most of the titanic and inexplicable earthworks of prehistory (Stonehenge, etc.) but had also left traces of their visit in the corpus of world myth, and even their portraits on cave walls and tombs. A bizarre kind of euhemerism. The old gods weren't really gods, no that was silly; what they were, really, were folks from outer space.

A lot of his students had liked this explanation for history too.

He opened the book to the middle. There was a photograph of a bare tor surmounted by a tower. *Glastonbury "lighthouse"?* asked the caption. *The ley-lines from all over Britain center on "Avalon" (p. 195).* Pierce flipped through to that page.

"The fact that mappable straight lines of enormous length traverse the whole of the British Isles, connecting churches, old standing stones, mountain peaks, and 'holy' sites of all kinds, was first established by researchers in the 1920s." Pierce always enjoyed the "researchers" and "investigators" of books like this one; readers were to imagine disinterested scientists, possibly in lab coats, and not the collection of cranks and odd numbers who actually compiled "research" like this. "At the same time, in the neighborhood of Glastonbury, gigantic astral figures were discovered in the earth, forming a circle many miles in diameter, and *unable to be perceived except from the air.* What purpose could the 'Star Temple of Glastonbury' serve? A sort of star map, guiding visitors who came by other means than land or sea . . . ?"

Good lord, Pierce thought, snapping shut the book and reinserting it in its row. Star temples and ley-lines, UFOs and landscape giants, couldn't they see that what was really, permanently astonishing was the human ability to keep finding these things? Let anyone looking for them be given a map of Pennsylvania or New Jersey or the Faraways, and he will find "ley-lines"; let human beings look up long enough on starry nights and they will see faces looking down at them. *That*'s the interesting thing, *that*'s the subject: not why there are ley-lines, but why people find them; not what plan the aliens had for us, but why we think there must, somehow, always have been a plan.

Julie would get it. She must. She had to.

He turned away into the central atrium (irritated, excited, seeing in his mind green hills and blue streams as from a height). Fiction, biography, science branched away. Meaning. He thought there were five basic needs a human being had: for food, and shelter; clothing, if that wasn't shelter; for sex, or love, if that was different; and for Meaning. Deprived of meaning a man might wither and die as surely as if deprived of food or water.

Not noticing where he walked, he had gone into the fiction

stacks, casting his eyes over those mostly unwanted things, they seemed sadder somehow than neglected science or thought. Down the way a young woman pulled one out, glanced within it, smiled, and carried it away; what, he wondered. Norton. Norris. Nofzinger. *The Way's Far Turning,* by Helen Niblick. Mitchell, well that one of course, in many copies. Mackenzie, Macauley, Macdonald. Ross Lockridge. Joseph Lincoln.

And well look at this.

When, just out of curiosity, he had gone to the New York branch library nearest him, he hadn't found a single one. And here were dozens, or a dozen anyway at least. The Complete Works. How do you like that.

Here was *Bitten Apples,* wasn't that the one about Shakespeare? And here was *The Book of a Hundred Chapters,* that had frightened and awed him as an adolescent. And a bunch more that he had not read, or didn't remember having read. Now why, he wondered, would a little library like this one have all these? Kraft had never, after all, been a Shellabarger, or a Costain. He touched one or two spines, drew out a volume, remembering the rich anticipation the arrival of one of them would start up in him when it showed up in the monthly box from the state library; how he would settle to it, as to a long meal, accompanied by milk and cookies.

Somewhere in these too, as in the book on Bruno, he might have come across matter, surely must have come across matter, that he had used to make Ægypt. Though he felt pretty sure that whatever he had found in them had only confirmed the existence of that country, and his discovery of it predated his discovery of Kraft. He was pretty sure.

How anyway *had* he discovered Kraft?

Once, one of these books had got into the box, filling some request of his or Sam's or Winnie's, though Winnie's taste was for escapes of a different order. What had he asked for, "stories of history," that had brought him Kraft? And which had been the first he got, was it Bruno or one of these fictions, that caused him to ask for more? Had he asked for more, or had they just arrived?

He pushed back the one he had drawn out.

When he had a card.

There were other resources he discovered; this cupcake building was raisined with good things. The DNB. Cambridge Modern History. Catholic Encyclopedia, a good old one filled with oddities that later editions were ashamed of or knew better than to include; a fine field for browsing in. And there were many huge and lavish old folios of prints and albums of pictures, multivolume botanical atlases and bird books bound in leather—the wealthy summer residents of other days must have bequeathed these things to their local library. The tall shelves around the reading room were full of them. Pierce was standing at the entrance of this pleasant room (tables of light wood, green lamps, dark portraits) when a woman who had been kneeling at a case on the far side rose, a thick volume in her arms, and turned to see him, or rather turned her dark eyes his way unseeing, and went to sit with her book at a table spread about with other books and papers.

Could it be? Of course that night had been dark and brief, and months ago. And it would be strange if very nearly the first person he came across in this town were one of the only two or three he had already met. But it seemed to be her. He went on looking at her, and when she glanced at him again, he smiled, but she made no sign of recognition.

Got to be her.

He made his way around the room's perimeter, and came up near her table. Besides the book—it was a biographical dictionary, open at Emerson—she was equipped with graph paper and pencils, and a calculator; she seemed to be casting curves of some kind, one axis of which was marked off in years.

"Hi," he said.

She looked up at him, pleasant face for meeting possibly bothersome undeniably male stranger.

"Mrs. Mucho?" he said.

The face changed. "No," she said.

"Sorry," he said. "My name is Pierce. I'm sure we've met."

"I don't think so," she said.

"Your name is . . ."

"My name is Ryder."

Good heavens. "Oh."

"I don't remember you."

"Sorry, sorry," he said. "I'm new in town, actually. You just look a lot like someone I know."

"Sorry," she said, her face now definitely closed, as though she had decided a trick was being played on her, or a move made, and she had had enough.

"Well," Pierce said. "My mistake."

"Uh-huh," she said.

He bowed a goodbye and moved away smartly, not to seem a masher. In some ways not really like her at all, or not like the picture of her he retained within, which the months had however no doubt heavily altered. And yet that dark rope of hair down her back, which he had seen her wring the river water from.

Negotiating with the lady at the desk for a card, he glanced once back at her, and caught her looking at him. She returned then, not instantly, to her book, and to whatever the work was that engaged her.

It could be, of course (he thought, climbing up the town home) that the partly jocular "Mrs. Mucho" he had greeted her with didn't strike her as a bit amusing and she had decided thereupon to cut him dead. Ryder—was that the name she gave?—might be the maiden name by which she now wanted to be called.

Or it might be—it was a thought that had occurred to him before, usually when he had just called one of his loves by the name of one of the others, a thing which he and all men did and which no woman that he knew of ever did—it might be that there was only one woman in the world to whom he was attracted, one woman for him, and she kept showing up in his life in different forms, with different names, disguised as herself.

En ciel un dieu, en terre une déesse, and here she just was again.

Not that it mattered much, of course. His vow was taken, and a year's long work was before him. When he arrived at No. 21, an ungainly chocolate-brown van was offloading boxes and boxes of his books, which had been much delayed in transit, and were here at last.

"You don't belong here," Beau Brachman said to Pierce.

"No?"

"No." Pierce stood with his neighbor in the sunlight of Beau's lawn; just for this moment the lawn was tender green, and from every twig-tip of every maple on Maple Street yellow-green baby leaves were extruding themselves. The problem of how these small but perfect jewellike leaves grow into identically shaped but very much larger leaves, a problem Pierce had left off pondering on a day in April some years ago, occurred to him again. In amid the leaves were bunches of those winged seeds that maples bear, which you could (he remembered) wear on your left breast as aviator's wings, or break carefully open and clip to your nose. Or both, for that matter.

"Even though you've forgotten it," Beau said, "you're really from somewhere else. This is not your world, even though it seems to be. This cosmos. You arrive into it, come from a long way away; sort of stunned from the long journey, you forget you were on a journey at all. You started out an astral body, but during your journey you come to be clothed in material reality; in matter, like an overcoat. Inside is still the astral body. But now bound and asleep."

"Uh-huh," Pierce said. "And from where did you start out then? Where did you come from?"

"Lifetimes ago?" Beau said.

"Lifetimes ago. Initially."

"Well suppose," Beau said, "that we, we souls, came from outer space. The stars. Suppose we lost our way; stopped here; adopted a form that would fit with this planet's like low level of evolution. And suppose we lived so long like that that then we forgot."

"Hm." These stars, Pierce thought, would be the same stars the kindly aliens came from in *Phaeton's Car,* who taught men arts.

"Back there they remember," Beau said, seeming to be improvising. "They think of us; they wait for *us* to remember, and turn homeward. They might even send messages, that can be heard by the astral body."

"Which is asleep."

"That's the message," Beau said. "Wake up."

A little red sports car had turned the corner at the end of Maple Street and was coming toward Beau's.

"But beyond all those stars," said Beau, "in this story, is God. And no matter how far back we travel, we won't reach home again till we reach God. From where we started."

The car at first shot past the lawn where Beau and Pierce sat, and then stopped abruptly. Out from the passenger side came a child of two or three, who ran toward Beau, already holding out to him the doll she carried, and calling his name. Sunlight in her golden hair, clear eyes happy, she struck Pierce as singularly beautiful. After her, struggling from the miniature car's bucket seat, came a dark and thickish man, who called after the child: "Sam!"

"Hi, Sam. Hi, Mike," Beau said mildly, not choosing to rise from the stump in the sun where he sat.

"H'lo," said the dour man, Mike, seeming burdened with thought or care. "Her mother will be by for her. Hey, 'bye, Sam." This a trifle reproachfully to the child, who was clambering into Beau's lap. She clambered down again and dutifully up her father, for a kiss; as she was given it, her father's doubtful eye fell on Pierce, and he nodded noncommittally.

"G'bye, Sam. Mommy be here later."

"Later," Sam echoed. From the red car now had come a tall woman, with thick dark hair; she was pushing back the canvas top of the car. First day of the year warm enough. Her eye—noncommittal also—looked sidewise momentarily behind her at the lawn, the child, Mike, Beau. Pierce.

Her man turned from his child and hurried down to where she struggled with the car, maybe inconvertible after all.

"His name," Pierce ventured, "is Mike Mucho."

"Yup," said Beau.

Mike roughly took charge of the comic top from her, and she resigned it to him. Her eyes again wandered across Pierce, without recognition.

Now damn if she doesn't look *exactly* like the woman in the library. Ryder? Ryder. *Damn* if she does not. His confusion had been understandable, it had been more than that, it had been almost necessary. "Her name is Rosie," he said to Beau, as with a swing of her dark hair she turned away and inserted herself neatly into the driver's seat.

"It's Rose anyway, I think," Beau said.

The toy car, open now, putted away, Mike Mucho's arm flung proprietarily over the back of his wife's seat. Still chums apparently.

"So you don't belong here," Beau said, lifting Sam with a professional fillip to his shoulders. "You only seem to. You can never say This is where I belong. The best you can say is This is *like* it. This day, this place. This is like the place where I belong."

If that were so (and Pierce did not at all believe it was, he knew what heresy was being spoken here, and knew now what Beau was too) then Pierce would have to say it: This is like, this is a *lot* like the place where I belong.

"Come on in," Beau said. "Have some tea."

"Thanks, no," Pierce said. "Back to the books." The child on

Beau's shoulders, carried toward the house, looked back, first leftward
and then rightward, at Pierce in frank curiosity. And from where had
she got those golden curls?

Laid out on Pierce's bed together, squared up in two ranks of
two, the four volumes of Frank Walker Barr's collected studies of
history showed to Pierce the whole painting that had been cut up in
four to make their covers. What it pictured, though, was anybody's guess: here a man pleaded before lictors; there, a mendicant
in rags had come to a classical temple; dark Miltonic beings with
bat wings fled away; a flight of angels, or anyway tall and noble
ladies, draped, and winged with heavy, pigeon-gray wings, climbed
en masse toward an obscurity in the picture's center, where four
corners of the volumes met.

Cockerel Books. "His" publisher. He hoped that his own
volume, if it was ever finished, and if really published, would be
pondered by the designer who had done these. If if.

He swept them up, Time's body, and pushed them onto a shelf
that ran along the left-hand wall; groaning he bent to another
boxful of books, and with his jackknife cut the tape that sealed it.
Groaning, because his back and limbs still ached from the un-
wonted exercise of moving furniture, then carrying these boxes up
the stairs, and then the lumber for the shelves that he had put up all
along the walls of the central room of his apartment, which would
be library, bedroom, and workshop all in one. He had hoped to
have Spofford's help with the shelves, but he had not been able to
reach him, and so he'd done it himself, quickly, testily, and not
excellently. And it had become evident already that there would not
be room enough on them for all these books.

He scooped out two big handfuls, glancing at their spines. His
books had gone into their boxes on the basis of size, not content,
and these were all little guys, including a paperback cookbook,
some old pocket diaries, his childhood Mass book (*Our Sunday
Missal*) and a little Bible, some volumes of the Yale Shakespeare,
and the *Monas hieroglyphica* of John Dee. These handfuls he roughly
shoved onto a shelf, extracting only the Dee to go with others of its
special kind on the left-hand wall: a small, thin book, bound in red,
with the sign, the Monad, stamped on the cover, and appearing
again on the title page, reproduced in this cheap edition from the
original of 1564:

In his own book he would have to make something of this sign—how it came to be, and Doctor Dee's high hopes for it, and its subsequent odd reappearances in the history of Ægypt. He would have to take a shot at explaining it, too, and the power such a thing could once have seemed to embody, a geometric conflation or universal puzzle-ring made of a dozen different glyphs, elemental, planetary, mathematical, a seal of silence and a promise of revelation.

To do so, of course, he would have to begin to understand it himself, and feel its power; and in fact he did not. He was not unique in this; the scholar who translated the little book had himself felt compelled to interpolate into Dee's closed-mouthed and gnomic Latin some guesses as to the sense:

> All will be forced to acknowledge it [an] exceedingly rare [event] that (for the everlasting memory of men) this [work] be sealed with my London seal of Hermes, so that in it there may be not even one superfluous dot, and that not one dot may be wanting [in it] to signify those things which we have said (and things far greater yet).

He turned the page. A warning: Some men may lose themselves in the "labyrinth" of Dee's thought, "torture their minds in incredible ways [and] neglect their everyday affairs"; others, "imposters and mere spectres of men," will rashly deny the truths contained herein. Hm.

What would be nice to have for his own book was a Baroque title page like this one: an engraved portal at once stern and ludicrous, with pillars, lintel, and bases all labeled and emblematic, Earth, Air, Fire, Water, quotes in Latin and Greek on ruffed banners, Mercurius with winged hat and feet, finger to his lips. Above the dedication (to the Emperor Maximilian!) was a motto:

Qui non intellegit, aut taceat aut discat.
Which would actually mean, let's see,

Let [him] who does not understand [this], either be silent [about it] or learn.

Well and which was his case? It might be, of course, that you could be both: both fool and imposter, knowing nothing, saying much. He shut the *Monas hieroglyphica* and slipped it in among the others with whom he would be consorting here, his Secondary Sources: with Kraft's Bruno, with Barr in his four fat volumes, with Thorndike in six fatter volumes; with Earl's old astronomy textbook, Lewis and Short's dictionary and a dictionary of angels; with dozens of others the logic of whose association on the left-hand shelf only Pierce for the moment could discern. Let others learn, or be silent.

And did he have a dedicatee? He didn't, though it struck him just then for the first time what a unique gift such a dedication made: so rich and flattering, so costless to give.

What his book *might* have (he thought, stepping back and with arms folded regarding the spines of his collection, some of them upside-down) was an author's note of some kind.

Yes. An Author's Note: *This book, more even than most books,* no, *More even than most books are, this is a book made out of other books. The author wishes to acknowledge. Out of whose great and real scholarship, out of whose daring speculations, out of whose. This fantasia on their themes.*

An apology, maybe, in advance, for the uses he intended to put them to, and the company he intended to have them keep.

He turned away, and opened another box. This one was full of big books: a big dictionary and a big picture book on clocks, some volumes of his 1939 *Britannica* inherited at Sam's death, a big Shakespeare and a great big Bible.

This last (Douai), heavy in his hands, tempted him to a sortilege.

He put it down on the bed, opened its cover, grasped the thick text, and with his eyes closed riffed the pages. Stopped. With eyes still closed, he put his finger on a text, and warily looked. Isaiah.

For you shall go out with joy, and be led forth with peace: the mountains and the hills shall sing praise before you, and all the trees of the country shall clap their hands.

T H R E E

▲

Like all of Fellowes Kraft's books, the little autobiography which Boney gave to Rosie had an epigraph. It was from *Love's Labor's Lost:*

> *Welcome the sour cup of prosperity!*
> *Affliction may one day smile again; and until then*
> *Sit down, sorrow.*

Which seemed to be a sort of joke when you thought about it; it might be, Rosie thought, that it was the source rather than the quote itself that was significant, because a big theme of the book was Kraft's search for an Ideal Friend, and the various disappointments, betrayals, forswearings, and lapses the search had entailed, all of them presented so delicately though that Rosie wondered whether he could have been unaware of the shape of his nature, was really innocently in pursuit of just a friend, and it was she who had a dirty mind.

If he was coy about the Ideal Friend, he was frank about royalties and the business of writing. He gave a full accounting of how much he had made on each book, which Rosie found illuminating; enough to live on, apparently, but not enough to live well. There was family money too, though Kraft was a little more secretive about that; and there was the Foundation. Certainly the royalties from books could not have bought the house in Stonykill, or paid for the restless travel Kraft recorded, always hopefully undertaken, always illuminated by art or architecture he found along the way, always leaving an ashen taste: that was because of the Friends,

Rosie thought, Nikos and Antonio and the Baron and Cyril and Helmut. There were cloudy photographs of one or two of these men tipped into the book, inside printed frames, with name and place and date; in fact—except for one of a gay and childlike woman a long time ago, in a big hat and summer frock, his mother—those were all the illustrations.

No, one other: Kraft and two other young men, in a sort of truck on a mountain road, with a picture-book castle white and vague far down the valley behind. Kraft and whoever these others were wore rough clothes, leather shorts and sweaters. Underneath, it said: *On expedition in the Giant Mountains, 1937,* which Rosie thought was remarkable. She hadn't come upon anything in the text about this expedition, and didn't know at all where the Giant Mountains were. Fairyland, maybe.

She wasn't, however, reading the book in any sequential way. It lay on her desk (a card table actually, which she had put up in a corner of the office, where she could work) and she would pick it up now and then when she was bored or didn't know how to go on; reading it, or looking at it, seemed sufficiently related to her job to fill the holes in a workday. She was reading in it on a morning late in May, sitting in Boney's chair, with her sneakered feet crossed on his desk, though this was not a workday but a Saturday. Boney himself was out on the lawn, bent over a croquet ball, mallet in hand. Deep green lawn, pride of old gardeners, blue-striped ball and mallet. Rosie could see him, when she raised her eyes from the book: practicing.

"However beautiful we make them, our nests are empty ones," she read; and she thought she knew who this *we* was. "We will be solitary, inevitably, like balls struck across a wide lawn, striking others now and then, and being struck by them. We must be glad of that striking; and keep up our courage and our cheer; and not forget the ones we have loved—no, and pray that our remembrance will in turn earn us a place, however little visited, in their hearts."

Hm. It struck Rosie that nowadays everyone—no, not everyone, but lots of people she knew—lived the way gay men like Kraft had always lived; in brief collisions, restless, among lovers whom there was no way to *fix* except for as long as you could hold their hands. And then what? And then remember them, and keep in touch: friends. Maybe there was a lesson there, or a hint: how not to end up empty-handed altogether, if that was the way you had to live.

She let the creamy pages fall through her fingers toward the last ones. Out on the lawn, Boney swung his mallet neatly, pendulum fashion, before him, and straightened bent knees. Sam, running delighted across the lawn, intercepted the rolling ball. Boney raised a finger; Sam ball in hand looked up to listen, then decided to carry off the ball anyway, shrieking with glee.

"There is, in Venice, in the church of San Pantalon, one of the most remarkable works of art I know of. It is a Baroque ceiling painting done in eye-fooling perspective by one Fumiani, whom I have heard of in no other context. His work covers the entire ceiling and its coffers as though it were one enormous easel painting; it must tell the story of the Saint, though what that story is I have never learned. Despite the convincing upward leap of its perspective, it doesn't have the vanishing lightness of Tiepolo, it has a hallucinatory dark clarity, the figures distinct and solidly modeled, the pillars, flights of stairs, thrones, tripods, and incense-smoke so real that their great size and swift recession from the viewer is vertiginous. Most remarkable of all is that, except for a central flight of angels, there is no obvious religious import to any of it: no Virgin, no Christ, no God or Dove, no cross, no haloes, nothing. Nothing but these huge antique figures, associated in a story more than portraying one; pondering, judging, hoping, seeing, alone. The flight of angels ascends not to a Godhead but to an empty, white-clouded center of the sky.

"Just before he finished this huge work, Fumiani apparently fell from his scaffolding and was killed. Imagine.

"I first saw the ceiling of San Pantalon (Saint Pantaloon, the old fool's church?) in 1930, when I was in Europe writing my very first book, *Bruno's Journey*. I have gone back to Venice often since then, and Fumiani's ceiling has been among the things that drew me back. If I could—if I didn't feel this old Waterman's I hold to be already running on empty—I would attempt one more book, a book like that ceiling; a book composed of groups ambiguous but clear, great solitudes that look on and look away from each other; a book solemn and darkly bright and joyous in its achievement, as that ceiling is joyous in the immense trick of its perspective; a book empty and infinite at its center. A book that would close the circle of my life as Bruno opened it; a book that I could die before finishing."

The hair rose on Rosie's neck. Actually, though, she knew, these enormous thoughts were a little premature, he'd written at least one more whole book after this memoir, was it *Under Saturn?* Or *Darkling Plain?* She'd read it, and it didn't seem very different from the others; just one more. The memoir, she thought, might have been written more at the onset of old age than in the shadow of death.

Apparently, though, he never did come up with the Ideal Friend. So love's labor was lost.

She put down the book, and took her feet from the desk. It was not a workday, but there were lots of things to be done: for this was the first day of the summer's floating croquet tournament, and the season opener, a premier social occasion, was to be played here at Arcady, on the lawn beyond the office.

Not all of the top-seeded players would be coming; some were summer people who hadn't opened their houses yet, some were setting out their tomatoes. She thought Beau and them would come. Allan Butterman had been invited. She hoped Spofford, whom she hadn't officially seen for some time, would be there; he had (he had said) a scheme to talk to her and Boney about.

A scheme. She tightened her sneakers' laces, and, though sure it wasn't really proper to do so, opened the tall casement and stepped out over the sill onto the lawn, calling her daughter for lunch.

Neither had Pierce been seeing much of Spofford since he had arrived, Spofford being busy on his land this time of year and having little reason to come into the Jambs. Pierce was making his own way, though, already aware that as a newcomer he was an object of some interest.

He had got on good terms with Beau and the women of his house, and at Beau's he had met Val among others; indeed it seemed likely that he would soon have a wider circle of acquaintance in this small town than he had had in the great city, in which he had come to be something of a recluse finally, and from which anyway most of the people he cared about had, one by one, escaped, as he had at last himself.

As he had himself. On a Saturday he sat in a deep armchair by his open window, able to smell lilacs (a vast old bush of them burdened the stick-and-wire fence that separated the yard of his building from the neighbors') and hear birds. He was waiting for Val to call up the stairs: for he was going with her and Beau to play croquet of all things. And he was writing in his record book.

"Persistence of magical thinking in this neighborhood is remarkable," he wrote. "My neighbor Beau explaining to me yesterday all about the various planetary characters people can have, mercurial, jovial, saturnine, martial, etc. And how good planetary influences can be attracted to counteract the bad ones. Talismans. Seals. He is *not* getting this from any kind of scholarly endeavor, from any old book; it's just available to him. Yet it's the same prescriptions Marsilio Ficino worked out for himself 500 yrs. ago. How?"

He put his pencil between his teeth like a pirate's dirk, and struggled to rise; he went to the left-hand shelf, sought among the books there, found one, and sought through it as he returned to fall again into the armchair.

"Val," he wrote, "is our astrologer, and apparently an extremely important character around here, just as the astrological doctor or cunning woman would have been in any Elizabethan village. She was explaining the other day at the Donut Hole the qualities or contents of the twelve houses of the horoscope. I asked her how she had come by the descriptions she has; she didn't really have an answer; she's studied, she says, but what she's studied seems to be magazines mostly; and she's thought, and felt—experience, she says, more than anything; but look how her descriptions match the ones Robert Fludd gives in his astrology, in about 1620:"

He propped open the book on the arm of the chair, to copy from it.

"Val says *Vita* is Life, psychological and physical character. Fludd says: life, personality, appearance, and childhood. *Lucrum* is possessions, money, jobs, Val says; Fludd says property, riches, and house (but Val says it's also beginnings; first steps; what you do with what you get in *Vita*). *Fratres,* Val says, isn't just brothers and sisters, it's about family relations and communication of all kinds; more than that, it's friendship too: your circle in effect. Fludd says" —he had lost the place, and had to search—"brothers and sisters, friendship, faith and religion, and journeys."

Well maybe not so exactly identical as he had imagined. How

did journeys come in under *Fratres?* Farther down the list, *Pietas,* the ninth house, had "travel" in Fludd's description. Was there a difference between "journeys" and "travel"? *Mors,* the eighth house, Val had said, isn't just death, it's coming to see the larger perspective on life, the cosmic perspective. Fludd's description was, "Death, work, sadness, inherited diseases, final years." In general Val's descriptions were, well, *nicer* than the seventeenth-century mage's, more meliorative, always conceiving difficulty and obstacle as growth and struggle on a higher plane.

But why after all did the houses have the characters they had, and not others? And why in the order they came in? Val could explain them as a series, a cumulative expansion out of childhood and personal concerns through socialization and family toward cosmic consciousness, a story in twelve chapters: but that wasn't really what Pierce was asking. Any twelve notions in a row could probably be satisfactorily *interpreted,* especially in that esoteric, anagogical way; but that didn't *explain* them. He had put it to Val in the Donut Hole: Why did Death come in the eighth place and not in the last? Why eighth and not seventh or ninth? Did *Lucrum* really deserve its place immediately after *Vita?* And why did the twelve end, not with the grandest expansion or the darkest finality, but with *Carcer,* the Prison?

Beau Brachman had sat listening to their discussion with a faint smile of amusement, as though knowing better, keeping quiet, while Pierce asked questions and Val put forth notions, laughing at her own unhandiness with logical intellection. "*Carcer,*" Val said, "sorrow, okay? And fear and restriction; but see it's the individual fate, and coming to *see* that."

"See what?"

"That your individual fate, *this* time around, is something you have to drop, and get out of, in death, and rejoin the universe. It's *understanding* that." She looked to Beau. "Right?" But Beau said nothing, only smiled, Pierce had begun to think his smile simply stood in the shape of his mouth, the curve of his neat satyr's lips, and not in his eye or mind at all.

Now what did Fludd have for the last house of all? "Hidden enemies, deceivers, jealous persons, evil thoughts, large animals."

Large animals?

Pierce had a sudden inspiration. It popped open in his mind like a bud, and immediately began putting forth petals, unfolding like a time-lapse flower in a nature film, even as Pierce groped for the pencil he had put down.

"Organize the book according to the twelve houses," he wrote, "each house a chapter or segment. Somewhere tell story of how 12 houses came to be, how changed meaning over time, but save this till late; let reader ponder, *Vita? Lucrum?* What's up, etc."

He heard the door below, his front door, open.

"In *Vita,* tell how you came to do this investigation. Barr. Childhood. Etc."

"Hey, handsome." Val's raucous voice from the bottom of the stairs.

"Okay. Coming." His pencil hovered over the page. *Lucrum,* hm. But *Fratres* the company of thinkers, historians, mages then and now. And Bruno's journey.

He got up, putting aside the journal but still writing.

Mors three-quarters through would be where Bruno burns. But then his legacy—Ægypt, infinity—expanding through *Pietas, Regnum, Benefacta.*

Carcer at the end. *Carcer.* Bruno's nine years in a cell the size of Pierce's bathroom. Nine years to recant, and he never did.

Why are we left at the end in prison?

He clattered down a few stairs, back up to snatch up his tobacco, matches, the sunglasses he had bought last summer in Fair Prospect. And out and down again to where Val arms akimbo awaited him with mock impatience. He didn't lock his door behind him, he hadn't locked his door since he had come to this small town; he had somehow instantly broken ten years of city habits as though he had not lived there at all, and was never to take them up again.

Some of the games of the summer's croquet tournament, played on the backyard courts of farmhouses up north, rocky and full of stumps and lost toys, had developed a unique character, and rules of their own; a sort of Obstacle Croquet that some players had got very good at, Spofford among them. But on the billiard-table ground at Arcady croquet was played according to stricter geometries; the crowd tended to be older, and the younger players to be a little abashed, by the whites that Boney's set wore, and Mrs. Pisky's pitcher of lemonade and silver tray of cookies. Pierce, climbing from Val's Beetle and seeing a warm-up round in progress beyond the rose bushes, expected almost to be handed a flamingo, to roll hedgehogs beneath hoops of playing cards.

Rosie Rasmussen saw him coming across the lawn with Beau and Val, a big ugly man in a knit shirt holding with odd delicacy a tiny cigarette stub. She knew who he was, for he had been described to her by Spofford and by Val, but she hadn't yet met him, the new man in the county.

And Pierce saw her, striking a pose with her mallet and with her hand displaying to him, and to Beau and Val, the lawn around her, the flowers and the day; a rangy, cheerful person, carrot-topped with curly hair, the kind of clear-cut almost horsey features that would keep her long looking pretty good. Not his type though. She shouldered her mallet and came across the lawn to meet him. A sudden burst of chagrined groans and laughter came from the white-clothed players near the post; Val cried out her party laugh; Rosie and Pierce took hands.

"Hi, I'm Rosie Rasmussen."

"Pierce Moffett."

"Right," she said, as though he had guessed correctly. "Welcome to the Faraways."

Val called out a hello to people she knew, and began rapidly muttering their histories to Beau beside her. Rosie pointed to the croquet ground. "You play this game?" she asked.

"I haven't," Pierce said. "Oh once or twice. I'm not even sure of the rules."

"I'll show you," Rosie said. "Couldn't be simpler." They walked that way. Pierce looked up at the gray heights of Arcady, its gingerbread and deep eaves, and into the broad veranda where wicker furniture consorted. There were, he was aware, many old houses of this size and age tucked into the hills and glens of the Faraways, turn-of-the-century summer places, modest back then, fabulous now. Spofford, on one drive last summer, had somewhere pointed out the road that led to a big place he said his Rosie's uncle owned. Somewhere. Eventually, Pierce supposed, the local geography would come to lie right in his mind, its hoops and posts and the paths that led among them.

"So Spofford got you to come here, right?" Rosie asked.

"Sort of," Pierce said. "Mostly. And luck. You know Spofford?"

"Real well," she said, smiling and lowering her eyes to the ball she was tapping into place. "How do you like it here?"

Pierce, soft May airs in his hair and shirt, and the chartreuse hills and changeful clouds in view, thought how to answer. "I'll tell you what," he said. "If I had three wishes, any wishes, I would think that one had been delivered already, just getting me here, getting me out of the city."

Rosie laughed at the silly extravagance of this. "Well and you still got two more."

"Those," Pierce said, "I know how to treat."

"You sure?"

"Oh yes." He outlined for her, briefly, his theories and conclusions in the matter of wishing, the preparations he had made, the traps he had foreseen.

"Boy you got all this figured out," Rosie said.

"You betcha," Pierce said. "Be Prepared."

"And what makes you think you've got to get ready? I mean what are you going to do to get these wishes?"

"I'm not sure you have to do anything," Pierce said. "Not to *deserve* them. They just are offered. Your number comes up. You buy an old lamp at a stall in a bazaar. Your fishing line pulls in the magic fish."

"Oh?"

"Sure. I mean the chances are slim, I admit, but still, why not take the trouble to be ready? The same way you always send in those magazine sweepstake things, even though it's millions to one."

"I never do," Rosie said.

"Well in fact," Pierce said, "neither do I." His face creased several ways in an asymmetrical grin. Rosie laughed, puzzled by his funny fantastical gravity. How old would he be, thirty or forty? Big hands, she noted; big feet. "Okay you start at the stake," she said, pointing it out to him. "What color do you want to be?"

"A matter of indifference."

"Spofford said you were writing a book?"

"I'm going to try to."

"Getting paid for it?"

"Not a lot. Some."

"Hey, good for you. About what?"

Pierce leafed rapidly through the several descriptions he kept within, suitable for different hearers. "It's about magic and history," he said. "About magic in history, and also about the history of magic, and magicians."

"Wow, interesting. History when?"

"Well, the Renaissance and a little later. Shakespeare's time."

"Magicians back then, huh," Rosie said. "Like John Dee?"

He looked at her in astonishment. "Well yes," he said. "Among others. How do you come to know that name?"

"I read about him in a novel. Are you a historian?"

"I taught history," Pierce said, unwilling to assign the larger word to himself. "What novel was this?"

"A historical novel." She laughed at the obviousness of this. "Of course. By Fellowes Kraft. He used to live around here, and wrote these books." A look of understanding had begun to cross Pierce's face, a big understanding, bigger than merely knowing the source of her knowledge of old Dee. Rosie suddenly remembered catching a glimpse of someone who looked like him on her last visit to the library. "Yeah, our local famous author. His house is in Stonykill."

"How do you like that," Pierce said.

"You've heard of him? He wasn't really so famous."

"I think I've read most of his books. Once upon a time."

Rosie said, "Huh," looking up at Pierce and experiencing a feeling very much like the feeling of conceiving a painting: the feeling of a number of things melding, turning out to be picturable as one thing. "Is there any chance," she said, "you might need a job? I mean a part-time temporary kind of thing?"

"I," Pierce said.

"And you were really a college teacher? Advanced degrees?"

He gave her a brief vita.

"Listen," she said. "Wait here, will you, just a sec."

He indicated he had no place to hurry to. He watched her go slowly, in thought, across the lawn, and drift almost to a halt, deeper in thought; and then, mind made up, go quickly toward a group of players in white.

He tried a few practice strokes, and then leaned on his mallet, alive in the middle of the day. Now those yellow flowers that had just been coming out when he arrived in the Faraways were gone; a bush of them there by the drive bore green leaves only, and a dusting of fallen petals at its base. The lilacs had come then, white and purple, and were themselves passing; and the rosebuds were heavy. And it was his, all his, the whole unfolding of it, he was *not missing it all* for the first time in years, for the first time since when? Since the tended quadrangles and cloisters of Noate at least.

His county, and Fellowes Kraft's too: and if *that* was some kind of omen, he must suppose it was a good one, though he was yet unused to seeing his life in such terms. The warmth of simple glee was all he felt so far, and astonishment all that he was sure of.

A job. He saw Rosie come back toward him, quick, her face alight.

"Boney thinks it's a *really great* idea," she said, taking Pierce's arm, "and it will turn out really great for you, I know, so come meet him."

"Boney?"

"Boney Rasmussen. Whose house this is."

"Your father."

"My uncle."

"Aha." Rich uncles were perhaps common around here, as in an old novel. "And the job?"

"Well listen," she said. "If you'll first just do me a favor. About Fellowes Kraft. There'll be a job in it, I'm just sure."

"Aha." He was being led toward a frail and bent and seemingly very aged man who rested on *his* mallet by the lemonade.

"And boy it's a relief to find you," Rosie said.

"Yes?" The old gent far off raised his hand in greeting, and Pierce raised his too, crossing the velvet lawn and, at the same time, feeling himself step across the threshold of an invisible portal: a portal through which there would be no going back again. He didn't know why or wherefore, but he knew that it was so, for it was a sensation he had felt before.

FOUR

▲

The first time Rosie had seen it, in March wind and rain, she had felt warned away; it was like a hermit's or a wizard's house, lonely on a wooded knoll at the end of a long dirt driveway, almost a causeway, that curled through bare and rocky fields. And it was one of those houses too that, to the right eye on the right evening, seemed to have a face: the hooded eyes of a pair of shuttered windows on either side of the nose and mouth of a door and its fanlight, chin of curved steps, mustaches of shaggy balsam. Rosie thought of the phrase from the poem, *Death's dream kingdom,* to which this seemed the gatehouse or keeper's cottage. And beyond it the dark pines gestured, impenetrable, and the hills rose up.

When Pierce first saw it, though, the weather had changed, and it was only a small mock-Tudor cottage, stucco and brick and timber, somehow unconvincing; the eaves were deep, and rounded like thatch, but they were of tarpaper shingle. The rosy-red chimneys and many chimney pots, the mullioned windows and rose trellises, all said 1920 and not 1520. The pines were still dark behind it, though, and the eyes still blind.

He was to go in it, with Rosie, and see what he could see; make a general assessment, sort of, she wasn't quite sure, but she was sure she had neither the competence nor the desire to do it alone. That was the favor. Putting in order the stuff they found, cataloguing it maybe, deciding to sell or not sell the books and stuff if they were worth it—that was the job. If he wanted it.

"While it's still light," Rosie said. "Just to check it out."

And so at evening (the croquet game having ended, Pierce coming in just barely last and much applauded) they climbed into the Bison with a couple of bottles of beer taken from the party offerings and tore away; Val called ironically after them, Rosie waved, the dogs in the back barked triumphantly.

"I've put it off and put it off so long," Rosie said, cradling the beer between her thighs. "You really didn't have anything planned?"

"Nothing," said Pierce. The huge car rolled terrifically down the roadway, as often as not taking more than its allotted half. "Isn't it usual," he said, "to have a mirror to look out the back with?" He pointed to the gob of stickum on the window where there was no mirror.

"You'll get used to our ways," Rosie said. She smiled sidewise at him. "So you think you'll stay? Yeah? Settle down here, huh. Maybe get married."

"Ha ha," he said. "You married?"

"No," she said, not quite truthfully. She had chosen to make no further reference to Spofford either. Not because she was hurt that he had in the end not come to play croquet, or called to explain. No. She just chose not to. No reason. No plan.

"It was kinda sad, I guess," she said, as they went through the town of Stonykill. "Boney says he got almost completely deaf toward the end there. And poor. He was a dapper little guy, and he sort of never quite went to pieces, but the show got a little thin. That's how I picture it."

"Hm," Pierce said, watching Stonykill pass: a mill town nearly depopulated, its mill in ruins—roofless walls pierced with ogee windows, which with the Gothic detail of chimney and clock tower suggested a ruined abbey, also unconvincing.

"He used to walk into town and order his groceries," Rosie said, pointing to a general store, "and buy a bottle, and the papers. With Scotty."

"Scotty?"

"The dog." She had turned off the main road, and sharply upward. "The saddest thing was when the dog died. That just about killed him. I think it was the saddest thing that ever happened to him. Oh, maybe when his mother, oh oops oops."

She had slammed on the power brakes, propelling Pierce into the dashboard. Craning her neck to look between the heads of the dogs who had come hurtling forward too, she backed up in a spray of gravel to a broad aluminum gate that, bolted into old stone gateposts, barred the drive. "Shot right past it," Rosie said, "but here we are."

She had been unable to find the key to the gate's padlock, so they walked to the house along the dusty causeway. Crows making their way toward the pines cawed. The silver-gilt summer evening, daylight savings time, had seemingly ceased to pass away, and might last forever.

"You want to see Scotty's grave?" she asked. "It's around back."

"I thought you hadn't been here before."

"I came once. I looked in the windows. I just didn't dare go in."

They passed around the still and observant house to the back, for it was the kitchen door Rosie had a key to, a round-arched dutch door. "Listen I'm just so grateful for this," she said, struggling with the stiff lock.

"No trouble," he said. "It's interesting. And I'm sure I could think of a favor to ask you. In return."

"Anytime," she said, and the key turned.

"Driving lessons." Not his type, no. But at least not married; at least not the girlfriend of his only friend in the county.

"Sure," she said. "You can drive back."

She pushed open the door, and they went into the cold kitchen.

"Okay," Rosie said when she had closed the door behind them. She felt an urge to take Pierce's hand for safety in the stillness. "Okay."

From being long shut up, the house had the musty smell of a reclusive animal's den, and the small light through the leaded windows made it the more cavelike. A bachelor had lived here, a bachelor once upon a time fussy about his arrangements and his surroundings but who had come to neglect them, growing used over time to the desuetude and no longer actually seeing it. The furniture was good and well chosen but soiled and even a little squalid, a lamp repaired with tape, an upturned umbrella stand to hold an ashtray by the big armchair. The animal denned here had curled up in that chair, it still held his shape; that pale path in the rug that led from chair to Magnavox to liquor cabinet had been worn by his slippered feet. Pierce felt embarrassed by the intimacy of it.

"Books," Rosie said.

They were everywhere, books in tall cases, books piled in

corners, on chairs and beside them, open books laid atop other open books; atlases, encyclopedias, brightly covered novels, broad glossy art books. Pierce took the path of least resistance which Kraft had worked out amid the shoals and islands of them, toward a locked glass cabinet which held still more.

He opened it with a key, which was in the lock.

"We should be systematic, I suppose," he said. "More systematic."

Several of the items in this case were carefully sealed up in the plastic bags in which rarities are kept; one seemed to contain leaves of a medieval manuscript. The typed label glued to it read PICA TRIX.

Pierce shut the door, suddenly shy. A man's best books.

"So," Rosie said. Her first apprehension had passed; she was beginning to feel oddly at home here, in this strange man's house, with this stranger. Watching Pierce touch the books in the cabinet had made her think she had introduced two men who could not help but be friends. "You want to poke around down here? I'm going upstairs."

"Okay."

He stood alone for a moment in the sitting room. There were cigarette burns, but why, all along the windowsill by the easy chair. The whole house seemed darkened with smoke, like a Mohawk's lodge. He turned. The path led that way, through the asymmetrical and eccentric layout which the architect had hoped would be picturesque, and into a small, a surprisingly small room at the back of the house whose use was evident and at whose threshold Pierce paused, even more shy than before.

It was as crowded as a cockpit, and as thoughtfully fitted out. There was just enough room for the desk, not a desk even but just a broad surface built in not particularly well under the mullioned windows; and some tall bookcases fitted in beside the windows; and two gray steel filing cabinets labeled in a way Pierce couldn't understand. There was an old electric heater, a stand-up hotel-lobby ashtray, an office lamp on an extensible arm which could be pulled out to shine down on that black Remington.

There he would sit; he would look out those windows at the day. He would put on the glasses he was too vain to wear elsewhere, and light the thirteenth cig of the day, and prop it in the ashtray. He would roll into the typewriter a piece of paper. . . . A piece of *this* paper: here convenient to hand was a ream box of that coarse yellow copy paper he would have used for initial drafts. Sphinx. Pierce opened it; the lid clung to the box beneath with the vacuum its pulling-off created; the box was nearly full of paper, but the paper wasn't blank.

It was all typed on, pages unnumbered but apparently consecutive, the draft of a novel. With both hands, a cake from the oven or a baby from its pram, Pierce lifted it out, and laid it on the desk before him. Out in the evening, a dog barked: Scotty?

There was no title page, though the top page had what might be an epigraph typed on it.

> I learn that I am knight Parsifal.
> Parsifal learns that his quest for the Grail is the quest of
> all men for the Grail.
> The Grail is just then coming into being, brought forth by a
> labor of making in the whole world at once.
> With a great groan the world awakes for a moment as from
> slumber, to pass the Grail like a stone;
> it is over; Parsifal forgets what he set out to do, I forget
> that I am Parsifal, the world turns again and returns to
> sleep, and I am gone.

This was attributed below (by a quick pencil-dash, as though in an afterthought, or a wild guess) to Novalis. Pierce wondered. He lifted the dry yellow sheet, fragile-seeming, its edges already browning. The second sheet was headed *Prologue in Heaven,* and its first words were these:

> There were angels in the glass, two four six many of them, they kept
> pressing in one by one, always room for one more; they linked arms
> or clasped their hands behind them and looked out at the two mortals
> who looked in at them. They were all dressed in green, and wore
> fillets or wreaths of flowers and green leaves in their loose hair; all
> their eyes were strangely gay, and their names all began with A.

A door thudded closed above his head, and Pierce looked up. Rosie's feet crossed and then recrossed the floor above. Prying. Pierce riffled a little farther through the soft stack of sheets; he found chapter one. Once, the world was not as it has since become, it had a different history and a different future, and the laws that governed it were different too.

At the bottom of this page was a name and a date he knew.

A past moment of his child-being returned to him, when, where, the kind of soft surge of nameless body-memory that can be caused by a smell or a sound. He drew out Fellowes Kraft's hard chair and sat in it; he put his elbow on the desk and his cheek in his hand, and began to read.

F I V E

▲

Once, the world was not as it has since become.

It once worked in a different way than it does now; it had a different history and a different future. Its very flesh and bones, the physical laws that governed it, were other than the ones we know.

Whenever the world turns from what it has been into what it will be, and thus earns a different past and a different future, there is a brief moment when every possible kind of universe, all possible extensions of Being in space and time, are poised on the threshold of becoming, before all but one pass into nonexistence again; and the world is as it is and not as it was, and everyone in it forgets that it could ever be or has ever been other than the way it is now.

And just as the world is thus turning from the what-has-been into the what-is-to-be, and all possibilities are just for a moment alight and one has not yet been chosen, then all the other similar disjunctures in time (for there have been several) can become visible too: like the switchbacks on a rising mountain road suddenly becoming visible to a climber just at the moment when his car swings far out on the apex of the turn he is taking, and he sees where he has come from: and sees a blue sedan far down there climbing too.

This is the story of one such moment, and about those men and women and others who recognized it. They are all now dead, or asleep, or do not figure in the history which the world has come to have; and their moment appears quite otherwise to us than it did to them. Today I pick up a book, a history of those times, and what it tells me doesn't surprise me; however these people misconceived their world (and apparently they misconceived it wildly, peopling it with gods and monsters, with non-existent lands having imaginary histories, with metals and plants and animals ditto, having powers ditto) they really dwelt in the same world I dwell in: it had these animals and plants which I know, this sun and these stars, and not other ones.

And yet, in the interstices of such a history book, between the pages, I discern the shadow of another story and another world, symmetrical to it, and yet as different from it as dream is from waking.

This world; this story.

In the year 1564, a young Neapolitan of the ancient town of Nola, making the great mistake of his life, entered the Dominican monastery of San Domenico Maggiore in Naples. It wasn't, of course, entirely his decision; his father was a retired soldier, landless and not rich, and the boy was brilliant (so the parish priest said) and a little wild, so there was really nothing for him but the Church. Still, the Dominicans, though the great and powerful order of the Kingdom of Naples, were not the order for this boy. Perhaps, if he had joined some smaller, less potent order, some hardworking Minorite or easygoing Benedictine or even cloistered Capuchin monastery, he might have been left alone to dream his dreams. If he had made his way into the Company of Jesus, they would have found some way to turn his pride and his strange gifts and even his distaste for Christianity to their own ends; the Company was well able to do that.

But the Dominicans: the order of Preacher-Friars, whose self-appointed mission was to keep pure the Church and the Church's doctrines; the Dominicans, who punningly called themselves *Domini canes,* the running dogs of the Lord, black-and-white hounds eager to bring down heresy like prey: that was not the order in which to incarcerate young Filippo Bruno, given the name Giordano when he put on his robe of black and white. The order didn't encourage independent thinking; it would never forgive the Nolan boy for turning his back on them, and carrying his heresies into the world; and in the end they would have him forever for their own, tied to a stake in Rome.

But there, for the moment, he is, in the monastery of San Domenico, going slowly up the right-hand aisle of the monastery church, avoiding the loiterers and the bravos and interrupting assignations. He stops at each side chapel, each statue niche, each architectural division, and stands before it long in thought before passing on to the next. What is he up to?

He is memorizing the church of San Domenico, piece by piece, for use as an interior storehouse or filing cabinet for remembering other things.

A hundred years before, books had begun to be made by the new *ars artificialiter scribendi,* the art of writing artificially, printing. Thousands of books have already been printed. But in the great monasteries of the Dominicans the age of the scribe, the age of the manuscript, the age of memory, is not over. Printed handbooks on how to preach sermons are appearing, printed breviaries and books of homilies and Scripture quotations for priests to use, but the order of Preacher-Friars is still inducting its novices into the mysteries of memory arts as old as thought.

Take a large and complex public space—a church, for instance—and commit it to memory, every side altar, chapel, statue niche, and arch. Mark every fifth such space, in your imagination, with a hand; mark every tenth space with an X. Now your memory house is prepared. To use it, say to remember the contents of a sermon you are to give, or a manuscript of canon law, or a confessor's manual of sins and their appropriate punishments, you must cast vivid images in your imagination to represent the different ideas you wish to remember. Aristotle says clearly, and St. Thomas follows him, that *corporeal similitudes* excite the memory more easily than the naked notions themselves. If your sermon then is the Seven Deadly Sins, cast them as evil ugly characters, displaying appropriate signs of their qualities (from Envy's mouth a loathsome viper protrudes instead of a tongue; Anger's eyes flame red and he is brutally armed). Then have your characters stand in their places in order around the church or city square or palace you have in memory, and as you speak each one in turn will prompt you, Now speak of me, now speak of me.

This was how the Scholastics had expanded and elaborated a rhetorician's trick mentioned briefly by Cicero and Quintillian; and by the time Brother Giordano was committing the church of San Domenico to memory not even its endlessly exfoliating spaces were sufficient to hold what he was given to remember. Patristics, moral theology, *summulae logicales,* hagiography, the contents of compendia, encyclopædias and bestiaries, the same tale in a thousand guises—the monkish passion for collection, dissection, division, and multiplication of notions filled the cathedrals of memory to overflowing just as those of stone were filled with gargoyles, saints of glass, passions, fonts, tombs, and judgments.

And as the amount to be remembered grew, so the means to remember it by expanded, divided, multiplied. Brother Giordano committed endless new rules of memory to memory. He memorized a system for remembering, not just notions and ideas, but the very words of the text, by substituting other words for them: so that the mental image of a city (*Roma*) reminds the speaker to speak next of love (*amor*). More: there were rules for remembering, not the words, but the *letters* of the words, an image for each, some corporeal similitude, so that the word *Nola* was formed in the Nolan's mind by an arch, a millstone, a hoe, and a pair of compasses, and the word *indivisibilitate* by a whole atticful of junk. Giordano found he could do such tricks with ease; he composed a bird alphabet of his own, *anser* the goose for A, *bubo* the owl for B, and so on, and practiced with it until he could make *In principio erat Verbum* flutter and settle on his shoulders like a flock. The only difficulty he had was in expelling what he had once put in place, and ridding the church of San Domenico Maggiore of its birds, hoes, shovels, ladders, allegorical figures with snakes for tongues, gesturing captains, anchors, swords, saints, and beasts.

—Is it lawful then, when you have no more places left to fill, to make in imagination further places attached to those places?

—It is, Frater Jordanus, if you do it correctly. You must imagine a line running from west to east, upon which you are to place imaginary towers to use as memory places. The towers are multiplied, as many as you like, by being changed, turned this way and that way through their faces, *per sursum, deorsum, anteorsum, dextrorsum, sinistrorsum.* . . . The brother instructor's hands turned and twisted an imaginary tower.

—Yes, said Giordano. Yes.

—Now, said the brother instructor, raising a finger: you are only to use such towers to exercise and strengthen the memory. Do you hear? Not to use in remembering. Do you hear, Frater Jordanus?

But a line of imaginary towers had already begun to spring up, stretching west from the door of San Domenico: towers very much like the ones that Brother Giordano remembered from his Nolan childhood. Every year in Nola, to honor the city's patron St. Paulinus on his feast day, the various guilds of the town built and displayed tall towers made of wood and lathe and canvas, called *guglie:* multistoried constructions balconied and steepled, pierced with windows and openings large and small displaying scenes out of the saint's life, or of the Passion, or scenes out of romances or the life of the Virgin. Inside and out they were painted, encrusted with cherubs, roses, stars, zodiacs, emblems, exhortations, crosses and rosaries, dogs and cats. On St. Paulinus's day the *guglie* were revealed to the town, and then—most marvelous of all—each *guglia* was lifted up by thirty strong young men, and not only carried through the thronged and decorated streets, but, in the square before the church, was made to dance. The boys who carried them, grunting and crying encouragement to each other, made them bow, tilt, turn round and round to music: dancing with each other amid the people who danced around them, their crazy contents appearing in window and door and disappearing again as the towers turned and twirled, left, right, bowing, tilting, *per sursum, deorsum, dextrorsum, sinistrorsum.*

And yet: he would think—looking out the narrow window of his cell at a pale strip of evening, one star alight—that even an infinite line of *guglie* running east to west and changed every which way would not be enough to hold all that he had seen and thought of in his short life, which to him seemed so endlessly long as to be without a beginning at all. Not every leaf whose shadow had crossed him, not every grape that he had crushed against his palate; not every stone, every voice, star, dog, rose. Only by committing to memory the entire universe, and casting on it a universe of images, could all the things in the universe be remembered.

—Is it lawful to use the spaces of the heavens, I mean the zodiac and its houses, the mansions of the moon, for the purposes of remembering? And the images of the stars for images to remember things by?

—It is not lawful, Frater Jordanus.

—But Cicero in his Second Rhetoric says that in ancient times . . .

—It is not lawful, Frater Jordanus. To stretch and exercise the memory by artifice is a good work; to seek for aid in the stars is not for the likes of you. You understand neither Cicero nor the stars. And for that *but* you will be a long time on your knees.

As well as learning to write inwardly with images in the way the Dominicans were famous for, Brother Giordano also learned to write with pen and ink; to write in a thick quick secretary hand a monkish Latin untouched by *umanismo,* a Latin learned from the books he was given to read. He read Albertus Magnus and he read St. Thomas, the great learned doctors of his order; he overlaid his own inward cathedral with the cathedral, divided into apse nave and choir, parts and parts of parts, of Thomas's *Summa theologica.* Through Thomas he came to him whom Thomas had called simply the Philosopher, Aristotle. Aristotle: a mass of manuscripts greasy from use, copied and recopied, glossed and interpolated, grown blurred from the accretion of tiny errors.

All things seek their proper spheres. What is heavy, as stones and earth, seeks the center of the universe, which is heaviest; lighter things, as air and fire, leap upward to their spheres, which are lighter.

The inmost heaviest sphere is earth, and next to it the sphere of water, ascending as dew, descending as rain. The spheres of air and fire are next, and then the sphere of the moon. All change, all decay and corruption, all birth and death, occur in the spheres of the elements, below the sphere of the moon; beyond the moon are the changeless regions. That which suffers no change is more perfect than that which is subject to change; the planets are perfect matter, unlike any we know, attached to perfect crystal spheres, which, turning, mark time. These seven spheres are contained within an eighth, the crystal sphere wherein the stars are set. And that is contained within the utmost sphere of all, the sphere that, turning, turns all the others: the Primum Mobile, itself turned by the finger of God. For nothing moves except what is moved by a mover.

Cheek in hand, amid the nodding brothers in the library, Brother Giordano assembled within himself Aristotle's heavens and earth, like a man building a ship in a bottle. *Time is thought to be movement of the Sphere viz. because the movements are measured by this, and time by this movement.* What? The brothers around him muttered aloud reading their books, a dozen voices reading a dozen texts, buzzing like stupid wasps. *This also explains the common saying that human affairs form a circle, and that there is a circle in all other things that have a natural movement and coming into being and passing away.*

He sighed, an ashen taste in his mind like the burnt summer day's. Why is changelessness better than change? Life is change, and life is better than death. This world of perfect spheres was like the world that painters show, where they pretend that some few leagues above the mountains a moon like a melon and stars like sparks go by, and just above them God bends down across the spheres to peek inside. It was a universe too small, made of too little; an empty trunk, bound in iron straps.

But there were other books.

Like many monkish libraries, San Domenico's was a midden of a thousand years' writing; no one knew all that the monastery contained, or what had become of all that the monks had copied, bought, written, commented on, given away, and collected over centuries. The old librarian, Fra' Benedetto, had a long catalogue in his head, which he could remember because he had composed it in rhyme, but there were books that weren't in this catalogue because they didn't rhyme. There was a Memory Palace in which all the categories of books and all the subdivisions of those categories had places, but it had long ago filled up and been shuttered and abandoned. There was a written catalogue too, into which every book was entered as it was acquired, and if you happened to know when a book was acquired, you might find it there. Unless, that is, it had been bound with another, or several others; for usually only the incipit of the first would be put into the catalogue. The others were lost.

So within the library which Fra' Benedetto and the prior and the abbot knew about there had grown up another library, a library which those who read in it did not catalogue, and did not want catalogued. Fra' Benedetto knew he had the *Summa theologiae* of Albertus Magnus and his book *On Sleeping and Being Awake;* he didn't know he had Albertus's *Book of Secrets* or his treatise on alchemy. But Fra' Giordano knew. Fra' Benedetto knew he had the *Sphere* of Sacrobosco, for every institution of learning had the *Sphere* of Sacrobosco, it was the universal textbook of Aristotelian astronomy. He had several copies, and some printed texts as well. He did not know that bound up with one manuscript was the *Commentary on the Sphere* by Cecco of Ascoli, he whom the Church had burned at the stake for heresy two hundred years before.

He didn't know it, but Fra' Giordano did. Fra' Giordano read Cecco's commentary shut up in the privy, swallowing it like sweetened wine. The stars alter the four elements, and through the elements our bodies are altered, and through our bodies our souls: in the stars are the Reasons of the World, and Jesus's own horoscope was set at his birth by God so that he would suffer the fate

that he did. Under certain constellations and conjunctions happy
divine men are born, Moses, Simon Magus, Merlin, Hermes the
Thrice-great (Giordano read this assortment of names with a deep
thrill of wonder, that they could be listed together, as people of the
same kind). Countless spirits good and evil fill up the heavens,
constantly in motion, criss-crossing the zodiac; founders of new
religions are actually born of them, of incubi and succubi who live
in the colures, the bands that separate solstice and equinox.

Those perfect spheres were coming to contain a busy populace.

In the library, Brother Giordano read the books that a doctor
of theology must read; he read the Fathers, he read Jerome and
Ambrose and Augustine and Aquinas. He chewed and swallowed
them like a goat eating paper, and excreted them in *examenes* and
recitationes.

In the privy he read Cecco. He read Solomon's book on the
Shadows of Ideas. He read Marsilio Ficino *De vita coelitis comparanda*,
on drawing down the life of heaven by talismans and incantations.
The privy was the secret library of San Domenico; there the books
were read, and changed hands; there they were hidden; there they
were traded in for others. Giordano was its librarian. He knew and
remembered every book, where it lay in Fra' Benedetto's cases, who
had asked for it, and what was in it. In his vast and growing
memory palace, the whole heavens in small, all that took up next to
no room at all.

His brothers marveled at Giordano's memory, and whispered
how he had come by it. Giordano let them whisper. Addicted to
gossip and sausages, they would never dare to put the stars to use:
but Giordano dared.

Meanwhile the enormous sun burned in the blue, blue sky;
pleasure craft and oared warships skimmed across the bay, the azure
bay prinked with silver points of wavelets. The Spanish viceroy (for
the Kingdom of Naples was a possession of the Spanish crown) rode
through the city dressed in Spanish black, in his little black chaise;
if he met the Host being carried through the streets to someone ill
or dying, he would get down and join the procession, following it
humbly to its destination. Every year the congealed blood of St.
Januarius kept in the cathedral melted and flowed on his feast day
as though just shed, and the people and the priests and the cardinal
and the viceroy wept and groaned aloud or held their breaths in

awe. Some years, the blood was slow in melting, and the mass of people pressed into the cathedral grew restive, and a riot would start to seethe.

There were always riots; there were always the poor, crowded in the tall close houses of the port quarters, in narrow alleys piled with refuse, where children grew like weeds, untended and wild and numerous. They begged with persistence, robbed with skill; they laughed equally at the *pulcinelle* in their booths around the Piazza del Castello and at the extravagant farewells of a brigand about to be hanged in the Piazza del Mercato. All day the naked beggars lay on the quays; at night, fisher-girls danced the tarantella on the flat roofs of cottages that ringed the bay under the moon.

The moon drew humid tears from the earth, attracting them upward by her own watery nature; by her action also, in the mud-flats of river estuaries and in sea-pools, frogs and crabs and snails were generated. When she was full, dogs all over the city turned their faces up to hers, and howled. When their own star Sirius arose with the sun, they went mad, and the dog-killers went out to catch them.

In the wood of dead trees, in the guts of dead dogs, worms were generated; from the guts of dead lions, bees were born—so it was said, though few had ever seen a dead lion. Horsehairs fallen in a horse-trough turned into snakes, and now and then you could see one starting: one hair beginning to whip sinuously amid the floating still ones. The sun shone, and the heliotrope in the gardens of the Pizzofalcone turned their faces to it, and the living lion in the viceroy's menagerie roared in his strength and pride. The moon drew the fogs, the sun drew the heliotrope; the lodestone drew iron, and Saturn in the ascendant tugged terribly at the brain of the melancholic man.

It was all alive, all alive, from the bottom of the sea through the air to the heavens, the stars altering the four elements, the elements the body, the body the soul. Brother Giordano sang his first Mass in Campagna, at the church of San Bartolomeo, whispering *Hoc est enim corpus meum* over the circle of bread he held in his anointed fingers, and in the warmth of his breath it was alive too. The heretics of the North said it was not alive, but of course it was; swallowed, it warmed Giordano's bosom with the small fire of its aliveness. Of course it was alive: for there was nothing that was not.

So the Nolan grew from boy into man, priest, and doctor; so

the stars turned over the changeful world; so the memory he had made grew full of treasure, too full for reckoning, yet all of it his. Brother Giordano amazed his brothers, filling the evenings in Chapter after supper with feats that seemed more than human. He had them read out lines of Dante chosen at random, here, there, in any canto; and then the next night he would recite them all, in the order they had been given to him, or backward, or starting from the middle. He asked them to name humble objects, fruits, tools, animals, articles of dress; over months and years the list grew hundreds and hundreds of items long, yet he could remember it all, or any part of it, in any order, starting anywhere: the brothers (who had them all written down) would follow along the lists as Giordano, hands folded in his lap, eyes slightly crossed, named each thing, seeming almost to taste it, to relish it, even as he took it from the hand of the kindly one who leaned from his tower window to proffer it: hoe, shovel, compasses; dog, rose, stone.

His fame spread. Among the Dominicans, at first, who were proud of the ancient art which they were well known for preserving and practicing; but then in the world at large as well. Giordano came to the attention of the *Academia secretorum naturæ,* the School of Nature's Secrets, and of the great magician of Naples who presided there: Giambattista della Porta.

When he was only fifteen years old, this Della Porta had published a huge encyclopædia of natural magic; then there had been trouble with the Church, and the young mage had come under the eye of Paul IV, and might very well have ended badly; he was exonerated at length, but now he kept his gaze firmly below the moon's sphere, and practiced only the whitest of white magics—and heard Mass daily, just in case.

He was an ugly, dog-faced, egg-headed man, swarthy and brutal-looking; at his temple a thick vein beat. As though in compensation, his voice was gentle and melodious, and his manners exquisite. With great kindness he led the young monk, defensive and rigid with unease, through the public rooms of the Academy decorated with allegories of the sciences and into an inner chamber where, at dinner, the fellows reclined in the antique style, wearing white robes and vine leaves in their hair.

They didn't giggle, or stare slack-jawed at him when he performed his feats; they considered, and asked questions, and put hard tests to him. One had made a list of long nonsense-words

almost identical but not quite—*veriami, veriavi, vemivari, amiava*—
thirty or more of them. Giordano broke them into parts, and for
each part he found some visual clue: birds *(avi)*, lovers *(ami)*, a
book of truths *(veri)*, a bunch of twigs *(rami)*. Then, hands folded in
his lap and his eyes with that far-off cast in them (for they watched
the scenes he had made out of the clues pass in his inward sight), he
gave them all, and again, and differently. A girl gave her lover a
white pigeon, in a cage made of sticks, and he sold it for a book. It
happened in the piazza before the church in Nola, in scorched
August; he could see the girl's shy look, smell the cracked leather of
the book, feel the bird's quick heartbeat beneath his fingers: years
later he would sometimes dream of these figures and their dramas,
the girl, the bird, the boy, the book, the sticks.

He did all that they asked him, and more that they hadn't asked
him—smiling at last, and leaning forward to see their amazement—
and later when the guests were gone and he sat alone over wine with
the ugly magician, he talked about how he did what he did.

—Places, and images cast on them, yes, Della Porta said, who
had written a little *Ars reminiscendi* himself which included all the
usual rules.

—Yes, said Fra' Giordano. The church of San Domenico Maggiore and the cloisters and the square before it. But it's not enough.

—Imaginary places can be used.

—Yes. I do.

—And images can be taken for use on them from our painters.
From Michelangelo. Raffaello. The divine ones. Images of good and
evil, strength, virtue, passion. These vivify the imagination.

Fra' Giordano said nothing, who had not seen their paintings,
though the names seemed to make paintings in his mind, and he
found a wall there to put them on.

—I use the stars, he said. The twelve houses. And their deni-
zens. Those are powerful aids.

Della Porta's eyes narrowed.

—That might be lawful, he said carefully.

—But they're not enough, Giordano said. Even now the figures
sometimes grow confused to me. Too few to do so much, play so
many parts. Like a comedy with too few actors, and the same ones
come on again and again in different cloaks and wigs.

—You may use the images of Ægypt, Della Porta said, clutching his knee in his hairy hands and casting his eyes upward. Hieroglyphs.

—Hieroglyphs . . .

—That is lawful. That much is lawful.

The monk was staring at him so fixedly that Della Porta felt compelled to go on.

—You see, he said, in their wisdom the Ægyptians made multiform images, a man with a dog's head, a baboon with wings. They were not so foolish as to worship such monstrosities. No. They concealed in their images truths for the wise to uncover. The baboon is Man, the Ape of Nature, who reproduces Nature's effects by imitation, but whose wings take him above the material plane as his mind pierces through appearances.

The monk said nothing, only still stared.

—A fly, said Della Porta. It means Impudence, because no matter how often it is driven away, it always returns. You see? And out of these images, linked, they made a language. A language not of words but of corporeal similitudes. Like your memory images. You see? In that book of Horapollo's there are seven dozen of them explained. Hieroglyphs.

The library of San Domenico did not have a book by Horapollo, or Fra' Giordano did not know of it. He felt—he had felt since Della Porta had begun speaking of hieroglyphs—a weird hunger at the bottom of his being.

—What other books? he asked.

The mage withdrew slightly from the monk, who leaned toward him with an intensity Della Porta disliked.

—Read Hermes, he said. Hermes who gave to Ægypt her laws and letters. It grows late, my young friend.

—Marsilio Ficino, said Giordano. He translated the works of that Hermes.

—Yes.

—Marsilio knew images too. Was he taught by Hermes? Images of the stars, to draw down their power.

—That is *not* lawful, the mage said, standing suddenly.

—He made them in his mind only.

—It is not lawful and it is not safe, the mage said, lifting Fra' Giordano by a hand on his shoulder, and propelling him toward the door of the chamber.

—But, said Giordano.

—Your memory is God's gift, said Della Porta, almost a whisper into the monk's ear as, arm linked in his, he walked him to the street door. Your memory is God's gift and you have improved it wonderfully. By natural art. Be content.

—But the stars, Giordano said. Cecco says . . .

Two servants had pulled open the double doors onto the piazza. Della Porta pushed Giordano out.

—They burned Cecco, he said. Do you hear me? They burned Cecco. Good night. God help you.

But why was it unlawful to push past accidents, and proceed to the reasons for things? Once put Venus in your mind to stand for Love—Venus with her dove and her green branch—and Love will glow in the mind with its own glow, for Venus *is* Love; place her in her own sign of Virgo and Love pours down through all the spheres, warm, living, vivifying, Love both inside and out.

Natural magic like Della Porta's allowed you to discern Venus in those things of the world most impressed with Venus's qualities: her emeralds, her primroses, her doves; her perfumes, herbs, colors, sounds. Venus and Venus-ness pervaded the universe, a quality like light or flavor; doctors and wise men and wonder-workers knew how to trace it and put it to use, and that was lawful. But to cut—in your mind or on an emerald—an image of Venus, dove, green branch, young breasts; or to sing, in her own Lydian mode, a song of praise to Venus; or to burn before your image a handful of her rosemary—dangerous. And why?

Why? Bruno asked of no one, honest eyebrows raised, palms open and reasonable. But he knew why.

To make an image, or a symbol; to sing an incantation; to name a name: that was not simply manipulating the stuff of the earth, however wisely. That was addressing a person, an intelligence; for only a person could understand such things. It was invoking the beings behind the stars, those countless wise beings Cecco talked about who lurked there. And to invoke such beings would put the worker who attempted it in mortal danger.

Cause Venus by your songs to take notice of you, to open her almond eyes and smile, and she may consume you. The Church was no longer certain that the potent beings who filled the spheres were all devils, as She had once thought. They might be angels, or dæmons neither good nor bad. But it was certain that to ask them for favors was idolatry, and to attempt to conjure and compel them was madness.

That was the answer. Bruno knew it, but he didn't care.

He had begun to assemble around him now a group of younger or wilder brothers, a loose association of devotees and hangers-on everyone called his *giordanisti,* as though Giordano were a brigand chieftain. They sat around him and talked in loud voices and said extravagant things or, hushed, listened to the Nolan expatiate; they ran errands for him, got into trouble with him, spread his fame. When Giordano enraged the prior by deciding to clear his cell of images, plaster statuary, blessed beads, Madonnas, and retain only a crucifix, the *giordanisti* did—or talked of doing—the same thing. The prior, unable to understand at all, suspected Giordano of northern heresies, *luteranismo,* iconoclasm: but the *giordanisti* laughed, knowing better. Giordano pestered the librarian, and got the *giordanisti* to pester him too, to buy the books of Hermes that Marsilio Ficino had translated; but Benedetto wouldn't hear of it. Idolatry. Paganism. But had not Thomas Aquinas and Lactantius praised Hermes, and said he had taught one God, and foretold the Incarnation? Benedetto was deaf.

When his monks traveled, Giordano gave them lists of books to look for, and sometimes he got them, borrowed or bought or stolen: Horapollo on hieroglyphs, Iamblichus on the Mysteries of Ægypt, the *Golden Ass* of Apuleius. And in the privy on a winter day a young brother, trembling with anxiety or cold or both, took from his robe and gave to Giordano a thick sewn manuscript without cover or binding, written in a crabbed quick hand full of abbreviations.

—*Picatrix,* the boy said. It's a great sin.

—The sin will be mine, Giordano said. Give it to me.

Picatrix! Blackest of the black books of the old times, and there was no doubt about the intentions of anyone found studying it, no way a doctor of theology might defend himself as he might if he was caught with Horapollo or even Apuleius. It was madness to keep such a book, and Giordano did not keep it long; every page memorized was torn out and cast behind him forever.

Man is a little world, reflecting in himself the great world and the heavens; through his *mens* the wise man can raise himself above the stars. So Hermes the Thrice-great says.

Spirit descends from the prime matter which is God and enters into earthly matter, where it resides; the different forms which matter takes reflect the nature of the *spiritus* that entered it. The mage is he who can capture and guide the influx of *spiritus* himself, and thus make of matter what he wishes. How?

By making talismans, as Marsilio had hinted: only here were exact instructions, what materials were to be used, what hour of the day was best, what day of the month, month of the zodiacal calendar; what incantations, invocations, lights were to be used, what perfumes and songs would most attract the Reasons of the World, the Semhamaphores all mind who fill up the universe. There were long lists of images to be used on talismans, and Brother Giordano, who had no materials to make them of, no lead for Saturn, tin for Jupiter, could nonetheless cast them inwardly and unforgettably:

> An image of Saturn: The form of a man, standing on a dragon, clothed in black and having in his right hand a sickle and his left hand a spear.

> An image of Jupiter: The form of a man with a lion's face and bird's feet, below them a dragon with seven heads, holding an arrow in his right hand.

Better yet, and more potent, were long lists of images for thirty-six gods of time, nameless, vivid, of whom Giordano had read in Origen and in Horapollo's hints: *horoscopi,* the gods of the hours known to Ægypt and then forgotten or ignored by later ages. They were called *decans* also, because each one ruled over ten degrees of the zodiac, three *decans* to each of the twelve signs. The images of the thirty-six, Picatrix said, had been cast by Hermes himself, as he had cast the hieroglyphs of Ægypt's language; Giordano hardly needed to memorize them, they stepped off the crowded page directly into his brain and took their seats there, where they had all along belonged, though he hadn't known it:

> The first *decan* of Aries: A huge dark man with fiery eyes, holding a sword and clad in a white garment.

> The second *decan:* A woman clad in green, and lacking one leg.

> The third *decan:* A man holding a golden sphere, and dressed in red . . .

He imbibed this weird congress like food, like a fiery liquor, and almost as soon as they had entered within him he began to dream of them and of their doings. Who was he who had discovered them, this Hermes?

There are among the Chaldeans very perfect masters in this art of images, and they affirm that Hermes was the first who constructed images by which he knew how to regulate the Nile against the motion of the moon. This man also built a temple to the Sun, and he knew how to hide himself from all so that no one could see him, though he was within it. It was he too, who in the east of Ægypt constructed a City twelve miles long within which he constructed a castle which had four gates in each of its four parts. On the eastern gate he placed the form of an Eagle: on the western gate the form of a Bull; on the southern gate the form of a Lion, and on the northern gate he constructed the form of a Dog. Into these images he introduced spirits which spoke with voices, nor could anyone enter the gates of the City except by their permission. There he planted trees, in the midst of which was a great tree which bore the fruit of all generation. On the summit of the castle he caused to be raised a tower thirty cubits high, on the top of which he ordered to be placed a lighthouse the color of which changed every day until the seventh day, when it returned to the first color; and so the City was illuminated with these colors. Near the City there was an abundance of waters in which dwelt many kinds of fish. Around the circumference he placed engraved images and ordered them in such a manner that by their virtue the inhabitants were made virtuous and withdrawn from all wickedness and harm.

The name of the City was Adocentyn.

The name of the city was Adocentyn.

Pierce pushed back the wheeled chair he sat in, and with the page (Adocentyn!) still in his hand he started out of the room. Then he returned, and put it back. He went out again, got lost in the toils of the tiny house, came into a second parlor matching the first, and thought for a bad moment that he had only imagined that glass-fronted bookcase and its key and its contents, for it was nowhere to be seen; got straightened around; went into the first parlor, opened the bookcase, and took from it the plastic envelope marked PICA TRIX.

Absurdly, his heart was beating hard. But the thick vellum

leaves he pulled out, covered top to bottom in double columns of manuscript, were in a dense black-letter script unintelligible to him, curt monkish Latin, or code for all he knew.

He locked it up again, and went through the house to the front hall and the stairs, calling Rosie's name.

"Up here!"

"I've found something," he said mounting the stairs. "Rosie?"

Down a corridor at the top of the stairs, a corridor whose walls were covered with framed etchings, people places and things, so many of them that the colorless paper behind could hardly be seen. He turned in at the door of a bedroom.

She stood with her back to him in the stuffy dimness, drawn blinds making a nighttime in the room, someone else's bedroom. Pierce felt suddenly caught in the toils of an awful pun, a misunderstanding, a rebus, a palindrome. Rosie turned; what light there was in the room gathered in her eyes.

"Satin sheets," she said, gesturing to the big bed with her bottle. "Check it out."

SIX

▲

"It's a novel," Pierce said to Boney Rasmussen. "Unfinished, apparently. It seems to end with a bunch of notes, and hints about further scenes."

"You've read it all already?" The rainy day outside the library was so silver, the sparkle of the new greenery so various, that it made a vague darkness inside, and Boney at his desk was hard to see.

"No," Pierce said. "No. I've started it. But we didn't want to move it." Like a corpus delicti. "So I quit reading when it got dark yesterday."

Boney was silent.

"Rosie's pretty sure it's not just a draft of one of the ones he published. It's all new."

Still Boney said nothing.

"It is," Pierce began, and halted; he wasn't sure he should make the claim, or the revelation, which he had thought to make, or reveal, when he was shown into this room; but then he said, "It is really a very strange and remarkable thing to find and a very unlikely coincidence." He fell silent himself then, and they both sat amid the tick and pop of raindrops outside as though under a spell, Boney thinking thoughts Pierce could not imagine and his own mind filled with the wonderment of what had befallen him.

Adocentyn.

"I," he said at length, "am at work on a book."

"Rosie told me."

"Well what's remarkable is," he said, "the things and the people in this book that are things and people I'd been thinking about and studying for a long time, in a completely different way. Doctor John Dee, for instance, the English mathematician. Giordano Bruno."

"He's written about them before."

"Well. Not quite in this way."

"What way?"

Pierce crossed his legs, and took his knee in his interlaced fingers. "This book begins," he said, "with John Dee talking to angels. Now in fact Dee left extensive records of the seances he held with a person named Talbot or Kelley who claimed to see angels in a kind of crystal ball. All right. Only in this book of Kraft's he's really seeing them, and talking to them."

Boney waited unmoving; but Pierce had begun to feel a kind of intensity of attention growing in him.

"Next comes a chapter about Bruno," Pierce said. "And all the biographical details are right, I think, and the milieu; only the *reasons* for everything happening are not the reasons we would give now."

"No?"

"No."

"What reasons then?"

"It's as if," Pierce said. "As if, in this book, there are angels but not laws of physics; as if theurgy could work, and win battles; prayer too. And magic."

"Magic," Boney said.

"Glastonbury's in this book," Pierce said. "And a Grail. The book might be about a Grail, somehow hidden in history." Leafing forward with the same horrid yet eager fascination he might feel if allowed to leaf through his own life to come, he had glimpsed Kepler's name, and Brahe's; he had seen kings, popes and emperors, famous battles, castles, ports and treaties: but he had seen also the City of the Sun, and the brothers of the Rose; the Red Man and the Green Lion; the angel Madimi, the Death of the Kiss, a golem, a wand of *lignum vitae*, twelve minims of best gold in the bottom of the *crater*.

"And your book," Boney said. "It's the same?"

"Not the same. This is fiction. Mine is not."

"But it deals in these same matters. This same period."

"Yes."

And maybe it wasn't so different, no not so different. Kraft's was only going to be the strong wine undiluted: no subtleties of qualification, no might-it-not-seems, no it-is-tempting-to-thinks, no it-is-as-thoughs. None. Only this extraordinary colored toy theater of unhistory.

"You would notice then," Boney said slowly, "if there was anything in this book about an elixir. Not medicine exactly, but."

"I know the concept," Pierce said.

"Anything about that?"

Pierce shook his head. "Not so far."

Boney rose from his desk, and helping himself with his knuckles along its edge, he went to stand looking out the window.

"Sandy knew so much," he said. "He joked all the time, and you never knew when he meant what he said. He knew so much that you were sure that behind the joke was something he knew. But he wouldn't tell.

"He said. He often used to say. What if once upon a time the world was a different place than it is now. The whole world I mean, everything, well it's hard to express; so that it worked in a way it no longer does."

Pierce held his breath to hear the small old voice.

"And what if," Boney went on, "there remained somewhere in this new world we have now, somehow, somewhere, some little fragments of that lost world. Some fragments that retain something of the power they used to have, back when things were different. A jewel, say. An elixir."

He turned to look at Pierce, and smiled. The Fabulous Monster. So Rosie had called him. "Wouldn't that be something, he used to say. If that were so. Wouldn't that be something."

"There are such things," Pierce said. "Unicorns' horns. Magic jewels. Mummified mermaids."

"Sandy would say: *they* didn't survive the change. But somewhere, somewhere there might be something. Hidden, you see; or not hidden, just overlooked; hidden in plain sight. A stone. A powder. An elixir of life." Standing had caused him—so it seemed to Pierce—to sink ever so slightly, as though his spine were slowly melting. "He was teasing, I suppose. I'm sure he was. And yet in the Giant Mountains once. . . ."

Nothing more followed. At length Boney left the window, and climbed into his chair again.

"So it's a good book?" he said.

"I've only begun it. The first chapters. Bruno. John Dee at Glastonbury. I think Dee and Bruno are going to meet, eventually. I doubt very much they ever did. But surely they could have."

"Maybe you should finish it," Boney said. "Finish the writing of it, I mean."

"Ha ha," said Pierce. "Not my line of work."

Boney pondered. "You could edit it. For possible publication."

"I'd certainly like to read it," Pierce said. "At least."

"I'm too, it's a little beyond me now," Boney said. "And I'm not sure I'd recognize it if I saw it there. But you. You."

Through the open door just then there came a bouncing rubber ball, a large one painted with red and white stripes, and white stars on blue. It bounced twice and rolled to a stop, vivid on the rug.

"Does it," Boney asked, "have a title?"

"It doesn't have a title page," Pierce said.

He thought he knew, though, what title it might have been intended to have; what title he, as editor, would be tempted to give it. He thought: there is not only more than one history of the world, one for each of us who studies it; there is more than one for each of us, there are as many as we want or need, as many as our heads and wanting hearts can make.

Rosie put her head into the room. "Ready?" she said.

"I won't go in with you just yet," she told Pierce as they went toward Stonykill.

"No?"

"I've got another house to break into," Rosie said. "Some errands. I'll drop you off, and come back."

In rain, Stonykill was hangdog, exposed and unhappy-looking. Someone stood by the gas pumps of the little store, under the sagging marquee, wiping the drops from his spectacles. "Anyway," Rosie said. "You know what you're looking at in there. I don't."

"Maybe yes," Pierce said, "maybe no."

They coasted to a stop at Kraft's barred drive, and for a moment sat in silence looking out the rain-speckled windows toward the shuttered house and the dark pines. "You know," Rosie said, "in his autobiography? Kraft said he wanted to write just one last book."

"Yes?"

"He says: a book he could die before finishing."

"And when," Pierce asked, "was it that he died?"

"Oh six years ago. I think. About 1970."

"Oh. Hm."

"Why?"

"Nothing, really. I was just thinking about this book, coming to be. I suppose it could have been in the works for a while. And then abandoned. I was just wondering."

Rosie extracted the key to Kraft's kitchen from her ring, and gave it to Pierce; he opened the great door of the wagon and put out first his black umbrella, which Rosie had laughed at when she had seen him with it; he in turn had claimed to think it was funny that no one around here had any use for umbrellas, and dashed through the rain bareheaded, a matter of pride it seemed.

"See ya."

"I won't be long," Rosie said.

The umbrella popped open. "Automatic," Pierce said.

She watched him step long-legged over the gate and walk the drive, avoiding puddles. His city mac was rumpled and gray.

She could have had him, yesterday, on Fellowes Kraft's satin sheets; only he seemed for some reason too stunned to participate. And Rosie had not pushed it.

She looked behind her, as best she could, and before her, and made a wide and clumsy U-turn. 'Bye, Pierce.

What had happened was that as she stood with him in the dim bedroom, she had felt herself, all in a moment, forgetting why you did this, seduced people, got into their pants. She just forgot; it vanished from her. And so she gave it up.

She might get him yet, of course. Not a warmth but a weird coldness went through her to think of it, the wrong tap turned on.

The house she had lived in with Mike lay on the other side of the wide township of Stonykill, the newest side: a flight of broad terraces, unwooded and windswept, upon which two-and-a-half-story houses were being built, all alike except that some were mirror images of the others, reversed left to right, and some turned front to back, for variety. It made them look oddly random to Rosie, scattered on the hillside, with their hopeful young birches tethered to the lawns. As though none was aware that others were

being built around it. The streets that wind through them are called
Spruce and Redbud and Holly, but the whole place has always been
called—perhaps after some now-lost village—Labrador.

She approached the house slowly, ready to turn back if there
was a car or cars in the driveway. There was none. Rosie had got
into a habit, which she reproached herself for, of getting into the
house when Mike wasn't there, to find things that she or Sam
needed, things she had never recovered, things she didn't want to
negotiate with Mike about delivering or replacing. She had at first
believed that none of it was important, but now and again over the
months had recalled this, or found herself in need of that, and a
picture would present itself to her of the thing lying just where it lay
in the Stonykill house; and she would come break in to get it.

Only it wasn't really breaking in. She just went up the stairs
from the garage; that door was never locked.

She wondered if Mike noticed the pilfering. He never said.

Parked in Redbud Street she pulled her little list from her
pocket. There was a hard stone in her breast, the leaden coldness
that had been there all day; all spring for that matter.

> R. view mirror
> Mice/balloons
> Pelican
> BCPs

She had done without a rear-view mirror for nine months, but
it was time to get the wagon inspected, and she wasn't sure it would
pass without one. Her Pelikan drawing pen lay (she could see it) on
the windowsill of the sun porch, behind the TV; she had been
writing letters with it on a summer night last year.

She thrust the list back into her pocket. The book about the
family of mice who go traveling in a balloon: it had taken her a
while to figure out what Sam meant by the bloon mice, until she
remembered the long-overdue, the already-paid-for lost library book.
Amazing Sam could remember it, so long ago. It was because of the
spring balloon festival up at Skytop tomorrow: and Mike's ridiculous promise to Sam, he'd promise her anything lately. Bloon ride.
Anyway she had to have the book. Had to.

The birth control pills, a three-month supply she had got the
day before she left this house and Mike, were in the little cabinet

beside the toilet, where there was also the extra baby powder, the twelve boxes of tissues Mike had abstracted from The Woods, the potpourri from the bath shop in the Jambs.

They would still be there, she was sure. Mike lived in the house like a squirrel or a caveman, some creature unable to think how he might alter his circumstances to suit himself. Nothing had changed since last summer; last time she had broken in her old nightie still hung on the back of the closet door. The pills would still be there. Rosie had gone off the pill the month after she'd moved out; now she thought she ought to go back on again, and the little pink dots were damn expensive, and she'd need a new prescription if she didn't come get these she'd already paid for: and standing in the damp and concrete-smelling garage she couldn't remember why she wanted them after all.

In the garage were Sam's trike, which sometimes traveled with her and sometimes got left behind; and Mike's ten-speed, not used as much as it had been on the flats of Indiana. The cyclist's body he had once had, heavy-thighed and round-backed, had pleased him more than it had her. The cold stone behind her sternum was heavy. The autumn rake; the summer lawn mower; the winter snow shovel. She had forgotten why it had been important to get away from all this, why she had gone to all the trouble she had gone to to break these connections; she had forgotten, just as she had forgotten why she had once tried hard to make them.

Love's labor's lost.

She had forgotten why: as though the heart inside her had been removed, and with it all knowledge of such things. What makes people love each other? Why do they bother? Why did children love parents, and parents children? Why did husbands love wives, and women love men; what did it mean when they said: he drives me nuts, but still I love him?

She must have known once. Because love had made her do a lot of things, and go to a lot of trouble. She had known once, she almost remembered knowing; she remembered getting along with Mike and Sam, and the getting along was powered by love; love was the necessity for getting along. Once she had known, and now she didn't; and not knowing now made it seem that not she or anyone really knew, they were all faking it, forcing it, even Spofford, even Sam, and why did they bother. A cold loss of knowledge and dark ignorance were where her heart had been, and were all that these commonplace things, innocent tools and toys, called to; her dog Nothing, the name of the stone in her breast.

You couldn't live that way long, of course. You couldn't live in that kind of ignorance. She'd have to remember, sometime. She was sure she would. Because she still had a whole long life to get through, Sam's growing up, Boney's death and her mother's and at last her own: and she couldn't get through it without remembering why you bother.

She would. She was sure of it. *Sure you will* she said to herself, and patted her own bosom: *sure you will.*

At the bottom of the stairs leading up to the kitchen, a flight of open bare wood steps still showing the carpenter's marks, she stopped, unwilling to go up. It seemed certain she would have an accident on the stairs, or that the door at the top would turn out to be locked after all. She stood for a long time looking up, and then went back out into the warm rain.

"So how's it going?" she asked Pierce, at the door of Fellowes Kraft's study, brushing the rain from her cheeks. "How's Bruno?"

"Off to see the Pope," said Pierce.

SEVEN

▲

The coach racketed over the bad roads out of Naples, two bright-
garbed men riding postilion to clear the way. Carters cursed at them
and peasants along the road took off their caps and crossed themselves. The friar in black and white opposite Giordano murmured
to him in Roman-accented Latin of what the visit would entail, how
long he would be with the Pope—*Sanctissimus* he called him, as
though it were a pet name—what Giordano should do and say,
whom he should speak to, and whom not.

—*Sanctissimus* will present His ring to you but you must only
come near it and not kiss it. Peter's ring would be worn away to
nothing if everyone who came to *Sanctissimus* actually pressed his
lips to it. *Sanctissimus* will see you in the afternoon, between Nones
and Vespers, after He has dined. His dinner is of the simplest. He is
as abstemious as He is pious. You must speak clearly and distinctly,
as His hearing is not what it was. . . .

The coach stopped at Dominican monasteries in Gaeta and
Latina, the horses lathered and weary; Giordano lay long awake in
the sultry heat, putting together the journey he had come already,
the longest of his life, and attaching the places, roads, shrines,
churches, and palaces he had seen to the Neapolitan places of his
memory: new spokes of the earthly wheel he had constructed,
centered on the church of San Domenico. Before dawn they started
out again, to travel in the cool part of the day, and before the
brigands—so the friar with him said—were awake.

Giordano's fame had spread to the widest imaginable circle:
the widest anyway that the monks of Naples could imagine. When
the abbot had come to his cell to tell him that the Pope had heard

of the young man with the astonishing memory, and desired to know more, and that the Pope was *sending a coach from Rome to bring him there,* his voice had sunk low in amazement and solemnity.

Giordano's first thought had been, irrelevantly, about Cecco of Ascoli. He had thought: I'll tell Him about Cecco. I'll tell Him: if what Cecco said about the stars is true, if the universe is as he thought it to be, then it can't have been heresy, can it? The truth could never be heresy. A mistake was made, that's all; it's clear that a mistake was somehow made.

The coach sped down the old Appian Way, the friar nodding in his sleep while Giordano's eyes ate up the tombs, ruins, churches along that impossibly straight and metaled road. The coach dove through the Porta San Sebastiano, and past the gigantic ruins of baths and circuses, and into the thronged heart of Rome. At the Tiber bridge the friar pointed out the Castel Sant'Angelo, which had been built as the Emperor Hadrian's tomb, and was now the keep and dungeons of the Papacy. An angel with a sword stood atop it, mobile in the shimmer of noon.

The coach did not stop even at the gates of the Vatican Palace, it went right through, and only came to rest at last in a garden of golden stone and green poplars, fountains and galleries and silence.

—Come, said the friar. Wash and refresh yourself. *Sanctissimus* is at dinner.

From that day forward this garden (it was the Cortile del Belvedere that Julius II had built) would mean Garden to Giordano Bruno. This flight of stairs would mean Stairway. These *stanze* he entered now, dark-brilliant in the flaming day, were the courts and chambers of a mind, a thinking, remembering mind.

—These are the *stanze* painted by Raffaello. There is the Triumph of the Church. Saint Peter. Saint Stephen. Aquinas, of our order. Come along.

—Who are these?

—Philosophers. Look more closely. Can't you see Plato with his beard, Aristotle, Pythagoras? Come along.

He tugged at Giordano's sleeve, but the young monk in wonderment held back. The painted crowd on the stairs of that cool edifice, those gowned men holding tablets, stirred; they blinked, looked down on Giordano, smiled, and resumed their conversation and their stillness.

The friar delivered him to other Dominicans, secretaries of the

Dominican cardinals around the Pope; they looked Giordano over, and put questions to him. And Giordano began to understand why he had been brought here.

Around Peter's throne now the jealousies and suspicions which tend to divide and inflame the busiest of Christ's servants were unusually raw, and Giordano was to be a counter, one small counter, in the game of influences and prestige waged between the *Domini canes* and the Black Company of Jesus. The Jesuits were famed for their adoption everywhere of the New Learning, and for putting its novelties and successes to the Church's uses in their colleges and academies. The Dominicans wanted to show off some knowledge that was theirs, and to remind Pius, who was after all a Dominican himself (though He seemed not always as conscious of it as He might be) that His black-and-white hounds guarded treasure as precious as any New Learning: the Art of Memory, which the order had so perfected. *Sanctissimus* would be amused to see how agile it had made a Dominican mind. *Sanctissimus* would be instructed as well.

Cardinal Rebiba himself returned Giordano to the Raffaello *stanze* when he had washed and eaten, and introduced him to the little dried pear Who was Pius V, Vicar of Christ on Earth. He lived in those rooms, beneath those pictures, amid these bustling monks. He sat on a pillowed chair; He was so short that His white satin slippers didn't reach the floor, and a monk hastened to slip a stool beneath them.

Giordano did his tricks. He recited the psalm *Fundamenta* in Hebrew after hearing it read aloud once; he named the tombs on the Appian Way in their order as he had passed them. The trick of *amiavi-amaveri-veravama* was tried, but *Sanctissimus* could not understand what was proceeding, and it had to be quickly given up.

—We studied this art when We were young, the Pope said to Rebiba, who nodded encouragingly. To Giordano the Pope said:

—Now We have no need of it. You see here are secretaries all around Us now, who remember for Us all that We need to have remembered. Perhaps you will be one of them, one day.

He nodded then, smiling sweetly, and said: Go on.

Under Rebiba's questioning, the memory artist (close-mouthed with stage-fright, and having forgotten Cecco) gave an account of his practice of the art, how he had built his palaces, and cast the images he used on them; he said nothing about the stars, or the *horoscopi,* but he told them how the hieroglyphs of Ægypt could be used, the signs made by Hermes.

—Is this that Hermes, the Pope asked, who gave laws and letters to the Ægyptians?

—It is, Giordano answered.

—And who in his writings spoke of a divine Word, Son of God, through which the world was made, though he lived many generations before Our Savior?

—I have not read his works, said Giordano.

—Come and look here, said *Sanctissimus.* Come along.

With a bustle of monks and Rebiba, the Pope went into the largest of the *stanze,* the *Stanza della Segnatura,* where He was accustomed to sign the decrees of the ecclesiastical court, and stood with Giordano beneath the painting of the pillared basilica, Plato, sunlight, truth.

—Look up there, said the Pope. Beside the man with the diagram, who is Pythagoras. Who is he in the white?

—I don't know, said Giordano.

—No one knows, said the Pope. Here is Plato. Pythagoras. Epicurus (who is in hell) with his vine leaves in his hair. Could this one in white be Hermes?

 Giordano looked up at the personage the Pope pointed to.

—I don't know, he said.

The Pope moved away, through the crowded room, crowded with the great dead, and Giordano followed.

—Ptolemy, He said, pointing. With a crown, who was a king in Ægypt. Was not that Hermes also a king in Ægypt? And look there. Homer. And Virgil. But who are these, these in armor?

Cardinal Rebiba marveled sourly at them, the little old man, the monk who with his bull neck and tense strut looked more like a brigand or a wrestler than a philosopher. They studied pictures that the cardinal himself had never thought to puzzle over. The afternoon was growing late, and had taken a useless turn; the Neapolitan, instead of astonishing with his art, was advertising his ignorance.

—We live in these rooms, *Sanctissimus* said. And so do these people. And We don't know who they are, or what brought them here. Well.

He proffered His ring, and Giordano fell to his knee and, as instructed, came close to but did not kiss the stone on His finger even as the Pope withdrew it.

—Now We must return to Our business. Is there anything you need? Ask Us.

—I would like, Giordano said, to read the writings of that Hermes.

—Is that lawful? the Pope said, and turned to Rebiba. Is it?

Rebiba, blushing, made an ambiguous gesture.

—If it is lawful, the Pope said, you may. Go downstairs. In Our library We have We-don't-know-how-many books. Hermes *et hoc genus omne.*

Turning to go, He raised His hand, and a secretary flew to His side.

—The *Index librorum prohibitorum,* He said as the secretary wrote. It needs looking into. We will appoint a *congregatio* of Our cardinals. They must take counsel about this. It has been much neglected.

He was gone, leaving Giordano and the others kneeling, and red-faced Rebiba bowing low.

—Go away, Rebiba then said to Giordano. The library is below. You have been worse than useless.

Behind Rebiba as he went out, as though caught up in the angry swish of his red satin skirts, went the rest of the priests, secretaries, guards, and servants who had filled the rooms. One only was left, standing by the far door, a young and smiling boy Giordano had not before noticed, fair-haired, his arms crossed before him. Without words, he crooked a finger, signaling Giordano to follow. Featly he went down the narrow stair, which after a long time debouched into a disused suite of rooms, all painted, empty and lit by the day.

—Look, the boy said, at that wall, beneath the zodiac. Who holds the book? Hermes.

Giordano looked. An armillary sphere representing the heavens hung over the head of a sweet-faced man, who spoke to others, Ægyptians perhaps, in a garden.

—Pinturrichio painted it, the boy said. Come. You will see Hermes again, in the farther room.

They went through connecting chambers, a room of Apostles instantly recognizable by the emblems they carried, Peter's keys, Matthew's book, Andrew's cross; and through a room of Arts—

Astrology and Medicine and Geometry and Grammar—all pictured
there much as they were pictured in their rooms in the memory
palace Giordano had within.

—Who do you see there? the boy said, bringing Giordano into
the last room. Who is on that wall?

—Mercurius, Giordano said.

—Who is Hermes too.

A young man with the same sweet face as the man beneath the
armillary heavens: with a curved sword he was striking down a
grotesque figure who grew eyes not only in his head but all over his
body, in his cheeks, arms, thighs. Behind these two a placid cow
looked on: Io. Transformed into a cow by Juno, she was put to be
watched over by Argus the thousand-eyed, but Argus was slain by
Mercury, and Io escaped into Ægypt.

—Look, said the boy. Ægypt.

Along the borders of the wall, all around the room, were
pyramids, hieroglyphic bulls, Isis, Osiris.

—It was Alexander the Sixth who made these rooms, the
young man said. His sign was the Bull; he studied magic; he knew
Marsilius, and loved him. He loved wealth, too. He was a very bad
man.

His clear laughing eyes directed Giordano's to another wall: a
seated queen, not Our Lady; a bearded prophet on one side of her,
and the same strong sweet-faced man on the other, pensive, smiling
faintly.

—Queen Isis, said the boy. Who was Io once. And Mercurius,
who went into Ægypt, and gave to the Ægyptians their laws and
letters. The other man is Moses, who lived then too.

—Yes, said Giordano. He looked from the clear dreaming wise
eyes of Mercurius in the picture to the clear laughing eyes of the
fair-haired boy, and a weird shudder flew over him.

—Come, the youth said. Down.

They went into a tiny and shabby chapel, and down a twisting
flight of stairs into a chamber whose smell Giordano knew at once.
Books.

—It is called the *Floreria*. Sit.

There was a broad scarred table onto which the light fell from
a high window; there was a bench before it. Giordano sat.

*   *   *

In after times he would not remember much of his sitting there, or even how many days he sat. He was brought food, now and then, to his table; a pallet was made for him, in a corridor, between piles of books waiting to be bound, and there sometimes he slept. And the smiling youth came and went, and put the books before him, and took them away, and brought more. It was he too who brought the dishes of food, and tugged at Giordano's hair when he had fallen asleep on the open pages.

Had there been others there? There must have been, other scholars, librarians, students harmlessly looting the Pope's treasure: some of the faces which, ever after, the speakers in the dialogues of Thrice-great Hermes would wear in Bruno's imagination must have been borrowed by him from the readers whom he saw there: but he couldn't remember. What he remembered was what he read.

They were great folio volumes, a hundred years old almost, Marsilio Ficino's translation into Latin of the Greek originals (which had come out of the Ægyptian somewhen): bound in gold and white, printed in a clear and smiling Roman type. *Pimander Hermetis Trismegisti.* He began with Ficino's awed commentary:

> In that time in which Moses was born there flourished Atlas the astrologer, brother of Prometheus the physicist and maternal uncle of the elder Mercury whose nephew was Mercurius Trismegistus.

He read how Pimander, the Mind of God, came to this Mercurius-Hermes, and told him of the origins of the universe: and it was an account strangely like Moses's in Genesis, but different too, for in it Man was not made of clay but existed before all things, was son and brother at once to the Divine Mind and sharer in Its creative power, sharer with the seven Archons—the planets—in celestial nature. A God himself, in fact, until, falling in love with the Creation he had helped to shape, Man fell: and mingled his substance with Nature's matter: and came to be earthy, bound up in love and sleep, and subject to Heimarmene and the Spheres.

Back upward he must go then, through those Spheres, taking from each of the seven Archons the powers he lost in his fall, and leaving behind the layers of material garment he has worn, until in the ogdoadic sphere he returns to his true nature, and sings hymns of praise to his Father:

Holy is God the Father of all, who is before the first beginning;
Holy is God, whose purpose is accomplished by his several Powers;
Holy art Thou, of whom all nature is an image. . . .
Accept pure offerings of speech from a soul and heart uplifted to
thee, Thou of whom no words can tell, no tongue can speak, whom
silence only can declare. . . .

What sort of journey was this, how was it made, how were the
powers to be acquired so that a man or his spirit could go so far?
Giordano read Pimander's words to Hermes:

All beings are in God, but not as though placed somewhere; no more
than they are placed in the incorporeal faculty of representation. You
know this yourself: Direct your soul to be in India, to cross the seas,
and it's done instantaneously. To travel up into heaven, the soul needs
no wings, nothing can prevent its going thither. And if you wish to
break through the vault of the universe, and see what's beyond it—if
there is anything beyond it—you may do it.

Do you see what powers, what speed you have? That is how God
must be imagined. All things are contained within God—the universe,
himself and all—just as thoughts are contained within a mind. Unless
you make yourself like God, though, you cannot understand God, for
like is only intelligible to like.

Therefore make yourself huge, beyond measuring; with one leap
free yourself from your body. Lift yourself out of Time and become
Eternity: then you will begin to understand God. Believe that for you
as for God all things are possible; conceive of yourself as immortal,
capable of understanding everything, all arts, all sciences, the nature
of every living being. Climb higher than the highest height; sink lower
than the lowest depth. Draw into yourself the sensation of all created
things, of fire and water, of wet and dry, cold and hot, imagining that
you are everywhere on earth and in the sea, in the haunts of the
animals, that you aren't yet born, in your mother's womb, adolescent,
old, dead, past death. If you can embrace in thought all things at
once, all times, places, substances, qualities, quantities, then you
might understand God.

All, all contained within the thinking mind, just as all the
things Bruno had ever seen or done, all the tools, birds, articles of
clothing, pots and pans on the lists of the brothers in Naples, were

all contained—separate, findable, distinct—within the circular memory palace of his skull. He knew. He knew.

> Say no longer that God is invisible; never say so, for what is more
> manifest than God? God has created all so that you may see an
> All in what he has created; it is the miraculous power of God
> to show himself in every being. Nothing is invisible, not even
> bodiless beings. The mind makes itself visible in the act of thinking,
> just as God makes himself visible in the act of creating.

Giordano read, his heart beating slow and hard; he read with calm certitude and the deep satisfaction of a child sucking the nourishment it knows it needs. He had been right, right, right all along.

Hermes, become a priest and a king, taught others what Mind had taught to him. There were dialogues between himself and his son, Tat, and one long one between him and his disciple Asclœpius, instructing him in the now fully formed religion of Ægypt and its cult. God dispenses life to all through the medium of the stars; he has created a second God, the Sun, an intermediary through whom the divine light is spread to all. And next the Horoscopes whom Giordano had read of already, the *decans* responsible for the persistence, through infinite diversity and constant changefulness, of the Reasons of the World: themselves changing form continuously like the talismanic images of Picatrix, but persisting nonetheless. And the name of the chief god of these gods was Pantomorph, or "omniform." Giordano laughed aloud.

> And there are other gods beside, whose powers and operations are
> distributed through all things that exist. . . .

The book of Asclœpius told how the priests of Ægypt were able to draw down dæmons from the stars, and cause them to take up residence in the zoomorphic statues of stone which the priests had had made, whence they would speak, prophesy, tell secrets. So well did those priests know how divinity permeated the lower world, which animals and plants were governed by which stars, which odors, stones, music the dæmons could not resist.

All that knowledge lost now, all that omniform heavens-and-earth, lost; as though that armillary sphere which Pinturrichio had floated above the heads of Hermes and the Ægyptians had been smashed, scattered, the ruins of it only to be come upon now by chance and puzzled over in this latter Age of Brass; surviving only in rumor, debased stories, cantrips, shards. Picatrix.

But how lost, why, why lost?

A time will come when it will be seen that the Ægyptians have honored the Divinity in vain. All this holy worship will become ineffectual. The gods will desert the earth, and return to heaven; they will abandon Ægypt; and this land, the home of religion, will be widowed of its gods and left destitute. Strangers will fill this country, and not only will men neglect the worship of the gods, but—still more terrible—so-called laws will be enacted, which shall punish those who do worship them. In that day this most holy land, this land of shrines and temples, will be filled only with tombs, and with the dead. O Ægypt, Ægypt: there will remain of your religion only fabulations, and your own children will not be able to believe them; nothing will survive save glyphs engraved on stone, to tell of your piety!

He read, and wept to read. *He* knew how the old religion had come to an end; he knew what strangers had come to supplant their pieties. When all the old gods had run to hide their heads, when the women wept that Pan was dead. When the Christ whose colors Giordano wore, whose soldier he was, had banished them all, all but himself and his Father and the emanation of the two of them that made three: a tangle of triplex Godhead too jealous to allow any mysteries but the mystery of itself.

Does it make you weep, Asclœpius? There is far worse to come. . . . In that day will men, in boredom, give up thinking the world worth their reverence and adoration—this greatest of all goods, this All which is all the best of past and future. It will be in danger of passing away; men will think it a burden, and despise it, this incomparable work of God, glorious structure, one creation made of an infinite diversity of forms. . . . Darkness will be preferred then to light, death to life, and none will raise his eyes toward the skies. . . . So the gods will depart, separating themselves from men—sad!—and only evil angels will remain. . . . Then the earth will lose its equilibrium, the

sea no longer hold up ships, the heaven will not support the stars. . . .
The fruits of the earth will moulder, the soil be fruitless, the air itself
thick with sadness. Such will be the old age of the world. . . .

Yes! Eyes clouded with tears, his nose running, Giordano brow
in hand made out the words. They had *not* been banished; they had
departed of their own free will, disgusted by the upstarts who
scorned and hated their knowledge and their powers, free gifts for
men, now withdrawn.

But if by their own free will they had gone away, then, one day,
they might return; they might be induced to return. They *would*
return!

That is what the rebirth of the world will be: a coming-back of all
good things, a holy and awesome restoration of the whole wide world
imposed by the will of God in the course of time.

He saw them as he read, returning, the godlike men or manlike
gods who are true inheritors of and sharers in God's restoring
power; he saw the turgid air clearing at their passage, the creatures
of night fleeing away, dawn bursting.

And if such a time had been to come all those centuries ago,
then why might it not be coming now, right now—now when this
old knowledge had come back to man again, and been cast in this
type, printed on these pages? Why not now?

—Now, said a soft voice behind him, and the boy who had
brought him this book sat down beside him on the bench. Now
listen carefully and don't be alarmed.

Bruno put his hand on the page to mark his place, to stop the
knowledge flowing for a moment.

—What is it?

—There is news from Naples. Proceedings have been started
against you with the Holy Office. Don't turn around.

—How do you know this?

—You are to be prosecuted for heresy. The Holy Office here
has been given notice. A hundred and thirty articles of heresy.

—Nothing can be proven.

—Did you, the boy said lightly, ever leave books in the privy?
Giordano laughed.

—Writings have been found in the privy, the boy said. Erasmus. The commentaries on Jerome.

—Erasmus? Nothing more terrible?

—Listen, the boy said. They have prepared this long and well. It will go hard with you. They have it all arranged, the interrogation, the witnesses, the evidence.

—They are men, Bruno said. They possess reason. They'll listen. They must listen.

—Believe me, Brother. You can never go back.

There was no one else left in the cool tall room except Bruno and the blond young man, who still smiled, his hands folded loosely in his lap. A fire caught in the dry tinder of Bruno's heart, and burned hot and painfully.

—The Pope, he said. I'll speak to Him. He said that I, He, He . . .

The boy's face didn't alter, he only waited for Bruno to quit, to finish in a hopeless stutter. Then he said:

—Stay here till dark. Then go out by that door, the small door at the far end. Follow the corridor. Go up the stairs. I'll meet you there.

He rose.

—At dark, he said; and he smiled down at Giordano, a smile of complicity, as at a joke both he and Giordano well knew was afoot; only Giordano did *not* know it, and the small hairs rose on the back of his neck, and his scrotum tightened. The boy turned and went.

Giordano looked down at the page where his hand lay. Already the long light of afternoon was leaving it.

> In that day the gods who once oversaw the earth will be restored, and will come to settle in a City in the extreme limit of Ægypt, a City founded toward where the sun goes to his setting; a City into which will hasten, by land and by sea, the whole race of mortal men.

He read until he could no longer make out words. Then he had read all of it that he would ever read, and night had come. He rose. He thought: Tomorrow is the sixth of August, the Transfiguration. He crossed the long vaulted room, past the scholar's tables set beneath the night-blue windows, and opened the small thick door.

✳   ✳   ✳

In darkness his feet found the steep stairs; he mounted toward
the landing where a lamp shone beyond the turning. The fair-haired
boy sat there on the stair, waiting for him. He had a bundle in his
lap.

—Get out of that robe, he said softly. And put on these.

Bruno looked from the boy to the bundle held out to him.

—What?

—Quick, the youth said. Be quick.

For an instant the solid stone beneath his feet seemed to tilt, as
though the building were toppling. He pulled off the black-and-
white robe and thick underclothes, trembling slightly. The bundle
was hose, boots, doublet, shirt, wrapped in a cloak. The boy sat on
the step above, chin in his hand, and watched the monk struggle
with the unfamiliar garments, trying to tie the points with shaking
fingers. The cloak last, long and hooded. And a belt with a purse,
and a little dagger. The purse was heavy.

—Listen, the boy said, standing. Listen now and remember all
I tell you.

He spoke mildly and clearly, sometimes striking one forefinger
against the other when he named a name, or raising a forefinger in
warning. He set out Giordano's route, the streets and gates and
suburbs, the roads north, the towns and cities. Giordano, clad in
someone else's clothes, heard all and would not forget.

—A doctor and his family there, the boy said. Ask them. They
know. They will help.

—But how, how . . .

The youth smiled and said: They are *giordanisti* too. In their
way.

He laughed a small laugh then, at Giordano unfrocked, and
tugged the cloak straight; he picked up the lamp, and led the way
by its light up the curling stairs to another corridor, a narrow one,
and along it to a double door.

—Now, he said.

He set down his lamp; he grasped the rings of the door and
turned them, and thrust the door open. Giordano Bruno looked out
into an empty cobbled square; a fountain gurgled in the center of it;
torches were carried away down a far alley, and he heard a shriek of
laughter. Night air in his face. Freedom. He stood, looking.

—Go, said the boy.

—But. But.

—Out, said the boy, and he put his soft boot against Bruno's hose-clad backside, and pitched him out; and the doors clashed shut behind him.

E I G H T

▲

It wasn't a small world: it was immense, made immense by the infinitesimal steps a man on foot could take, or a man on muleback for that matter, or borne in a litter or even astride a fast horse. The long road went ever on, a faint track sometimes and nearly lost in swamp or mountain, but always reappearing eventually. Which way is Viterbo? Siena? Another river to wade, wood to pass through (eyes wide, looking from side to side, knuckles tight on dagger hilt), always another walled town to come to: Siena, Vitello, Cecino, to a weary walker seeming to be only the same town repeated over and over, like the single tiny woodcut that in geographies stands variously for Nuremburg, Wittenburg, Paris, Cologne: a steeple, another steeple, a castle, a plume of smoke, a gate, a little traveler stunned and wondering.

He went north, at first, like all Italian heretics went north; to the last of his Roman places he attached the first of his Tuscan places, to the last of his Tuscan places the first of his Genoese places. He followed the instructions given him, and was handed over from one household to another, one refuge to the next, never without help, and not marveling particularly at his good fortune either: he hadn't known what the world beyond Nola and Naples would be like, and was not surprised that it contained the kind helpers that it did.

For many days he walked, to save his purse, and the new hose he wore chafed his thighs until he nearly wept with pain and irritation. The only thing monks had ever done for the world was to invent a reasonable dress for man, and no one used it but them.

Not until he reached the new city of Livorno did he dare to

take ship, and pass the scrutiny of harbor officials: for Livorno was a free port, and all nations and religions were at liberty there. Giordano went down through the town to the docks, looking side to side, marveling at the painted house-fronts that showed the victories of San Stefano over the Turks, the incidents passing on from one house-front to the next.

A free port. Free. Jews did business in the shops and chandleries without any yellow badge; at noon from a tiny minaret a man in a turban leaned out and crowed a long unintelligible prayer: for even the Turks were allowed to have a mosque for their people. But in the market the shipmen of many nations gathered to argue over the galley slaves for sale there, for Livorno was also the great slave market of the Christian world, and Moors, blacks, Turks, Greeks, a wild confusion of humanity, some sleeping, some weeping in their chains, were being bought and sold as Bruno passed. Following the inward map the blond boy of the Vatican had given him, he found the dock he needed, spoke the right name, and, almost unable not to cry aloud in astonishment, glee, and fear, was handed down into a long and narrow felucca just putting out to sea: *Avanti signor. Avanti.*

The felucca fled up the coast, putting in often to take on and to offload an endless variety of wares, casks of oils and wine, furniture, bales of cloth, packets of letters, passengers, a cage of cooing doves. (Years later, in prison, he would sometimes pass the time trying to reconstruct the list of them, the casks, the boxes, the people, the ports.) The grunting oarsmen seemed stupefied by their own rhythm, blind with sun; at noon the craft put in at some nameless harbor, and the oarsmen slept where they sat, under the shade of the lateen sails; their bodies, of several colors, shone with sweat.

Giordano Bruno, Nolan, lay on his satchel and did not sleep.

Genoa, a city of palaces and churches, orgulous and gay. He went up from the harbor along avenues of palaces, palaces half-built or half-rebuilt; every one different. He took the lefts and rights he had in memory; he found an archway into the gardens of a palazzo, he crossed a geometric pleasure-ground, he walked between ranks of dark topiary beasts (centaur, sphinx) down to a grotto where water dropped musically: there he found the man he had been sent to, master of these gardens, who was supervising the installation of a waterwork within the grotto.

To this man he spoke the phrase he had committed to memory,

a meaningless but odd little compliment. The man's face did not change, but he held out his hand to Bruno.

—Yes, he said. Yes, I see. Welcome.

He drew Bruno within the clammy cool shell of the grotto, stuck full of glittering stones, bits of mirror, shells, crystal. A leaden statue had been set up above the marble pool; workmen fussed with the pipes that led in and out of it, but the god took no notice of them, he looked down at Giordano, arched brows witty and wise, goat's feet crossed.

—Pan, the gardener said.

—Yes.

—And with the water, brought up from below by these pipes, and circulating *here,* and then *here,* Pan will play his pipes. Syrinx.

He looked deeply into Bruno with ash-colored eyes, light in his garden-brown face.

—*Magia naturalis,* he said, smiling like his Pan.

—Yes, said Bruno.

The workmen opened their pipes; a spectral hooting sounded within the grotto. Bruno shivered. The aquatect took his wrist, and Giordano saw that he wore a gold seal-ring on his strong brown hand, a seal-ring carved with a curious figure.

—Now come, he said. Come to my lodge, and tell me what you need.

He was fed and bedded in Genoa for a few days; then he was handed on to the family of a doctor in the Genoese town of Noli, and a place was found for him in the shabby little *accademia,* lecturing to whoever wished to listen on the *Sphere* of Sacrobosco.

—You have traveled much? the doctor who had taken him in asked at dinner.

—No.

—Ah.

The doctor passed him wine.

—I should say *yes,* said Giordano. I have traveled infinitely. In my mind.

—Aha, said the doctor, without a smile. In your mind.

His lectures on astronomy began simply enough, spherical geometry, the colures and equators, Giordano was not particularly easy with this; then he began to draw on Cecco, and attendance improved. His fame spread. Only a few months had passed when the doctor came to him in his little room and said that it would be best if he moved on now.

—Why?

—Travel broadens, said the doctor. Travel not only in the mind.

—But.

—You have been noticed, the doctor said. Our little town is not often in the eye of the Holy Office. But you have been noticed.

—I've said only the truth, Giordano said, rising. The truth.

The doctor raised a hand to calm him.

—Best to leave after a moonset, he said. I will come then to wake you.

Another sleeping courtyard, another wallet full of bread, a pouch of coins, a book. Night. A frontier to cross. It was a world full of dangers: and to all of them a young man on foot, with a monk's robe in his satchel and a headful of notions, not used to keeping still, was subject.

Southward he could not go. Northward, in the Spanish kingdom of Milan, the Inquisition was busy and the Spanish soldier, the *tercio,* stood—grinning and most likely drunk—astride every road Giordano might take. Giordano had known the *tercio* all his life, had laughed at him in the *commedie* in his old city: *Capitano Sangre y Fuego, El Cocodrillo,* the eternal bragging soldier, ragged fiery and mad, loyal only to a Spanish honor incomprehensible to all the rest of the world, and to a Catholic church whose every moral law he flouted. Killing heretics—and their servants and children if necessary, their oxen and geese for his sustenance—was what the *tercio* lived to do; after that to drink, and lie, and have his way with women. The Milanese girls didn't leave their shuttered houses even to go to Mass.

So Signor Bruno (new sword at his side) went west, skirting the Milanese borders, and up to Turin in the kingdom of Savoy: which was just as Hapsburg as Milan but not Spanish at least, having fallen to the Holy Roman Empire when old Charles had broken his vast inheritance in two, half for Phillip of Spain, half for Maximilian of Austria. In Turin Giordano taught Latin grammar to children until he could stand it no more; then he packed books, papers, habit, and, one step ahead of the parents who had paid him in advance, found a place on a boatload of Alpine timber going downriver to the Po. The Po went east to Venice. So did Bruno.

*   *   *

It could seem in those years that half the world was in motion, put to flight by the other half. From square to square across the chessboard of the Hapsburg possessions the *tercios* crossed and recrossed, billetted on households in Naples and Milan, rifling the warehouses of Protestant merchants in Antwerp (who packed their goods in trunks and fled to Amsterdam and Geneva); shipped by Armada to the New World, slaying Indians, who had no souls, and looking for El Dorado in Guinea and Brazil; battling the Turks in Transylvania and Crete, holding open the doors of a Spanish corridor from Sicily to the Baltic, starting fugitives like hares wherever they passed.

But there were other armies abroad who also admitted of no boundaries, either geographical or in the hearts of men; forces that could likewise abide no compromise, could not even conceive of it.

—They come out from Geneva with books hidden in the false bottoms of their trunks, said the lean passenger who shared Giordano's perch upon the timber. They come into a city, and never reveal themselves. They are merchants, agents, goldsmiths, printers. They begin to attract others by their secret preaching—the father of a family, who brings in his wife, his children, his servants. In this way many small congregations are established, like the cells built by a honeybee, linked but sealed off from each other; if one is broken into, no matter, others remain whole. They know only the names of those who share with them, so torture cannot wring the names of others from them. And so they grow, in secret, like worms inside a fruit, until one day they are enough; they reveal themselves, the fruit bursts to show the roiling mass inside, the city falls to them. Just in that way.

—How do you come to know so much of it? Giordano, irritated, asked him.

—In France, the lean man said, the Huguenots (which is only another name for them) are now debating whether the believers are justified in killing a monarch who oppresses them. *Killing a monarch.* Why not the Pope then? Why not Jesus Christ himself again?

—Hm, said Giordano.

He pretended to sleep. The riverbanks, crowded with people and carriage, went by him, or he went by them. Later he saw the lean man take from his clothes and open a black book Giordano recognized; his lips moved as he read, and his hand now and then sketched a cross on his bosom.

They were soldiers, and in motion too: the Company of Jesus, soldiers loyal to no crown, no bishop, no territory. No more than the Genevans did they believe that Christ's church could be divisible, and at every breach from Scotland to Macao they were there. They could stab a monarch, Giordano was sure: or pay to have one stabbed. They could. They already had.

In Venice he again found help: a name he knew led him to another name, and that one to a scholarly doctor with a room to spare; there was an academy where he could lecture, money for books.

He lectured on the *Ars memoriae,* and let it be whispered that he had fled a Dominican monastery: the reputation of his order for possessing potent memory arts was old and wide. To his students at the academy he began to seem—as he would seem to many others from that time onward—to have a secret he could impart, a secret that had cost him not a little in the learning, if they would just sit still to hear it. He drew hearers, not all of them sympathetic. He lost—discarded, threw away in a few terrific moments—his old virginity, in a closed gondola rocking on the autumn Adriatic.

His powers continued to grow. Offered a counterfeit coin—not a silver ducat but cast glass silvered with mercury—his fingers knew the difference. Mercury, trickster and thief, speaker and laugher, his own Hermes, was burning to his touch: silver, the moon's metal, was cool and liquid. If he drew on Venus, blew on Venus inwardly as on a coal, then other powers were his: women turned to watch him pass, men deferred to him, there was no hesitancy in him when words needed to be whispered into a small pink ear, when masks—hers frilled and black, his white and long-nosed—were put aside.

(He found, after those exertions, as he lay still and glowing beside a sleeping woman, that something was loosened within him; for a few moments or an hour he would perceive the packed contents of his consciousness on the move, streaming together, like with like, rank on rank, like the different troops of an army, horse and foot, artillery, pikemen, fusiliers: each kind in different bright coats and caps, all under the command of the different captains he had set for them, the Reasons of the World; and their general the god Omniform. He would think then: There is only one thing in the universe, and that thing is Becoming. Endless, timeless, ceaseless

Becoming, infinite generation exfoliating from the ideas within the mind of God and casting these bright moving shadows in his own soul—and colored, all colored, for if the shadows in his soul were not colored, then nothing is. In a Venetian *bagnio* on the last night of the feast of the Redentore he lay listening to the soft inhalations beside him and the distant revelers, watching within himself the pulse and scintillation of Becoming, like the silver tips of wavelets endlessly becoming on the sea.)

Venice in rain sailed its broad lagoons like an ark of Noah (so he described it in a sonnet) bearing all kinds, two of each. Venice was indulgent: a man could live here, and think. In the bookstalls around the piazza San Marco, amid the smudgy almanacs and books of prophecy, the pamphlets and *novelle,* he came upon books he had long heard of but had never seen between covers. Iamblichus on the Mysteries. Agrippa, *De occulta philosophia.* Here were the wild hymns of Orpheus to the Sun that were sung in the young age of the world. Here was the *Ars magna* of Ramon Lull, an art of memory like his own but not like his own: he stared at its branching trees and climbing steps and wheels-within-wheels.

Who was publishing these things newly? How did they know he needed them? Why was he seeing books like these in the book presses and cabinets of the kind doctors and scholars who sheltered him? He raised his eyes from the page to see the bookseller, leaning on the back of his bin of books, cheeks in his hands, smiling at him. On his finger he wore a gold ring, a ring cut with that same curious figure the gardener in Genoa had worn:

Seeing Bruno baffled and uncertain, the bookseller put before him a thick German volume, sewn but unbound, wrapped in parchment covers. He opened it to the title page.

—Cosmography, the bookseller said.

The book was *On the revolution of the orbs of Heaven* and was by Nicholas Copernicus of Poland.

Copernico. That was another name Giordano knew, a figure of fun in his Neapolitan schoolrooms, the man who, to explain the heavenly motions, had set the solid earth revolving and staggering around the spheres. He had seemed almost imaginary to Giordano, but here was his book. Nuremburg, A.D. 1547. Dedicated to the Pope. Giordano turned the big pages.

> Saturn, the first of the wandering stars, completes its circuit in 30 years. After him comes Jupiter, moving in a duodecennial revolution. Then Mars, which rolls around every two years. The place fourth in order is occupied by the annual revolution of (as we have said) the Earth, carrying with it the orbital circle of the Moon as an epicycle.

He had begun to feel very strange. It was as though, when he read Copernicus's placements of the planets, he felt the same planets in the heavens he kept within him (and their tutelary gods and spirits) open their eyes, and move to their proper places. And then the earth moving too, and all its contents.

> In the fifth place, Venus, who completes her revolution in 7½ months. The sixth and final place is occupied by Mercury, who goes around in 88 days. But in the center of all rests the Sun.

As though all the *guglie* of his memory system had been lifted up, at a signal, and put in motion—a motion they had always had, potentially, a motion without which they were asleep, or stopped, like a stopped clock. Giordano laughed. From the sparkling piazza beyond the arcade a flock of pigeons arose, as though suddenly shaken out like a banner: the view of the square was shattered in an instant into a thousand flying particles, fluttering bodies hurtled through the arches of the dark arcade and out again into the light, rousing others to flight.

Wings. Taken wing.

What if it were so? What if it were really so?

—He says, the bookman said in a low voice, he says that it's not new knowledge he has found. It's old knowledge he has brought back again. Pythagoras. Zoroaster. Ægypt. So he says.

> And who would place the lamp of this most magnificent of temples anywhere else, who could find a better place for it than there from where it can illuminate all that is at the same time? That's why some,

and not improperly either, have called it the Lantern of the World, others the Mind, others the Pilot. And Trismegistus calls it "God visible."

The bookseller had gently put his hands on the book to take it back, but Giordano would not give it up.

—I have no money now, he said. But.

—No money no Cosmography.

Giordano gave the name and street of the house where he was lodging.

—Send it there, he said. You'll be paid. I promise you, you . . .

The bookman grinned.

—I know the man, he said. Take it to him. With my compliments. I will put it on the account he keeps with me.

He released the book.

What glyph was that he wore?

Giordano carried Copernicus with him through the rainy streets, wrapped in his cloak like an infant.

In the spring he heard that the Venetian Inquisition, so slow to act, had at last noticed him. Spies had reported his lectures and his boasts. The bookseller on the piazza shuttered his shop. By now, Giordano's old Dominican habit provided more of a disguise than the signor's hose and sword; so the doctor cut his hair, and put him into his own gondola at the water-stairs, and wished him luck.

Eastward from here there was only the Turk. Frater Jordanus put his hands within his sleeves, and went west again.

"Pierce," said Rosie. "Gotta go."

Pierce—looming large in Kraft's miniature study—whirled around on the swivel chair, looking guiltily surprised. "Oh?"

"Mouths to feed." He only stared at her, though not perhaps seeing her leaning there in the doorway, a bunch of Kraft's papers in her arms for Boney to look at, letters from long ago. She wondered if it was a face like that with which she had used to look up from the books into which she escaped. That wild absent blind look. "Okay?"

"What?"

"If you're near a stopping place," she said. "Soon."

"Yes," he said, "yes," and turned back to the typescript. A

small stack of it on his left-hand side, a big pile on his right. He cupped his chin in his hands and sighed.

"It's stopped raining," Rosie said.

While Pierce read, his old teacher Frank Walker Barr at Noate stood up before his senior seminar on the History of History, and, talking as he worked, opened the classroom windows; for the rain that was ceasing in the Faraways had passed from here too, and the sun was hot.

"What, then, grants meaning to historical accounts?" he asked, for the last time in that semester. "What is the difference between a history and a register of facts, of names and events?" He had taken from the corner a long oaken pole, with a brass finger on the end of it; this he was inserting into the brass sockets set for it in the frames of the windows, and drawing them down. Many in the classroom remembered grade-school teachers doing the same, in past classrooms, and they watched Barr with interest.

"What we might do to conclude," Barr went on, "is to try to think how meaning arises in other kinds of accounts or narratives." The finger engaged the hole of the last westward-facing window. "It seems to me that what grants meaning in folktales and legendary narratives—we're thinking now of something like the *Nibelungenlied* or the *Mort D'Arthur*—is not logical development so much as thematic repetition, the same ideas or events or even the same objects recurring in different circumstances, or different objects contained in similar circumstances."

The window he tugged at yielded, and slid open, admitting a crowd of breezes which had been pressing for admittance there.

"A hero sets out," Barr said, not turning back to his students but facing the sparkling quad and the air. "To find a treasure, or to free his beloved, or to capture a castle or find a garden. Every incident, every adventure that befalls him as he searches, *is* the treasure or the beloved, the castle or the garden, repeated in different forms, like a set of nesting boxes—each of them however just as large, or no smaller, than all the others. The interpolated stories he is made to listen to only tell him his own story in another form. The pattern continues until a kind of certainty arises, a satisfaction that the story has been told often enough to seem at last to have been really told. Not uncommonly in old romances the story just breaks off then, or turns to other matters.

"Plot, logical development, conclusions prepared for by intro-ductions, or inherent in a story's premises—logical completion as a vehicle of meaning—all that is later, not necessarily later in time, but belonging to a later, more sophisticated kind of literature. There are some interesting half-way kind of works, like *The Faerie Queene*, which set up for themselves a titanic plot, an almost mathematical symmetry of structure, and never finish it: never need to finish it, because they are at heart works of the older kind, and the pattern has already arisen satisfyingly within them, the flavor is already there.

"So is this any help in our thinking? Is meaning in history like the solution to an equation, or like a repeated flavor—is it to be solved for, or tasted?"

He turned to face them.

"Is this a parable? Have I simply repeated our seminar in another form?"

The air in the room had all been changed now for the air outside, burdened with June, whatever that was exactly, something heavier than warmth or odor or vapor. It was the last day of classes.

"No?" he said, regarding their mild faces, absent already, and no wonder either. "Yes? No? Maybe?"

NINE

▲

Out of Turin the roads west and northward rose quickly into the mountains, climbing toward the passes of Little St. Bernard and Mont-Cenis; and an endless train of wagons, carts, mules, and men unwound from the Piazza del Castello and upward, carrying mail, news, jewels, and specie (well hidden in the pack trains or sewn in the linings of merchants' coats, not mentioned at inns and borders) and luxury goods of the Levantine and Asian trade valuable enough to make the overland journey worth the cost—ostrich feathers, drugs, silks, plate. The outlaws, the fugitives and spies, the friars and common people, went over the Alps on foot; the great were carried in litters, surrounded by clanking men-at-arms.

The road they followed went up into the high Savoy, through meadows lush and spangled with flowers, into a country of dark firs; beside rivers now rushing and dangerous; between beetling walls of gorges where snow still melted. Snow: Giordano pressed a handful to his lips. He heard someone say that it was from drinking snow-water continuously that the natives of these mountains—the strong squat men and long-armed women whose cottages hung on the points of crags, whose sheep danced from steep to steep—were so often hideously goitered.

He supposed that these must be the mountains where witches lived as well, the witches who were prosecuted so relentlessly by his Dominican brothers; stories of the witch-hunters and their dangers and triumphs were the lore of Dominican houses. Down those deep passes perhaps; in those black cave mouths; in those low cottages, roofs piled comically thick with snow, a breath of dark smoke from their chimney-holes. He thought maybe he should go find them, and live with them. Raise winds, and fly. There was a wind rising even then, harsh and searching, and a few snowflakes blown in it like cinders.

That night in the cold guest cell which he was allotted in a Dominican hospice in the Val Susa he lay awake before dawn, between Matins and Prime, remembering Nola.

Brother Teofilo had told him that the earth was not flat, like a dish, but round, like an orange; it seemed right that Teofilo would know this, round as he was himself. Giordano listened to him; he watched the friar draw with a burnt stick the circle of the world, and the outlines of lands on it, a *mappamundi*—and was content to believe it. Teofilo did not know that the round world which Giordano had instantly conceived and assented to when Teofilo drew his picture was a hollow sphere, and contained the lands and peoples, the mountains and the rivers and the air, as an orange contains its meat; what the boy thought Teofilo had drawn a picture of was its outside surface, marked like a plover's egg, the view God had. Inside was the earth we see. Along the bottom half lay the fields and vineyards; the mountains rose up the curved sides; the sky was the inside of the top, whereon the sun and stars were stuck.

Bruno laughed, remembering, and laced his hands behind his head.

When Teofilo at last realized what sort of world Giordano imagined, then the struggle began. Giordano's world was just as round as Teofilo's, and it made better sense; it was to him so obviously the case that it took him a long time even to grasp what Teofilo was laughing at, and then expostulating about. And when he did grasp it, the difficulties of it seemed overwhelming: What held the air and the light in? How could we live, sticking out into the nothingness? Why did the peoples in the Antipodes not fall off, and keep falling forever? It was absurd.

And then on a golden day he sat eating an orange in the winter ruin of the garden, and he turned—it felt like cracked knuckles or crossed eyes all through his being—he turned the round world inside out, like the skin of the orange he was peeling; and all the mountains and rivers, the vineyards and farmsteads and churches, turned with it. The sun and stars flew out to fill the nothing where God lived. The world was outside itself. The world was round.

Softly through the hospice of Susa the low bell sounded for Prime.

That—that sense of the world turning inside-out like the peel of an orange—was what he had felt standing in the rain in Venice at the stall of the bookseller with the curious ring: that was what had made him laugh.

If he put the center of the universe in motion, then what became of its circumference? If he turned the outer spheres inward, what became of spheres? In the center of the old universe had been the earth, in the center of the earth himself, in the center of himself the spheres of the heavens he had built within himself, in the center of them. . . .

If he turned the small universe within him inside-out, then what would happen in the one outside him?

He heard the sandals of the postulant whose duty it was to wake the monks for prayer. The sandals approached his door, the postulant struck his door and passed on, calling at each door: *Oremus, fratres.*

Snow was still falling in the spring air as the caravan Giordano joined went up through Novalese to Mont-Cenis. The travelers coming down from the top rode on sledges, a strong *marron* in front with a strap around his chest pulling, and another up behind with an alpen-stock to steer; on the slick path the sledges shot by, the *marrons* stoical, the faces of the fur-wrapped foreigners wide-eyed with alarm. All day the snow swirled heavily down from the heights; stuck carts began to burden the trail, the tough little mules waded in snow to their knees. Giordano, terrified and elated, felt his senses swallowed up in it.

His caravan called a halt at last at a carter's village just short of the Col; the villagers expertly tucked all the travelers in among themselves, every cranny could contain a sleeper; the animals were penned and the carts covered. Giordano paid high for a bowl of milk and bread and a share of a mattress stuffed with crackling beech leaves, not far from where the fire glowed.

It was still night when he awoke amid the snorers. The inn was a lightless cave. Giordano struggled out from the pile he was ensconced in, and pulled a fur robe with him; he wrapped it around his monk's robe, and—stepping over and around and sometimes on sleeping dogs and children on the floor—he found a door to go out by.

The air was shocking, as still as if all crystal, corrosive in his nose and throat. The storm had passed, and the sky was clear, more clear than he had known it could be: as though he were high up, away from the earth, and within the sphere of air itself. His warm breath hung before his face in a cloud. He gathered his robes and his fur around him and stepped into the yard; his rag-bound feet left black holes like pools behind him in the starlit snow.

But was there a sphere of air above the earth, if Copernicus was right? The old earth of Aristotle, black thick and base, collected at the bottom of creation, within finer spheres of water, air, fire. Whatever was lighter—sparks, souls—rose up. But Copernicus said the earth itself rose up, lighter than air, and went sailing; and so which way was up?

His heart was full. In the moonless sky the stars and planets stared down or stared away and burned. Burned. There was Cassiopeia's great chair. Lyra. Draco. The Bear standing on his tail, looking at the North Nail on which the heavens turned. Only they didn't. The eighth sphere of stars only seemed to turn because the earth turned around once a day, spinning on its toe like an *arlecchino*.

Perhaps there was no eighth sphere.

With a sound of not-being, a kind of tinkling indrawn breath, the eighth sphere went away. The stars, liberated, rushed away outward from the earth and from one another; the smaller ones (rushing away even faster) were perhaps not smaller, they were only farther off. Yes! And there might be—must be!—others, too far off to be seen at all.

His heart might burst, filled with cold starlight. The Milky Way, a powder like snow, might be stars simply too far away to distinguish from one another, like the blue haze of a far-off vine-yard, which is nothing but all the blooming grape-globes seen together.

How far off?

What could mark the limit? What reason could there be for them to end?

Infinite, Lucretius said, who could think of no reason. Cusanus said: a circle, whose center is everywhere, whose circumference is nowhere.

No. Cusanus had only spoken so of God. It was he, Giordano Bruno, who was saying it of God's creation, the shadow of God that was the universe. If there was an end to the stars then God was not God.

It was not only clear to him, neck bent staring upward, as clear as this air, it was self-evident; he seemed to have always known it, and had simply never said it aloud. Infinite. He felt its infinity tugging at his heart and eyes, and he felt an answering infinity within himself: for if it was infinite outside, then it must be infinite inside as well.

Infinite. He stirred his cold feet in the snow, and turned back toward the hostel. The little ponies stamped in their pens, breathing whitely, their shaggy manes powdered with hoarfrost. In the windows of the hostel, candles flickered, and furry smoke filled with sparks rose from the chimney; someone laughed within. Wake up.

It wasn't far from the village to the top of the pass. The sky had only begun to pale, and the dimmest stars—or those farthest off— had disappeared, when the caravan began clambering up the path toward the summit. The great starless darknesses on either hand were not sky but mountains, coming suddenly clear as though they had just awakened and stood up. Between them in the azure there flamed the morning stars. Mercury. Venus. Wet to the knees with snow-melt, Giordano climbed toward them.

Earth was a star as they were; and the bright beings who inhabited them, looking this way, saw not a cold stone but another like themselves, aflame in the sun's light. He hailed them: Brother. Sister. A strange and soundless hum seemed to be filling up his ears and his being, as though the dawn itself were to make a sound in breaking, continuous and irreversible. The star he rode was turning pell-mell toward the sun with all of them aboard it, dwarfish stolid carters, chairs, animals, and men; Bruno laughed at his impulse to fall and clutch the hurtling ball with hands and knees.

Infinite.

You made yourself equal to the stars by knowing your mother Earth was a star as well; you rose up through the spheres not by leaving the earth but by sailing it: by knowing that it sailed.

Sunlight struck the lifting white heads of the peaks, though the snow of the pass was still blue. Giordano had been taught that on the highest mountains the air is eternally still, but dawn winds pierced his robes here, and from the summits glittering streams of snow were slowly blown like banners. The peaks all had names, and the huffing carter who climbed beside Giordano named them, pointing. They sailed too.

The caravan stumbled and slid through the cold roaring throat of the Col, out of sight of the dawn, passed by a multitude going the other way, all jostling as in a city alley. Then they came out onto a field of shattered flints and a steep path downward. They had crossed the ridge. The sky was huge and blue, but the far lands Bruno looked out over were still soft and asleep, mountains folded rank on rank, the rest of his life. The path that way—it brought his heart to his mouth to trace it—traversed the mountainsides switching back and forth like a whip; you could see, far far below, the turns you would have to take, and the travelers there who toiled upward. Along the fingernail of silver path that edged the precipice a shepherd walked his sheep along in a single file.

Earth turned, coming about like a trireme, beating East; and thus the sun rose, gigantic spark, God visible. Bruno, stock still, hum in his ears and heart in his throat, felt its smile on his cheek.

Hermes said: make yourself as God. And Bruno could feel his smile too, like the sun's. Make yourself as God: Infinite. And Bruno had been infinite even as he had read the words and longed to understand them.

Earth gave up its valleys to the sun. The burdened men, cheeks warmed, laughing with relief and apprehension, started downward. Day had come.

The next morning Bruno reached the Dominican monastery at Chambery, in France: he was Brother Teofilo, witch-hunter of Naples. As he stood explaining himself to the puzzled prior in the sunstruck garden, the earth took a sudden northward tilt, and the flagstones rose up to meet his darkening sight. He woke in the infirmary, where he spent Holy Week, sticking-plaster over his eye, head and heart empty, as still and weary as though he had moved the sun all by himself. He could take nothing but broth, and the Host; he slept long, and when he slept he dreamed of Ægypt.

They *were* returning, as he had seen them returning: they were returning now. The new sun of Copernicus was the sign of it; Copernicus might not know it, but Giordano Bruno knew it, and would cry it now like a bantam cock through the world. Sunrise.

Once back on the road, Bruno was rarely to cease journeying his whole life long: but even as he walked the old tracks and high roads of Europe he walked in Ægypt too, its painted temples, the glitter of its sands, its blue skies dark. Sleeping and dreaming, working and wooing, he walked toward a city built in the east or in the west of Ægypt, in the region of the rising or the setting sun, a city whose name he knew.

Those who everywhere took him in—in Paris, in Wittenberg, in Prague—those *giordanisti* who furthered his fortunes, or dressed him, or printed his books; who won him interviews with the great; who fed him; who hid him: they seemed often to recognize him too, or to remember him from some other time or place, to have once known but forgotten him or forgotten that it was he who was to come and not some other: *Oh yes I see* (holding out slowly their hands to him, eyes searching him) *yes I know you now yes yes come in.*

He left the house at Chambery as soon as he was well, bored to madness by the monks' thick stupidity, the endlessness of their talk, like prayer, and their prayer, like talk. In 1579 he reached Geneva; he won the protection there of a Neapolitan nobleman, the Marchese de Vico, who told him for God's sake to get out of those robes of black and white, and who bought him a suit of clothes; but Bruno dismissed with a joke the Marchese's Calvinism, on account of which the Marchese had given up all he had. He registered at the University under the name Phillippus, and there began to read the Reformers, with a mixture of amusement and contempt. What poor stuff. He stood in a lecture hall full of ticking automata, planetary clocks, moon machines, and listened to a puppet-boned fellow tell how he was attempting to make a machine, an automaton, that would somehow so exactly replicate in its geometries the workings of the universe that when something happened in the universe an identical thing would be caused to happen in the model, however differently manifested: another universe, in fact, only smaller, like the image in a mirror.

But Giordano knew that such a machine, such a model, already existed. The name of the machine was Man.

The Genevans didn't like him; no more did he like them. The Marchese interceded for him when he insulted the famed theologian Antoine de la Faye and got himself arraigned before the Theological Consistory, men in deep black who had no use for notions; he wasn't tried, but he was pitched out of town and down the Rhone. Enough of Calvin's city.

Lyon, a center of the book trade, but he could gain no living there, a cold wind seemed to be blowing through the world of learning, anyway Giordano felt it. Shake the dust from his feet. He did better at Toulouse; he was elected to the University (guided by good advisers and just for the moment willing to say and do what he was advised to say and do) and for a year and a half taught philosophy and the Sphere.

In the quiet Languedoc months he began casting what he had learned so far into the form of gods and goddesses; not only the great planetary gods and their *horoscopi* but lesser gods too, Pan and Vertumnus and Janus and he who swaggers drunk on his ass, Silenus. On these small gods—still and pale when he set them up within as old statues along a Roman road—he would work Ægyptian magic, he would feed them from his own storehouses, and flush their cheeks, and make them speak. Had not Hermes said that a multitude of gods were distributed through all things that exist? Then they were distributed through his own shadow universe within as well, the small gods of endless becoming.

Toulouse was a Huguenot city, and in that year the armies of the Catholic League were advancing on its walls; there were riots in town and outrages at the University; Bruno moved on.

He was in Paris in 1582, the largest city in Europe but not too large to fit within the walls of Bruno's city inside. He lectured at the University, a free lance, tilting with pedants, Aristotelians, followers of Petrus Ramus; he published at last his enormous book, an Art of Memory which anyone who dared look into it could see was a work of *magia* deep-dyed and horribly potent: he even gave it a title taken from that book of Solomon's he had hidden in the privy long ago: *De umbris idearum,* About the Shadows of Ideas.

Now his universe moved as the universe outside him moved: they were the same. And so if he chose to cause a thing to happen in his world within, then . . . He laughed, he laughed and could not stop: had he not moved the sun from its sphere? There was no knowing what he might not do if he chose.

The King heard of him and invited him to the Louvre, and opened Bruno's book upon his knee in wonder; he was given a glass of wine with the Queen Mother, and the Queen Mother sat him down with her astrologer and cunning-man, whose name was Notredame or Nostradamus. Bruno thought the man a fraud and a fool, but asked him: In what country will my bones be buried? And the answer of Nostradamus was: In no country.

In no country was a good answer. Perhaps he would just go on circling outward forever, sailing the earth like a ship, not ever to die at all.

At spring's end in 1583, in the entourage of the new French ambassador to England, he took ship from Calais with his books, and his systems, and his knowledge; with a purse fat with *louis d'or;* with a mission from the King engraved on his endless memory. The English ambassador in Paris wrote to Walsingham: *Doctor Jordano Bruno Nolano, a professor of philosophy, intends to pass into England, whose religion I cannot commend.* But what religion did he carry?

The ship raised sail, Bruno stepped on its deck, the mate whistled, the lines were loosed. Bruno for the first time lost sight of land, and with the sight felt something fall away from him; something that would not ever be taken up again. Wherever he went from here he would never be going back. Æolus sang in the rigging, cold spray dashed in his face; the crew was aloft, the captain asleep below, his belly filling and luffing like his sails; the little ship clambered through the flinty seas, crowded with animals, people, and goods, a red Mexican parrot furious and swearing out the forecastle window.

—And a fire burning on its yardarms, Mr. Talbot said. St. Elmo's fire, one flame on the right side, one flame on the left. Castor and Pollux, the Twins.

—*Spes proxima,* said Doctor Dee.

The angel who showed them this ship within the showstone (she was a laughing and changeable child, and named Madimi) bent the skryer's head closer to the stone and the ship and the man in the bows holding tight.

—He, said Mr. Talbot.

—*That is he,* the angel said. *That is he of whom I told you.*

—Can she speak more plainly? Doctor Dee said. Ask her.

—*The one I told you of,* said the angel Madimi. *The Jonah that the fish spat out, the brand to be plucked from the burning, the stone rejected by the builders that will be the corner of the house, the last house left standing. Our adorp, our dragon flying in the west, our philosophical Mercury. Our Grail of the quintessence, our* sal cranii humani, *for if the salt has lost its savor, wherewith shall it be salted? Our pretty rose. Our Bruin sleeping in a cave through winter. Our Mr. Jordan Brown whose religion I cannot commend. He has stolen fire from heaven and there are spheres where he is not loved. He is coming to this house, though he knows it not; he is not going back the way he came; and nothing now will ever be the same again.*

T E N

▲

The only way to experience the semiannual festival sponsored by the Faraway Aerostatic Society and held at Skytop Farm high up on Mount Merrow is to be up before dawn, and drive to Skytop early enough to see the daybreak ascensions: for lighter-than-air flight, improbable in the best of cases, is most possible at dawn, and at evening, when the air is cool and still.

So, shivering somewhat in the chill of predawn, Pierce Moffett sat on his front steps, waiting for the lights to come on in the house opposite and Beau Brachman to come out, ready more or less for this adventure but thinking chiefly of the gray box of yellow paper on Fellowes Kraft's desk in Stonykill miles away. It seemed to glow, in his mind, like a hooded sun.

Maybe it was only because he had read so little fiction in recent years, had read nothing but what at least purported to describe what was in fact the case, that he felt in his breast this weird warmth, this satisfaction in some deep part of him that had not for a long time been satisfied; this vision of the book's contents as of morning mountains, receding row on row into pale distance, all new, all to be explored, yet somehow already known.

What a simple conceit, though, really, what a metaphor, the most revelatory of all: that once, once upon a time, the world actually was different. Was not the way it is now.

And Bruno the harbinger, messenger to the future, sure that the age to come will bring in more magic, not less: like those who cried the new age in Pierce's own time.

Bruno, cheek in hand at John Dee's table, drawing with a chip of chalk the circles of the next universe, the revolution of the orbs of heaven. Once it wasn't this way, but now it is, and from now on will be.

Dee, though. Dee knows better, forewarned by his angels, themselves due to pass away. He'll lay down his wand and (empty) globe at last, Pierce guessed, drown his books like Prospero. All over now.

A huge shudder, but why, covered Pierce and made him grin.

What if it were really true?

Time's immense body now and then waking from sleep, shifting its massy limbs, disposing them differently, groaning, sleeping again. Hm. And nothing ever the same thereafter.

He remembered how once at St. Guinefort's he had been beguiling the time in study hall with a volume of the Catholic Encyclopedia, and had come upon a condemned opinion of Origen's: that this world we know, in which Adam sinned, which Christ had come to redeem, to which He would return in the glory of the final battle—this world, after it was rolled up like a scroll, would be succeeded by another, in which none of that would happen; and that world, after its end, by another; and so on endlessly—and Pierce reading it had felt for a moment the purest sense of relief, a gust of something like freedom, to think that this might actually be so.

Might actually literally really be so.

He laughed. The greatest secret story of all, the container and explainer of all secret stories whatever, explainer too of why they were secret. He rolled a cigarette and lit it, harsh in the breakfastless dawn; and he perceived a corollary.

If then was one such time, now must be another.

Yes. In order for him to entertain the notion, the world must just now be on the turn again: for it would only be in such moments of turning—when not only all possible futures come into view but all possible pasts as well—that the previous moments of turning become visible, Time awaking and rubbing his eyes, *Oh I see, I remember.* Wasn't that really what Kraft was saying, or rather leaving to the reader to discern? Then was one time; now is another.

Now; the white decade just past; the children in motion, the days when a closed world like Dante's had opened, and the still earth moved, both rotating and revolving; and Pierce had found himself at a sudden crossroads, dawn winds rising as night turned pale. And this book of Kraft's coming to be, yellow page by page, a book like no other he had ever written.

Pierce thought of Julie, sitting on the bed in his old apartment, the hubble-bubble on the floor beside her, painting her nails in stars: *It makes a lot of sense.*

The sky had lightened now, and there were oblongs of yellow lamplight in the face of Beau's house across the street. A dog barked. Beau's screen door banged, and Pierce rose from his chilly seat. What if it were so.

Wouldn't Julie be knocked out, he thought, wouldn't she be astonished if the book he was writing for her were to make the claim that it *was* so. Kraft's book was, after all, only a novel, a metaphor; but what if his own book could actually adduce evidence that it was so. God. A world more lost than Atlantis, perceived again beneath the sea, recovered, its treasures told. His own fortune made, and Julie's too.

He laughed again aloud. You cut it out now, he counselled himself; you be careful. He was still laughing softly when he entered Beau's yard, and his puzzled neighbors smiled at him.

"Hi, hi," he said, and set to helping them fit picnic baskets and children into Beau's car, a large dented Python that did not always function.

"Ready? *Ready?*" said one of the kids to him, horribly excited.

"Ready," said Pierce, climbing in. He found it funny that while he had been out of the world of auto travel, the nature of jalopies had changed. This was not a humpbacked Nash like Sam had owned, or an old winged DeSoto; this Python was one of the sleek predator-like cars of, well, of the recent past; a new-car type of car, and yet no, it was already old, a junker, it had that smell of burnt oil and damp upholstery and it had the plaid rug thrown over the back seat. Funny.

At the Donut Hole there were two or three pickups parked in the yellow lamplight, but otherwise town was still and seemed strangely nonexistent, the morning and the river so large around it and so real and odorous. They cruised out the Shadow River road and upward: and even the excited child in Pierce's lap was hushed by the white river's breath and the ghostly pines and the wet wind pouring through the car.

But what if it were so, Pierce went on thinking, or perhaps only saying in his heart, *what if it were so: that the world could be, and had once been, different than it is.* And the more he thought or felt it, the more he understood—without any real surprise—that in fact he had long supposed it to be so. Had always supposed it to be so: yes: had never truly believed that History lay behind him in the same stream of time he floated in, that all those people places and things colored like the nine digits had ever actually occurred in the world in which he had his own being, where water flowed and apples ripened. Never. Whatever he had told himself, or his students or his teachers, what he had really sought for in those pieces of past time which he had picked over and examined with such diligence and attention was confirmation of what he longed to know for sure: that things do not have to be the way they are.

The last wish: the only wish, in fact. That things could be, not as they are, but some different way instead. Not better, really, or not better in all ways; a little larger maybe, more full of this and that, but mostly just different. New. That I, Pierce Moffett, could know that it had once been as it was and is that way no longer, that I could know it to have once been remade and so able to be remade again, all new, all other. Then perhaps this grief would at last be lifted from my heart.

"Oh look," said the woman in the front seat. "Oh look there's one."

The mist had risen, and the sky was clear behind it; the balloon was hanging in the air, not far away, where it had not been before, insolent in its improbability—an unreal blue globe with an orange stripe, a white star, and a wicker basket full of folks. The Python took a sweeping turn, and every head within it but the driver's turned to look back at the balloon, which seemed to look godlike down on them. *Deus ex machina.* A jet of flame arose within it, making a noise like a dragon's long exhalation, and it mounted smoothly up the clearing sky. Day had come.

Skytop Farm really was once a farm; then it was a summer camp for years, and is now a closed camp. Its central lodge is opened only occasionally now, for a game supper, a balloon festival. The lodge is at the top of a long varicolored blanket of meadows spread over the knees of Mount Merrow, and sees a wide circle of the Faraways.

The parking lot was already filling when the troop from the Jambs arrived; Beau had to leave the Python far from the flying field. Passing through the lot Pierce noticed Spofford's truck, and a little red Asp that looked a lot like the car he had seen Mike Mucho and his ex-wife struggle with.

"Some folks we know here," he said to Beau.

"Oh yes," Beau said. "Oh you bet."

A hot day was succeeding the cold dawn. The aeronauts—who had slept here all night in tents and campers or tucked within their special ballooner's trucks—were up and about, sipping coffee at refreshment wagons, zipping up their coveralls, checking their gear. Some had already got aloft; others' balloons were beginning to sprout from the grass, tumescent and slowly erecting. A whole field of balloons was comically heart-lifting, lighter than air, and made the child who tugged at Pierce's hand leap up in imitation, and laugh exultantly. Pierce laughed too, unable not to, when just then another one of them left the earth, not suddenly but calmly, and ambled outward in the air over the meadow.

"Thought I'd see you here," said someone at his elbow as he gaped.

"Spofford," Pierce said. "I saw your truck. Hey where *have* you been?"

"Around," Spofford said mildly.

"Well hell," Pierce said. "Hell. You might visit."

"Hey, likewise," Spofford said. "I'm usually up at the place."

"You forget I don't drive," Pierce said.

"Oh yes," Spofford said, grinning even more broadly at Pierce, as though still relishing a trick he had played on Pierce some time ago. He held out to Pierce a book he had had behind his back. "I brought this along," he said, "on the chance you'd be here. You left it last year."

It was the *Soledades* of de Góngora, the twisted pastorals Pierce had never retrieved from Spofford's cabin. He took the book from Spofford. A rich chain of past moments was forged within him, link by link, and he remembered how he came to be here now. "Thanks," he said.

"I looked into it," Spofford said. "Interesting, but tough."

"Well," Pierce said. "They're not really meant to be read, I mean I mean . . ."

"One of those shepherds," Spofford said, "used to be a soldier."

"Yes?"

Spofford took the book back from Pierce and opened it. "'*When I, who now wear homespun, went in steel.*' Do I guess right?"

"I guess."

"He fought once in a battle, on this same mountain he guides the shipwrecked guy over. Right? Once a long time before. See:

> *Round the bare stones of these dejected heaps*
> *Now pitying ivy creeps;*
> *Time which heals every woe*
> *On ruins green endearments can bestow.*"

He gave the book back. "Interesting," he said. His eyes narrowed in the sunlight, looking out over the Faraways. "I remember how quick the jungle came back."

"Hm." Pierce tucked the book under his arm, shamed somewhat, shamed that his old pupil could find true matter in the written word, however much the writer might have preferred it not to be sought there.

They walked together through the crowds at the perimeter of the field, upon which now most of the balloons had been at least unfurled and laid out, a heraldry of checks, bars, chevrons, and targets in savagely gaudy colors, like knights' tents pitched on a jousting field—enormous, though, tent flag and charger all in one.

"It's a funny thing," Pierce said. He waved to a dark-haired man in tailored shorts who had waved to him, a lawyer he thought, whom he had met playing croquet. "When I first moved up here, I was afraid there wouldn't be many people to know. I thought I'd be making regular trips back to the city, for, for . . ."

"Sparkin'."

"Entertainment. I haven't though. And now I'm getting introduced around, and really there are lots of people. Good people too. Interesting. I've met more and more. I was surprised."

"Yep." Spofford raised a brown hand himself, and nodded a greeting to someone.

"But," Pierce said. "Look now. This field is filling up with people I've already met, or seen at least. The same ones. I must have been introduced to oh a fifth of these people. A lot of the others I know by sight."

"Uh-huh."

"I'll run out soon. They aren't endless like the city. I'll come to the end of them."

"Ha," said Spofford. "Wait'll you've been married to one or two, and had kids by another; and your kids' mother is the lover of your ex-wife's old husband, et cetera. *Then* you've come to the end of them. And it's time to move on."

"Yes?"

"Well they just don't leave you a lot of room to maneuver," Spofford said. "They think they know all about you, and what they've decided you are, that's what you gotta be. Small town, y'know?"

Pierce supposed he did know. He had grown up in a town in most ways far smaller than any in these parts, smaller because more remote in time and space from Possibility. There, character really had been fate. The town drunk, the flinty mine-owner and his degenerate son, the hypocrite preacher and the kindly doc. And the simple moral tales acted out by this brief cast over and over, as in a movie. Continuous showings.

It didn't seem to him, though, on this morning in the Far-aways, such an unfortunate thing, that kind of small-town determin-ism. True, he had himself clambered out of it as fast as he could and into the Great World seeking growing-room and air to breathe; but he had in fact languished in the city, not growing but shrinking over time into a strange form of invisibility. Almost no one that he'd known there knew anyone else he had known, and so to each new acquaintance Pierce was able to present a separate and partial character, an ad hoc personality specially adapted to the circum-stances (bar, bookstore, Brooklyn) but too flimsy to support more than a single other person at close range, or two at the most. Freedom of a kind, that changeful dandy's life, but thin, thin.

Things would be different now. He had long lived solitary as a pinball, despite all the collisions of so-called love, but now maybe real connections might begin to be made. Maybe. Of what kind, though, he couldn't really know; for they would not be entirely his doing. Whomever he would become for these people over time, whatever sort of *exemplum* their communal comedy required and that he could plausibly embody, they would participate in deciding on.

A part to play. Okay. All right.

"There," he said to Spofford, "just for an instance of what I'm talking about, is Mike Mucho, right, standing next to the basket of that balloon."

Spofford glanced that way. "Right," he said.

"Now I haven't met him, exactly, but I know him. He's a fixture." And someone with whom Pierce was, in more than one way, already connected. QED. A warmth, weirdly fraternal, arose in his bosom. "And see there with him is his wife, Rosie."

Spofford's head snapped quickly from Pierce to the black balloon far off, and back to Pierce. "No it isn't," he said.

"No?"

"No."

"It must be the other one, then," Pierce said. "It sure does look a lot like his wife."

"It doesn't," Spofford said. "Not a bit."

Well, she was a ways away, and allowance had to be made, Pierce thought, for the eyes of love. She sure looked like Rosie Mucho to *him*.

"Her name," Spofford said, "is Ryder. Rose Ryder."

Ryder was Rose too? A popular name around these parts; that made three he knew of already. Roses were thick on the ground.

"She and I," Spofford said, "had a brief thing a while back. A good while back. And now look."

Rose Ryder was being helped into the basket by Mike.

"You see what I mean?" Spofford said, clasping his hands behind him, and turning away. "You see what I mean."

It might be, Pierce thought, that Mike Mucho was another like himself: one girl for him, the same girl in different guises, under different names—or in Mike's case nearly the same name. "And here again," he said, pointing the other way, down the meadow. "Another instance."

"Yep," Spofford said.

"That woman is my new boss," Pierce said, "and her name too is Rosie."

"Rosalind," said Spofford. "I heard about this. You working for the Foundation."

"You did?" Rosie Rasmussen waved to the two of them; she was following a child of two or three, who seemed to be in a tearing hurry. "You know her, I guess."

"Yes," Spofford said. "I introduced you two. Didn't I? Maybe not as such." He began to turn his head toward the black balloon up on the flying field behind him, but then seemed to think better of it. "I know I've talked about her to you. My plans and all. Rosie. Rosie Mucho."

He struck out down the meadow toward where the golden-haired child toiled upward. Pierce did not follow. His head too turned partway toward the Rose behind him, Ryder; and then thought better of it, and turned again to the Rosie before him.

"She's a little nutso," Rosie said to Spofford.

They had taken hold of Sam together, Sam having tripped in the grasping weeds knee high to her and surrendered to despair. "Daddy's not going without you, kid," Rosie said to her. "Don't worry."

Spofford, grinning, hoisted weeping Sam to his shoulders, from where she still reached out histrionically toward her distant father.

"Going for a balloon ride, huh, Sam?" Spofford asked.

"It's amazing to me," Rosie said. "She can't think about anything else. *I'd* be scared shitless."

Spofford laughed aloud, and the boom of it stilled Sam on his shoulders. "Hey," he said then. "I'm sorry about the game."

"Yeah, well." Pierce Moffett, solemn on the hillside, raised a hand to her. "So what was this big scheme?" she said. "You said you had a scheme."

"It's about sheep," Spofford said. "I'll tell you later. I talked to Boney. He likes it."

Pierce, hands in his pockets when she reached him, staring oddly at her, looked even more stunned than he had the other day. "Hi," she said. "You never met my daughter Sam, did you? Samantha. Say hi, kid, aw don't start crying again."

Pierce stared up, at Sam aboard Spofford. Maybe stunned was his usual mode or mood: he looked like he had just awakened in a strange bed, and was wondering how he had got there. A pleasant bed, a strange room. It was appealing, sort of. "So," she said. "We're going back tomorrow? To old Kraft's?"

Pierce only went on studying her, as though deaf; at last he said, "Yes. Yes. If I can."

"I talked to Boney more," Rosie said. "You know he's very interested in your, what you're up to."

"He seemed to be," Pierce said.

"He told me to tell you that you should apply for a grant. From the Rasmussen Foundation." She felt suddenly absurd, a character from television, altering some innocent's life. "He said not to let you get away."

"Oh yes?"

"Really. There's money there."

Now from the balloon, restless on the hillside, tugging at its moorings, Mike called out to Rosie. Spofford was already carrying Mike's daughter to him.

"So listen," Pierce said as they fell in behind. "Can I ask you a question?"

"Well okay." Pierce seemed of a mind to hang back, looking up the hillside in something like wonder.

"The man in the balloon is your ex-husband?"

"Yes." As of today, in fact; as of today.

"And the woman with him in the balloon is his present wife?"

"Rose? No. Just a friend."

"Aha."

"I'm his once and only. So far."

The vast black balloon, much vaster when you could look up into the void within, bent like a punchable inflated clown in a breath of breeze; the best flying weather was already past. Spofford had handed Mike's daughter over to him; she seemed now, clutching Mike with arms and knees, less certain of her desires than she had been.

"Okay, okay," called out the skipper, tanned and haggard, great glove on his hand like an old-time motorman's. He organized the bystanders, including tall Pierce and Spofford, into a ground crew, who were to lay hold of the basket, and hold it to earth until his command.

"Michael," Rosie said. "Did you get your letter today?"

"Yes."

"I got mine. Just today."

"Okay, Rosie, okay."

With his gloved hand the balloonist tugged at the rope of his burner as at a steam whistle or a trolley's bell, but the noise produced was shocking, like a blow. The basket rose, turning, lighter than air, and in turning brought the woman Rose around to where Pierce stood ready to lay hold.

"Hi." She had a bottle of beer in her hand despite the hour.

"Hello," Pierce said. "Rose."

"I remembered you," she said. "At last." The awful roar came again, the balloon rose up, Pierce grabbed hold; the girl Rose closed her eyes and her mouth, as though embraced from behind, and opened them again when the noise ceased. "The party at the river," she said. "The boat."

"Yes."

"The little flask."

"Right." The brand name of this balloon was printed on a tag sewn to the canvas lip of the basket. It was a Raven. "Right."

"You were getting into sheep." The icy shimmer had come over her eyes again: about that there could be no mistake. "Do you live here now?"

"In Blackbury Jambs." The basket had begun to move outward across the field. Pierce and the rest went with it.

"I might see you there," she said. "I'll be at the library a lot."

"Me too," Pierce said.

"Oh yeah really?"

He was running now to keep up with the Raven; Rose looked down at him and laughed. "Okay," she said.

" 'Bye," Rosie Rasmussen called out. " 'Bye. 'Bye. Hold tight."

The ground crew one by one let go, the short ones first, and then the taller; for some reason they continued running after it as it rose. The burner roared. The laws of physics, like a joke, pulled up the vast taut bag out of reach.

"Okay," Rosie said, out of breath. She looked at Pierce, and then up at Spofford, and Pierce saw in her look something like abandonment, a shadow of the panic of abandonment, or thought he did.

"I think I'll go find a coffee," he said.

"A thing I've noticed," Spofford said to Rosie as they both stood watching the balloon grow smaller. "A thing I've noticed is that a woman who loves a man often will call him by his whole name."

"What?"

"Everybody else in the world can call a guy Bob or Dave, but the woman who loves him calls him Robert. David. Michael." He went on looking up.

"What's that supposed to mean?"

"If you don't know," Spofford said, "then very likely it don't mean a thing."

"Hm." She crossed her arms before her. She could see that Samantha in the wicker basket would not lift her face from the crook of her father's neck; Mike tugged laughing at her curls.

"What letter was that," Spofford said, "that you both got? Was that . . ."

"From the court," Rosie said. "The divorce. It says it's registered now, and we have a decree nisi."

"Oh." Spofford took a small step closer to her, and clasped his hands behind his back; he studied the sky. "Oh."

"Yep." *A new beginning,* Allan had said in the kind and courtly letter he had sent with the notice, but Rosie had no sense of what it might be the beginning of. Not an ending but a beginning, or The Beginning, like *Bitten Apples:* THE BEGINNING strung teasingly across the blank bottom of the last page, the rest of her life.

For herself it wasn't so bad, she could just keep on somehow, she thought, Ship of the Desert, not knowing where she walked. But for the daughter she had so thoughtlessly taken charge of she could project only a gloomy and loveless imaginary future, cared for or rather tended by a woman who had forgotten, if she ever knew, what love was, what people wanted or needed in order to live; some kind of alien being, a Mother from Another World.

Maybe she could die. Before everyone found out, Spofford, Boney. Sam might cherish her memory then, remember the good times, never discovering her secret.

"A decree nisi," Spofford said, as though tasting the phrase. "And is that, like, a final judgment?"

"Not exactly." Without seeming to have moved, the balloon stood at a further remove already, shrinking with distance. "It's a decree nisi. Nisi is Latin. It means unless."

"Unless what?"

"Unless a lot of things. Unless nothing, really. It's just a formality. You have to wait six months, basically, to get the final papers. That's all."

"Reminds me of a story I read somewhere," Spofford said. He went on studying the sky, but not as though seeing anything there. "Seems there's this guy about to have his head cut off by a king. He's been caught fooling around with the king's wife. And he says, Wait a minute: If you will spare my life for six months, in that time I can teach that horse of yours to talk. Guaranteed."

Maybe, Rosie thought, they should climb in the car, and chase the balloon. Maybe it would get lost, fall into the Blackbury. Never come back.

"King says—why not? You've got six months. And he locks the guy in the stable with the horse. This is actually a very old story. So the king's wife goes to him there and asks him, How come you made this crazy promise? You can't really do it, can you? And the guy answers, Hey: A lot of things could happen in six months. The king could get sick and die. He could change his mind. The horse could die. *I* could die. And maybe the horse . . ."

"Oh Christ," Rosie said, and grabbed for Spofford's arm. For some reason of the air's the balloon had suddenly sunk sharply before the burner lifted it again. Rosie felt a black rush of anger at them, at their danger, at their distance from her. "Sorry," she said to Spofford, suddenly aware of his patient waiting for her attention to turn his way. "Were you telling a story?"

"Don't matter," he said, smiling down at her.

"Sorry," she said, and tears gathered painfully in her throat. She wanted to tell him: that she was sorry, that she really wanted nothing more than to turn back the way she had come, but that there was no way back. Whatever it was that lay on the other side of this, and she could not even tell if anything at all lay on the other side, that was the only direction she could go in, and alone.

How far into the forest can you go? The old grade-school puzzler. The answer is: Half way. Then you start coming back out. But how would she know when she had gone halfway? Until she knew, each step was only farther: each step a beginning.

"Sorry," she said again, and patted his big shoulder, and turned away.

It was actually simpler this way, Pierce supposed; no needless multiplication of entities. And yet for a long time thereafter he would go on feeling the presence of one other, at least one; someone not either of those two, or both, or one or the other with a different story. No recounting of the facts could ever quite erase her.

Mike's wife and Spofford's girlfriend: one. Mike's girlfriend and Pierce's boatmate: two. All the others were only the one or the other in a different aspect, morning and evening stars, full moon and crescent moon.

He must have been wrong, he saw, to think he had had intimation from Rosie, Rosie Rasmussen, Rosie Mucho, in Fellowes Kraft's bedroom, that he, that he and she. No. Wrong. That was only his own Adam, growing restive; a blind man, whose misperceptions Pierce would have to get used to correcting for.

What if, unwelcome, he had, he had. Spofford's woman, too (was that right? That was right). He felt a hot rush of comical shame, of guilt twice unwittingly avoided, and laughed suddenly aloud. If these people he had come to live among—these sensible and happy people, mild as the day and the meadow—were to go on

fooling him that way, quick-change artists, then he was surely wrong
to say to Spofford that he would soon come to the end of them.

Day was full, and hot. He found a coffee, and sat with it at a
table by the refreshment stand, under a striped umbrella, and
opened the *Soledades* that Spofford had returned to him.

The First Solitude. In the sweet flowery season. It began with a
shipwreck, and ended with a marriage: like a lot of good romances,
Pierce thought, like more than one of Shakespeare's.

Not his, though.

A kind of blow of awful wonder that this might really really be so
was struck somewhere well within him. It was so. Slowly, carefully, he crossed his legs, and let the pages of *The Solitudes* fan
closed.

Celibacy, though—even the more strict celibacy of the heart
and the intentions which Pierce had enjoined on himself—didn't
mean chastity, necessarily. Probably would not, he thought, not
given the caucus race apparently proceeding in secret all around
him here. He lifted his eyes. The whole flying field—all the craft
that were fit, anyway—seemed to be aloft now; they stood at varying
distances from him through the air, large globes and small, like a
lesson about the third dimension. There, the figures within too
small to be seen, was the black one, the Raven.

He would have to be very careful, that's all; knowing himself,
knowing how he was.

There were other stories, anyhow, he thought. There was the
one about the shipwrecked man, naked and with nothing, who
makes his way by his wits and his readiness (maybe his magic
helpers too) and after many adventures comes to be king of the
kingless country into which he has come.

And then, at length, sets out again.

From far above him, from aboard the Raven, the things and
people below had also come to have an illustrative look: that clean
and toylike aspect they have when seen from planes, the model cars
moving soundlessly, the lawns and houses tidy and artificial-seeming.
Relativity. Rose Ryder looked down, hands resting lightly on the
canvas-covered wicker, feet too resting lightly on the nothing between her and earth.

She had noticed Pierce walking away from where Rosie Mucho
and Spofford still stood together, but could not see where he had

gone. She thought she might wave, if she could see him looking up. No she would not.

Pierce Moffett, funny name, both sharp and soft at once.

Sam cried louder whenever the balloon's burner was fired, hooting into the crook of her father's neck; otherwise she was just rigid, and Mike couldn't get her to raise her head to look. "See the center?" he said. "See where Daddy works? Aw Sam."

If ever *she* were to have a child, if ever she were to find herself pregnant, Rose had decided, she would never tell the father. He would never see the child, borne by her in secret; never know it existed. Rose imagined talking to the guy years later, the child's father, say at a restaurant table, chatting, idly, about the past; and the child elsewhere, at play, growing. In secret.

The aeronaut beside her fired his burner again; the noise of it struck Rose like a blow, causing something deep within her to vibrate with it. Earth withdrew further. According to the science of Climacterics, whose method Rose had applied to her own life, this blue day was the first of her new Up Passage Year, heading for the plateau of twenty-eight: and despite Mike's warnings that Climacterics wasn't prophecy, she was sure sure sure that this was going to be a good year for her. Change for the better. She could feel it, like the shocking certainty of the burner's firing, at the root of her being.

"See, Sam. Rose isn't afraid. Rosie wants to look. See?"

The Woods turned a corner of its mountain and was gone. The chartreuse Faraways, seamed by the silver Blackbury, went on west and south, looking to Rose Ryder in the new morning like the interlaced fingers of a pair of patient hands folded on the torso of the enormous earth.

That was the last day of spring, as the days of spring are counted in the Faraways; and the next week Spofford drove his flock down by the byways and discontinued roads to Arcady. *Transhumance* was the word he thought about as he walked, a word he had learned from Pierce, a word meaning the movement of pastoral peoples from winter to summer grazing lands; for that, sort of, was what Spofford considered himself to be doing.

The scheme had, for him, several advantages, and advantages too for Boney Rasmussen, advantages which Spofford had largely emphasized when putting the plan to Boney. His grounds, in danger of reverting to woods under the tight budgets of recent years, would be kept cropped and lawnlike (to say nothing of fertilized, and for free; "golden hooves, Mr. Rasmussen," Spofford had said, illustrating with two prodding forefingers the sheep's useful way of treading her own pellets into the soil). There was the picturesque aspect. And a share in the eventual product, as well, neatly wrapped in butcher paper, packed in dry ice at the shambles in Cascadia. All flesh is grass.

What Spofford would get out of the transaction, he said, was wider and lusher grazing, first of all; and a barn in good repair, his own makeshift byres would have to be torn down and rebuilt to accommodate new lambs; and the (occasional) help of Rosie, who Spofford was sure would like to get the exercise, and the chance to train her two dogs before they got too old and lazy to learn to make a living.

"Well, of course you'll have to ask *her* that," Boney said.

"Oh I intend to," Spofford said. "I intend to."

In fact on hearing the plan Rosie had not seemed so pleased, nowhere near as pleased as Sam; she implied she had a lot to do, and didn't like being presented with a partnership she hadn't asked for. But Spofford had not been surprised at that. He had even taken it into account when conceiving the plan, one restless May night, the first night his window had stood open till morning.

So he walked the perimeters of Arcady's back lawns, and found the walls of red sandstone crumbling in places but all sheep-proof, and closed the circle he had been allotted with some inconspicuous electric wire; and on a green morning herded his puzzled and complaining flock into it through a large carved gateway (grapes and faces) no one any longer used. Spofford had got a job upstate, cabinetry on a string of vacation houses going up on the marge of Nickel Lake, and would be passing Boney's drive every morning and evening; no trouble to look in, and check.

The sheep were soon calm. The grass was sweet beneath the oaks of Arcady, each calm too in its pool of shade, a crowd of grave eminences standing at respectful intervals. Spofford looked up into them.

You couldn't be a real classical shepherd, Pierce had told him, unless you ate acorns, and were in love.

"Well a bread *made* from acorns," Pierce said. "I guess not the nut itself."

"Uh-huh," Spofford said, sure that his leg was being pulled. Acorns.

The sheep wandered, shy guests at a big lawn party, and he wandered too. The house came into view, brown and many-angled, ensconced in yew and rhododendron; its empty towers roofed in scalloped tiles pink and blue. It was the sort of house his mother always called for some reason a Sleeping Beauty house.

The house he himself was building, up in the bright mountain orchard, would be different, not a secret; plain and able in a glance to be understood. This summer the foundation, cleaned out, pointed, and sealed. Long afternoon light for him to work in.

He *didn't* know anything about love; what people meant by "in love" had always baffled and annoyed him. Taking flight was what they seemed to mean. What he knew about was something else, something that only came into being by degrees, a quid pro quo; you didn't take a step unless there was enough road there to step on, but however much road appeared you took. That's all.

He found a good tree to sit under, in view of the house, and sat, and crossed his high-top sneakers. He would stay on his feet, his own four feet, and see where they led. It would have to do. He took out his old Kohner, and blew the pocket dust from it, listening with his mind's ear for a tune.

It was just then, the sun crossing the meridian on his old journey, that Pierce Moffett in Fellowes Kraft's house in Stonykill turned facedown on the pile at his left-hand side the last page of what Kraft had written, and sat back in the hard chair (how had Kraft spent so many hours in it?) before the desk.

He lit a cigarette, but then sat motionless with it in his hand, the smoke rising in a continuous and manifold ribbon, like the warmth rising from Pierce's loins up to his bosom. He knew now that his whole life up to this time, the religion he had been born into, the stories he had learned and made up and told, the education he had got or avoided, the books somehow chosen for him to read, his taste for history and the colored dates he had fed it on, the drugs he had taken, the thoughts he had thought, had all prepared him not to write a book at all, as he had thought, but to read one. This one. This was what he had once upon a time expected and hoped of all books that he opened, that they each be the one book he required, his own book.

For this book was not different after all from his own book, unfinished also (unstarted for that matter); for that matter his own life seemed the same, the unwritten, unwritable book of his own whole lived life, only another edition, with the same title too. A confusing title, Julie had said, and hard to file.

He regarded the staggered heap, all facedown, over but not done with. What public, he wondered, had Kraft thought he was writing for, who had he supposed would want to read such a thing? No one, perhaps, which is why it lay still on his desk, unfinished, unpublished, lying in wait for its single ideal reader.

For it wasn't a *good* book at all, Pierce supposed, considered as a book, a novel; it was a philosophical romance, remote and extravagant, without much of the tang of life as it really must have gone on in the world—as it really *had* gone on if you meant *this* world, this only one in which, metaphors aside, we all have really and solely lived in. The characters were hungry ghosts, without the cheerful lifelike rotundity Pierce remembered from Kraft's other things, from like *Bitten Apples* or that one about Wallenstein. The dozens of historical figures, none except for the most minor as far as Pierce could tell made up, the actual incidents great and small in which they in fact participated, all reduced to a winter's tale by the springs their actions were imagined here to have: the birth-pangs and death-throes of world-ages, the agonies of potent magicians, the work of dæmons, of Christ's tears, of the ordering stars.

No no no, he had said to Julie, no, these Rosicrucians preserving their secret histories, passing them down through the ages encoded in secret books that mean the opposite of what they say, working to alter the lives of empires, lurking behind the thrones of kings and popes—come on: secret societies, Freemasons, *illuminati* haven't had real power in history. Can't you see, he'd said, the truth is so much more interesting: secret societies have not had power in history, but the *notion* that secret societies have had power in history *has* had power in history.

And yet. And yet.

Finish writing it, huh. Unlike histories, stories need endings; the pages of notes at the bottom of Kraft's manuscript only carried the story far forward, massing more years and books and characters, enough (it seemed to Pierce glancing through them) to fill another two, another three volumes without coming to an end.

But Pierce could imagine an ending; he could. Could imagine how, after the great change had all gone by—a Noah's flood, a storm of difference sweeping all the old world away, a storm composed of the Thirty Years' War, of *tercios,* Wallenstein, fire and sword; of Reason, Descartes, Peter Ramus, Bacon, and of Unreason too, the witches on their gibbets aflame—after it had all been swept into the unrecoverable again, Rosicrucian brothers fleeing, the Stone, the Cup, the Cross, the Rose all blown away like leaves—he could imagine that under a fuliginous and pitchy sky (dawn due to come, but otherwhere and elsewhen than there and then) they would be gathered up, the heroes of that age which would be by that time already growing imaginary, gathered up one by one by an old man, his beard white as milk and a star on his forehead. Gathered up. Come along now, for our time is past. One by one, from workshops and caves in Prague and philosophical gardens in Heidelberg, from cells and palaces of Rome and Paris and London. All over now. And where then shall they go? The wind is rising with the dawn; they step onto the deck of that ship restless at anchor, whose sails are already filling, the sign of Cancer painted on them. They are for elsewhere, a white city in the farthest East, a country once again without a name. Set out.

With a sudden awful certainty, Pierce knew that he would sob.

Good Lord, he thought, when it had come and passed, good God where within him had that come from, wrenched from him all unexpected as though by a hand. He wiped his eyes on the shoulders of his shirt, left side, right side, and looked out the mullioned window, his breast still trembling. Out there, Rosie Rasmussen and her daughter tended Kraft's neglected garden. Sam was crying too.

Why must I live in two worlds, Pierce asked, why. Do we all, or is it only some few, living always in two worlds, a world outside of us that is real but strange, a world within that makes sense, and draws tears of assent from us when we enter there.

He stood. He squared up the pile dead Kraft had left, and inserted it again into its box.

It wasn't true. Of course it wasn't. For if this moment was a moment when it *could* be true, this moment was also fast passing; and when it had passed all this story of Kraft's not only would no longer be possible, it would not ever have been possible. There was no way, if the world kept rolling, to save these nested stories; they slipped one by one again into the merely fictional—Hermes's false Egypt, and Bruno's false Hermes; Kraft's false Bruno; Pierce's false history of the world, the doors that had once blown open blowing closed again one by one down the corridor into the colored centuries.

The rift was closing; this year might be the last year it could even be sensed, this month the last month; and once it had closed there was no messenger from thence who could be believed, *I only am escaped to tell thee,* for the messenger would be a fiction too, a crazy idea, a notion.

The moment of change, Pierce's moment, was not itself to survive the change, that's all. It retreated with the rest into the ordinary, this only world, this actual, which would now be paying out backwards endlessly, all of a piece, all like itself.

Yes.

Except that from now on, not often but now and then, those who have passed through that moment might experience the sharp sense that their lives are in two halves, and that their childhoods, on the far side, lie not only in the past but in another world: a melancholy certainty, for which no evidence can be adduced or even imagined, that the things contained therein, the Nehi orange and the soiled sneakers, the sung Mass, the geography book and the comic book, the cities and towns, the dogs, stars, stones, and roses, are not cognates of the ones the present world contains.

Pierce left the study, and went out through the dark house and into the noontide. Continuously, unnoticeably, at the rate of one second per second, the world turned from what it had been and into what it was to be. Rosie tilted up her sun hat to see Pierce striding from the house, and Sam ceased crying; Spofford at Arcady lifted the instrument cupped in his palms to play.

"Done," Pierce called. "All done."

"Us too," said Rosie; and she held out for him to see what they had looted from Kraft's garden, huge armfuls of blossoms that would otherwise have fallen unseen, rank poppies and roses, ox-eye daisies, lilies and blue lupines.